P9-DGB-913

PRAISE FOR
HARD COUNTRY

"To those who have become fans of Michael McGarrity's police novels, *Hard Country* is a welcome addition to the author's published works. This newest book doesn't star lawman Kevin Kerney. Instead, it traces the lives of his ancestors as they settled in New Mexico. Just as the Kevin Kerney series is among the best of modern crime novels, *Hard Country* joins the ranks of superior historical novels . . . worthy of the great writer of Westerns Eugene Manlove Rhodes. And happily, Rhodes is a character in the book."
—Robin Martin, *The Santa Fe New Mexican Pasatiempo*

"As anyone familiar with his excellent crime novels knows, Michael McGarrity really gets—and loves—the Southwest: its colors, its rhythms, its blessings, its cussedness. Here McGarrity moves back in time to explore New Mexico's frontier past and in the process gives us something most unusual these days: an expansive, lyrical, period Western in the tradition of A. B. Guthrie Jr. and Larry McMurtry. Savor this one—they don't make cowboy epics like this anymore."
—Hampton Sides, bestselling author of *Hellhound on His Trail*

"*Hard Country is* aptly titled, and the reader will take a spectacular journey with real people settling the West. There is inescapable action of the gun, the earth, the sky, and the heart. This is a Western that women will love."   —Max Evans, author of *One Eyed Sky*

"*Hard Country* is the evocation of real people in a real land. McGarrity is an accomplished storyteller, and he writes with clarity, perception, and authenticity. Those who read this novel will find it engaging, and they will come away with a deeper understanding and appreciation of the Old West and of the part it played in forging the American imagination."
—N. Scott Momaday, Pulitzer Prize–winning author of *House Made of Dawn*

continued . . .

"*Hard Country* by Michael McGarrity is a 'Western' in the sense that *Lonesome Dove* was a Western. It transcends the genre, a great and true American novel of the West with immense power, beauty, and sweep. It is an unforgettable book. I loved it."

—Douglas Preston, coauthor of *Gideon's Corpse*

"*Hard Country* is a stunning saga of the Old West—a tale rich in both heartbreak and the uplifting spirit of the brave men and women who settled the territory against all odds. It's the great storytelling of Michael McGarrity, one of my favorite writers, that brings the past alive with such superb authenticity. Saddle up with McGarrity and let him take you back—I loved going to the wild New Mexico territory with him."

—Linda Fairstein, *New York Times* bestselling author of *Night Watch*

"A compelling and richly imagined epic told by a master storyteller. Michael McGarrity has his finger on the pulse of the Old West and a knack for drawing the reader in. He also has a marvelous way of illuminating the human heart in characters tough and determined enough to stake a claim on a wild and hard country. I didn't want the story to end. It is just that good."

—Margaret Coel, author of *Buffalo Bill's Dead Now*

"Michael McGarrity's epic Western, *Hard Country*, is awesome in its scope. There hasn't been anything like it in quite a while. I was taken back to sagas such as A. B. Guthrie Jr.'s *The Big Sky* and *The Way West* as well as Vardis Fisher's *Mountain Man* and Larry McMurtry's *Lonesome Dove*. This is a big story with big characters in a big land."

—David Morrell, *New York Times* bestselling author of *The Brotherhood of the Rose*

"McGarrity tells a sweeping Western family saga with the same straight-ahead prose and eye for detail that makes his Kevin Kerney novels so compulsively readable. The characters breathe authenticity as they step in and out of the pages of Tularosa Basin legend. Raw, exciting, and always surprising, *Hard Country* is historical drama at its best."

—Kirk Ellis, writer/coexecutive producer, HBO miniseries *John Adams*

ALSO BY MICHAEL MCGARRITY

Tularosa

Mexican Hat

Serpent Gate

Hermit's Peak

The Judas Judge

Under the Color of the Law

The Big Gamble

Everyone Dies

Slow Kill

Nothing But Trouble

Death Song

Dead or Alive

Backlands

The Last Ranch

HARD
COUNTRY

A NOVEL

MICHAEL McGARRITY

DUTTON
— est. 1852 —

DUTTON
— est. 1852 —

An imprint of Penguin Random House LLC
375 Hudson Street
New York, New York 10014

Previously published as a Dutton hardcover and NAL paperback.

First Dutton paperback printing 2016

Copyright © Michael McGarrity, 2012
Penguin supports copyright. Copyright fuels creativity, encourages diverse voices, promotes free speech, and creates a vibrant culture. Thank you for buying an authorized edition of this book and for complying with copyright laws by not reproducing, scanning, or distributing any part of it in any form without permission. You are supporting writers and allowing Penguin to continue to publish books for every reader.

DUTTON—EST. 1852 (stylized) and DUTTON are registered trademarks of Penguin Random House LLC.

Dutton Trade Paperback ISBN: 978-0-451-41714-5

THE LIBRARY OF CONGRESS HAS CATALOGUED THE HARDCOVER EDITION OF THIS BOOK AS FOLLOWS:
McGarrity, Michael.
Hard country : a novel / Michael McGarrity.
p. cm.
ISBN 978-0-525-95246-6
PS3563.C36359H37   2012
813'.54—dc24   2011041881

Printed in the United States of America

Set in ITC New Baskerville Std.
Designed by Leonard Telesca

This is a work of fiction. Names, characters, places, and incidents either are the product of the author's imagination or are used fictitiously, and any resemblance to actual persons, living or dead, businesses, companies, events, or locales is entirely coincidental.

For Mimi

The American Southwest, 1888

PAINTED DESERT

ARIZONA

HUALAPAI MOUNTAINS

Prescott

MOGOLLON RIM

MAZATZAL MOUNTAINS

Phoenix

SAN FRANCISCO PLATEAU

Colorado River

Gila River

Yuma

MOHAWK RANGE

GALIURO MOUNTAINS

DRAGOON MOUNTAINS

Willcox

Tucson

FLYING W RANCH

Tombstone

MEXICO

Gulf of California

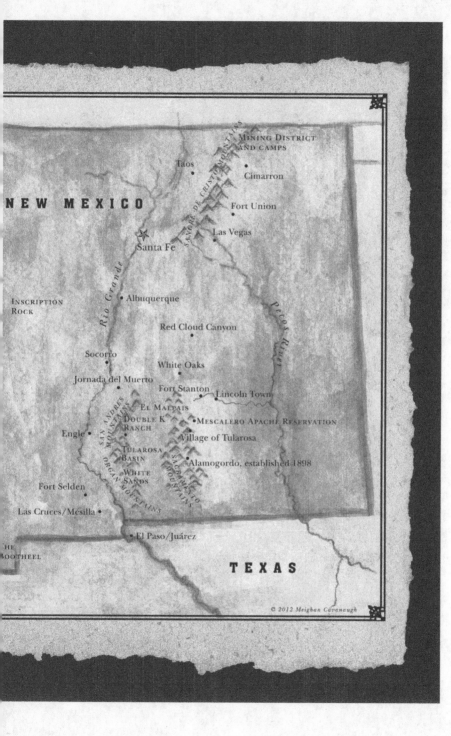

⊹ONE⊹

John Kerney

John Kerney

1

M ary Alice Kerney spent the late afternoon hours of a dry September day cleaning the one-room cabin her husband, John, had built upon their arrival in West Texas. They had settled on the land soon after the U.S. Army had defeated the Indians in the Red River War and the buffalo herds that once roamed the Cheyenne-Arapaho Reservation had been mostly wiped out.

It wasn't much of a place: half cabin, half dugout, with a low ceiling, a sod roof, a hard-packed dirt floor, and no windows—just slat openings on both sides of the door wide enough to aim a long gun through. The only sunshine that penetrated the cabin came when the door was open during warm daylight hours. Even then, without the kerosene lamp lit and a fire going in the fireplace, the light inside was always dim. It felt more like a dungeon than a home.

Keeping it clean took hours out of her day. Dust from the packed-earth floor, wind-blown sand from the West Texas plains, dirt that seeped down from the sod roof, and fireplace soot coated every crack and cranny. She dusted constantly; otherwise an inch of grit covered everything within hours. She hated the dirt, the dust, and the never-ending wind.

She had little furniture in the cabin. A rough plank table with four stools sat in front of the squat stone fireplace. Opposite the fireplace against the sloped wall stood a sturdy cupboard traded to her husband by a family traveling west. It protected her food-stuffs from the mice and rats that found their way inside the cabin no matter how many tiny holes in the walls she plugged with mud. That cupboard was one of the few things in her life that made her work easier, and she was grateful to have it.

She'd prepared a stew with fresh vegetables from her garden and meat from a steer John had recently slaughtered. It simmered in a pot over a bed of embers in the fireplace. The chimney John had built drew poorly, adding to the soot that accumulated in the cabin.

She glanced uneasily at the ceiling as she wiped down the stools with a damp cloth. Soon after they'd moved into the cabin, at sup-pertime a small rattlesnake had fallen onto the table from above. John had quickly crushed the rattler's head with his supper plate, splattering most of his meal on Mary Alice's face and dress. She ran outside and refused to go back until he searched the roof for more snakes and convinced her it was safe to return. From that day on, she feared a rattler would fall on her while she slept, or strike her without warning. She frequently woke up in a panic after dreaming about it.

She stirred the stewpot and added a pinch more of salt and pepper to the beef, turnips, potatoes, peppers, and onions. John liked his food far too salty for Mary Alice's taste. Like clockwork at mealtime, he sat, took one bite, grumbled about her cooking, added a handful of salt, and then ate everything in front of him.

He worked hard to keep the ranch going and needed more than one big meal a day, so Mary Alice was constantly cooking, filling his plate at breakfast, dinner, and supper, with seconds to be had for the asking, if there was food enough in the house. On summer days when the cabin was unbearably hot, she cooked over an outdoor fire pit she built herself, carefully lining the hole with rocks she'd dug up from the plot that became her garden. But today she wanted nothing to do with the world outside the cabin door, even though the heat from the fireplace drenched her in sweat that soaked her dress.

Feeling faint and unsteady, she stopped cleaning and sat on the narrow bed at the back of the cabin. It was scarcely big enough for the two of them, especially when John tossed and turned in his sleep, which he did most nights. But even when he lay quiet, she squeezed herself against the rough mud wall and prayed to be released from her life.

She ran her hand over the cradle at the foot of the bed. John had built it during a late winter blizzard that kept them inside for three days. He spent time working on the cradle until the storm broke and the weather cleared, joining the wood perfectly and rubbing it smooth to the touch. He wanted no splinters or rough edges to harm the baby boy he hoped to see sleeping there. Never had he made anything so nice for her.

When the storm passed, it took a week to count their losses. In the bone-cold days that followed, harsh northern winds blew across the vast West Texas plains, exposing the dead animals buried under snowdrifts. To Mary Alice the grotesque, frozen carcasses scattered across the land was a scene from Hades. As the carcasses thawed, the wolves, coyotes, vultures, and crows congregated to feast. The screeching and squealing of the feeding animals, their howls, yips, and caws, made her uneasy and fretful.

Outside the cabin, the stray dog John had found on the open

range started barking again. Mary Alice didn't bother to get up to see what had set it off. It barked all the time at nothing. John let it sleep in the cabin, and most mornings it left a mess that had to be cleaned up before she started breakfast. She kept hoping a coyote or wolf would make a meal of it, but it stayed close to the cabin, barking, barking, barking.

She hated that dog. John had given it a name, but Mary Alice refused to remember it. More than once, she'd considered shooting it, burying it far away from the cabin where John wouldn't find it, and telling him it had run away.

She absentmindedly caressed the cradle again, trying to remember what she'd been thinking about. Ever since the fifth month of carrying the baby, she'd felt deathly tired. Her legs ached from morning to night and she had constant pains in her back. The heat of late summer days, with not a trace of rain for weeks, had worn down her thin, small-boned frame even more.

The baby had kicked hard all day but suddenly shifted and stopped moving about the time she'd started dusting. Although her water hadn't broken yet, earlier she'd sent John to fetch his sister-in-law, Ida, to help with the delivery. The angle of the sun through the open door told her they should arrive soon.

She wasn't looking forward to having the baby. She had tried hard to match John's happiness over the prospect of a son, if it was to be a boy, but secretly she felt no attachment to it. Living on the empty, lonely Texas plains had carved a hole inside of her. She forced herself to act glad, but it was all make-believe.

She didn't fear childbirth. She'd seen her mother and an older sister go through it and knew what to expect. The baby would come when its time was due. It would be painful, bloody, and she would be sore for days, but that was simply the way of it, and nothing could be done to change it. What she fretted over and feared the most was the stark reality that she had no interest in the child at all. Was she mad? Daft?

She dreaded the rest of her life. The dark cabin, the empty world outside, the endless work with little sleep, caring for John and the baby day in and day out, the possibility of more children. She had tried repeatedly to make the baby real in her mind in the hopes that she could learn to love it. She thought about nursing it, caring for it, dressing it, playing with it, teaching it, but her indifference never went away.

She closed her eyes and tried to picture a happy baby, but all she could think of was how big and uncomfortable her breasts felt, how alien her body had become. She didn't like it at all.

She opened her eyes and looked through the door at the small barn John had built after he'd finished the cabin. She'd begged him to put it where she could see it from the door so that it broke the emptiness of the West Texas plains and enormous, never-ending horizon.

The dog suddenly stopped barking. She stretched out on the bed remembering the blindingly hot, early April day when John stopped their wagon near a clear, shallow pond fed by a live spring on the pale green, windswept plains. On a hillock behind the pond, small bushes with tiny yellow flowers waved in the breeze.

John jumped down from the wagon, spread his arms wide, spun around on his heels, and declared it was here they'd build their ranch. "The Running Springs Ranch we'll call it," he said, his eyes sweeping the landscape.

He dropped to his knees at the edge of the pond, plunged his head into the water, and stood up with his face dripping wet, hair plastered against his forehead, grinning from ear to ear. She laughed at the sight of him with such a boyish look of happiness on his face, and he took it to mean that she approved, when in truth she did not.

At thirty-two, John was twelve years her senior. She'd married him three years ago, herself barely a year off the boat from Ireland. He was an energetic man, with little use for words, who got pleasure from hard work and seemed content with his life. He'd fought as a bluecoat in a volunteer Illinois regiment during the Civil War, tried farming afterward, lost his crops to floods, and traveled west to Kansas with his brother to seek a new life. Other than that, she knew little about his past. Neither John nor his brother, Tom, a veteran himself, talked about their childhood, and as far as Mary Alice knew, their parents were dead and buried somewhere back in the old country.

It was in Kansas that John had met her, living like a servant in the farmhouse of a cousin who told her mother back in County Mayo he would take good care of her. Within a month John had won her hand solely on the promise of a life away from Cousin Charles, who looked at her with greedy eyes, tried to fondle her when his plain, pious wife wasn't in the house, and would beat her for the slightest hint of disobedience.

Although John could find fault with her for not working hard enough, not seasoning his meals properly, or not having his food ready the moment he walked in the door, he'd never raised a hand against her, not even after a nip or two of whiskey. In bed, when his needs arose, he wasn't rough and finished with her quickly. It was more than she had expected from marriage, yet it didn't serve to end her misery.

At first, the wagon trip west had been an adventure, and Mary Alice had high hopes for a bit of happiness. But when they reached the vastness of West Texas, a haunting feeling of loneliness settled over her that never went away no matter how hard she tried to shake it off. Even after John had started to build the cabin next to the spring, she hoped that he would give in to the isolation and decide to move on, perhaps to New Mexico, where there were mountains, forests, fertile river valleys, and villages like Santa Fe. But John had little need for other people, and the open plains suited him.

Mary Alice coughed and turned on her side to ease some of the pain in her back. The dryness and the dust had worked into her lungs, and her throat was parched and raw. Too tired to get up for a sip of water, she closed her eyes again and tried to think pleasant thoughts. But frozen in her mind was the image of the land she'd come to hate.

They had settled south of the Canadian River on the panhandle, where the land was mostly tabletop flat; an in-between country of neither plains nor desert, where until recently buffalo herds and warring Comanches and Kiowas had held sway. The land was covered with a ragged carpet of grass, and good water from underground springs bubbled to the surface. In some of the shallow vales near water, stands of cottonwoods or groves of scrub oak flourished, freshening the view, but it was never enough to make it seem like a place where people should live.

In their first spring after a wet winter, countless flowers blossomed, many Mary Alice had never seen before, and for a brief time the plains burst with color that lifted her spirits. But the scorching sun and dust storms of summer baked out the color and blew it all away.

There were still dangers. Old-timers had warned John against settling too far west. Yes, the land was for the taking, but the Comanches and Apaches still considered it theirs and weren't too friendly about intruders. And a stampede of what was left of the buffalo herds could wipe them out in an instant, as could a thunderstorm or a wildfire. Or they could lose their livestock to bands of rustlers passing through.

John had taught Mary Alice to use the shotgun for protection when he was away, and it stood loaded next to the door in case trouble came calling. But more often it was nature that threatened. There were blinding snows, fierce lightning storms, prairie wildfires, raging tornados, torrents of rain that turned the earth into mud and the gullies into brown rivers. And the endless, ceaseless wind that drove her to distraction.

Even the best autumn days of soft light and cool breezes were poor by comparison to the rich, green farmlands of Kansas and rugged shores of County Mayo. Nothing seem settled or rooted to the land. They were a hard three days' ride from any settlement, a half-day ride to the neighboring ranch where John's brother, Tom, his wife, Ida, and their son, Timmy, lived.

Surrounded by the absence of almost everything comforting to her, Mary Alice lived in exile. She rose each morning determined to make the best of things, but her longing to leave only grew stronger.

When they first arrived, before an early winter set in, she saw only a few people other than her husband, all of them on their way to somewhere else, looking to water their horses and bed down for the night. In early spring, a few more travelers stopped by, in a hurry to move on while good weather held.

Lacking the company of others, Mary Alice began talking to herself, letting her mind wander and her thoughts spill out whatever way they occurred to her. Mostly what she mumbled was idle chatter, but sometimes a word stuck in her head and she would whisper it over and over again as she went about her day. Other times her hatred for her life in this godforsaken place made her hiss out loud like a snake. When John was around she carefully guarded her tongue so as not to upset him.

Today she had repeated the name John had picked for his baby, murmuring "Patrick, Patrick, Patrick," in the hopes it would improve her disposition about the infant. But if it was to be a girl, he'd refused to pick a name, leaving that to her. She'd given it no thought until now, suddenly deciding Margaret would do. When he came home, she'd tell him Margaret.

The dog started barking again and she looked out the open door hoping John had arrived, but there was still no sign of him. Thousands of bits of dust floated in the air on the shaft of light that shone on the dirt floor. Her skin felt dry and dead. All she wanted was for the baby to be born and the aches and pains to stop.

After the spring thaw, they'd made a wagon trip for supplies to the army cantonment on the banks of the Sweetwater River. In spite of her urging him to remain at least a couple of days before returning to the cabin, John had started them home the following morning. Over her shoulder, the sight of the tidy rows of military buildings fading in the distance as they rattled over the ruts of the wagon road chilled her heart.

Soon after they'd returned to the cabin, John's brother and his family arrived, and for a while she enjoyed their company. But as time passed, she found Ida dull, Tom more boring than John, and their half-wild son, Timmy, a loud little devil. When they left to start a ranch nearby, she didn't miss them at all. Yet, who was she to be so highfalutin? She was no better, was she?

The dog's constant barking agitated Mary Alice's mind. Hadn't she killed it with the shotgun and buried it? She got up, walked outside, and stared at the animal, chained to a post ten yards from the cabin door. The dog returned Mary Alice's stare as it barked frantically. The day was blinding hot, with not a bit of shade, and no cooler outside than in. The sun pounded into her head while the dog snarled and yanked at the chain as if to attack her. She could feel something wet running down her legs. She raised the hem of her dress and saw dark red blood dripping onto her shoes. She sank to her knees and hugged her belly as pain seized up inside her.

She felt sleepy and wanted go inside to lie on the bed. She tried to raise herself, but the pain came again, stronger, holding her down. She could feel the blood against her thighs.

The dog howled with excitement.

The contractions came faster and faster and she wondered if both she and the baby would be dead before John arrived with Ida.

She decided it didn't matter. She lay back and let the sun blind her open eyes.

2

John Kerney dug into the sun-dried, cracked earth at the base of the small hill that sheltered the spring and the small, sweet-water pond. Eight weeks of drought had about dried up the water, and the pond was but a third its normal size. His sweat-soaked shirt clung to his back and the sun burned his neck. He loosened the hardpan with thrusts of the shovel blade and threw the clumps of dirt into a pile that a steady southwesterly wind blew back into his face. The wind made the searing hot early evening even worse to bear.

John Kerney paused, gauged the depth of the hole, and figured he had another two feet to go before he could bury Mary Alice deep enough to keep the wolves and coyotes away. He rammed the shovel into the ground repeatedly, hoping to hit some soft earth, and struck a big rock instead. He loosened the soil around it, pulled it free, and heaved it out of the hole.

Inside the cabin, Ida tended to John's newborn son. Mary Alice lay dead on the ground outside the door, covered in threadbare linens from the bed. Buddy, the mongrel dog she'd hated, strained against his chain. It had been barking with barely a pause ever since John and Ida had found Mary Alice lying in a pool of blood breathing her last, the baby about to be born.

Most times the dog didn't bother him, but today it set John Kerney on edge. He threw the shovel aside, got his rifle from the wagon, shot the dog where it stood, and returned to digging without a twinge of remorse.

From inside the cabin, he could hear the weak, raspy cries of his son. With Mary Alice gone, what in the world would he do with a little one? It was a sorrowful day.

John Kerney ran a sleeve across his forehead and looked over at the covered form of his wife. Had he ever really known her? Back in Kansas, she'd eagerly taken him as her husband, and for a while he thought she loved him. That notion passed when they reached Texas and a coolness settled over her. After a spell of getting used to her indifference, he'd found to his relief that it suited him. She never minded his silence, left him to himself, made few demands, gave herself to him without complaint in their bed, and had none of the sharp-tongue faults of the other men's wives he'd met, including Ida.

She had been a wee lass, with a tiny waist and a pretty face, puzzling and odd in her ways, and although he couldn't say why, he would miss her. Best he could figure was she was not like most, and he wouldn't come across the likes of her again.

Finished with his digging, he went to Mary Alice, knelt down, picked her up, and carried her to the grave. She was light in his arms. Gently, he lowered her into the ground and uncovered her face so he could take one last look at her. The time in Texas had roughened and reddened her fair skin, and her blue eyes were pale and empty. He closed her eyes, covered her face so as not to throw dirt on it, and placed the big rock he'd dislodged from the grave at her feet. He thought about putting the dog in with her and decided against it. Although he'd long ago stopped believing in an afterlife, it was better to lay her at rest alone in keeping with her faith. The dog could stay where it fell for the coyotes or wolves to fight over come dark.

He filled in the grave, made a mound over it, and fashioned a wooden cross from two pieces of wood he ripped from the barn wall. With the cross in hand, he led the milch cow to the wagon, tied it off, went to the grave, and stuck the cross in the dirt. At the pond, he shed his shirt and hat and dunked his head in the water. As he rose, he remembered Mary Alice's laugh the day they'd found this place. Had he ever heard her laugh again? He couldn't recall one more time that she had.

He stood for a moment at the foot of the grave. The baby's crying had stopped, and John wondered if it too had died. He turned and looked at the cabin, half expecting Ida to appear holding the lifeless infant. A swarm of flies buzzed around the body of the dog like a small dark cloud. He more or less liked Buddy and wasn't sure why he'd shot him. Maybe because he didn't want the mongrel following along once he left. Maybe because killing Buddy would have pleased Mary Alice.

Inside the cabin, Ida sat at the table with the baby wrapped in a blanket in her arms. She was a stout woman with a broad face, a thick back, and arms as big as a man's. Sturdy stock she was, as his brother liked to say with a laugh. A blood-soaked rag on the table and a bucket of red water at her feet told him that she'd washed the infant.

"Why did you shoot the dog?" Ida asked, looking over at him.

"No reason," John said. "Does the wee one live?"

"Yes, your son is sleeping."

"Thank you for your help."

"If we'd gotten here a little sooner, perhaps I could have done more."

John had almost killed a good team of horses driving at a murderous pace to fetch Ida back to the ranch, and there she sat accusing him of being partially to blame for his wife's death. He clamped his jaw shut, crossed the room, and picked up the cradle. "Get ready; we're leaving," he said.

Ida's lips narrowed. "The baby needs quiet, sleep, and to be fed. Best we stay here till morning."

"We're leaving," he repeated flatly.

Ida stared hard at her brother-in-law. Maybe he was smarter than her husband, and at first glance more appealing to the eye, with his tall frame and broad shoulders, but he wasn't steady like Tom and he always seemed a bit brash in his manner.

"You're not coming back here, are you?" she asked.

"I have the milch cow hitched to the wagon," John said as he headed to the door. "Bring the baby and let's be on our way."

Ida stood and followed John outside. "Did you say words over Mary Alice? She gave her life to give you the son you wanted. It would be the least you could do."

John turned and faced Ida with her stinging tongue. "I'm no preacher. I gave her a proper burial. That will do."

"Pray tell me how you will care for your child," she called shrilly as he strode toward the wagon, carrying the cradle.

"I do not know." He returned to the cabin for the bundle of baby clothes Mary Alice had made and stored in the back of the cupboard.

"Leave the child with us," Ida said when he came back. "To raise."

John stopped in his tracks. "Did you talk to my brother about this?"

"Mary Alice was frail and childbirth can be difficult. It was worrisome to me."

"Did you reckon Mary Alice would die?"

Ida flushed a deep red. "I thought no such thing." She thrust Patrick at John. "You haven't even looked at him. Take your son. Hold him."

Gingerly, John took the baby. The tiny child almost fit in one of his hands. He peeled back the blanket. His head was covered in soft dark fuzz and he had a round little belly. Ida had neatly clipped and tied off the umbilical cord. The baby's tiny fingers reminded John of Mary Alice's dainty hands.

"He looks healthy." He handed Patrick back to Ida and helped her into the wagon.

"He's a strong one," Ida said in a slightly more pleasant tone as she settled down on the plank-board seat. "What do you plan to do now with Mary Alice gone?"

Kerney shook his head as he led the horses to the pond. "I don't rightly know."

By the time he'd watered the horses, sunlight had faded fast behind a thin curtain of dust, throwing out a last glint of gold that stretched like a narrow ribbon across the horizon. He took one more look at the cabin and Mary Alice's grave before turning the team away at a slow walk. Silently, he hoped Ida and the baby would stay quiet so he could do some hard thinking. In the space of an afternoon, his world had turned upside down.

The horses knew the way to his brother's spread, so John gave the reins some slack and watched nightfall mask the plains he'd come to love. During his time on the panhandle, he'd marveled at happening upon occasional small lakes, round as pie pans, that broke the plains, discovering thick groves of trees that stayed hidden in the creek beds until you crested the last hill, or watching an ocean of rolling green grass whipped by the wind after the spring rains brought the land back to life.

But those feelings were now somehow changed with Mary Alice gone. The land no longer seemed to mean as much to him. Had he loved her without letting himself feel it? He felt remorseful about the possibility.

He glanced over at the shape of the baby asleep in Ida's arms. From the moment Mary Alice had told him she was pregnant, he'd thought mostly about the baby and hardly at all about her. But she was always meant to be there caring for their son. Now Tom and Ida would need to look after the child until John could find a way to do it on his own.

He wasn't about to search for another woman to take as a wife, and even if he did, he'd have to scout far afield to find one. On the frontier the chances of finding an unmarried woman who wasn't a soiled dove or a saloon girl were about plumb zero. Moreover, the idea of marrying again held no appeal.

The wagon ride was uneventful, and in the quiet of the night John Kerney tried to clear his mind. Patrick woke up once, crying, and Ida made Kerney stop for some fresh milk from the cow. She wet her fingers with it and let Patrick suckle, and soon he was fast asleep again. When they crested the small hill that sheltered the valley where Tom had built his home, they could see lamplight through the open door.

"Appears my menfolk have waited up for us," Ida said, trying to sound cheerful.

John wasn't so sure. In the light of a half-moon partially masked by a thin band of clouds, he could see the empty horse corral with the open gate. He hurried the team along and reached for his rifle.

"What's wrong?" Ida asked.

"When I stop the wagon, you stay put," John said as they rattled down the rutted incline.

As they neared the ranch buildings, the moon broke through the veil of clouds, shedding enough light to reveal Timmy lying on the ground near the corral gate. Inside the corral, Tom was stretched out facedown, unmoving.

The scream that came from Ida's mouth was a sound John had never heard before. Clutching the baby, she flung herself off the wagon, raced first to Timmy then to Tom, and collapsed on her knees next to her dead husband. Her screams turned to gasping sobs.

John Kerney went to Ida, took Patrick from her, and lifted her to her feet. He led her away from the bodies to the cabin and told her to sit in the rocking chair his brother had made out of cottonwood.

When her sobs lessened, Kerney asked if she was able to care for Patrick while he tended to Tom and Timmy.

She nodded and held out her arms for Patrick.

"Stay here," he said, handing Patrick to her. "Don't come outside."

She nodded again, eyes wide with pain.

"From the smell of it, he's soiled himself."

"What are we to do?" Ida moaned.

"First, care for the baby," John Kerney replied. "That's about all we can do."

He brought the cradle and baby clothes that Mary Alice had made in from the wagon, and he took a look around outside. Not only were all the horses gone, but the saddles and tack had been stolen from the barn. From the shod hoofprints he counted five riders. Neither Tom nor Timmy had been mutilated, which meant the murdering horse thieves weren't Comanches, Kiowa, or Cheyenne. The killers were most likely white men, and were probably gathering Tom's cattle for a trail drive to the nearest market.

He looked in on Ida and Patrick to see how they were holding up. Dressed in some of the new clothes, Patrick slept in his cradle. The sight of him looking so peaceful made the dreadful day seem unreal. He could think of no worse way for a child to start life.

Ida rocked gently in the chair with tear tracks on her cheeks, eyes dark and rimmed with pain. She looked half crazy. John hoped she wasn't.

"I'll be outside for a time," he said. "I'll come get you when I'm done."

She gave him a blank stare and rocked a little faster.

He carried the bodies in turn to a nearby arroyo, fetched a shovel from the barn, and began digging. With dawn about to break, he finished burying his brother and nephew. Too tired to think or feel, he walked slowly to the cabin to fetch Ida so she could say her good-byes. A brief thought of revenge seeped into his head and faded like a passing fog. *Against who?* he wondered. He'd talk to the army and tell them what happened. Maybe they knew who was out killing and stealing.

He paused outside the cabin and looked at his hands. They were dirt black and sticky with dried blood. He washed up at the water barrel, trying to sort out what to do next. Nothing came to him.

Ida was asleep in the rocking chair, as was Patrick in his cradle. Hunger pangs made John's stomach grumble. He hadn't eaten since breakfast yesterday. Sometime back, he'd helped Tom build a meat smoker out of an inverted barrel, with a bunghole for a vent and another hole used to keep a low, slow fire burning. Smoke-cured meat was suspended at the top of the barrel, but it still needed to be cooked before it could be eaten.

He lifted the barrel lid, took out a fresh smoked slab of beef, took it to the cabin, got a fire going, cut the beef into strips, and put them in a skillet to sizzle. On a shelf above the fireplace was a jar filled with bread dough yeast. He kneaded some of it, knocked it down, kneaded it once more, pressed it flat, and put it on a bake-stone to be cooked over the fire once it rose. He found coffee, put the pot on to boil, and stood at the front door watching sunrise wash over the land. The sight didn't move him as it had many times before.

Behind him Ida stirred, and he turned. "We'll have some break-fast soon," he said.

"I'll tend to it," Ida said without emotion, rising stiffly from the rocker, her face a blank mask. "But first, take me to Thomas and my Timmy."

John picked up Patrick from the cradle and led the way. He had buried father and son side by side under a young cottonwood that grew in the arroyo.

Ida started sobbing as they approached and threw herself down between the two mounds, arms outstretched, embracing the graves.

"No harm can come to them now," John said.

Ida called out to her husband and son, her fingers clawing the fresh dirt as though she was trying to unbury them.

"No harm," John repeated softly as he stood at the head of Tom's grave. The early morning sun was hot in his face, but there were no tears in the corners of his eyes. Did he really care about nothing?

He looked down at the baby boy in his arms, now awake and staring up at him. If he had a mind to believe there wasn't much to live for, little Patrick made it a foolish thought.

* * *

Two days later, John, Ida, and Patrick arrived at the army cantonment by wagon, carrying Ida's personal possessions and some clothes John had gathered up on a return visit to his ranch. While there, he went to Mary Alice's grave once more. As he stared at the simple cross he'd fashioned, a sudden yearning for her hit him square in the stomach like the kick of a mule. He caught his breath and stifled a sorrowful sigh.

The settlement outside the cantonment had grown considerably since John's last visit. A trading post, livery stable, restaurant, Chinese laundry, several saloons, and a hotel now stood where buffalo hunters had once encamped to sell their hides to the Dodge City buyers.

The military post had also expanded. New barracks had been built to house a detachment of recently arrived Negro soldiers, and permanent officers quarters were under construction.

During the long trip to the post, John and Ida had talked over their situation and come to an agreement on how to deal with their predicament. They would sell both ranches, including the remaining livestock and improvements, and divide the proceeds. John would handle the transaction, and when the cash was in hand, Ida would take Patrick and her share of the money and go to Dodge City, where her brother owned a mercantile store. She had taught school before marrying and probably could do it again.

John decided he would trail south to the Texas brush country, find ranch work, and look for a place to make a fresh start. If all went well, he'd fetch Patrick in a year or two. It was the best plan for all concerned. Patrick would give Ida a reason to keep going, and for Kerney she was the only person he knew and trusted enough to care for his son.

The arrangement hadn't improved Ida's outlook much; she still had crying fits, then fell silent and wouldn't talk at all. John worried he might be leaving Patrick with a madwoman but didn't see a way around it. It was either Ida or strangers, or take the little button with him, which was impossible.

He got rooms at the hotel, left Ida and Patrick, stabled the horses, and went to the fort to report to the military authorities the murder of Tom and Timmy by rustlers. He gave the officer detailed descriptions of the horses that had been stolen. The officer knew of no other recent depredations and didn't hold out any hope the bandits would be caught. There was too much open range, too few pony soldiers, and too little law to make it likely. He promised John to send out a scouting party to search for signs.

Finished with the army, John went looking for buyers for the ranches. With newcomers arriving daily and a small land rush going on, he figured the prospects for selling were good. But he soon found that most of the greenhorns were as strapped for cash as everyone else, and those who had some money weren't willing to offer what the two ranches were worth. A land speculator who was buying out nesters who'd quit or gone broke when their farms blew away during the drought offered slightly less than half of what the land was worth and not a lick for the improvements or the re-maining livestock.

Disappointed, he returned to the hotel to find Ida sitting on the bed next to a sleeping Patrick, crying and talking to herself. John shook her hard to get her to stop.

"You should be lying in a grave," she hissed as she pushed his hands away, "not my Thomas and Timmy."

"Probably so," John said, not willing to discuss the matter further. "Seems I'm not going to be able to bargain a fair price for the ranches."

"You just get me some money," Ida snapped, her eyes flashing. "I don't want to stay here one day longer than I have to. And I'm going to have to pay my brother in Dodge City for our keep until I can get settled there."

"I'll make sure you have enough to do that."

"You'd better. Now that you're here, I need broadcloth to make diapers for the baby."

John Kerney looked perplexed. "The trading post is across the way. I'll walk you over there."

Ida shook her head. "I'm not setting a foot outside this hotel until it's time for me and Patrick to leave for Dodge City. Not a foot."

John thought about forcing Ida to go to the store with him and decided against it, figuring it would only agitate her more and set off another crying fit.

She started sobbing again anyway as John left. He tracked down the land speculator who'd made the cash offer on the ranches, talked to him again, and agreed to his terms. They shook hands and settled on a time to sign the papers in the morning. At the trading post, he arranged for Ida, Patrick, and their few possessions to travel on the next supply train to Dodge City, due to leave in two days.

With three yards of cloth under his arm, he stopped at the livery stable and traded the wagon and team of horses to the proprietor for a good saddle horse and some cash, which would cover the cost of the hotel rooms and their meals, with a bit left over.

He walked the milch cow to the military post and sold it at a fair price to the quartermaster, who was happy to get it. On his way back to the hotel, with money in his pocket, he stopped at a saloon for a drink. It wasn't much of a place. Sharpened cottonwood poles stuck into the ground and covered with adobe plaster formed the walls. Larger logs fastened at the top, and long ceiling logs held everything together. The roof was packed sod, the floor earth, just like his cabin, and the bar was a long plank table, waist high. A few tables and chairs were scattered around, barely visible in the dark interior, heavy with cigar smoke. Some men were playing cards, drinking whiskey, and carrying on with a saloon girl who had seen her better years slip away some decades ago.

He laid down a coin, ordered a whiskey, nursed it, and thought about the tight spot he faced. Maybe Ida was touched in the head, and maybe she wasn't. Either way, if he gave her most all of the money from the sale of the ranches, perhaps she could make the best of a bad situation until he could come for Patrick.

Deciding he could do no less, he finished his whiskey. He could scrape along, but a woman with a baby needed more than a few dollars to survive. He'd stay and see them safely off on the supply train to Dodge City, take what money remained in his pocket, drift south to find work, and keep an eye out for the stolen ponies. He knew every one of the stolen horses by sight. With a million square miles of open country, the odds were against finding the men who'd murdered Tom and Timmy. But if he ran across any of the horses, he might have a slim chance of doing that.

Soon, ranchers would be gathering their herds for the fall

works, so it was likely he could hire on somewhere, although the job probably wouldn't turn into anything permanent.

John and Tom had both used the Double K brand on their livestock, figuring their spreads were all part of the same family. On his way south, he'd stop by Tom's ranch, put the Double K brand on his new pony as a reminder of what he'd lost, and say his final good-byes. It was almost too much to think about.

He hoisted the bundle of cloth Ida needed for Patrick's diapers and stepped outside into the blazing hot afternoon. In a matter of days, he'd lost almost everything and everyone dear to him. He couldn't help wondering if in the end he might lose his son too.

3

The dusty settlement along the bone-dry riverbed had sprung up to supply outfits trailing cattle west, and from the looks of it John Kerney guessed it would melt back into the sunbaked earth long before anyone decided to give it a name. No more than a wide cow track at a bend in a hard-packed trail with a few hastily thrown-up buildings, it already appeared half-abandoned.

During the past year, Kerney had drifted through half a dozen or more similar outposts already fading from sight and memory. This particular hamlet of civilization sat in the middle of the West Texas brush country, an expanse of land that was hell and gone from nowhere, a vast semiwilderness of caliche hills, sandy pastures with ragged grass carpets, cactus patches that rose up to worry a horse and rider, and wooded creeks with ancient live oaks that offered brief respite from the relentless sun. In some places rugged, twisted mountains touched the sky, but in all of what Kerney had seen it was a thorny scrubland with thickets mostly impenetrable by man and beast.

It was also, as Kerney discovered on his last job, a land where working cattle was most times downright dangerous and otherwise hard, exhausting work at best.

He had yet to see all of the brush country, for it stretched roughly between the San Antonio River and the Rio Grande, ran on to the Gulf Coast, and took up a considerable amount of land south toward Old Mexico. Some of the hands he'd ridden with said it was roughest between the Nueces and the Rio Grande. But even with their stories of old bulls with horns wider than the spread of a man's arms and cactus savannas so thick cows and calves refused to be driven through them by men on foot, Kerney had a hard time imagining how it could be any worse than what he'd already experienced. He looked forward to the day when he could get far away from it.

Until then, he was still stuck square in the middle of a hardpan, drought-stricken swath of brush country, and he'd been eating its dust for two days. So he was glad enough to see the lopsided saloon that leaned southerly, the general store with its wind-whipped, ragged piece of canvas covering an unfinished roof, and the small stable with a corral that held a neglected broomtail pony. He wanted a drink, a meal, some grub to pack in his saddlebag, and a nickel's worth of feed for his horse. With any luck, the store would have some green coffee beans to carry him through until he reached a real town.

Kerney badly needed work, and a traveler he'd passed by sometime back had told him that a rancher fixing to move his herd out of the drought was hiring hands in the area. But from his perch on a small rise overlooking the settlement, he saw no activity that gave him any hope of a job.

He guessed no more than a dozen folks made the place home, living in several wagons scattered near the buildings. The only people in view were some barefoot children sitting under the welcoming shade of a wagon in front of the saloon watching an older boy skin a pink coachwhip snake.

Kerney tied his horse to the saloon hitching post next to a thrifty-looking bay with a flame of white hair in the center of its forehead. His brother's brand on its shoulder had been altered, but not enough to hide the original back-to-back Double K marking.

Seeing the animal made Kerney pause and take a cautious look around. It was the first time since he had sold the ranches, sent Ida away to Dodge City with Patrick, and started working at any job he could find that he'd come close to anyone or anything connected to the murders of his brother and young nephew.

The horse sported a fine, hand-tooled rig that no saddle tramp or hired hand earning an honest wage could afford. He considered asking the boy skinning the snake who had ridden into town on the bay but thought better of it. Best not to show any interest too soon.

He stepped through the open door to the saloon and waited for his eyes to adjust in the dim light. There were no women to be seen, most likely owing to a lack of sufficient paying customers to keep a saloon girl busy. The only liquor in sight was a row of brown bottles lining a single shelf on a wall. At the back of the room a moth-eaten blanket hanging from a rafter partially hid the kitchen cookstove. The lingering smell of fried beefsteak made Kerney's stomach rumble.

Two men made up the establishment's congregation: a barkeep as bald as a man could get, with a belly to match his round head, and an older, wiry fellow with a neatly trimmed beard, high forehead, and broad nose.

A long, waist-high table served as the bar. Kerney stepped up to it next to the bearded man and asked the barkeep for a bottle and a glass. The man didn't move until Kerney laid his coins on the counter.

"Passing through?" the barkeep asked with a thick southern accent as he poured a shot in a glass and placed it in front of Kerney.

Kerney nodded. "Unless I can find a piece of work."

The man with the beard looked over at Kerney with interest but said nothing. Kerney smiled in return, thinking the fellow didn't have the look of a cattle-rustling, murdering horse thief. But then a lot could change in any man's life to make him seem respectable and law-abiding.

"Who might you be?" the man asked.

"John Kerney."

"Weren't you busting longhorns out of the brush on the Lazy Z for a time?"

"I was," Kerney allowed. "But you have me at a disadvantage, sir."

"I'm Sam Wilcox," the man said with a smile. "I run the Robertson outfit. The Rocking R."

Wilcox stuck out his hand and Kerney shook it.

"I hear tell you didn't want to stay on at the Lazy Z and help trail the cattle to Louisiana," Wilcox continued.

Kerney drained his glass, poured another shot, and looked Wilcox in the eye. "Truth be told, traveling farther south holds no appeal to me. That aside, it seems from what you know about me, I've misunderstood how interesting I am to folks hereabouts."

Wilcox laughed. "Hell, with so few people living hereabouts, everybody is interesting one way or another, John Kerney. Some say you wore a blue coat in the war."

Kerney gave Wilcox a measured look. "I don't deny it, although it remains a curiosity and devilment to most Texans I meet."

Wilcox slapped his hand on the bar and laughed again. "I didn't know you Union fellows had such a refined sense of humor. I like that in a man."

"I'll allow that a light tongue has kept me out of a few arguments and fights, but it hasn't helped me get work these last few weeks."

Wilcox shook his head sympathetically. "I guess most people in these parts are still smarting over the war. But I'll criticize no man who fights for what he believes in. It seems downright unchristian to do so. Now, if you've an interest, I'll soon be trailing cattle west, if you don't mind moseying in that direction."

Kerney smiled at Wilcox's friendly rag over his reluctance to travel any deeper into Johnny Reb country. "Are you offering me a job?" he asked.

"I allow I could use another hand or two. I pay a dollar a day, plus grub and browse for your horse, if you've a mind to sign on. You can pick out a string of broomtails to use once we get to the ranch. We've got a real fine remuda."

Kerney nodded his agreement. "I'm obliged to you. How far west do you propose to go?"

"New Mexico Territory," Wilcox replied. "My boss wants free grass, open range, and ready buyers. Plans to sell to the army and Indian agents. Haven't been there myself, but those who have say the grass is belly high to a horse and the land has never been grazed."

Wilcox laughed and pushed his glass aside. "Course, I don't believe a word of it. Those stories about a cattleman's paradise come from old-timers who pushed cows to California ten years before the war, fighting Comanches and Apaches along the way."

"It sounds a mite embellished," Kerney allowed.

"Embellished," Wilcox echoed. "Now, that's a word you don't hear too often around a trail-drive campfire. But I'm told you're a man good with words, although you don't appear to waste them just to fill up empty air."

"Less said, the better," Kerney replied.

"Now, that's an idea I can take a hankering to," Wilcox said. "I'd like to ask you a personal question, if you're agreeable."

"I've got nothing to hide," Kerney answered, wondering if the same held for Wilcox.

"No offense, but is it true that you lost your wife and had to leave your baby boy with a half-crazed woman up in Dodge City?"

"I wouldn't call her half-crazed, but the rest is true. The woman was my sister-in-law."

Wilcox nodded. "I've got a hand who works for me, name of Cal Doran. He trailed up to Dodge City a while back. Talked about meeting up with the brother of the woman caring for a little one, not even a scamp. Seems the man asked about you, wanted to get in touch. You might want to jawbone with Cal about it."

"I surely will, and I appreciate the information."

"Glad to pass it on," Wilcox said as he adjusted his hat and glanced out the open door. "Best we get started. We've got a considerable ways to ride."

Kerney drained his drink and followed Wilcox out into the humid, hot Texas sun of a late April morning. His last meal had been in a cold camp the night before last, but he pushed down the cramps that gnawed at his empty stomach. He'd been hungry before, and with a new job and a new boss, food could wait. He watched Wilcox climb onto the back of the bay that had been Tom's favorite pony and mounted up beside him.

Wilcox seemed an open-minded, tolerant man, but during the course of their conversation Kerney had learned nothing at all about him. Was all his charitable talk about Kerney's blue-coat past nothing more than blowing smoke? And why had Wilcox been so quick to ask him about Ida and his son in Dodge City?

In the brush country of southwest Texas, a man's past was considered his own personal business, unless he was otherwise inclined to talk about it. Wilcox had prodded where most men would have sidestepped. Was that just his nature, or did he have another motive?

Kerney didn't try to swallow his doubts about Wilcox. His goodwill toward men had turned brittle and withered the day he'd buried his wife, brother, and young nephew. He'd need a hell of a lot more convincing before he would believe that the man sitting astride Tom's bay was an honorable, trustworthy man.

For now, he'd ride along with eyes wide open, hoping to learn something about his son from this waddie that Wilcox had mentioned. The letters he'd written to Ida had all gone unanswered, leastways as far as he knew. Maybe she'd written back and the letters had gone astray, been scattered to the four winds after a Comanche raid on a mail wagon, or just never caught up with him. Or maybe she'd fallen ill, or something bad had happened to the boy and she couldn't bring herself to tell him. Knowing nothing, he hungered for any news, no matter how old, unreliable, or distressing.

Wilcox didn't talk much on the ride to the ranch, which suited Kerney just fine. He held his own tongue about Wilcox's bay and tried to avoid dwelling on it. But the horse was a powerful reminder of that dreadful day. The memory had continually flooded through his mind, along with painful stabs of guilt he carried for not saving

Mary Alice or being there to stand and fight side by side with Tom. There were times the memories were so godawful that he wished he could have died with them.

Kerney hoped the pony Wilcox was riding would lead him to the murderers. He surely would like the chance to gun them down.

4

They arrived at the ranch at early dusk, just in time for a supper of beef, beans, biscuits, and hot coffee. Wilcox introduced Kerney to the rest of the hands as they drifted in and lined up by the cook pot next to the chuck wagon. While he waited for his first meal in two days, he learned that Cal Doran, the cowboy Wilcox had mentioned, and three other hands were camped ten miles distant, bedding down several hundred cattle that had been chased out of the brush over the past week. It deflated him a bit to know that he'd have to wait to hear what Doran knew about Ida and his son, if anything, but the smell of hot grub restored his spirits.

He ate his meal perched on a log with two fellows he'd worked with up north a ways on other spreads, and learned that the ranch had been sold and the drive west to New Mexico would start in a matter of days. Except for a shed and a low-slung cabin, about the only other improvement on the land was a large corral that held the remuda.

After his meal, he washed his plate and went to the corral to look over the horses. It was a mix of the usual nondescript, hard-working stock found on any ranch; some of the animals appeared to be half-broke, others looked sturdy and relatively gentled, and none seemed paunchy or unsound. On the far side of the corral, he spied a broomtail roan not much bigger than a pony that drew his attention. He ducked into the corral and made his way to the animal. It had horny growths on the inside of its front legs, and a sharp, arched back. In spite of the shoulder brand being altered just like on Wilcox's bay, it was young Timmy's pony sure enough.

In the morning Kerney would watch with interest to see who cut out the roan. Wilcox was small enough to ride the pony, but so were several other hands he'd met. But no matter who saddled the broomtail, two horses stolen from his brother, both with the same altered brand, were on this ranch. That made for some sober speculation that he might be working side by side with one or more of the killers.

He left the remuda in time to see Wilcox walking in the light of a full moon toward the cabin, where a man stood framed in the open doorway, backlit by the flames of the fireplace. Kerney figured it was the rancher Robertson, who'd sold out to move west.

Kerney didn't discount Robertson as a suspect just because he bossed the outfit. Many a man in West Texas had grown respectable after whipping a tired horse out of a town in some other state where the law had a jail cell or a hangman's knot waiting for him.

Had he chanced upon one or more of the murderers? If not, maybe he could at least learn the name of the men who'd sold his brother's stolen horses.

Kerney had grit but was no shootist when it came to gunplay. He wore his hogleg high and strapped tight, not low and loose like the *pistoleros*. He spread out his bedroll thinking he could easily end up dead if he didn't bide his time, get the facts straight, and keep his temper. He'd never bushwhacked anyone but wasn't opposed to doing it if that was the only way he could put the killers in their graves.

Wilcox walked up as he was about to bed down.

"I'm sending you and three other men east at first light," he said. "Work the timber and brush rough country around the water holes and gather as many cows as you can. Most are mavericks with long-horn blood that have been running wild for so many years that moss is growing on their horns. You've got two days. Bring in what you gather and watch out for the bulls."

Wilcox pointed to a snoring man stretched out near the embers of the campfire. "That's Buck Moore. You'll ride with him. Do what he tells you."

"As you say," Kerney replied.

Wilcox nodded and left.

Disappointed that he'd be delayed meeting Cal Doran yet again, Kerney pulled off his boots and settled down with a full belly to get some sleep.

* * *

Let down to see Tim's pony remain unsaddled in the corral the next morning, Kerney picked out a fresh mount from the remuda and trailed his own horse behind as he lit out with Buck Moore, the ramrod, and two other waddies named Ed Pearl and Charlie Gambel. For two long days, they worked the brush in dense chaparral, with thickets of prickly pear impassible in places.

Passage at times had to be on foot to reach the cows deep in the brush. They fought their way through undergrowth that poked, stabbed, jabbed, and cut, skirted angry six-foot-long rattlesnakes, and faced mean, wild, long-back bulls that charged straight at them before veering away to vanish into the brush. They worked a parcel of bottomland where the mesquites grew large and the hackberries provided some shade, but not even the shade could cool ground so hot that it almost scorched the hand to touch.

Some of the cattle they worked were descended from stock brought to the New World by the Spaniards. Born wild during the war years, when ranchers and cowboys left the land to fight as Johnny Rebs, the animals had never known a rope around their necks or the searing heat of a branding iron. In among the bovines were a few mean mother cows that could kill a man or a wolf with their horns or hooves, survive a summer drought or a winter freeze, drop a healthy calf like clockwork every year, and never suffer a day's sickness. They were rough, rangy, and lanky, and many could outrun a man on horseback.

Some of the cattle were unbranded mavericks of mixed blood, not quite as wild and a bit easier to gather. But no matter the breed, busting them out of the brush was so perilous and painful that at the end of each day the men removed thorns and spines from their horses' legs before tending to their own cuts and bruises.

At one point they almost lost every animal they had gathered when a herd of fifty or more deer scampered through the cows and sent them stampeding for the breaks.

During all of it, Buck Moore, who had a cleft palate that badly affected his speech, gave his orders with hand signals, which let him avoid talking.

When they had seventy cows and calves corralled in a makeshift pen, Buck left to bring a few more men back from the ranch head-quarters to help trail the animals to the main herd. Without the extra hands, they would lose most of the stock back into the brush, making it impossible to round them up in time to start the drive west.

At camp that night, with Buck gone, Charlie and Ed were more talkative.

"We don't chew the fat much when we're around Buck," Ed Pearl explained in his gravelly voice. "It frets him that he can't wag his tongue like an ordinary person."

"Gets angry 'cause he thinks he sounds stupid," Charlie Gambel added. He held a stained, tightly folded piece of paper in his hand. "One of the boys you worked with on the Lazy Z says you can read."

"I can," Kerney said.

A boy of no more than sixteen years, Charlie had a button nose and cheeks that had yet to feel the sharp edge of a straight razor. He thrust the paper at Kerney. "I'd appreciate it if you'd read this to me. I've heard it read twice before but would sure like to hear it again."

Kerney unfolded the paper and in the light of the campfire scanned the one-page letter before reading it to Charlie. It was from a sister in Tennessee writing about the birth of her first child and the improving health of their mother, who had caught a bad chill that had laid her up over the winter. She closed by asking for news about Charlie and his older brother, Frank. The letter was nearly a year old.

Kerney read it slowly as Charlie sat beside him, smiling and nodding his head.

"Seems you and your brother are uncles," Kerney said as he folded the letter and handed it back to Charlie. "Is Frank with the outfit?"

Charlie's smile vanished. "He's dead. Cal Doran shot him down. I'd kill Doran myself, except he's too good with a gun. Maybe I'll bushwhack him."

Surprised to hear Charlie say exactly what he'd been thinking to avenge his own brother's murder, Kerney gave him a long look.

"It wouldn't be such a bad thing," Charlie said, flinching under Kerney's stare, "him being a shootist and all."

"I can see how a fella might want to do that," Kerney said.

"I've told him not to talk that way," Ed Pearl said with a disapproving shake of his head. "Either fight Cal square or let it be, is what I tell him."

"Who is this Cal Doran?" Kerney asked.

Ed grunted. "A gunfighter by trade but a decent hand when he puts his mind to it; I'll give him that."

It wasn't unusual to have a hired gun on a trail drive. Oftentimes rustlers, criminals on the run from the law, ne'er-do-wells, and petty thieves worked as waddies and brushpoppers right along with the honest cowboys. And if the hard cases and ruffians weren't working for an outfit, they were close by, ready to steal what they could from it any chance they got.

That Cal Doran was a *pistolero* made the man all the more interesting to Kerney. "What happened between Doran and your brother?" he asked Charlie.

Charlie shook his head sadly. "Cal called Frank out for stealing money from his bedroll."

"Was there any truth to it?"

Charlie's face turned red. "I won't say nothing bad about my brother. Maybe Cal thinks he had cause, but he knew Frank was no match with a six-shooter. He could've just given him a good hiding and been done with it."

Ed nodded in agreement. "Big as Cal is, he could have whipped Frank good to teach the boy a lesson, kicked him off the ranch, and let it go at that."

Kerney considered young Charlie Gambel. "Might be best for you to go home to Tennessee."

"No, sir," Charlie said emphatically as he stirred the campfire with a stick. "There's nothing for me there anymore, and I'm bound to travel west."

Across the clearing, some of the cattle started milling and snorting.

"That pen we threw up won't hold those critters back if they decide to run," Ed said. "Go calm them down, Charlie."

Charlie grabbed the reins to his pony and walked it out of the light of the campfire toward the pen.

"He's a good kid," Ed said when Charlie was out of earshot, "but he's got a ways to go to make a hand."

"Maybe so, if he sticks at it," Kerney replied.

Ed nodded. "After Cal gunned Frank down, Charlie took him to town to be buried. He lost a week's wages doing it and gave the undertaker half a month's wages to have him buried proper with a preacher saying words and a marker placed and all. Now, that's brotherly love."

"Losing close kin can be hard," Kerney said, "especially a brother."

"True enough." Ed smiled, showing the gap where his two upper front teeth used to be, and spit a wad of tobacco juice on the ground. "I watched you eye that broomtail roan pony back at the remuda before we struck out."

"Did you?"

Ed laughed and nodded. "Couldn't wait for you to mount up. Wanted to see if your feet drug along the ground when you rode it. You weren't for sure thinking of cutting it out to ride, were you?"

"No," Kerney replied, smiling back at Ed. "I just liked the look of it and thought about a young boy I knew it would suit." He remembered the image of Timmy, who sat a horse just like his father, galloping that pony across the plains. The memory dug into him like the thorns of a Texas ebony. "Is it owned by the outfit?" he asked.

"It surely is," Ed answered. "I was there when Sam Wilcox bought a string of horses for the ranch, including that pony. Sam picked out that bay with the flame on his forehead that he favors and paid his own hard cash money for it. Got the best of the lot."

Kerney held his breath to keep from prodding Ed with more questions, hoping he'd volunteer additional information.

Ed cocked an ear and listened. "Appears Charlie has those cows settled down," he said.

Kerney swallowed his disappointment and nodded in agreement.

"He's an easy boy to like," Ed added, "although he gets riled if you call him that."

"I'd say his boyhood days are pretty much behind him," Kerney replied.

"That's the truth of it." Ed paused again to listen for a spell. "Yep, everything's nice and quiet."

Kerney stood and reached for his saddle. "I'll take first watch."

"Fine by me." Ed stretched out on his blanket.

Kerney gave up his attempt to be cautious. "Who sold those horses to Sam Wilcox?"

"Don't rightly remember his name. But Cal Doran seemed to know him. Both cut from the same cloth, I'd say—men intent on doing no good."

"Does anyone ride that roan pony?"

"Cook does once in a while when he goes deer hunting. I ain't seen anyone else on it."

In the light of the full moon, Kerney saddled his horse and mounted up. "I'll send Charlie in. Tell him he's got third watch."

"That boy has taken a shine to you," Ed added, "and he may need as many friends as he can find."

"Meaning?"

"I think Cal Doran has a grudge against Charlie over what his brother done."

"Can Charlie count you among his friends?" Kerney asked.

"Yes, indeed, but I don't plan on getting killed on account of it."

"That's prudent," Kerney said as he turned his horse and trotted away.

Ed Pearl watched Kerney and his horse fade into a ghostly shape in the pale light of the full moon and then disappear. The sky was clear and full of stars. The night would cool down some, but tomorrow promised to be a scorcher. He wondered what held Kerney's interest about those horses. He dozed off thinking the man had something pressing on his mind.

5

J ohn Kerney finally met Cal Doran at dawn on the morning
Sam Wilcox started the herd west to New Mexico Territory.
He'd brought all the cowboys together, and as the men drank their
coffee and ate breakfast, he told them to divide the herd into thirds
and keep them apart on the trail until they reached good grass
and water. Each drove would have a separate crew and trail boss,
who'd report directly to Wilcox. Along with some other hands,
Kerney, Charlie Gambel, and Ed Pearl were put under Buck Moore
and given the job of herding the tailing bunch, which prompted
Ed Pearl to whisper that they'd be eating dirt and dust for a month
or more.

After Wilcox finished, Kerney sought out Cal Doran and sized
up the man as he approached. Except for his low-slung pistol, nothing about him seemed hard case. He matched Kerney's six-foot
height and in spite of a bushy mustache had a boyish look about
him. Kerney introduced himself and Doran responded with an
easy smile and a firm handshake.

"I hear you might have some news for me out of Dodge City,"
Kerney said.

Doran nodded. "A shopkeeper was asking his customers about you by name. He wanted anybody who crossed your trail to pass on a message that your widowed sister-in-law had run off with some man and took your son with her."

"Did he say where she'd gone?"

Doran shrugged. "North a ways, if I recall correctly. Nebraska or Wyoming. I don't think the shopkeeper was sure himself where she'd lit out for. But he seemed glad to see the last of her. Said she was a little touched in the head from what had happened to her family and all."

"Did he say who she'd left with?" Kerney asked.

"I don't recollect him mentioning a name," Doran replied. "But he did say that he expected you to settle accounts for your son's room and board."

"I'll surely do that," Kerney said, wondering if Ida's brother had run through all the money Kerney had given her to care for the baby when he'd sent her off to Dodge City on the wagon train. Or maybe Ida herself, in a weakened state of mind, had let her coin purse spring a leak.

Kerney changed the subject. "I understand you know the man who sold Sam Wilcox some horses for the remuda a short while back."

Doran's pleasant expression vanished. "Maybe I do, but I'd need to know your business with him before I give you a name."

Kerney shrugged. "From the way Ed Pearl described him, I thought he might be a friend I served with during the war."

Doran's agreeable expression returned. He shook his head and chuckled. "Now, I hear you were a blue coat in the war, so unless you shook hands with a Johnny Reb across a picket line during a pause in the fighting, I surely doubt it. He's a true son of Texas by the name of Dick Turknet, and he rode with a band of Confederate raiders who weren't known for their genteel nature. He's got a hard crust, if you get my drift."

"I do," Kerney said. "Mind me asking if you have a grudge against Charlie Gambel because of his brother's thievery?"

Cal Doran laughed. "That boy Charlie surely has a fanciful turn of mind. I don't know how many brushpoppers he's convinced that I'm itching do him in. I put his brother, Frank, in his grave because of the stealing he did, and that's the end of it. And while I think young Charlie isn't the innocent little peckerwood he makes himself out to be, I've no personal reason to call him out."

Doran pulled his gloves out of his belt and started walking toward his horse. "It appears you and Charlie will be at the back end of the drive, eating trail dust for a time."

"Appears so," Kerney replied as he kept pace.

"I noticed that Double K brand on your horse," Doran said. "Someone handy with a running iron wouldn't have much trouble altering it, if he were a mind to. Bet it might even come out looking like the brand on Sam Wilcox's fine new bay. But then I've always thought Dick and his cousins admired other people's horseflesh too much."

"Do Turknet's cousins have names?" Kerney asked.

"I'm done talking about Dick and his lot," Doran replied. "I've no need to get myself in a squabble with him."

"I had no mind to drag you into my business," Kerney said.

Cal nodded. "I appreciate that."

Over at the remuda, Buck Moore was signaling Kerney to get a move on.

"I'd keep an eye peeled on that boy Charlie, if I were you," Doran added as he swung into his saddle. "He's useless and prob-

ably ain't fit to shoot at except for target practice. Still, he might
need some killing before we get paid off at the end of the drive.
See you when we reach water."

Kerney touched a finger to the brim of his hat in response,
mounted, and trotted his horse toward Buck, who waited at the
corral. Although he didn't think Charlie Gambel was as bad a kid
as Doran made him out to be, the boy lacked the gumption needed
to make a hand. Kerney decided it might be wise to keep Cal's
words in mind. He found himself inclined to like the man in spite
of his outlaw reputation.

* * *

Charlie Gambel sorely missed the company of his brother, Frank,
laid dead by Cal Doran. Days back, he'd considered asking John
Kerney to write his mother telling of Frank's death, but he let the
idea die unspoken for fear that the news might put the law onto
him.

Truth was, no matter how lonesome he felt without Frank
around, Charlie wasn't about to head home, not after all the stealing and robbing they'd done coming west. And even if he did avoid
the passel of lawmen looking for him in Arkansas and East Texas,
all that waited for him in Tennessee was backbreaking work on a
farm that barely made a dime and a dollar in a good year and a
drunken father with a mean streak who'd whipped his two sons
one too many times.

Even before he buried Frank, Charlie decided he'd stay with
the outfit until it got to New Mexico Territory, draw his pay, and
strike out for the gold camps around Silver City. He'd stake a claim
and, if luck was with him, find a vein of silver or pan a stream filled

with gold nuggets. If that didn't work out, he could always return to thieving for a stake and ride down into Old Mexico to avoid the law, or push on farther west to California.

But now Charlie wasn't so sure about staying with the drive. He'd originally thought that working from the back side of a horse would be a lot easier than wrestling a plow behind a team of cantankerous mules. Fact was, it was worse, especially riding drag day in and day out, prodding a bunch of weak, hungry, and thirsty cattle that trailed behind the two main herds several miles ahead.

He wanted to shoot the starving mother cows, their bony calves, and the scrawny half-dead yearlings that made up the herd and be done with it. Then if he had his druthers, just for fun he'd shoot the pack of gaunt coyotes that followed close behind.

Today he rode left drag, and it was well nigh intolerable with the wind blowing dust from the herd straight at him. Even with his neckerchief over his face and his hat pulled low, it wasn't enough to keep the sand out of his eyes. His mouth and throat felt like he'd been eating dirt and chewing cactus thorns for a week or more. Not only were the wind, sun, sand, and dust about all a body could bear, but he itched from top to bottom, to the point of painful distraction.

Four thousand animals were strung out over ten miles of nothing but parched grass, dry water holes, and thick brush, and the pace was damnably slow. By noontime each day the cattle kicked up so much dirt that even with no wind to speak of, the haze was thick enough to weaken the glare of the blinding sun. Every night Charlie looked skyward, hoping for a sign that a rip-roaring gulley washer would come along and give everything a good soaking, but the sky held nary a cloud.

Across the way, he could make out John Kerney working a reluctant mother cow and her calf back toward the slow-moving, lowing animals. Up ahead, Ed Pearl rode flank with a few other boys to keep some cattle from breaking for the brush, where they'd be lost for good.

The stragglers that couldn't keep up were left behind for the coyotes, wolves, and buzzards to pick over. When the coyotes made a kill, the wolves closed in and drove them away with enough yipping, barking, snarling, and howling to wake a man up from a sound sleep. Charlie figured Robertson had lost about twenty cows so far.

Charlie was choking on some dust in his gullet when Ed Pearl rode up and told him there was water one day's drive farther on.

"You look a sight," he added with a smile. "Push them critters along, now. Wilcox wants the herd bedded down by dusk. Cook is bringing water back from the river."

"Enough water so I can wash my face?" Charlie asked.

"Doubtful," Ed replied. "Besides, you look more agreeable when no one can see that ugly mug of yours."

"You're a whole lot uglier than me, old man," Charlie shot back with a snarl.

"No need to get put out, Charlie," Ed replied with a chuckle. "You're as touchy as a riled rattlesnake. Now, move those cows before Buck comes back here and gives us both a tongue lashing."

When the herd was settled and the early night riders sent out, the cowboys that remained in camp talked over a meal of warmed-up beans, biscuits, beef, and coffee thick enough to eat with a spoon about the prospects of freshwater come one more sundown and what the cattle might do once they caught scent of it. Stories of past stampedes circulated among the men, most with dire warnings of deadly consequences suffered by careless cowboys.

Not about to wait another day for water, Charlie left the waddies to their stories and pondered a plan. If he lit out before dawn on a fast horse he could make the river crossing with nobody missing him till he was long gone. And if he did take off, there would be no coming back, so he'd first need to steal a few things he could sell for ready cash.

He'd been eyeing John Kerney's long rifle, a Springfield Model 1873 that would fetch a good price, and he'd been hankering for Buck Moore's Colt .45-caliber pistol ever since he'd laid eyes on it. Also, there were several sound horses in the remuda he could rustle that were worth twenty dollars each, Ed Pearl kept some folding money in his left boot, and another boy had a pouch that jingled with silver coins. Whatever he could steal quickly and easily would have to do, until he got to a place where the pickings were better.

The idea of being done with the whole damn outfit lifted Charlie's spirits considerably. He'd grab what he could in the dark of night and be gone. He could almost taste cool water in his mouth.

* * *

In the darkest hour before dawn, John Kerney woke with a start from a restless sleep. He'd been dreaming that Mary Alice was running away from him clutching their baby, and no matter how far or fast he chased after her, he couldn't catch up.

Off in the distance, the cattle were lowing softly but not stirring enough to worry about. He heard someone rummaging around at the chuck wagon and sat up to turn and look, but it was too inky black to see a thing. If it was Cook, he'd yet to light the fire and start the coffee boiling.

The sounds stopped, and Kerney figured it was probably just a hungry cowboy looking for something to eat. Unable to go back to sleep, he put his head down anyway and closed his eyes. After some time, he heard soft footsteps coming his way and looked to see a figure reaching for the Springfield carbine that he always kept at his side.

He clutched the arm, swung hard with a balled fist, hit Charlie Gambel square on his button nose, and rammed his shoulder into the boy's chest as he sat up.

"Jesus, I just came to wake you," Charlie moaned as he rocked back on his haunches, a hand over his nose trying to stem the flow of blood.

"And you needed my Springfield to do it," Kerney said, standing over Charlie. He reached down and pulled Gambel to his feet. Stuck in the boy's pistol belt was Buck Moore's Colt .45.

On the ground was a gunnysack from the chuck wagon. Kerney kicked it open to expose some hardtack, beef jerky, a coin purse belonging to a cowboy everybody called Brother Thomas because of all the endless preaching he did about hell and damnation, and some folding money that probably belonged to Ed Pearl.

"What else have you got that doesn't belong to you?" Kerney asked as he tossed the Colt and Charlie's pistol on the ground.

"Nothing, I swear," Charlie said, his voice cracking.

Kerney looked around. Dawn was fast approaching, and Cook had the fire going. Off a ways he spotted Charlie's saddled horse. He dragged the boy to it by the scruff of the neck, took Charlie's rifle from its scabbard, and told him to get mounted.

"What are you going to do?" Charlie asked as he swung up on his horse, blood still dripping from his broken nose.

"Give you a five-minute head start before I tell everybody that you're a no-good thief and I ran you out of camp," Kerney replied.

"I need my pistol and rifle before I ride out," Charlie said.

Kerney shook his head. "So you can come back and shoot me? Leave unarmed now, Charlie, or I'll pull you off that horse and let every man you stole from give you a good thrashing."

Charlie wiped the blood from his nose on a sleeve, gave Kerney a dirty look, spurred his horse, and galloped away.

That evening at the river, after the cattle and horses had drunk their fill and a number of the men were still bathing and clowning around in the water, Cal Doran walked up to where Kerney was giving his pony a good brushing.

"I just heard you've made an enemy for life out of Charlie Gambel," he said.

"Maybe so," Kerney replied as he plucked a burr off the horse's flank. "But you were right about that boy; I'll give you that."

"Mark my words," Cal said. "You should have shot him down."

* * *

After a day of rest at the river, Wilcox pushed the men and cattle hard across the Staked Plains, a vast, featureless stretch of empty country broken only by a sea of yucca stalks. On the second day out, trailing the herd late in the afternoon, Kerney spotted Cal Doran's riderless horse, Patches, off in the distance. Going to investigate, he found a fall had put a crease in the cowboy's forehead and his pony had come up lame. Nearby was a dead rattlesnake, minus its head.

"I'm obliged," Cal said after Kerney doctored his noggin. "Patches got spooked."

"I can see that," Kerney replied. "Your pony is lame."

"I know that, dammit," Cal snapped back, his head spinning.

Kerney got Doran to his feet. "No cause to get surly. Climb on my horse."

"I can walk."

"You're wobbly. Get in the saddle." He gave Doran a leg up and started out in the direction of the herd a couple miles distant, leading Cal's lame pony.

"You're gonna be sore footed when we reach camp," Cal said. He blinked his eyes to stop seeing double, but it didn't work.

"I've lived through worse," Kerney answered.

"That rattler was a good eight feet long."

"Six," Kerney corrected.

"Eight, dammit."

Kerney shrugged. "I ain't gonna argue with a man who's been knocked silly off his pony."

"How is my pony?" Cal asked.

"He'll mend."

"My head sure aches."

"Least you didn't break anything important," Kerney said.

Cal laughed. "You do to ride with, old son."

"Maybe we'll do that someday."

"That would be fine with me," Cal replied, thinking John Kerney was a damn good man, better than most.

6

Ignacio Chávez had heard the story of his birth countless times, told over and over by his family and every adult in his village. Even little children who hadn't been alive at the time knew the tale by heart.

Each time Ignacio's father, Cesario, recalled his son's birth, he spoke of it with great dramatic flair, for it occurred on the very night a rampaging flood had wiped out farming settlements up and down the Rio Grande south of the *villa* of Socorro. As the despondent families huddled together on higher ground, surrounded by the few possessions they'd salvaged from the raging waters, with the angry currents still lapping at their feet, Ignacio entered the world with lusty cries.

Whenever the subject came up, Ignacio's mother, Señora María Candelaria Chávez, who was not given to storytelling as was her husband, simply liked to say that out of all her six children, his birth had been the most unusual since it had been witnessed by everyone in the village.

In the harsh light of the following day, when it was clear to all that everything of value had been lost, their homes and livestock alike

buried by a thick carpet of brown mud, the men of the village gathered in serious conversation. After much discussion, they decided to
leave the fertile bottomlands of the Rio Grande—a river that sometimes slowed to a trickle, occasionally trapped man and beast in
quicksand, often wandered, flooded unexpectedly, and seemed to
change course at will regardless of the season—and start anew along
the banks of the much smaller, less turbulent Tularosa River.

Situated across a vast basin on the other side of the mountains,
the Tularosa was so small and timid a stream—more a creek than
a river—that it wandered out into the basin grasslands and disappeared underground. Except, of course, when the rains came and
waters crested the banks and filled the floodplain.

The decision to move was made with grave misgivings. Two years
earlier several families had left the Rio Grande to settle along the
Tularosa, only to be driven out by the Apaches who lived high in
the mountains to the east, which loomed over the valley.

The Indians had burned their crops, destroyed their homes,
and killed two men during the battle. As the survivors fled in fear
for their lives, the Apaches attacked once more and made off with
a small child who had fallen out of his mother's arms in an overturned wagon. So there was great risk in the move, and none took
it lightly. Yet, with everything lost except life itself, the threat of
nearby Apaches paled in comparison to the need for survival.

Once again on the night of the annual fiesta celebrating the
founding of Tularosa, Ignacio endured a shower of stories about
his birth. Some, like the devout grandmothers of the village, who
considered Ignacio's arrival on earth a miracle, reminded him that
they had prayed over his pregnant mother during the raging flood.
Surely, their prayers and God's hand had spared mother, son, and
all the villagers on that dreadful night.

Others, mostly friends his own age, teased him about the old
ones treating him like he was the favored son of the don of a great
ranchero, and taunted him about his mother's often-stated prophesy that someday he would achieve high station, perhaps as mayor
like his father, sheriff like his uncle José Candelaria, or even—
could it be possible?—a priest to be feared and respected by all.

A few of the grandfathers rubbed his head as if he were a good-
luck charm as they wandered off to find friends to drink with, while
others stopped to tell him *their* version of the great flood and the
subsequent dangerous resettlement. As he listened, Ignacio never
ceased to be amazed at the subtle changes each storyteller brought
to the tale.

After nightfall, when the roasted goat and the calf had been
carved and served with tortillas and beans, when the feasting was
over and the fandango had begun, Ignacio turned his attention to
Teresa Armijo, dancing with her as often as possible. Although she
was still not old enough to marry and Ignacio had said not a word
to her of his intentions, in his mind she was already his betrothed.
Barely five feet tall, she was the most beautiful girl in Tularosa,
with round, inviting eyes, a long, thin neck that made her seem
taller, a tiny waist, and full lips that were always ready with a smile.
As children they'd played in the shade of the courtyard trees and
chased each other through the cornfields when the men of the
village were close by to watch over them. In more recent times, he
read to her under the shade of the cottonwood trees from a book
on the lives of saints left behind by a priest who'd passed though
the village on his way to Santa Fe.

Not once had she ever teased him about being the miracle baby
born during the flood, or for being the favored village son, or for
his studious nature. And she admired his seemingly amazing abil-

ity to learn English from the *americanos* who'd recently moved onto the basin, although she found the few words he taught her to be harsh upon her tongue.

During a lull in the dancing, Ignacio's father took him outside the granary, which had been cleaned and decorated for the dance, gave him a sip of whiskey from his cup, and told him in the morning he would be driving one of the wagons leaving for the army fort on the other side of the mountains.

It was a moment Ignacio had been dreaming about for years. At sixteen he was now considered a man. The days when he had ached to ride out to skirmish with the raiding Apaches were behind him. Now, not only would he continue to work in the fields, tend to the sheep and the cattle, cut wood, and do all of his ordinary chores, but he would also get to make the dangerous wagon trips reserved only for men of fighting age. Finally, he would get to travel through the high peaks of the Apache lands and see the army fort on the east side of the mountains. Soon he'd get to make the long, hard trek west across the basin to the villages of Las Cruces and Mesilla on the banks of the Rio Grande, where staples and supplies could be purchased, news of events in the world could be heard, and books could be found. He had hopes of having enough money someday to purchase one, perhaps even two books.

Henceforth, he'd be armed with a rifle and one of his father's pistols and required to help guard the crops, the livestock, and the village against attacks by marauding Apaches.

With the arrival of the Texans a few years ago, danger from the Apaches had diminished, but there were still sporadic clashes. Now he'd be able to prove himself to be a man of courage.

"Starting tomorrow you can no longer act as a willful, spirited child," Cesario Chávez admonished, "or spend hours reading. You must be reliable in all ways. No idling over the stories of the saints when you are a sentry, no visits to the *americanos* when you should be working, no stealing away to speak to Teresa when you have chores to do. Do you understand?"

"Yes, Father," Ignacio replied solemnly as he handed back the cup of whiskey. The harsh taste of it burned his throat.

Cesario sipped from the cup and returned it to his son. "Let us have one more drink between us to celebrate the first night of your manhood. But when you kiss your mother good night, do not tell her it was I who gave you the whiskey."

"On my honor, I promise not to tell her," Ignacio replied, trying hard not to make a face as he swallowed.

Cesario looked into his son's eyes. At sixteen he was already taller than Cesario by at least an inch and still growing. Someday Ignacio would be the tallest man in the village, almost as big as the *americanos*. Already he was the smartest, although Cesario had no plans to tell him so.

"Good," Cesario said. "Now, go and dance with somebody other than Teresa Armijo so she won't treat your attentions lightly when you are able to announce them to her."

Surprised that he'd been found out, Ignacio opened his mouth to speak, saw the smile on his father's face, blushed, and said nothing.

"Go," Cesario repeated with a laugh as he pushed Ignacio toward the open granary doors. "And tell your mother I'll be sharing a drink outside with your uncle José and will dance with her shortly."

Inside the granary, Ignacio passed on his father's message to his mother, who laughed and quickly returned to her conversation with María Romero, the village gossip. No secret was safe with her. Across the room, Patrick Coghlan, the big, red-faced, bearded

Irishman who owned half of the vacant lots in Tularosa, was talking to Perfecto Armijo, Teresa's father. Coghlan, who had bought his lots from Señor Armijo, spoke pretty good Spanish, so Ignacio wasn't surprised to see the two men conversing.

Ignacio knew the four *americanos* with Señor Coghlan only by their first names. The Irishman was building a store on the main road through the village, and Ignacio had seen the vaqueros come and go many times. Dick, an older man, perhaps in his forties but certainly not as old as Señor Coghlan, had a nasty scar that ran from below his eye to his jaw. He seemed to be the *jefe* of the crew. The two cousins, Bill and Walter Clossen, who were surly to Ignacio upon occasion, stood to one side watching Charlie, a slender cowboy not much older than Ignacio. Charlie was talking earnestly to Teresa, leaning close to her, smiling and laughing, while Antonio, Ignacio's fourteen-year-old brother, stood nervously nearby. Alarmed at such a sight, Ignacio made a beeline for them.

"The señorita doesn't speak English," he said to Charlie as he approached.

Charlie laughed. "I got that figured out all right, but I can tell she likes me anyhow." He glanced at Teresa with the look of a hawk about to swoop up its prey. "Now, you go on and talk Mexican to the little lady for me. You tell her I like her *mucho bueno,* and that I'm gonna borrow me a horse and buggy on Sunday and come calling to take her for a ride."

"I cannot speak that to her," Ignacio replied, glancing at Teresa. Although her eyes were lowered, she smiled sweetly at the cowboy.

Charlie's grin disappeared. "Sure you can. Just be a good Mexican and do as I say."

Ignacio shook his head. "Her father will not allow you his permission."

Teresa pulled at Ignacio's sleeve. "What is he saying?" she asked in Spanish, her eyes fixed on the *americano*.

For an instant Ignacio wished he had Charlie's straw-colored hair and blue eyes. He switched to Spanish. "Nothing of importance."

Teresa's mother was steps away, deep in conversation with some of the village women. He pulled Antonio along with him, walked over to Señora Armijo, and politely asked if he could dance with Teresa again once the music resumed.

"Of course," Señora Armijo replied with a smile, a bit perplexed by Ignacio's request. There was no need to ask her permission.

As she glanced around for her daughter, her smile froze when she caught sight of Teresa talking to the blond *americano*. She broke away from the chitchat, took Teresa by the arm, and led her away from the gringo.

Charlie shot Ignacio a hard look and edged over to him. "You shouldn't have done that, boy. I wasn't finished talking to the lady."

"*Excusa, señor?*" Ignacio said innocently as he stood his ground and tried to keep his apprehension at bay. Sweat trickled down the back of his neck.

Charlie bared his teeth. "Ain't you just a sight, acting slow-witted and such. Don't get uppity on me, boy, unless you want to go home, borrow your daddy's *pistola*, and meet me outside."

Ignacio stiffened. "I have no *querella* with you."

Charlie smirked. "I bet you fancy that little *chica* yourself, don't you, boy?"

Ignacio could feel a blush spreading across his cheeks. He glanced at the *pistola* strapped to Charlie's leg, swallowed hard, and said nothing.

"Next time I tell you to do something, you jump to it, hear me, boy?" Charlie patted his pistol for emphasis. "Now, get."

Ignacio slowly turned away, angry at himself for not standing up to Charlie, certain that in his first test of manhood he'd failed dismally. Behind him he heard Charlie and the gringo Clossen cousins laughing at him. On the other side of the dance floor Teresa gazed at Charlie, that coy smile still on her lips. Never had she ever smiled at him that way. There and then Ignacio vowed that when he had money, instead of books he would buy a pistol and learn how to use it.

The music started up again. He walked over to Teresa and asked her to dance. She refused and would not talk to him for the rest of the night.

HARD COUNTRY

7

John Kerney had been on the Tularosa for nearly a year, and the land still amazed and awed him. Mountains rose east and west of the wide basin, making for endless brilliant sunrises and astonishing sunsets. Under crystal-clear, deep blue skies, he could see in sharp detail a hundred miles up and down the range, from the northerly lava badlands the Mexicans called the malpais, past the gleaming waves of blinding white sand dunes that stretched for miles over the basin, beyond to the southerly nameless mesa grasslands and the faint outline of the mountains near the El Paso border town.

The basin and the mountains that confined it were a land impossible to ignore. Kerney had seen beautiful places before; the endless Texas prairie that stretched a man's vision to the distant horizon, the rich farmlands along the wide Missouri that seemed to be cast in every imaginable shade of green, the deep forests of the Kentucky blue mountains. But on the Tularosa—where sentinel mountain ranges hid fresh running streams coursing down narrow ravines, where bunchgrass grew as high as a horse's belly, where massive creamy clouds gathered thousands of feet above vertical spires—here his spirits soared, and the sadness that had dogged him the last few years lessened.

The basin was vast, inspiring, daunting, filled with plants and animals that stung and bit, harsh and windswept, ravaged by floods and parched by drought, and mostly empty of people. It suited John Kerney just fine.

Trailing five horses he'd picked up for his employer from a rancher trading livestock at the army fort two days ago, he'd camped overnight on the Apache lands in the high country without incident and had just passed Dead Man's Mountain when he spotted a convoy of four supply wagons winding up the rocky wagon road from the village far below. He continued on until he reached the slow-moving wagons and then halted his small remuda. The Mexicans from Tularosa likewise reined their horse teams to a stop. Kerney greeted them with his slowly expanding Spanish vocabulary.

"Señor Kerney, your Spanish is improving little bit," Ignacio Chávez said with a smile. "Why we don't see you in the village anymore?"

"I parted ways with Pat Coghlan," Kerney replied as he opened his saddlebag and pulled out a small parcel. "I've been working for John Good over at La Luz. Haven't been back this way since he took me on."

He leaned out from his saddle and handed the parcel to Ignacio. "This is for you."

"What is it?" Ignacio asked, surprised.

"I know you like to read. It's a book of stories by a writer named Hawthorne. It's pretty beat-up, but most of the pages are there, and some of the yarns aren't half bad if you can stand all the fancy words he uses to get the job done."

With Ignacio in mind, Kerney had bought the tattered book for a five-cent piece from a soldier's wife at the fort.

"Is it written in *americano?*" Ignacio asked, almost unbelieving.

"Yep, so your English can get better, *poco a poco.*"

Ignacio laughed and grinned with pleasure as he unwrapped the parcel and slowly sounded out the words of the title. *"Twice-Told Tales.* What means that?"

Kerney shrugged. "I don't know."

Ignacio carefully tucked the book inside his shirt. *"Muchas gracias,* Señor Kerney."

"Por nada," Kerney replied. He touched the brim of his hat, waved good-bye to the men in the wagons ahead of Ignacio, and started down the road trailing his small remuda.

A good mile farther on, Ignacio suddenly remembered that the gringo Charlie had asked him several times if he knew of Señor Kerney's whereabouts. And although he had no knowledge that Charlie wished Kerney harm, Ignacio had an urge to stop the horses, turn the wagon around, and warn the señor about the *pistolero.*

Over his shoulder he could see only dust on the trail kicked up by Kerney's remuda. Ignacio hoped there would be no trouble waiting for him in Tularosa.

* * *

As John Kerney drew near Tularosa, the village spread out before him. The low, flat-roof adobe houses with chickens running loose in yards behind low walls, the orderly irrigation ditches filled with clear running water that fed the carefully tended fields, and the cottonwoods along the riverbank spreading welcoming shade made for a pleasant view. Beyond the village, the hot sun on the still basin and the shimmering mountains to the west etched by a cloudless blue sky promised a dry, windless day.

He entered the peaceful village through the main road and passed by two old men unloading a cart of firewood near an outdoor kitchen, where several women were busy at a table near an *horno* preparing food for the midday meal. From the river he could hear the sounds of children playing under the cottonwood trees, and in the grassy rangeland farther on a small herd of sheep grazed under the watchful eyes of a man and dog.

The village of La Luz, where Kerney's employer, John Good, had his ranch, was still a twelve-mile ride away. He stopped to rest and water the horses at the river before moving on past the unfinished store and saloon Pat Coghlan was building on the main road. Steady progress to the buildings had been made since Kerney had left Tularosa: Chimneys now poked through finished roofs, and a plank sidewalk joined the long porches that fronted both structures.

Once Coghlan opened for business, every cowboy and rancher within fifty miles would be coming to Tularosa for supplies, liquor, and whatever else they needed, including the favors of the soiled doves that were sure to be drawn to the town. Soldiers from Fort Stanton would gladly make the long ride to frequent the place, and in no time the villagers would stop making the arduous wagon trips to Las Cruces and Mesilla for supplies and start trading with Coghlan instead. The man was poised to get rich.

Tularosa's days as a sleepy Mexican village were numbered. Some folks were already calling Patrick Coghlan the king of Tularosa, and there was talk he had bought up a large stretch of land upstream from the village in the sweetest valley on the basin. If that was true, Coghlan now controlled the water that supplied the

Michael McGarrity

village and could run cows on a half million acres. That made him a force to be reckoned with.

Up ahead in the open country, four horsemen rode hard in his direction, kicking up dust. Unsure of what their hurry might be, Kerney veered the string of ponies off the road, ran a quick picket line, pulled his rifle from its scabbard, saddled up, and waited. As the riders came close, Kerney recognized Charlie Gambel. His grip tightened on the rifle.

"Well, well," Charlie said, almost sneering as he pulled his horse to a stop. "If it ain't John Kerney."

"Charlie," Kerney said evenly, eyeing Gambel's companions as they joined up with the young outlaw. Although he'd never met the other men before, he guessed Charlie's pals were Dick Turknet and the Clossen cousins. The cousins were dull-eyed boys without much spark, and Turknet had a vicious look about him. He gazed at Kerney's string of horses with great interest.

Aside from Charlie, this was the bunch that had sold Tom's stolen horses. Kerney had wondered what he would do if he met up with them. From the hard looks he was getting, asking about Tom's ponies didn't seem like a good idea.

"Aren't you glad to see me, old friend?" Charlie asked with bravado, eyeing Kerney's rifle.

Kerney turned his horse slightly so that the rifle barrel pointed directly at Charlie's belly, but he kept his eyes locked on Dick Turknet, who would obviously call the play.

"I heard you'd showed up hereabouts recently," Kerney replied, "but I don't have time to palaver, and you boys seemed to be in a big hurry when you rode up."

He started silently counting, figuring if he got to ten he'd probably be a dead man lying at the side of the road.

"True enough," Turknet said just as Kerney counted nine and was about to shoot Charlie Gambel.

He nodded at Kerney and wheeled his horse against Charlie's mount. "If you got business with this cowboy, Charlie, it will have to wait. Let's go."

Turknet lit out for the village at a gallop.

"I ain't forgetting what you did to me," Charlie called out as he and the cousins chased after Turknet.

John Kerney watched until they were out of sight, let out a sigh of relief, and put the rifle away. As he gathered the small remuda and struck out for La Luz, he wondered if there was anything at all that might change Charlie's mind about being an outlaw. He doubted it.

In the tense few moments during his encounter with Turknet and his gang, Kerney had managed a quick look at their horses. None had belonged to his dead brother which didn't mean much one way or the other. What did matter was that Turknet was without a doubt a killer who'd once had Tom's stolen horses in his possession. That made him three-fourths guilty of horse thieving and murder in Kerney's mind. He looked forward to seeing Turknet again in a more peaceable setting.

* * *

John Good's ranch was a few miles above the village of La Luz in a canyon that ran down the west slope of the mountains through a narrow gorge that opened onto broad meadows with tall, abundant grasses. In fact, the grass was fragile and easily overgrazed, a lesson John Good had learned the hard way by letting his cattle browse a higher pasture down to bare soil and dead roots.

A wide, perennial creek with headwaters in the mountains flowed through the canyon to the carefully tilled fields in the Mexican settlement below.

According to the story recounted by La Luz villagers, two Spanish missionaries stopped on their way to Santa Fe in 1719, baptized a group of Indians, and built a chapel, which they named Our Lady of Light before moving on. La Luz—"The Light"—remained a forgotten place for well over a century, until Mexican settlers moved in, followed a mere fifteen years later by Texas ranchers trailing cattle into the territory.

The ranch was a family operation. John Good had a passel of sons to help him, along with a son-in-law and a brother. He also had a wife and several daughters to care for domestic matters. As the only hired hand, Kerney pretty much got the chores none of the male family members aspired to, including cutting wood for the cookstove, drawing water from the well, and helping the ladies in the kitchen when called upon to do so.

He'd been given the job of fetching the new mounts from the fort because the menfolk had gone to Lincoln to testify in a hearing about John Good's killing of a cowboy allegedly caught stealing cattle from the ranch.

Kerney had heard that the dead man in question had been bushwhacked by Good because of some old feud back in Texas. Given the way Good bridled at any perceived slight or wrong, Kerney didn't doubt the possibility.

So far, he'd avoided Good's mean streak by holding his tongue and doing his job, but he wasn't happy with the situation and planned to move on after drawing his pay at the end of the month. To where, he wasn't sure.

The absence of horses in the pasture told him that Good and

his kin had not yet come back from their visit to the circuit court. He turned the horses out into the corral, stripped to the waist, and cleaned up at the water trough next to the barn. Across the way, John Good's wife, Jewel, watched him from the ranch-house porch.

She was a tall, stern-looking woman with thin lips, a square jaw, and a quarrelsome personality that contradicted both her names. She turned and went inside without so much as calling out a howdy or giving a wave in Kerney's direction.

After feeding his horse some oats and putting it in the corral, Kerney chopped firewood, carried it to the cookstove, and hauled well water to the kitchen without one word passing between him and Good's wife and daughters. When he finished his chores, Good's plumpest daughter served him a meal of fried chicken and beans, again without a word spoken. He ate it on the porch stoop with the western sun hanging large over the distant mountains.

As he sipped the last of his coffee, a horseman came into view on the lower meadow, approaching at a slow pace. Kerney squinted and recognized Cal Doran's paint horse, Patches. Smiling, he stood, waved, and waited.

Robertson's hired gun on the cattle drive that brought Kerney from Texas to the Tularosa, Cal Doran had become a good companion on the trail, and over the past year their friendship had deepened.

"Haven't seen you since I quit Pat Coghlan," Kerney said as Doran pulled up and dismounted.

"I quit him myself soon after. I can't abide a man who expects loyalty without earning it." A rangy man with intelligent and watchful eyes, Cal took off his gloves, slapped some dust from his chaps, and looked over Kerney's shoulder. "Who's the woman standing at the door inside the house?"

"Mrs. Jewel Good, the rancher's wife, I imagine," Kerney answered. "She seems to think she needs to keep an eye on me. Dick Turknet is working for Coghlan now."

"Now, that's disturbing news," Doran replied with a rueful smile. He'd shaved off his mustache since last Kerney saw him and now looked even more boyish. "I heard that Charlie Gambel is riding with Dick and the cousins," he added. "That's a group of compañeros to stay shy of."

"Too late for me," Kerney replied. "I met up with those bright lads gone bad earlier today. Charlie promised to see me again real soon."

Cal laughed. "So Charlie's a hard case, is he?"

"He'd have me believe so," Kerney replied. "What brings you up the canyon? Looking for work?"

"Nope," Cal said. "I've got something for you." He took an envelope from his shirt pocket and handed it to Kerney. "A mule skinner down in El Paso was asking around about you. When I allowed I might know you, he gave me this to pass along."

Kerney's name on the grease-stained envelope was misspelled and barely legible. "What else did he say?"

"Said this fellow in a mining camp up north was asking anyone heading south if they knew you."

Soon after arriving on the Tularosa, Kerney had sent a letter to Ida's shopkeeper brother in Dodge City with money to settle the account for the care of his son. He'd also enclosed a letter to Ida asking that it be forwarded if her whereabouts were known.

Quickly he tore open the envelope and read the note:

Ida dead eight weks ago come Sunday. I cain't care your
boy no more myself. Come get him or I give him away to
someone who can.

Virgil Peters

Kerney's expression hardened. "Did he say where he met this man?"

"Arroyo Hondo, north of Taos," Cal replied. "You look like something bit down on you terrible."

"I need to get up there pronto." Kerney stepped off hurriedly toward the corral.

Cal kept pace. "Mind telling me why?"

Kerney handed Doran the letter as he got his saddle and entered the corral.

Cal read it quickly and gave it back. "How old is the boy?"

"Coming on four years." Kerney heaved the saddle over his horse's back and tightened the girth strap. "His name is Patrick."

"What in blazes are you gonna do with a four-year-old boy?"

"Be his pa, which I haven't been for one damn day of his wretched life so far."

"That's a heavy load for a hired hand on horseback," Cal said. "You're going to need some considerable help to raise up that pup."

"If I don't go get him, then I'm the sorriest man who ever forked a horse." Kerney led his mount out of the corral, looped the reins loosely over a railing, and turned for the barn. "I'll get my gear and bedroll."

"Better hold up there, horse," Cal said with a nod at the ranch house. A woman came toward them at a hurried pace. "Seems your leaving has raised some curiosity. Is that rancher Good's wife?"

"It is." Kerney touched the brim of his hat when she drew near. "Ma'am."

"Where are you going?" she demanded indignantly, dismissing Cal Doran with a stern look.

"Mrs. Good," Kerney said. "I don't like leaving you short, but I need to draw my pay and be on my way."

"Draw your pay?" Jewel Good snapped. "You know my husband's rule. No wages paid until the end of the month."

"I can't stay. I'm in a tight spot. I need to fetch my son from a man who has been caring for him and now threatens to give him away. Surely you understand."

"Humph," she said in a huff, giving Cal a hostile glance. "Going drinking with your friend is more likely the truth, I'd say."

"Just hold up one minute, ma'am," Kerney said. "I don't appreciate your words, and I'm owed my wages."

"I have no money to give you."

Kerney knew better. He bit his lip to keep from calling the woman a liar and mounted up. "I'll get my bedroll and be gone."

"I'll ride with you a ways," Cal said. He gave Mrs. Good a winning smile, removed his hat, and said, "Ma'am, if I may say a word or two?"

"What is it?" she replied tartly.

"The way I see it, the only good thing about you is your name, which you plainly don't deserve."

Mrs. Good turned livid. "Get off this ranch."

"Gladly," Cal said with a broad, courtly sweep of his hat.

* * *

During their time in New Mexico, neither Kerney nor Cal Doran had strayed far from the basin, but they knew that the mail coach came to Tularosa from the village of Las Vegas, on the high plains, a far ways north of Fort Stanton. Because the road was a well-traveled route, Kerney figured he'd be able to make good time. Once in Las Vegas he would find out the quickest and best way to reach the mining camp at Arroyo Hondo before striking out for the high country.

After riding through most of the night and stopping for a few hours' sleep before traveling on, they arrived at Fort Stanton late in the day, where Kerney expected he and Cal would part company. Instead, after the colors had been retired for the evening and the troop formation dismissed from the quadrangle, Cal grinned at him, clicked his heels together, saluted, and said he'd decided to sign on for the duration.

"Are you sure?" Kerney asked. A small group of Mescalero Apaches wrapped in blankets came out of the squat administration building and sat on the ground in front of the building. The Indian agent stepped out and tried to wave them away. The Mescaleros didn't budge.

"You're good to ride along with," Cal replied, "and I've got a hankering to see Santa Fe. I understand the town is dirt ugly, but some of the women are fetching and a good game of chance is easy to come by. After we find your boy, I'll say adios and leave you to get in trouble on your own."

"I appreciate the company," Kerney answered, pleased to have Cal's companionship and his gun hand.

They left the quadrangle and found a stage driver who told them the wagon road to Las Vegas was passable and mostly tolerable except in wet weather, when the mud made for a blasted muddle. He mentioned that a good day's ride would get them to the stage stop and tavern in Red Cloud Canyon.

While Cal watered and fed the horses, Kerney went to the trader's store and stocked up on provisions. As he settled up with the clerk, Ignacio Cháves walked in and hurried over. He had *Twice-Told Tales* clutched tightly in his hand.

"I saw your horse outside with Señor Doran's," Ignacio said, smiling broadly. "This book is *maravilloso*, when I can make out words."

Kerney took a guess at the word. "Does that mean marvelous?"

"*Sí*. But I tell you now a man named Charlie has asked about you. Not be *importante* maybe, but I think he is not your friend."

"No, he's not," Kerney replied. "Stay clear of him, if you can."

Ignacio stuck his chin out defiantly. "Perhaps no."

"Have you had a run-in with Charlie?"

"It is for my concern only."

Kerney nodded gravely. Private matters were not to be questioned, and although Charlie wasn't a hard-nosed outlaw yet, Ignacio would be no match for him. "Use caution, my young amigo."

"First, I prepare myself." Ignacio tapped his forehead with a finger. "I will be, how you say, smart."

"Good."

"Will you come back to Tularosa?"

"I plan to."

Ignacio smiled as he slid his book inside his shirt. "I see you again."

Kerney nodded in agreement. "Your English is getting better."

Ignacio beamed. "I've been practicing. Talking only *americano* at the fort. It making my father loco."

"Perhaps not," Kerney replied, knowing full well how proud Cesario Chávez was of his son.

Outside the store, Cal waited with the horses. They said good-bye to Ignacio and rode out in the twilight. Soon they would be under a full moon in a clear sky and if they kept a steady pace would reach Red Cloud Canyon by dawn.

They crossed the river and at moonrise were past the flats north of the mesa. They topped a ridge above a narrow gorge and caught their first glimpse of a vast rangeland, the wagon road cutting through it, darkened by the shadow of close-at-hand mountains that ran east-west and dwarfed the lowlands.

"Now, that's a sight," Kerney said as his horse picked a careful way through the rocky wagon ruts.

"A nice piece of country," Cal said, following behind.

"More pleasing come sunup, I imagine."

They rode silently for a time, their eyes focused on the rough road as they made the steep descent to the great valley floor.

"I've been thinking on your predicament after we find young Patrick," Cal said as they resumed riding side by side.

"Have you, now?"

"Yep, and I've come up with a solution. You're gonna have to round yourself up a wife."

Kerney brought his horse to a stop. "Not this old boy."

Cal likewise drew rein. "You've got no choice, as I see it. Well, I guess maybe you could take Patrick along while you're out on the basin gathering shaggy cows with a mind of their own. Although I doubt any rancher would hire you riding double with a young squirt. Without a wife, you might have to turn to crime and thievery to care for that boy, and I know you're not inclined in that direction."

"You're thinking way too far ahead for me," Kerney growled, uneasy with the truth of the matter. He flicked the reins and his horse moved on.

Steady riding throughout the remainder of the night brought
them to the stage stop in Red Cloud Canyon just as the full moon
set to the west and the fiery sun spread yellow light through a stand
of tall trees.

Built with rough logs, the place was nothing more than a one-
room tavern with a small kitchen attached to the back. A cowboy
was passed out on the sawdust floor, his head pressed against a
piece of firewood, and an old man slept on a cot in the kitchen
next to the still-warm stove. Cal woke up the old man, who soon
scratched together a breakfast of cold biscuits, beans, and bacon
served on battered tin plates, and hot coffee as thick as molasses.
As they ate, the man invited them to sleep on the floor for two bits
each until the stage rolled in at noon.

Cal quickly turned down the offer before Kerney could open
his mouth to say no.

Outside, away from the smells of sour-mash whiskey and rancid
bacon grease, they unsaddled their tired horses, watered them,
and turned the animals out into a fenced pasture. In the deep
shade of the tall pines, they stretched out their bedrolls and let the
sounds of the squirrels and birds foraging for food lull them to
sleep.

As he drifted off, Kerney pondered how he'd be able to take
care of Patrick once he found him. He didn't have a notion in
mind, not even one glimmer.

* * *

There were wonders to behold on the road to Las Vegas: distant
mountains to the north and to the west; grassy, windswept rangeland as far as the eye could see; and stair-step mesas that dotted

the horizon. The nights camped beside the road for a few hours' sleep were quiet and peaceful, and during the day few riders passed them by.

The wagon road gradually climbed, then dipped again until it bordered a canyon riverbed thick with nesting birds, where the water ran fast and cool. They passed through small farming settlements where the villagers spoke a different kind of Spanish than that of the Mexicans on the Tularosa.

The thickly forested mountains that rose from the plains behind Las Vegas folded back into even higher peaks, still white tipped by the last of the winter snow. Deep gorges scored the mountains, which filled the skyline. From a distance, the range seemed impenetrable, and Kerney wondered if it augured a hard, toilsome ride through the high country to reach the mining camp at Arroyo Hondo.

Las Vegas wasn't much of a town. A scattering of adobe houses, some with tin roofs and a few with tiny windows, sat near an oval patch of dust six inches thick that served as the town plaza. A two-story mercantile store next to a low adobe bank building bordered one side of the plaza, where some small willow trees had been transplanted in front of the store, each protected by a slat-board fence. Beyond the plaza were low-lying hills stripped bare of all the trees by village woodcutters, and here and there adobe buildings sagged amid crumbling mud walls with signs announcing rooms, whiskey, tobacco, baths, and food.

They stayed overnight, and in the morning they reprovisioned at the mercantile with the last of Kerney's cash and some money Cal threw in. With advice from the store owner on the best route through the mountains to the mining camps, they left Las Vegas with a stiff prairie wind whistling at their backs and dust clouds swirling on the barren foothills.

For three days they worked their way through the rough high country on a road that faded to a trail and sometimes petered out completely. They passed through stands of pine, fir, and spruce trees, groves of tall, stately aspens, and crossed clear, cold, rocky streams. As they topped an open ridge with a slender river valley in sight, a thunderstorm pelted them with hail that stripped the leaves off nearby aspen trees. That night the temperature dropped so perilously low that not even the campfire kept them warm.

They rode into the valley soon after first light. Several prospectors, all working different parts of the stream, were strung out down the canyon, panning for gold and breaking rock along the riverbed. Kerney stopped and asked each man for Virgil Peters, but none of them knew him.

"How far to Arroyo Hondo?" he asked the last man at the bottom of the canyon.

The man raised his pick and pointed westward. "One day."

"Hallelujah," Cal said with a smile.

"And a night," the man added, returning his attention to the boulder he was trying to dig out of the riverbank.

Cal's smile dimmed considerably.

"Are you wearing down?" Kerney asked as they rode away with the sound of metal on stone echoing through the valley.

Cal shook his head and patted his horse's neck. "No more than you. Patches and me have miles left in us, although I'll admit all this good land and wondrous country we've ridden through has made me a shade lonely for a touch of civilization."

John Kerney nodded in agreement and broke his horse into a trot.

* * *

In Arroyo Hondo, a booming area with a stamp mill for crushing ore running at the lower end of the canyon, all Kerney found was disappointment. Virgil Peters had moved on, to where nobody knew, and while some said Patrick was with him, others weren't sure. For the better part of a week, Cal stuck with Kerney, bankrolling the search for Patrick once he learned his friend was busted. They went to every mining camp in the district—Willow Creek, San Cristobal, Arroyo Seco, Moreno Valley, some of the smaller camps that had no names, and finally Red River.

In Red River, Kerney decided to ride east across the mountains to Elizabethtown to look for Patrick. Although the town was just twelve miles from the headwaters of the river, it would be a forty-mile crossing on a bad road and a perilous rocky trail.

"I'm gonna part ways with you and head down to Santa Fe," Cal said as the two friends sat at a table in a saloon that was nothing more than a tent and knocked back a whiskey just shy of not being fit to drink.

"But let me grubstake you," he added, sliding a small coin pouch to Kerney. "I want no back talk or twaddle from you, now. I won a pretty big pot down in El Paso before I rode up to La Luz to deliver that letter to you, and I'm still flush."

"On my word, I'll pay you back," John Kerney said.

Cal grinned. "Make me a silent partner in that ranch you're looking to start once you've rounded up Patrick and get back to the Tularosa. I figure the day will come when I'll probably need a safe place to hide out."

"Partners fifty-fifty," Kerney said, extending his hand.

They shook hands and had another drink to seal the partnership.

"Don't go bust down in Santa Fe with all the women and gambling," Kerney cautioned as Cal mounted Patches.

Cal laughed. "I'll hide some traveling money in my boot. I still think you're gonna need a good woman to help raise up that son of yours."

John Kerney's expression clouded. "First I have to find him."

8

After the money Cal lent him ran out, John Kerney took jobs as he found them, working just long enough to get a stake and start looking for Patrick again. He had no luck hiring on as a ranch hand, so he labored on a crew building a road to a new ore site, drove a wagon over the mountains hauling parts of a stamp mill shipped from Chicago, worked as a chore boy at a high-country summer sheep ranch, and signed on with a construction gang to build a water flume a hundred feet above the ground that spanned half a mile.

During the working stints, he often slept in filthy, cramped tents or on the hard ground with drifters of every sort, who'd come west to get rich in the New Mexico gold and silver fields. Outwardly, he looked like any other muckman: bearded, shabby, and dirty. But instead of a motherlode strike, he sought a son he couldn't describe who was with a man he didn't know and might never find. He stopped at every settlement, mine, camp, and town, no matter how big, small, or remote. He talked with town marshals, merchants, preachers, mine officials, assay masters, womenfolk, and the mountain men he happened on in the wilderness. He trekked the length and breadth of the northern New Mexico and southern Colorado high country, digging for any information about his boy and Virgil Peters, putting up posters as he traveled, asking the same questions over and over again.

For his efforts he got lots of secondhand stories, not one of them the same, most of them unreliable. From a drunk in a whiskey tent, he heard Peters was living in Taos with a Mexican woman. A hard-rock miner in the Moreno Valley told him that Virgil and Patrick were somewhere up in the Leadville mining district. A grocer re-called that Virgil Peters had disappeared into the backcountry to prospect, leaving Patrick in the care of a traveling preacher and his wife, who'd moved on to Willow Springs along the Santa Fe Trail. Another tale had Peters shot dead in a bar fight in Elizabeth-town, the boy with him taken in by a Mexican sheepherder who lived somewhere out on the vast prairie of the Maxwell Land Grant. The most troubling story he heard had Peters selling Patrick to a Ute Indian before leaving the territory for California.

John Kerney followed every yarn as far as he could, but as the months passed and each trail turned cold, he became more and more disheartened. No longer did the peaceful mountain meadows and the shimmering, sky blue high-country lakes lift his spirits. Deep in the gloomy woods or traveling through the narrow, dark canyons, he felt hemmed in and jumpy. In towns he found no friendship with other men. He yearned for the open desert grass-lands and big sky of the Tularosa, but now his dream of proving up a spread on the eastern slopes of the San Andres seemed no more than a trifling whimsy beyond his reach. About the only good thing was he hadn't had to sell his saddle yet.

When a fierce storm brought winter to the mountains, Kerney dropped down into the deep shade of a canyon of spruce and aspen that led to the town of Cimarron. A watering hole and stomping grounds for cowboys, rustlers, gunslingers, outlaws, and mountain men, the town sat along the Santa Fe Trail on the edge of a boundless short-grass prairie that rolled eastward through hills and river valleys.

During his search for Patrick, he had been in Cimarron once before, and the town was passing familiar to him. A two-story adobe with a wide veranda filled one side of a plaza ringed by cottonwoods. Not far from Lambert's Saloon on the road through town, a three-story stone gristmill powered by water from a deep ditch stood near the Cimarron River's edge. Outside the plaza, adobe dwellings were scattered about in slapdash fashion. Away from the dirt houses, a small church with a cross nailed to a wooden belfry marked the town's cemetery grounds.

Kerney had a month's wages in his pocket and a thirst, so he hitched his horse to a post and went into Lambert's Saloon. He made his way to the bar through a crowd of cowboys, traders, road agents, travelers, and miners playing cards and jawboning, found elbow room next to a whiskered old-timer, and looked around the room for familiar faces. In a corner at a monte table he spotted Dick Turknet and the two cousins, Billy and Walt Clossen. Charlie Gambel was nowhere in sight. Turknet glanced his way but showed no sign of recognition.

Kerney had wanted to see Turknet again, but not now while he searched for Patrick. He couldn't risk riling the gunfighter and jeopardizing his own safety. Uneasy that Charlie might show up and make a play, Kerney downed a quick drink, left the saloon, stabled his horse, and rented a room at the big adobe hacienda on the plaza. He paid extra for a bath and scrubbed and soaked in the water until it cooled down and he started to shiver. He dried off, dressed, and took scissors to his beard, cutting it to a nub. Peering closely in the mirror, he shaved the rest of his beard off and then hacked at his hair with the scissors until he could see the tips of his ears. Figuring he looked almost civilized again, he went to bed feeling better about himself than he had in months.

Come morning, after a sound night's sleep and a dime breakfast, he made the rounds, asking merchants and any strangers he happened to pass about his son and Virgil Peters. As usual, he made a point to question the womenfolk of the town, who might be more inclined than their husbands to notice a young boy and a man traveling alone.

At midday, with nothing to show for his effort, he went to the saloon with the waning hope he might learn something from customers still sober enough to wag their chins. It was half-crowded, mostly with gamblers and hard-bitten miners at the tables, and they surely wouldn't cotton to any uncalled-for interruptions on his part. At the bar, Dick Turknet was talking to the saloon owner, Henry Lambert, a Frenchman who'd once been Abraham Lincoln's chef and had official letters framed over the bar to prove it.

Kerney looked cautiously around for the cousins and Charlie Gambel, but he didn't see them. He turned back to Turknet, who eyed him with interest, said something to Lambert, and walked to where Kerney stood.

"You're John Kerney," Turknet said, showing yellow teeth stained brown by tobacco juice.

Kerney nodded and looked around again. "I am. Where's the rest of your outfit?"

"If you mean young Charlie Gambel, he's still down on the Tularosa, lovesick over some little Mexican gal. He sure doesn't think kindly of you."

"I know it."

"And he's turned himself into a fair hand with a .45 in the hopes y'all will meet up again," Turknet added. "Course, the question is, does he have the grit for killing? I think he does. What did you do to rile that boy?"

"Saved him from a hiding or worse," Kerney answered.

Turknet shook his head. "Some folks just don't take to being treated fair and square. It gets them out of sorts."

"Charlie's a bit chuckleheaded."

Turknet smiled. "Yep, he's short on brainpower, but that doesn't make him less bothersome to a peaceable man like yourself."

"I expect you're right."

"Cal Doran said you had an interest in how I came by some Texas horses I sold to Sam Wilcox."

"I am, if you're inclined to tell me," Kerney said guardedly. Turknet hitched his thumb in the belt above his low-slung holster, which made Kerney a mite more nervous.

Turknet shrugged. "Not much to tell. Those horses along with some others were part of Bud McPherson's remuda at his hideout in the brush country. Don't know how Bud came by them exactly, but I've never known him to put good money in an honest man's pocket for an animal he admired. His boys got captured by Texas Rangers and wound up hanged and in shallow graves, but Bud got away and was looking to shuck Texas and ride north to Montana. I gave him half what those animals were worth and he gladly took it, eager as he was to make tracks."

"Bud McPherson," Kerney said.

"That's the man to talk to," Turknet said. "But be careful if you cross his trail. He's got snake blood and will strike fast if you accuse him of having a long loop."

"Did he spend any time up by the panhandle?"

Turknet shrugged. "Can't say I know for sure, but him and his boys covered a lot of country."

Kerney thanked him for the information, and Turknet took his leave, joining the cousins, who had just entered the saloon and had sidled up to the bar. He made quick work of asking questions about Patrick to patrons willing to hear him out and left Lambert's empty-handed, wondering if Dick Turknet had spun him a yarn or told the truth about Bud McPherson. He guessed the truth but wasn't completely sure and didn't see much sense in drifting north to Montana to find out.

But for the first time, thanks to Cal, John Kerney felt like he had some reliable information about Tom and Timmy's killers. He wondered what made Turknet come to figure he was such a peaceable man. Likely by way of Cal Doran, Kerney supposed, smiling at the thought. Or was Turknet just pointing out that he held the upper hand when it came to any thoughts of gunplay?

The sunny, cool day had turned dismal and cold, with a stiff wind running down the canyon and heavy gray clouds ringing the mountains. Earlier, Kerney had found the small adobe church locked, but now smoke rose from the chimney. He rode over and found an Indian woman inside cleaning a wooden altar under the watchful eye of a young friar.

"Do you speak English, Padre?" Kerney asked as he removed his hat.

"Of a sort," the priest replied softly with a Spanish accent. He had a long, thin nose, red hair, and a heavily freckled face. "How may I help?"

"I am looking for my son, a boy of four. He was in the care of a man named Virgil Peters, who wrote me he would give him to strangers if I didn't come fetch him. I've been searching for them ever since."

The padre looked at Kerney sympathetically for a moment and then nodded. "Yes, I have met this man, at Fort Union. He asked me to take a young orphan boy and find him a new home. He said he could no longer care for him."

The priest smiled slightly and made a helpless gesture with his hands. "But my duties require me to travel to many parishes, so I could not take the child. I told him my superiors in Santa Fe might find a family willing to adopt the boy. I advised him to go there."

John Kerney could barely contain his delight. "When was this, Padre?"

"Two months ago, but he did not wish to go to Santa Fe, as he planned to leave for Dodge City as soon as he could find somebody to take the child."

The thought of following another long, cold trail turned Kerney's delight to dismay. "Do you know what happened to the boy?"

The priest shook his head. "Sadly, no, but I have prayed for his safekeeping."

"Thank you, Padre."

"Go with God," the priest said as he made the sign of the cross, "and may he grant that you find your son. I will pray for you both."

"*Gracias*, Padre."

Outside, John Kerney mounted up in thick snow falling from a low cloud that almost clipped the treetops. The wind had stopped howling, and nary a breeze touched his face. He cast a wary eye skyward. The storm had settled over the prairie. The whole country was about to get downright swampy before it froze rock solid.

He hadn't been to Fort Union before but knew it was a ways

south on the Santa Fe Trail, a good fifty miles or more. Two days' travel certain in this weather, with cold camps at night and poor browse for his horse.

He chewed on the idea of bedding down in Cimarron until the storm broke but decided to move on. Fort Union was the main hub along the Santa Fe Trail for goods and supplies traveling to all points of the compass. Thanks to the priest, he now knew Patrick was alive and not a slave to some savage Ute Indian or living in a Mexican sheepherder's hut out on the prairie. Leastways, that was fact two months ago.

Best to get back on the trail before he gave in to the dark suspicion that Patrick was so far gone from the territory that he would never find him, no matter where he traveled or how long he looked. Although he was closer than he'd ever been to finding his boy, he felt no better for it.

He got his gear together, bought some provisions, including a small bag of oats for his horse, wrapped his blanket over his coat around his shoulders, and started out for Fort Union. The thick, wet snowfall dampened all sound except the slight creaking of his saddle leather and the soft fall of his horse's hoofs. Ahead, he could see no more than ten feet through a curtain of snow now falling harder. He pulled his hat down to his ears and spurred his horse into a trot.

It was loco to be traveling in this weather, and he knew it. He could freeze to death, get his scalp lifted by Indians, or be robbed and murdered by a road agent for his horse, gear, and the twenty dollars in his pocket before he got ten miles out of town. If that happened, Patrick would never know who his people were or where he came from. The thought didn't sit well with Kerney, so he silently vowed to write everything in a letter to Patrick once he got to Fort

Union. The boy might never get to read it, but at least the truth of things would've been told.

The storm worsened into a whiteout, and a little more than ten miles along the trail, Kerney found refuge in the village of Ryado. Given shelter by a family who lived in an adobe house that had once belonged to Kit Carson, he sat over a home-cooked meal and told the rancher and his wife the whole story from beginning to end of why he came to be traveling in such a dreadful blizzard, starting with the birth of his son, the death of his wife, and the murder of his brother and young nephew.

He'd never spoken of it before in detail to anyone, and telling it to strangers he might never see again made it easier. In the back of his mind he knew he was practicing out loud for the time when he would set it down on paper.

He finished his tale, and with hot coffee in hand, Kerney and the rancher talked about the coming of the railroad up near Willow Springs, where he'd gone to look for Patrick earlier in the summer. A tunnel had been blasted and cut through the mountain pass, and soon tracks would be laid south toward Santa Fe. Both men predicted it would change their world, but other than turning the Santa Fe Trail into a forgotten wagon road, neither could say exactly how.

In the morning the storm had passed and Kerney set out under a clear sky, bright sun, and a blanket of snow that nearly blinded him with reflected light. Underfoot the ground was soggy, and at times his horse sank above its fetlocks in the mud. He passed by a low butte with snow still clinging to the sheer south face, and soon the village of Ryado faded into a blur behind him.

It would be slow going to Fort Union, but Kerney didn't mind; he rode with the wind at his back and a wee bit of renewed hope that he still might find Patrick.

* * *

A cold camp and a clear, freezing night got John Kerney up and back on the trail long before dawn. He made good time on the hardened trail, which in places was more than a hundred yards wide, and by first light spotted the fort in the distance, the buildings harsh against the horizon, in stark contrast to the rolling, snow-covered prairie. He arrived early enough to find mule teams and freighters in the wagon yard readying to leave to take advantage of the improved conditions.

The fort was a huge compound, far bigger than Fort Stanton, with rows of company barracks, officers quarters, married enlisted quarters, stables, shops, sheds, quartermaster storehouses, offices, and a hospital. Constructed out of adobe, fired bricks, milled lumber, and dressed stone, it was the finest set of buildings Kerney had seen since coming west. At the headquarters building he introduced himself to a company clerk and asked to speak to an officer. The corporal escorted him to another office and introduced him to Lieutenant Hendricks, the regimental adjutant, a stocky, bearded man with a clipped eastern accent.

He started to explain his purpose and the lieutenant quickly cut him off.

"Your name, sir, is enough to tell me why you are here," Hendricks said sternly. He remained seated behind his desk and did not show the slightest courtesy. "Straightaway I can tell you that your son is with the post surgeon, Dr. William Lyon, and his wife. Dr. Lyon is on a leave of absence but asked me to advise you—if you presented yourself—that he and his wife wish to adopt your son. Your consent to allow them to do so would be most welcome. Virgil Peters told the doctor that the child was never in your care since his birth and you would likely welcome the opportunity to see the boy adequately cared for and properly raised."

Kerney looked at Hendricks in silence, trying to take in and size up what he'd been told. All he could hear was the ticking of the wall clock. He reckoned he'd been marked as a no-account who had abandoned his son, and nothing he might say to this officer, or the good doctor and his wife for that matter, would change that opinion.

He felt no pleasure or relief, knowing Patrick was alive and safe. What circled around in his brain was the singular fact that Patrick had a chance for a good home and future, things Kerney held in short supply.

"Mr. Kerney," Lieutenant Hendricks prodded, his tone harsh.

Kerney thought about his dead brother and young Timmy, about Ida, who—barmy or not—had cared for Patrick as her own, and Mary Alice, whom he should have loved better. "Patrick's my son and I will not give him up," he finally said.

"I see," Lieutenant Hendricks said flatly. "Do you read and write?"

Kerney nodded.

"Good." From a desk drawer Hendricks took a paper, wrote on it, and gave it to Kerney. "That is the address of the War Department in Washington. You may write to Dr. Lyon there, if you wish to do so. Use the sergeant major's desk in the outer office, but make haste, as the mail leaves at noon."

"You have no other address for him?"

"I do not," Hendricks replied. "The doctor and Mrs. Lyon are traveling extensively, visiting family throughout New England and Maryland. If you write to him at the War Department you are assured he will receive your correspondence."

"When will the doctor be coming back to Fort Union?"

Hendricks shook his head and stood. "He won't be returning. He is on leave pending new orders."

"What are his new orders?" Kerney asked.

"I wouldn't know," Hendricks answered.

"Do you have word of Virgil Peters?"

"You'll find his gravesite in the post cemetery. He fell ill and died of a disorder of the blood soon after putting the lad in Dr. Lyon's care."

Hendricks put on his great coat, adjusted his forage cap, buckled his saber belt, and picked up his gloves. "I have duties to attend to. When you've finished, leave your letter with the corporal."

Hendricks gestured toward his office door. "Now, if you please." In the outer office he told the corporal to supply Kerney with paper, pen, and ink.

"This man is writing to Dr. Lyon at the War Department. Rather than sending it by mail, I will include it in our official dispatches so that it can arrive there with all due speed."

"I'm obliged," Kerney said.

Hendricks nodded curtly and left without saying another word.

He sat at the sergeant major's desk and wrote the same story he told to the rancher in Ryado, adding to it as his memory served. It took hours to put it on paper, and his hand was stiff when he finally finished. He read it, decided it would have to do, and wrote a note to the doctor.

> *Dear Dr. Lyon,*
>
> *I take up this pen to write you with thanks for your kindness to my son, Patrick. With this I send the story I put down on*

paper so that he might know how he came to have so much
hardship. Please read it to him. I searched for Patrick over
many months and I cannot give him over to you to be
adopted. I will do my all to raise him right. Write care of
Coghlan's Store, Tularosa, New Mexico Territory, and I will
come and fetch him.

    I now close. Obliged and in your debt,

                                       John Kerney

He sealed and addressed the letter, left it with corporal and went outside, wondering if he'd just taken from Patrick the best chance the boy would have for a fortunate life.

Across the way he could see a lot of activity in the wagon yard. Fort Union served as the main quartermaster depot for the territory, supplying all the other posts in New Mexico. Maybe he could find work. He stepped off briskly to find out.

* * *

As he approached headquarters, Lieutenant Hendricks watched John Kerney cross the quadrangle in the direction of the quartermaster stores and wagon yard. He knew precisely where his dear friends William and Polly Lyon were staying while on leave of absence. He knew they couldn't have children and he had seen how much that little boy had brightened their lives in such a short time, especially Polly's. But William Lyon was a stickler about doing things right, and Hendricks knew he'd turn that child over to John Kerney no matter how many protests Polly made or tears she shed.

Why should a worthless drifter with no prospects other than a dollar-a-day job be allowed to spoil their happiness and ruin a child's opportunity to be brought up in a decent family?

Inside headquarters, the company clerk handed Hendricks a packet of documents with the envelope containing John Kerney's letter to Dr. Lyon at the War Department on top. He sent the corporal away to get the daily troop muster reports, went to his office, and burned Kerney's letter in the woodstove before sealing the documents in the courier's pouch.

Hendricks had a good feeling about it. It was the Christian thing to do for all concerned.

9

At the wagon yard Kerney talked to a freighter named Joseph Cooney, who hired him as a driver for a quartermaster supply train leaving for Fort Marcy in Santa Fe under military escort. It was the first time in months he would have a job with more than five dollars left in his pocket, and that felt good. In fact, the whole damn day felt good.

Kerney loaded and tied down the cargo, inspected the wagon to make sure the wheels and brakes were in order, and was about to hitch his team of mules when Cooney came up to him.

Near Kerney's age by his looks, he had a thick brogue, a nose that had been broken at least once, big hands, and long arms that hung down almost to his knees. He glanced at the loaded wagon and gave Kerney a brief nod of approval.

"Now, where in Ireland were you born?" he asked.

"County Clare," Kerney answered.

" 'Tis a charming part of our fair land."

"As long as the English rule it," Kerney replied, "it's only a lovely place to be from."

Cooney chuckled. "True indeed. Now, are you the John Kerney poor Virgil Peters was looking for?"

"I am. Did you know him and my son?"

"I knew both man and boy. Virgil worked for me for a time until he took sick, and the post surgeon could not save him. Not a jovial sort; sad he was to have lost his woman and bad tempered to have fallen on hard times. Now, your boy Patrick, he's the quiet one. Looks a bit like you. Same chin, and the nose too, I'd say. Busy with his hands he was, always making things out of bits of wood and tiny sticks. Liked to take things apart. The doctor's wife took quite a shine to him."

Cooney paused and looked up and down the line of wagons. "Best to hitch up your team."

"What kind of man was Peters?" Kerney asked as he guided the mules to the coupling tongue of the wagon.

"A good man when sober, he was," Cooney replied. "A bit surly at times, as I said, but drunk or sober I never saw him lift a hand to the boy. He took no notice of the lad most of the time, which made the wee one lonely. The child was left to his own devices, but Peters fed him and always made sure he had a place to rest his head."

The post quartermaster stepped out of his office and waved to Cooney. Cooney waved back.

"Look lively there, now," he said to Kerney. "Not a moment to lose."

Grateful for the job and for knowing Patrick was alive, and wanting the time to arrive quickly when he would hear from Dr. Lyon, Kerney tied his horse to the back of the wagon and climbed onto the driver's seat.

* * *

The wagon train made good time for the remainder of the day. By the next dawn, the snow on the prairie was mostly gone, melted by yesterday's sun and strong, tepid evening winds that came out of the southwest. Back on the trail, the day turned unseasonably warm and the rutted road became thick mud: a gooey, slippery sludge that slowed progress.

With the sun low in the west and a chill in the air, the caravan entered a sheltered valley and crossed two rivers running full from the recent storm. At dusk they made camp under a grove of tall cottonwoods near the settlement of La Junta, where a railroad crew was laying track.

At mealtime, the drivers sulked about the railroad, none of them happy about the loss of jobs sure to come when the trains started running all the way to Albuquerque next year. Kerney left them to their brooding and walked out into the prairie. The mule teams and the army horses had been settled down in a vale between two small hills, and a couple of the pony soldiers were riding night herd.

Kerney didn't mind at all the impending arrival of the railroad, since it meant he'd be able to quickly get Patrick when the time came without having to spur a tired horse for hundreds of miles to reach a railhead.

He'd need money to fetch the boy, and even more before that to make a place for them to live. He wondered what kind of work might be had in Santa Fe. Cattle and sheep ranches wouldn't be hiring this time of year, but maybe he could get taken on at a wheel-wright shop or with a blacksmith. He had some experience with both trades. He decided not to get to niggling his head over it.

According to Joe Cooney, they would have a long day on the trail tomorrow to Las Vegas, and maybe two or three days more, depending on the weather, to reach Santa Fe.

The full moon was up in a clear sky, casting a weak glow on the distant white-capped sierras the Spanish called the Sangre de Cristo Mountains—"Blood of Christ" in English—supposedly named because of how the light sometimes flashed bloodred on the peaks.

Kerney had crossed over that high country and knew the rough terrain could be fearsome. But after Las Vegas the wagons would veer south past mesas and buttes, skirt the mountains through a narrow, low-lying pass, and traverse foothills to reach Santa Fe. He wondered what the territorial capitol looked like, and for the first time in a while felt eager to face a new dawn.

* * *

In Santa Fe, Kerney got paid, and at a dusty mercantile store on the plaza he bought clothes and a new pair of boots. He found a lodging room to rent from an elderly mestizo woman who had a small house near an old adobe church on the other side of the river, where he cleaned up, changed into his new duds, and went looking for work.

All in all, Santa Fe was a disappointment to him. There was nothing grand or notable about it, nothing that gave the town any distinction as a civilized seat of the territorial government. The building where the governor resided was an ancient fortress a block long with four-foot-thick exposed adobe walls that faced the plaza. A rickety wooden portal ran the length of it, and only the front side had been plastered and whitewashed.

On a small rise a block away, a cathedral was under construction, several modern homes had been erected on residential streets near the governor's residence, and some new commercial buildings and hotels had gone up on the square. But aside from those improvements and one or two stately old haciendas with courtyards, the town was mostly a hodgepodge of ugly, mud-plaster adobe houses and outbuildings much like those in the isolated mountain villages Kerney had passed through over the last few months.

Dirt-roofed peasant houses were tucked into the roll of land above the town site on bare, treeless plots, and small farmsteads were spread along the banks of the river a short distance from the plaza. Farm animals and horses roamed free through a large marsh and communal pastures adjacent to the town, often running at large through the streets, chased by their owners.

There was active commerce in the core of the town, and most successful businesses appeared dominated by a group of American traders, lawyers, merchants, and government officials, along with a few prominent Mexican families, who acted for the most part like Spanish grandees. For residents and travelers alike, public gambling seemed to be the most popular sport in town, and the consumption of cheap liquor the most common diversion.

From Kerney's perspective, Fort Marcy was Santa Fe's saving grace. It provided much to the cultural life of the city and even had a regimental band that gave free concerts, played at fandangos and dances, and paraded through the streets on patriotic holidays.

The fort was a marvel. Located behind and next to the governor's residence, it was laid out with military precision. Built mostly of adobe and brick, it had several rows of new officers quarters, with large windows, fireplaces, and wide porches. The parade grounds were well tended, and there were separate quarters for the band and noncommissioned officers, a barracks for enlisted men, a hospital, and the usual assortment of stables and shops.

After three days of looking for work with no luck, Kerney sat in his room and counted out the money he had left. If he remained in Santa Fe and kept paying for lodging, meals, and the cost of stabling his horse, he could last two weeks before going bust.

But he had no intention of staying. He needed to get back to the Tularosa pronto to wait for a letter from Dr. Lyon to arrive at Coghlan's store. He had enough to get there with a little left over and was about to feel glum about it when he suddenly remembered that John Good owed him almost a month's wages.

He counted his currency and coin again. His first night in town, out of curiosity he had poked his head into a number of the gambling dens. Some were splendorous, with sparkling chandeliers and fine furnishings, and some were nothing more than smelly mud huts with earthen floors. Not much of a gambling man by nature, he had avoided the lure of wasting his money on games of cards.

Except for the necessity of new clothes and boots, he'd been penny-pinching since the day he left the Tularosa. After all, he was in the hole to Cal Doran. He'd been eating on the cheap, trying to conserve every dime. He looked at the greenbacks and silver and decided that he had cause to celebrate and treat himself to a good dinner. With Patrick alive and being well cared for, that was reason enough.

The Exchange Hotel on the corner of the plaza had a dining room that offered expensive meals. He had decided not to stay there because of the cost, but the dinner menu looked good, all the chairs in the room matched, there were clean napkins on the tables, and the crockery wasn't chipped or cracked.

He brushed his hat, dusted his boots, put some money in his pocket, hid the rest in his bedroll, and walked across the river to the hotel. In the dining room he ordered a cut from a saddle of mutton frosted with cooled meat drippings, a coronet of peeled

vegetables, a slice of mincemeat pie, and a pail of beer. When his
dinner came, he dug in with gusto and hardly lifted his gaze from
the plate. He couldn't remember better eating since the day Mary
Alice had fixed a pie and a roasted beef to celebrate the arrival of
Thomas and his family in the Texas panhandle.

He dawdled over the best cup of coffee he'd had in years and
listened to the laughter and chatter of men and women arriving at
the gaming rooms on the other side of the small lobby. He paid
for his meal and with three dollars still in his pocket had a growing
itch to spend it. Why not on a game of chance? If he could win a
few hands, maybe he'd have enough to pay his debt to Cal Doran
the next time he saw him.

It was Friday night, and the big gaming room at the hotel had
attracted a crowd. There were fancy ladies on the arms of young,
off-duty officers from the fort at a craps table and a group of
prosperous-looking businessmen playing poker in a corner. The
rest of the crowd was made up of traders, wagon men, a few cowboys, several slick gamblers wearing string ties and brocade vests,
some tough-looking hombres sporting fancy six-shooters, and a
number of painted ladies.

Kerney started at the blackjack table and drew two tens in his
first hand. An hour later he was up fifty dollars. He slipped a
month's pay into his boot and took a seat as the seventh man at a
five-card draw poker game. He lost his first two hands but started
with a pair of eights in the next deal, drew another eight, took the
hand with three of a kind, and from then on kept winning. By
midnight, three men had dropped out, new players had taken their
places, and he was up by five hundred and twenty-five dollars,
which was way more than he could ever earn in a year.

Ready to leave the game with his winnings, Kerney looked at

the men sitting at the table. He'd come out unarmed, figuring to
have a good meal and then go straight back to his room. One of
the players, a man with a waxed mustache, soft hands, and the look
of a professional gambler, had been at the table since Kerney joined
the game and wasn't happy about his losses. He figured him for a
hidden gun. Two others wore six-shooters waist high but seemed
peaceable enough. The rest weren't showing any iron, but that was
no comfort.

The cards were dealt. Kerney bet, then folded before the show-
down even though he had a strong hand. The gambler took the
pot.

"I'm done, gentlemen," he said as he stood, put the greenbacks
in his pocket, and scooped up the silver.

"That's not very sporting of you," the gambler said. "Sit down
and let's play a few more hands."

Kerney smiled at the man. "The cards fell my way tonight. No
need to get ornery about it."

"I said sit down," the gambler repeated as he placed a Colt Dragoon .44 on the table and covered it with his hand.

"The man said he was done for the night," a familiar voice behind him said, "so unless you want to get hauled off to the undertaker, get your hand off that Colt, push back from the table, and
stand up."

Kerney turned to find Cal Doran at his shoulder, his eyes riveted
on the gambler. He had a deputy sheriff badge pinned on his shirt.

The gambler scrambled to his feet.

"That's good," Cal said. "Pick up your money and leave the pistol where it is. You can claim it at the sheriff's office in the morning.
Now, skedaddle."

As the gambler fled the room, Cal took the Colt, stuck it in his waistband, and grinned at Kerney. "Let's go into the saloon so you can buy me a drink."

"Or two," Kerney said, smiling back. "I never figured you to still be in Santa Fe, and a lawman to boot."

People moved aside as the two men made their way to the saloon. "Hell, this town about broke me in less than two weeks," Cal said. "I drifted south and got hired by Pat Garrett as a deputy. I brought a prisoner up from Lincoln to a judge who plans to hang him, and I'm headed home tomorrow."

At the bar, Kerney ordered a bottle of rye whiskey, paid for it, and pushed some bills over to Cal. "That's what I owe you. Thanks for the loan."

Cal looked at the money but didn't touch it. "How much did you win tonight?"

"Over five hundred, plus another thirty in my boot."

Cal let out a low whistle and pushed the money back toward Kerney. "I thought we were gonna go partners on that ranch when the time came. I've got some *dinero* to contribute to the cause from rewards I've collected, so I can match you dollar for dollar."

A thousand dollars was a fortune. It meant enough money to build and fully stock an outfit. "You certain you want to do that?" Kerney asked.

"Damn right I do. Now, did you ever find that boy of yours?"

"I found him, but I still have to fetch him." He told Cal about the priest in Cimarron, what he'd learned at Fort Union, and the letter he'd written to Dr. Lyon at the War Department. "It's just a matter of time."

"That's real fine," Cal said as he raised his glass. "Here's to getting Patrick home to our ranch safe and sound."

The two men clinked glasses and drank.

"I ran into Dick Turknet in Cimarron," Kerney said, "and I'm thinking you may have told him I'm a peaceable man."

Cal chuckled. "You are, mostly. Did he say where he got those horses?"

"First, how did you get him to agree to tell me?"

"Dick's a scoundrel and a thief, but we go back a ways. I caught him and the cousins trailing some ponies that a rancher up by the Organ Mountains had reported stolen. I gave them the choice of leaving the county or trimming a tree once a judge and jury got through with them. What did he tell you?"

"He gave me the name of Bud McPherson, who lit out to Montana after his crew had been strung up by some Texas Rangers."

"That squares." Cal poured himself another drink and one for Kerney.

"You think Turknet told it to me straight?" Kerney asked.

"Yep. Are you planning to hunt McPherson down?"

"I can't see chasing him to Montana, not with Patrick needing to be fetched when the time comes. Maybe McPherson will lope south, and then I can settle accounts."

"That's being a bright boy," Cal said. He called the bartender over, gave him the gambler's pistol and four bits, and asked him to leave the gun with the sheriff in the morning.

The barkeep nodded, put the pistol under the counter, slipped the coins in his apron pocket, and went back to serving drinks to loud cowboys at the end of the bar having a high-heeled time.

"I'm staying here tonight," Cal said. "You can bunk with me."

"No need," Kerney said. "I've rented a room from an old lady just across the river."

Cal shook his head in strong disagreement. "At least three hombres followed you in here and are waiting for us to part company and go our separate ways. You step outside alone and unarmed and I guarantee you'll be robbed and murdered before you get ten feet. You bunk with me. Let's have one more drink and call it a night."

Kerney poured the shots.

"We can have a good breakfast in the morning, buy victuals, and be heading south before midday," Cal said. "There's a hacienda down a ways on the *camino* where we can put up tomorrow night."

"That's all right by me," Kerney said after downing the shot.

"So where are we gonna start this ranch of ours?" Cal asked as they left the bar.

"In the San Andres most likely," Kerney replied. "There are some wide canyons with good grass and year-round springs."

"Old Apache camping grounds by the sound of it."

"Could be," Kerney replied. "When we get back to the Tularosa, I need to visit with John Good about wages owed to me."

Cal smiled broadly as he unlocked the door to the room. "I'll gladly ride along with you to see his charming wife again and make sure he fights you fair and square when he refuses to pony up."

"Think it will come to that?"

"Maybe so," Cal said.

10

Cesario Chávez, the alcalde of Tularosa, called the men of the village to a meeting in Perfecto Armijo's large parlor. As was custom, Ignacio stood at the back of the room with the younger men while his father and the other village leaders sat at the front of the *sala* facing the gathering.

A heated discussion had broken out concerning what to do about gringo troublemakers who were streaming into Tularosa to patronize Señor Coghlan's store and saloon. Women of the village were being accosted on the roads, drunks were riding wildly through the village shooting their *pistolas* and scaring the children, there were brawls and fistfights almost every night, painted women were whoring in the saloon, and some horses, cattle, and sheep had been stolen from the communal pastures.

"José's efforts to stop these troubles have failed," Cesario said, nodding at José Candelaria, Ignacio's uncle and the village constable. "Señor Coghlan and the *americanos* do not listen to him. We must take stronger action."

"Do you remember the last time we did such a thing?" Perfecto retorted. "After the *americanos* dammed the river to irrigate their farms in the mountains and slowed our water to a trickle? They would not listen when we talked, so we took up arms, destroyed their dams, and got into a big fight. And what happened, I ask you? The army soldiers came here with a cannon and threatened to reduce our village to nothing. They pointed that cursed thing at my house with my wife and children inside."

"Yes, we all remember," Cesario replied. "But to this day no one has tried to deny our water to us again. If we do not stand up against Coghlan, Tularosa will only become more lawless and more dangerous as more is taken from us."

Perfecto snorted. "And if we oppose him, the army will not protect us from Coghlan's banditos. They are all *americanos*."

"The soldiers will do nothing," José Candelaria responded. "Nor will the county sheriff."

"They are Texans who despise us," Perfecto said. "Spit on us."

"What do we do?" Cesario asked. "We built this village. We defended it against the Apaches before the Texans came."

"True, but we are not *pistoleros*," Perfecto said. "I do not wish to see any of us shot down on the street."

"Is it that, or do you not want to offend Coghlan?" Cesario said. Perfecto's sale of his village lots to the Irishman had made him the richest villager in Tularosa.

Perfecto shook a fist at Cesario. "Do not insult me, Cesario. I am no man's peon. I have fought by your side many times."

"That is true," Cesario said. "I apologize."

"As constable, I will go to Mesilla and speak to the territorial judge about the lawlessness," José Candelaria suggested.

Cesario nodded and said, "A good idea. I'll also go to ask him to come here to see our troubles for himself."

A murmur of approval greeted the idea.

"First, we speak to Coghlan," Cesario added. "So that the judge knows we have tried to solve our problems with the *americanos*."

Ignacio stopped listening. He knew, as they all did, that nothing would come of it. The territorial judge was a gringo and would side with Coghlan, who now owned most of the town. Aside from the store and saloon, he had also built a large wagon yard with rooms at the rear that he rented to travelers, cowboys, soldiers, and the painted women who pleasured them. For his wife, he'd built a spacious new house in the village, larger than any hacienda Ignacio could imagine, and his Three Rivers Ranch with the big casa northeast of the village stretched for miles. He controlled most of the water, which made him almost a king of the basin.

More times than he could count, Ignacio had seen the men in this room, including his father, Perfecto Armijo, and Uncle José, remove their hats and step aside when Coghlan drove his team of matched *caballos* down the street. He had seen his mother and the other village women forced to wait in line at Coghlan's store while the clerks served the Texans and other gringos first. And like the Negro Buffalo Soldiers, Mexicans could not enter the saloon.

He knew the men of Tularosa were brave and proud, but Coghlan had beaten them. Not by force, but through greed, thievery, hired guns, and ill-gotten gains. Tularosa no longer belonged to *la gente*, and to speak to Coghlan only saved face, nothing more.

At that moment, Ignacio came to a decision that had been building in him for some time: He would leave Tularosa. His reasons were many, and not least was the fact that Teresa no longer showed any interest in him. Her affections were increasingly drawn to Charlie Gambel, who had been denied Perfecto's permission to court her but still persisted.

Although Ignacio did not fully understand her fascination with

Gambel, he realized that Charlie's wild, outlaw ways appealed to her spirited nature. With the cowboy gone on a cattle drive to California, Ignacio had tried to win back Teresa's attention but to no avail. He would leave in the hope that he could make his fortune and return to seek her hand after she gave up her girlish fantasy about Charlie.

He had but a year to do it. Next month, Teresa would be fifteen years old and of an age to marry. He believed Perfecto favored him as a potential son-in-law, but he also knew Perfecto valued money and would not turn over his daughter's dowry to a suitor with no means to support her.

To improve his English, he'd read the book Señor Kerney had given him over and over again, sounding each word out slowly at first. He listened carefully whenever he was around the Texans and other *americanos* so he could say the words correctly. Now he understood the gringos' speech almost perfectly and could reply in English without great difficulty.

Perhaps he would go to Las Cruces, a town of more than two thousand—many of whom were Mexican—where a young man who spoke both English and Spanish surely could find employment. Or maybe he should go to Mesilla, the county seat, where even more opportunities might exist.

He had been to both places once, and the visits had fired his imagination for adventure. True, they were far away, across the wide basin, through the blistering sea of white sand near the shallow salt lake, and over the pass near the mountains that cast a dozen or more jagged spires into the sky. It would be a long journey and perhaps dangerous now that some of the Apaches had escaped from the Fort Stanton reservation. But once he got there he was certain he could find work. First, however, he would travel to La

Luz, where Manuel Gutierrez, a distant cousin, lived, to see if there were any jobs there. If he could earn some *dinero* quickly, then he would move on.

Ignacio said good night to Perfecto and the others and walked into the cold night air behind his father and Uncle José, who were discussing when it would be best for them to meet with Coghlan and make the trip to Mesilla to see the judge.

Again his thoughts turned away from the troubles caused by Señor Coghlan. Now that winter had arrived on the basin, it would only get colder, especially at night. He would need warm clothes and a bedroll for his journey, as he planned to camp out if necessary, with enough food to sustain him during the first few days. With only three dollars in silver coins, he would have to be very frugal until he found work.

Tomorrow he would tell his parents of his decision and make preparations to leave. He was determined, excited, and at the same time anxious.

* * *

The long ride to Tularosa took John Kerney and Cal Doran first to a hacienda stage stop in a small farming community south of Santa Fe. The next day they dropped down a steep, rocky butte and traveled to the town of Albuquerque along the Rio Grande. From there they continued south in rough winter weather through an Indian pueblo and past small Mexican settlements perched on slender ribbons of fertile river bottomland. After four days and more than a hundred and twenty miles on horseback, they arrived in Socorro, a village west of the river situated at the base of a line of inviting mountains, barely visible under a low winter sky.

The town was booming, with two new mercantile stores opened in advance of the pending arrival of the railroad, and Americans pouring in every day. On the town plaza, miners in their red shirts, with wagonloads of silver concentrates bound for the smelters, and ox teams hauling processed silver-lead bullion from the smelters filled the streets.

Days of riding with a cold, snowy wind in their faces had them both cussing the weather. They took a four-bit room at a hotel and ate a good meal in the dining room, where well-heeled speculators and out-of-town financiers sat at a large table filling the air with cigar smoke and talking business.

In the morning, clear skies and a warmer day greeted them. They bought fresh victuals and reached the stage road to Fort Stanton well before noon. As they rode, Kerney discussed his plans for the ranch. He had his eye on the east slope of the San Andres Mountains, where there were some wide canyons with good grass and live water from year-round springs. Stockmen looking for fresh range hadn't strayed there yet because of the Apaches, but with most of the Indians back on the reservation and quiet, unclaimed land was there for the taking.

He wanted to put up a suitable house for Patrick, not a one-room, dirt-floor, earth-roofed cabin. To start out, he would build stock corrals, dig a well, and quarry rock for the house foundation and fireplace.

It was an ambitious plan. If Kerney was plumb set on building a proper house, he would have to first build a road to cart wagon-loads of lumber across forty miles of basin. But Cal said nothing about the difficuties ahead. Kerney was holding on to an idea of how he wanted life with Patrick to be the way a Saturday night sinner went looking for Sunday morning salvation. Besides, Cal cottoned to the idea of having a stake in a place he could call home with a partner he liked and trusted.

His friendship with Kerney had been forged on the trail. Work for a spell with a man under harsh conditions and you get to know his true nature. Unlike most cowboys, Kerney wanted something more than just riding for the brand. He was smarter than most, levelheaded, and inclined to lend a helping hand when needed. Cal had learned that the day Kerney found him dazed from a fall on the Staked Plains.

Maybe he wasn't fun loving and sociable when it came to raising a little hell, getting a little drunk, or spending his money on women or cards, but he was about as reliable as a man could get and as loyal a friend a man could ever hope for. That was good enough reason for Cal to throw in with him.

Patches had settled into a smooth, easy gait. There was nothing better than sitting a good horse on a fine day without a care to trouble a soul, and Cal let his thoughts skirt away from Kerney. Behind them the wide Rio Grande was a fading ribbon in a sea of sloping grasslands and hidden valleys. The oxbow curve in the river with the wide sandbar was no longer visible. Up ahead, hills decorated with scattered groves of trees promised thick forests beyond where the stage road climbed painfully along a ridge. Tomorrow, they would skirt the cliffs of the Oscura Mountains and cross Lava Gap through the dangerous malpais. From there it would be but a long day's ride to Fort Stanton.

Cal was happy to be out of the cold and snow and heading back to the stark beauty of the Tularosa which tested man and beast. It was a great pocket of sun-scorched land of alkali flats and white sand dunes where your eye could travel a hundred miles with nary a glimpse of any welcoming shade in sight. Cal was partial to it, even though it could sandblast body and soul. It was a clean, dry country, little touched by civilization, that kept the timid and faint of heart at bay. Cal liked that.

Kerney called to him from up ahead at the foot of the hill, where the stage road began a perilous climb. Cal gave Patches a light touch with his spurs and cantered to where Kerney waited.

* * *

The sun nosed over the snowcapped Sierra Blanca, where winter had claimed the mountains. On the Tularosa a mile or more below the summit, dawn promised a sparkling-clear, mild day. Yesterday, when Ignacio had announced his decision to leave, his parents had tried to discourage him from going. But once it was clear that he would not change his mind, his father fell silent and his mother sighed a great deal. Although his brothers and sisters were in awe of his boldness, they could not imagine what life would be like without him. Antonio, the next oldest, was both excited and anxious about the new role he would have in the family.

A light breeze caressed the bare branches of the cottonwoods as Ignacio made ready to leave home. His mother had washed, mended, and bundled his clothes. He carefully tucked the book Señor Kerney had given him inside the bundle. His little sisters had prepared another bundle of fresh tortillas, some hard candy from Coghlan's store, frijoles with a packet of fat to cook them in, dried chilies, piñon nuts, and delicious, steamed prickly pear leaves called nopalitos. He would eat those first, at midday.

In the chilly early morning, the family went to the church the villagers had built to fulfill their promise to God for their victory over the Apaches at the battle of Round Mountain. Together they knelt in front of the altar and prayed for Ignacio's protection during his journey and for his safe return.

Back home, his father presented Ignacio with the pistol he'd owned for many years, wrapped in an old piece of oilcloth. He also gave him two dollars in silver coins. His mother gave him a small cross on a chain to wear around his neck.

On foot, carrying his parcels and bedroll, Ignacio set out for La Luz. The sun cast the mild light of early winter across the basin, rolling back the darkness of the distant mountains to the west. The day would warm but remain comfortable, unlike the searing heat of summer, and by evening he would be at his cousin Manuel's house.

With the village no longer in sight, in the vastness of the basin, along the lonely wagon road, a stab of apprehension gripped Ignacio, and for a brief moment he considered returning home. He slowed his pace until pride overcame misgivings, and then he walked on without looking back.

* * *

The once tranquil village of Tularosa had changed during Kerney's absence. The hitching posts outside of Coghlan's newly opened saloon and store were crowded with horses, and the wagon yard was full up with high-sided wagons and harnessed teams of docile oxen flapping their tails. There were more people along the road through the village than Kerney had ever seen before, most of them Texans and soldiers, and somebody had thrown up a huge house that towered over a nearby adobe casita. Kerney didn't doubt for a moment that the palatial residence belonged to Pat Coghlan.

They stopped first at the store, where they found a message

waiting for Cal Doran and nothing for Kerney. He masked his disappointment by pretending to study the vast array of merchandise and goods stocked on the shelves and floor. No longer would the villagers need to trek once a year to El Paso or Las Cruces to stock up on salt, axes, powder and lead, matches, bolts of cloth, coffee and tobacco, or iron and steel. It was all here, including saddles, pistols, long guns, hard candy and trinkets for the children, and brightly colored ribbons for the women.

Cal read his message, tucked it away in a pocket, and told Kerney they would have to part company for a time.

"Seems some Texas boys shot up the streets of Lincoln, lit out, but promised to return soon to continue their jamboree," he explained. "The sheriff wants me over there pronto to help keep the peace."

"Has the feuding started up there again?" Kerney asked.

Folks in Lincoln had been outright killing each other with some regularity over the last several years and getting away with it scot-free. It had gotten so bad that soldiers from the fort had been called in more than once to settle folks down. A young cowboy known as Billy the Kid seemed to be smack-dab in the middle of the quarrel right from the start. Kerney had met Billy during the time he'd worked for Coghlan, and he seemed a likeable sort, although some thought him a cold-blooded killer.

Cal shook his head. "No, seems this is a fresh bunch of ruffians. But I've got no squabble about heading over there. Fact is it works out perfect. My reward money is locked in the sheriff's safe and I'm gonna need it if you want me to put up my share of our ranch."

"Are you done being a lawman?" Kerney asked.

Cal grinned. "Yep, I believe I'm just not suited to the job. Besides, sooner or later, I'd have to arrest some of my friends, and that just doesn't sit well with me."

"Then, let's celebrate you being done with the law," Kerney said with a smile. "I'm buying."

"I like that notion," Cal replied.

They stepped to the nearby saloon and pushed through the swinging doors into a busy, smoke-filled room. Although the day was no more than half gone, the place was doing a lively business in anticipation of the evening performance of a play, *The Union Spy*, announced by a poster on the wall and scheduled to start at eight o'clock. Admission cost a dollar and two bits, and the troupe would be performing nightly for only one week. A few pretty hurdy-gurdy girls were working the customers at the gaming tables. Kerney figured they'd either followed the thespians to town or were part of the troupe.

At the bar, Kerney ordered shots, asked the bartender the whereabouts of Charlie Gambel, and learned he was on a trail drive west. Over drinks, Cal agreed to meet up with Kerney three weeks hence in Tularosa. Kerney would use the time to scout the east side of the San Andres in hopes of finding good land and a reliable source of water. But first, he'd visit John Good to settle up for the back pay owed him.

"Be careful of that red-eyed wife of his," Cal cautioned as they left the saloon. "She's a true daughter of the devil, guaranteed."

Kerney laughed as he climbed into the saddle. "I will if you make sure those fun-loving Texas boys in Lincoln don't shoot too many holes in you. I'd hate to lose a partner. Adios."

"So long," Cal replied as he walked back to the saloon in search of another drink and some attention from one of the hurdy-gurdy girls.

John Kerney gigged his horse and trotted south, mulling on how long it would take before he heard from Dr. Lyon. He had no way of knowing, but he was anxious to go get Patrick. At the same time, he was vexed that he didn't even have a roof to put over the boy's head. Besides all that, how would he manage to raise him without help? He was a greenhorn when it came to children, about as ignorant as they came.

It was a tight spot with no surefire answers, but he was determined to make it work. In Cal he had a good partner, and between them they had enough money to get an outfit started and stocked, so it was best to keep thinking on the sunny side.

He raised La Luz before nightfall and found it sporting a new cantina, a new livery, and a passel of tough-looking pilgrims. He stabled his horse for the night, paid for a bed of fresh straw to sleep on next to a haystack, and in the faint light of dusk walked toward the cantina, hoping for a decent meal. He turned the corner and almost stumbled over a Mexican lying at the side of the road.

"Help me," the man said in English.

Kerney recognized the voice and bent down. "Ignacio?"

"Sí. Yes."

Kerney bent down. Ignacio had a bloody gash on his temple and his right eye was red and swollen. He helped the boy sit up. "What happened?"

"I've been robbed." Ignacio pointed in the direction of the creek behind the livery. "Where I was camping. One hombre, a Texan, maybe. He took my money, my father's *pistola*. Even the book you gave me. He hit me two times with his gun. When I tried to follow I fell here. *Desvanecido*." He made a circular motion at his head.

"Dizzy," Kerney guessed.

"Sí."

"Do you know the man that robbed you?"

Ignacio shook his head.

"Can you stand up?"

"I think yes."

Kerney got Ignacio to his feet, walked him back to the livery, and cleaned his wound with water from the trough. It wasn't a deep gash, and when the bleeding stopped, he applied a mud plaster to it. The eye had shut completely, so Kerney used his neckerchief to make a wet compress and had Ignacio hold it against the swelling.

"You'll live," he said. "Now, tell me what you're doing alone in La Luz."

Ignacio told John Kerney everything: Teresa's infatuation with Charlie Gambel, his decision to leave home, coming to La Luz only to find his cousin had moved away, his hopes to go to Las Cruces now smashed, as he had no money to get there, and the shame he felt about his humiliation.

"Tomorrow I will go back home to my family in disgrace," he said, head bowed in shame.

"Don't worry about tomorrow," Kerney replied as he took Ignacio into the stables and had him stretch out on a bed of straw. "Rest here. I'll go rustle up some grub at the cantina and bring you a plate. Some food, some rest, and you'll be good as new come morning."

After Ignacio ate, Kerney questioned him about the holdup. Five dollars had been taken along with the book of stories and his father's old pistol. From Ignacio's description, the revolver was likely a black-powder Colt Dragoon revolver that shot a ball. Probably an early model a good thirty years old, it had Cesario's initials carved into the stock. Somebody toting the sidearm should be easy to spot, although Kerney doubted anyone would want to carry such a relic for self-protection.

Soon, Ignacio slept. Kerney left him just long enough to gather up the boy's remaining possessions at the creek bed and tote them back to the stable. He covered Ignacio with a blanket and sat in the darkness listening to the boy's breathing. Near moonrise a storm came waltzing up from the southwest, bringing nothing but a lazy cold wind until a gentle rain started. Inside, warm and out of the weather, with the soft sound of raindrops on the roof of the stable, Kerney fell asleep.

* * *

At dawn, John Kerney examined Ignacio's face. His eye was still swollen shut, and the cheek below had puffed up and blackened a bit. Gently he rinsed away the mud plaster covering the gash at Ignacio's temple, cleaned it with water, and wrapped an improvised bandage around his head.

"You look considerable better," he lied as he helped Ignacio to his feet. "How about I make us some breakfast?"

"Yes, I'm very hungry."

Kerney moved everything to the creek bed, got Ignacio covered with a blanket and comfortable under a tree, made a fire, and cooked a breakfast of coffee, eggs he'd bought last night at the cantina, and beans he'd found in Ignacio's food bundle. They ate in silence as the sun winked above the brow of the mountains.

"You have been kind to me," Ignacio said after wolfing down the last of his eggs. "*Gracias*."

"No need for that," John Kerney replied. "I just lent a helping hand. Can you ride a horse?"

"Yes, a little bit. Maybe not like a vaquero, but I can ride."

"Good." Kerney hunkered down next to Ignacio. "I already know you can drive a wagon. Seen you do it. Have you been west to the San Andres?"

"*Sí*, yes, with my father several times when our sheep wandered away, and once when some were stolen."

"*Bueno*," Kerney said.

"Why do you ask?"

"I'm thinking I need to hire a hand and maybe you'll do."

Ignacio's good eye brightened. "You have work for me?"

Kerney nodded. "Hard work, lots of it, and not much *dinero* to start with."

"Doing what, Señor Kerney?"

"Ranching," John Kerney answered.

He gave Ignacio the lowdown on his plan to start a ranch with Cal Doran on the western slope of the basin below the San Andres peaks. Maybe under a ridgeline where the grass was thick and water ran in a clear spring, or in a shallow basin protected from the wind, with good grass and an underground stream that bubbled to the surface sweet and pure. He needed to get cracking and find just the right piece of country to lay claim to. After that would come the hard work.

"I'll start you out at half wages until you make a hand," Kerney proposed.

"How much is that?" Ignacio asked.

"Fifteen dollars a month, plus room and board," Kerney replied. "If you stick, when you're a hand, you'll get a dollar a day. That's thirty dollars a month."

Even though his face hurt when he did it, Ignacio smiled lopsidedly. Fifteen dollars a month was a lot of money; thirty was almost a fortune. "I will work hard for you."

Kerney stood. "Then it's settled. I've got some business to take care of before we can light out. You stay here and I'll be back by noon."

Ignacio nodded. "I wait here, *jefe*."

"It's 'boss' in *americano*," Kerney corrected with a smile.

"Okay, boss," Ignacio replied with the lopsided grin still plastered on his face.

11

The smoke that drifted from the ranch-house chimney and the number of saddled horses in the corral told Kerney that John Good and his kin were home. Some good-looking ponies and a few mares grazed in the nearby open pasture, and Kerney slowed to give them a once-over before stopping at the porch to the house. John Good stepped outside, followed by his brothers and one of his sons. Tall at six-three, he was an arrogant man who expected people to do as he said, no questions asked.

Not knowing what to expect and with a nod to convention, Kerney stayed mounted. He could see Good's wife glaring at him through the partially open front door, her arms folded across her chest.

"Are you here for your back wages?" Good asked.

"I am."

"I hear you've been up north searching for your lost son. Is that true?"

"It is," Kerney answered.

"Did you find him?" Good demanded.

Kerney shook his head. "I know he's alive and living with an army surgeon and his wife, but I haven't been able to find them yet. I wrote them a letter and I'm hoping to hear back."

"How old is your button?"

"He's four."

Good nodded. "How much wages do I owe you?"

"Three weeks' worth," Kerney answered, somewhat surprised by Good's accommodating tone. "But I'll take it in horseflesh if it's all the same to you. That blue roan in the pasture will do."

Kerney had saddle broke the pony when he'd worked at the ranch and knew it to have a gentle disposition and an easy gait.

Good pointed at the roan. "That pony?"

"Yep." Kerney pulled out some folding money. "And I'd like to buy that sorrel mare."

"That mare ain't a cow pony," Good said.

"I know it," Kerney replied. "But she'll make a good pack animal. How much?"

Good named a price. Kerney shook his head and put his money in his shirt pocket. "Just the blue roan, then," he said.

Good squinted hard at Kerney. The mare was past her prime and barren. "Give me ten dollars for the mare and I'll throw in two halters, free."

"Done." Kerney handed Good the money.

Good examined the bills before folding them into his pocket. "I didn't run you off today because you had reason enough to quit me and go looking for your son," he said gruffly. "But the next time you come here I *will* run you off for causing my wife grief. My boy Ivan will cut out those horses and give you those halters. Then you git. I'll have no further truck with you."

Kerney touched the tip of his hat. "As you wish."

Good and his brother turned and stomped silently back into

the house as Ivan hurried to his horse to chase down the roan and sorrel. In ten minutes, Kerney was on his way down the canyon to the village. At the livery, he left the horses in the corral, paid the stable boy for their keep and oats, and went to the creek bed where Ignacio waited.

"Let's mosey over to the store," he said. "We need to get you outfitted."

Ignacio turned his hands palms up. "I have no money."

"I'll pay and you'll work it off at five dollars a month."

"But I still get some dollars each month?"

"Yep, ten, and then fifteen when you've paid me back in full."

At the store, Kerney bought a used twenty-dollar double-rigged stock saddle, a bridle, a new fourteen-dollar packsaddle, a five-dollar pistol that came with a belt and holster, and a box of cartridges. He gave the pistol, belt, and holster to Ignacio and told him to pick out a pair of boots, a shirt, a rain slicker, and a hat to replace his straw sombrero. After Ignacio made his choices, Kerney paid the clerk and they carried everything back to the stables. He brought the blue roan out of the corral and told Ignacio to saddle it.

"This horse is mine?" Ignacio asked.

"Only to ride for now," Kerney said. "Treat it right and I might sell it to you someday."

"And the saddle?"

"That's yours. No self-respecting vaquero would hire on as a hand using another man's saddle."

Ignacio stroked the cantle. "It is very nice."

"Stop admiring it and put it on the pony. Tighten the front cinch first."

"*Por qué?*"

"Because the horse requires you to do it that way."

"A joke—as you say—no?"

"Not a joke. He'll chuck you off if you don't. It's a matter of good horse sense."

Ignacio shrugged and saddled the horse as he'd been told.

Kerney inspected the cinches, adjusted the stirrups, and handed Ignacio the reins. "Now ride it," he ordered.

As Ignacio swung into the saddle, Kerney slapped the roan hard on its flank and it took off at a gallop. Ignacio managed to keep his seat without grabbing leather, but it was nip and tuck for a while as he bounced around. He reined the horse to a stop in the middle of the road and came back to Kerney at a walk.

"Well, you can ride, sort of," he said. "A couple of months in the saddle every day should get the kinks out."

"What are kinks?" Ignacio asked.

Kerney carefully considered his reply. "You need to learn to keep your seat and smooth out your ride."

"I'll do better," Ignacio promised.

"I know you will."

He showed Ignacio how to put the packsaddle on the mare and told him to practice doing it several times, then change into his new duds and wait for him.

Back at the general store, Kerney stocked up on two weeks' worth of victuals, new blankets for the bedrolls, cartridges for his rifle and pistol, two good lengths of rope, two shovels, a spanking-new coffeepot, and some sturdy canvas sacks. He was settling his bill with the proprietor when a young man entered the store, unwrapped a Colt Dragoon revolver from a dirty oilcloth, and placed it on the counter.

Kerney studied the man as the proprietor continued counting

out the change due him. A smooth-faced lad, he dressed as a cowboy, but Kerney doubted the genuineness of his getup. Under his open woolen coat he wore a red miner's shirt, a sure giveaway, and when he tilted his hat back there was no telltale white forehead above a tan face, which branded every true waddie that lived and worked in the out-of-doors. His six-shooter hung in a brand-new holster without a scratch on it, and his broad-brimmed hat showed no sweat stains at all.

"Now, that's some six-shooter," Kerney commented cordially. "Looking to sell it?"

The young man smiled and nodded. "I surely am."

"Mind if I give it a gander?"

The tenderfoot handed Kerney the pistol. Over four pounds and more than twelve inches long, it was big and unwieldy. The initials CC were carved on the stock, and the cylinder had USMR stamped on it for United States Mounted Rifles. He smiled at the lad. "How did you come by this old gun?"

"It was my pappy's," the pilgrim said.

Kerney grabbed the pilgrim's gun hand to keep him from clearing leather and raked the barrel of the Colt Dragoon hard across his cheekbone. "You're a liar and a thief. Undo your gun belt or I'll kill you where you stand."

With shaking hands and blood pouring down his face, the kid did as he was told.

The storekeeper started to move away. Kerney told him to stand pat and poked the kid in the stomach with the Colt. "What's your name?" he demanded.

"Sam, Sam Nash."

"Turn out your pockets."

"I've got no money. I lost it all at faro."

Kerney poked him again. "Do as I say."

Nash turned out his pockets. Sure enough, he was busted.

"You stole a book," Kerney said. "Where is it?"

"I burned it."

"Back up to the door," Kerney ordered as he stuck the Colt Dragoon in his waistband and drew his pistol.

"Don't shoot me," Nash begged as he raised his hands and inched backward.

"I'm taking your gun belt and six-shooter as payment for the pistol, money, and book you stole from my hired hand. If you come looking for me or for him I will kill you."

"I won't. Swear, I won't."

Kerney waved his pistol. "Git."

Nash turned, crashed through the door, and ran helter-skelter down the street.

Kerney holstered his revolver and turned to the shopkeeper. "Do you know if young Sam Nash has any kin hereabouts?"

"None that I know of. He's a newcomer out of Kansas, as I recall. Been here about a week." He held out Kerney's change.

Kerney pocketed the money and scooped up the holstered pistol and gun belt. "I'll be back for my victuals and supplies in a bit."

"Take your time," the shopkeeper replied, his voice a bit shaky.

* * *

Ten days into his search for a homestead, Kerney had yet to find what he was looking for. He'd been in and out of canyons and flats along both sides of the San Andres, had trailed down draws and arroyos, traversed pastures twenty miles long, and climbed ridges and gaps in the high country. Nothing yet approached what he wanted, and he was starting to think that he might have to settle for less.

After a hard, difficult ride into a wide canyon that coursed east toward the Tularosa, Kerney called a halt for the day. While Ignacio got busy caring for the horses and setting up camp, he grabbed his rifle and followed a footpath that led to a rock outcropping at the base of a ridgeline. There he found painted images of mounted warriors and miniature drawings of cougar, javelina, deer, and dragonflies. It was an Apache camping ground for certain, perhaps even a sacred site. A well-worn trail close to water from a spring at the foot of a peak to the north probably ran from the mountains west of the Rio Grande all the way east to the Apache lands and Fort Stanton. The canyon was thick with dormant bunchgrass that waved in a lazy breeze, and there were stands of scrub oak scattered about, but the soil was poor and rocky, not fit as a permanent livestock pasture.

He returned to camp, where Ignacio had a fire going and the coffeepot on. He hunkered down, poured a cup, and drank it thinking that taking on Ignacio had been the smartest thing he'd done in a while. The boy made good coffee and was turning into a hand faster than Kerney thought possible.

"Does this place have a name?" he asked Ignacio.

"Hembrillo Canyon," Ignacio replied. "It is a word for a seed or nut."

"What kind?"

Ignacio shrugged. "I'm not sure." He glanced around the broad canyon. "The only thing I see that bears a nut are the small oaks. Is this the place you pick for the ranchero?"

"I'm not partial to it, although it's a nice slice of outdoors."

Kerney picked up his rifle, mounted his horse, and gestured at the bald mountain to the north. "There's enough daylight left for me to have a closer look at the source of the spring. Appears to be higher up in that crevice."

He followed a narrow ledge and reached the crevice where the water flowed, but it wasn't the source of the water. The gap widened enough for a horse and rider to pass, and Kerney followed it to a pool that bubbled out of the hard rock on the mountainside.

He knelt and sipped the water. It was cold and pure. Would the stream dry up in the summer? If he dug a well down on the canyon floor, would he hit bedrock before he reached water? Was there other water nearby that might be easier to get livestock to?

He walked his horse to the gap and froze. Below, two riders were at the camp. One rider held a pistol on Ignacio while his partner watched off to the side like a spectator, hands resting on his saddle horn. The man with the pistol motioned to Ignacio, who slowly dropped to his knees, crossed himself, and lowered his head. Kerney didn't wait to see more. He pulled his rifle from the scabbard, knelt, sighted carefully, and shot the cowboy with the six-gun out of his saddle. Quickly, he swung to fire on his partner, as the man's hands jerked off the saddle horn and flew into the air.

"Don't shoot," the rider called out. "I've got no part in this squabble."

"Keep your hands where I can see them, and call out your name," Kerney ordered.

"Bill Bonney," the rider shouted, looking up at the mountain.

"Billy, its John Kerney here, and I'll gun you down if you so much as twitch a hair."

"I ain't moving, John," Billy the Kid yelled.

Slowly Kerney mounted, his rifle trained on the kid. "Who's your partner?"

"That there was Charlie Gambel," Billy replied, "and you shot him clean through. Mind if I liberate my gun belt and climb off this horse? I sure could use a cup of coffee."

"Drop the gun belt, but stay put until I get there."

Kerney waited to ride into camp until Billy's gun belt hit the ground.

Billy smiled as he rode up. "It's been a while, John. Now, how about that cup of coffee?"

"Climb down," Kerney said.

Billy jumped out of his saddle, went over to Charlie Gambel's body, and prodded it with the toe of his boot. "Dead, sure enough. I expect you want me to help bury this old boy?"

"That would be neighborly." Kerney swung off his horse. "If we plant him now, you can stay for supper."

"I'd be obliged," Billy said.

"Seems you didn't care if Charlie did some killing here today."

Billy smiled. "Weren't my business." He took Charlie's legs and dragged him into the tall bunchgrass.

"Was old Charlie your pard?"

"Can't say that he was," Billy answered. "I was just wandering back from Arizona with him. We quit a trail drive there. Didn't feel like riding on to California."

Kerney grabbed two shovels and handed one to Billy. "Dig," he said.

"I never did like old Charlie much," Billy said as he started digging. "He was just about as useless a cowboy there ever was."

"That he was," Kerney replied.

Behind them, Ignacio's breathing had slowed to normal. His

heart no longer thundered in his chest and his ears had stopped ringing. In the space of a minute he'd gone from being almost killed to seeing Charlie Gambel fall off his horse dead.

He was glad Charlie was dead. He thought about Teresa and smiled.

12

Throughout the winter and into the first chilly days of spring, from sunup to sundown, John Kerney and Ignacio Chávez labored to start Kerney's ranch in a meandering valley north of Hembrillo Canyon. Formed into a horseshoe shape that dipped to low, rolling foothills, it had good grasslands watered by a spring-fed pond surrounded by reeds and cattails. An intermittent stream shaded by cottonwoods wandered through the tall grass and disappeared in a flat-bottomed arroyo that coursed into the Tularosa Basin.

From the upper reaches of the valley, Kerney could look out on the barren alkali flats, the blinding, sugar white sand dunes, the ink black lava fingers of the malpais, and the far-off eastern mountains, which cast powerful sunrises over the land most every morning.

Above the pond, a wide, level shelf nestled against the valley's north slope. With a commanding view of the basin, it was a perfect spot for a ranch house. Once built, he'd plant a windbreak of trees but leave the panorama open so he could rest on the veranda and enjoy the view after long days in the saddle. He imagined the cheerful sounds of birds and animals at the pond and the sight of lazy ponies grazing in the pasture below.

West behind the valley, the San Andres rose up in deep canyons with thick stands of pine trees and sheer rock falls. During the winter months, Kerney and Ignacio cut timber, snaked the logs to the valley, and built two sturdy corrals with strong gates. They hauled rock by the wagonload and built a saddle shed with a three-foot-high stone foundation finished with notched logs and topped off by a slanted wooden roof chinked with mud to keep out moisture and wind.

When the shed was finished, they dug a cistern at the back of it to catch rainwater. They hit bedrock four feet down and split it open by lighting fires against the granite and dousing the rock with cold water. Twenty feet wide and six feet deep, the cistern held a good amount of water.

As promised, Cal Doran put his money into the enterprise and showed up now and again to lend a hand. He was gone more often than not, working as an army scout hunting a band of Apaches led by a chief named Victorio. They were raiding from east to west, north to south, into Mexico and back again, stealing livestock and killing settlers and miners. The army skirmished with them time and again and claimed victory after each engagement, but Victorio and his people continued to avoid capture.

John Kerney figured Cal would get more interested in their partnership once the Indian troubles settled down, but for now ranching just didn't provide the amusement to be found chasing Victorio.

Although the Apaches had not bothered Kerney and Ignacio, the constant threat made them keep weapons close at hand at all times. Over the course of several months, they saw a number of small groups of Apaches at a distance traveling over the alkali flats toward Hembrillo Canyon. They took up their rifles and prepared for an attack, but none came. Once near dusk, a large band of women, children, and warriors on horseback crossed a mite closer to them, moving quickly. At first it looked like a small pack of dogs was running behind the riders, but it turned out to be six braves on foot keeping pace with the riders. Kerney watched them through his field glasses, amazed by their speed and endurance.

On one of his infrequent visits, Cal brought two sturdy cow ponies recovered from some rustlers that had gone unclaimed. Kerney promptly gave Ignacio the choice of keeping the blue roan as his own or taking one of the ponies. Ignacio, who'd become a good rider, wisely kept the roan. They used the cow ponies to pull a wooden scoop Kerney had fashioned to carve out a dirt water tank in the arroyo where the streambed disappeared. It would trap a good amount of runoff when summer rains came.

On his trips to the village of Tularosa, Kerney stopped first at Coghlan's store, hoping for a letter from Dr. Lyon or his wife, but none came. Each time, he sent another letter to them in care of the War Department, asking their whereabouts so he could fetch his son, and then returned to the ranch with a heavy heart he hid in hard work.

Occasionally, anger about the whole damn situation made him crabby with Ignacio. He didn't know much about the law, but he knew that nobody had the right to keep Patrick from him without his consent. Leastways he figured that was the way it should be.

When the weather began to warm, he put pen to paper and did some figuring on what it would cost to build the ranch house. Milled lumber was dear and hard to get and would need to be hauled a long way over a difficult route, so he decided to build with adobe and stone instead, except the roof would be pitched, not flat, and the floors would be wood, not dirt.

In late March they traveled to Tularosa and found it crowded with Buffalo Soldiers camped outside the village. While Ignacio went off to visit Teresa and his parents, Kerney stopped in at Coghlan's store and asked if there was a letter for him. The clerk searched quickly through the mail and shook his head. Disappointed, Kerney wrote another note to the doctor, paid the postage, and left it to be sent out with the next mail wagon. Outside at the hitching post, Cal Doran waved him down and slipped out of his saddle. He was covered in dust, and Patches, his horse, looked jaded from a long ride.

"When I didn't find you at the ranch, I was dreadful afraid the Apaches might have put the kibosh on you," he said.

"Here I am, fit as a fiddle," Kerney said with a smile. "No reason to worry over me."

"I swear someday you'll get yourself scalped out there in the hell-and-gone."

"I reckon that wouldn't trouble your mind unless you had a good reason to fret," Kerney said jokingly. "What's got you so all-fired interested in my welfare?"

Cal grinned sheepishly. "I'm caught fair and square. You've put a lot of horse tracks in the San Andres. I doubt there's a white man hereabouts who knows those twisted canyons and knuckled ridges better than you. I'd be obliged if you'd guide me and some pony soldiers into those mountains. Victorio and his braves are holed up there, and we'd surely like to find him before he decides to slip back across the border to Mexico again."

Cal had never asked Kerney a favor before, and he was loath to turn him down. "Killing Victorio won't be easy."

"You don't have to do any of the killing, just the scouting."

Kerney laughed. "Seems to me it's one and the same thing. When do we leave?"

"Right now, if you're able."

John Kerney looked confused. "Shouldn't we wait on the army boys?"

"They ain't moving a lick until we report back on Victorio's whereabouts," Cal replied as two soldiers strolled by. "We've got four days to get the job done and hightail it back here."

"That's a long, rough ride through hard country," Kerney allowed. "Best we get us a string of fresh ponies and some grub."

"Consider it done." Cal eased into the saddle. "Will hardtack, bacon, and black coffee serve you, or do you want something fancier for victuals?"

"I'm hankering for canned oysters," Kerney replied as he threw a leg over his horse. "And I'm powerful hungry for a mince pie."

Cal shook his head in mock disbelief as he led the way to the army encampment.

* * *

Within the hour, they were ready to make tracks on fresh horses. Kerney found Ignacio and told him to stay in Tularosa until he returned.

"Where are you going, *jefe*?" Ignacio asked.

"Looking for Victorio."

"I go too, *jefe*," Ignacio said stubbornly, "to defend my village."

"Victorio ain't anywhere near your village," Kerney said, worried about the boy's safety.

"I will go," Ignacio repeated, stiffening his back.

Kerney shrugged. "Then you'll have to stop wasting time." He spurred his army pony and rode away with Cal, leading a string of cavalry horses.

Quickly, Ignacio returned to his parents' house, got his six-shooter and rifle, saddled his horse, and caught up with Kerney and Cal before the village was out of sight.

The three men rode with the sun in their eyes until the night turned the sky black. They camped at Malpais Spring on the edge of the fify-mile black lava flow, got up before dawn, and skirted far north of Hembrillo Basin through a pinched canyon pass thick with brush. The sun was still at their backs when they broke through the hogback ridges of the San Andres Mountains, dropped into a boulder-filled arroyo, and began a trek down the Jornada del Muerto, the Journey of the Dead Man, a wide stretch of parched land where many Spanish settlers had died of thirst, starvation, and Apache raids during the long-ago days of the conquistadors.

At a small rainwater pond that in summer was no more than a faint, dry dimple on the flats, they watered their horses before pushing on to the mouth of the deep pass that led to Hembrillo Basin, where Kerney called a halt. Behind a rocky hillock covered in sage, greasewood, and a stand of sotol plants, they saddled fresh horses.

"Here's where you wait for us," Kerney told Ignacio.

"But, *jefe*," Ignacio protested.

"No buts," Kerney said. "I need you to stay here and look after the animals. Stay put and stay quiet. A lot of Apaches have come this way recently, and I don't need you to get yourself scalped."

"If you hear gunfire," Cal said, "you skedaddle back to Tularosa and tell the army to come pounding leather." He took some gunnysacks from a saddlebag and covered his horse's hoofs.

Kerney did likewise and threw a leg over the saddle. "Cold camp tonight, Ignacio, savvy?"

"Savvy," Ignacio said glumly as he unsaddled his horse. "When are you coming back?"

Kerney checked the angle of the sun, now sliding westward over the hazy Caballo Mountains, casting light on the gap that led to the shallow Rio Grande valley and the tiny Mexican farming settlement of Las Palomas. "Before midnight."

He led the way into the mouth of the canyon and veered quickly up a ridgeline that paralleled the trail.

"You sure Victorio is camped in here?" Cal asked.

"Almost dead certain," Kerney replied. "I judge the Apaches have been using this place as a hunting ground for a mighty long time. There's good water, good grass, good game, fuel for campfires, and it can be easily defended from high up. I spotted breastworks when I passed though with Ignacio."

"The army thinks Victorio has a hundred braves, women, and children with him."

"More than that, I reckon," Kerney replied. "I've seen a number of bands crossing the Tularosa from the east. Probably Mescaleros leaving the reservation to join him."

"We need to get a gander before nightfall; otherwise, we're gonna be spending the night huddled behind some boulder."

Kerney nodded. "There's a game trail that drops down to a pool that feeds a spring. We can scramble above it on foot and get a good look-see."

The trail wound behind a solitary peak and up the backbone of an adjacent east-west canyon that dropped off into the Tularosa. They followed the narrow, rocky canyon through a stand of thick pine trees, picked up the trail again, and stopped when they heard the distant whinnying of horses.

"We walk from here," Kerney said, dismounting.

"Those Indian ponies are a far piece away," Cal complained as he swung out of the saddle, "but I guess sore feet are better than an Apache haircut."

They tied off their mounts at a pine tree, followed the game trail into a valley that ran against the base of a lone mountain, and paused when they heard the sound of voices.

Kerney nodded at a sharp point well below the mountaintop and gestured at the faint trail that climbed toward it. "That's where we need to be," he whispered.

They moved slowly, careful not to dislodge rocks that might signal their presence. At the top of the rock-strewn trail they took a cautious look beyond the pool that fed the spring on the basin below. Dozens of wickiups and a whole caboodle of Apaches were in plain view. Evening campfires were lit, venison roasted over the flames, children played nearby, and horses were idly grazing under the watchful eyes of some young bucks.

"Maybe two hundred fifty," Cal whispered, a bit astonished by the sight. He'd never seen so many Indians off the reservation at one time.

"More likely three hundred," Kerney replied.

Cal's eye followed the sweep of land to the next lone mountain. "That's a hell of a big stretch of land down there."

"Do you see the breastworks?" Kerney asked.

"I got them fixed in my mind."

"Good, 'cause I'd surely like to know how the army plans to fight here without getting themselves ambushed," Kerney said as he slid behind the brow of the outcropping.

Cal joined him and shook his head. "You got me there, partner. I guess we'll have to leave that to the officers. How do you plan to get them soldier boys here?"

"From the north through Sulphur Canyon." Kerney looked skyward. Early dusk had arrived, and there would be no moon to guide them along the trail to their horses. "Best we get moving; otherwise, that damn Ignacio will come looking for us if we're not back on time."

"He sure is mutinous for a Mexican," Cal said, "but I can't help liking him anyway."

* * *

In Tularosa, Ignacio went to see Teresa again while Kerney and Cal rode on to the military encampment.

"Two bits that boy is gonna brag on his adventure to his young señorita," Cal said as he dropped the reins, groaned, and dismounted. His bones ached and his muscles were sore from the long, grueling days of hard riding.

"I hope he does," Kerney said as he climbed wearily off the army horse that had carried him back from the San Andres Mountains. "He deserves to win Teresa's hand. We're gonna lose him when he marries and moves back to town. That'll be a damn shame. He makes a hand."

"He'll do to ride with," Cal agreed. "Is Teresa old Perfecto Armijo's daughter?"

"That's the one," Kerney replied.

"She's gonna be one fine-looking filly," Cal predicted.

"She already is," Kerney said, remembering the last time he saw Teresa and how she reminded him of Mary Alice.

They turned the horses over to a private at the corral and went to meet the commanding officer, Captain Henry Carroll, who waited for them at a map table in front of a tent in the center of the encampment. A stern-looking man with a square jaw and a drooping mustache, Carroll gave his full attention to their report, including Kerney's estimate that no less than three hundred Apaches were camped with Victorio.

Carroll raised an eyebrow. "That many?"

"Afraid so, Captain," Cal answered. "More than half I'd figure to be braves."

Carroll stroked his mustache. "Show me on the map."

Kerney stepped to the map table and pointed out the route they'd taken to Hembrillo and what they'd spotted during their reconnaissance.

"There is high ground with breastworks that make strong defensive positions," he added. "I can get you there from the north, but Victorio will have the advantage once you enter the basin. In fact, he'll likely see us coming."

"That won't necessarily work against us, Mr. Kerney," Carroll said. He turned to a Negro sergeant who'd been standing quietly off to one side. "Sergeant Fletcher, have two couriers ready to leave with dispatches within the hour."

The sergeant saluted, turned, and hurried away.

"There are Sixth Cavalry troops and Apache scouts from Arizona encamped at Las Palomas on the Rio Grande," Carroll explained. "And the Tenth Cavalry out of Texas is currently moving toward the San Andres to cut off any Apache retreat once we engage Victorio. We will attack them from the west and the north and force the survivors into the guns of the Tenth waiting to the south. All told, we have over five hundred and fifty troopers in the field against him."

He pushed the map aside, sat at the desk, and picked up a pen. "Thank you, gentlemen, for your valuable assistance. Mr. Kerney, when Sergeant Fletcher returns, he will take you to the paymaster to enroll you as a scout for the duration of the engagement. We'll leave at first light for Hembrillo and camp overnight at Malpais Spring. With an early start, in three days we should be in position to attack. Now, if you'll excuse me, I have dispatches to write."

After Kerney finished enrolling and swearing to obey all lawful orders, the two friends headed down the road to Coghlan's saloon for a drink or maybe two. Along the way, Cal explained in his soft Texas drawl that generally he didn't care much for darkies, but he sure thought better of those who served as Buffalo Soldiers. "Most are fine fighting men," he allowed.

"They'll need all their courage and sand at Hembrillo Basin," Kerney said.

"That's a fact sure enough, especially with Victorio," Cal said, pushing through the saloon doors. "Best we make certain not to get scalped."

"I'll drink to that," Kerney said as he sidled up to the bar and called for whiskey.

13

Early in the morning, four companies of Buffalo Soldiers left Tularosa traveling light. By Kerney's count there were one hundred troopers and officers under Captain Carroll's command, nowhere near enough of a fighting force to dislodge Victorio from his stronghold. He voiced his doubts to Carroll, who reminded him that two larger columns were also converging on the Apaches and the combined forces would heavily outnumber even the most optimistic estimate of Victorio's fighting strength.

While Carroll's reasoning sounded good, Kerney knew how punishing and unforgiving the Tularosa could be to man and beast, how easy it was to get lost in the twisted canyons and boulder-strewn ravines of the San Andres Mountains, how quickly a lack of water could lay a man low; and how the temperature could go from boiling hot to freezing cold no matter what the season.

Ignacio had insisted on accompanying the column as a volunteer, and he rode with Kerney and Cal Doran as they scouted ahead of the mounted troops for any signs of trouble. They cut the recent trail of two small bands of Apaches headed toward the San Andres and figured another ten or twelve Mescaleros had jumped the reservation to join Victorio.

At Malpais Spring, Carroll called a halt for the night. In the morning, he ordered Kerney and Cal to accompany a detachment of thirty troopers commanded by Lieutenant Conline, an officer who had served as a private in the Civil War before graduating from West Point.

West of the spring, deep inside Sulphur Canyon, they cut a larger trail of at least fifty Indians. The lieutenant sent a courier back to inform Carroll and pressed on in spite of Kerney's warning that any element of surprise would be lost if they engaged the Indians too early.

They sighted the Apaches with the sun low on the horizon and within the hour the small column was engaged. Under a cloud of dust the Apaches vanished behind a sharp bend in the canyon only to reappear, firing down on the troops from rock outcroppings and low ridgelines. Almost simultaneously, a dozen or more Apache riders led by Victorio feigned a charge in an attempt to draw the column closer. Lieutenant Conline gave chase until the troops came under heavy fire from Apaches in hidden positions behind a rock fall, which forced a retreat to a shallow arroyo at the edge of the canyon wall. Side by side with the Buffalo Soldiers, Kerney, Cal, and Ignacio put their horses on the ground, pulled their rifles, and from the lip of the arroyo, fired on the Apaches bearing down on them. Thirty yards out, several bucks jumped off their ponies, took cover behind two dead cavalry mounts, and laid down a steady barrage, their bullets digging into the sandy rim of the arroyo.

For no apparent reason, suddenly both sides stopped firing and a momentary hush fell over the battlefield, only to be broken by a chorus of Apache war cries that echoed off the canyon walls. All at once, on horseback and by foot, the Indians attacked the troops from three sides. A yell went up from the arroyo as the troops fired into the charging Apaches. The smell of gunpowder hung in the still air, dust rose like puffballs from the hoofs of the Indian ponies, and the percussion of constant rifle fire reverberated like thunder, mixed with the screams of wounded men and animals.

Four bucks fell no more than a dozen feet in front of Ignacio before the rest retreated, some bloodied and wounded.

Next to him a corporal moaned in pain, clutching his side, trying to stem the flow of blood that squirted from a bullet hole.

In a voice that sounded strange to his ears, Ignacio called for help. Sergeant Fletcher crawled over and pulled the corporal away.

Ignacio wiped the sweat from his eyes and took a quick look at the battlefield in the fading light, waiting for the Apaches to attack again. Rifle fire kept them pinned down in the arroyo, but that was it. As he waited for the next volley of shots to ring out, the silence deafened his ears. Every muscle in his body felt like stretched rawhide. His leg twitched uncontrollably, his hands shook, and his mouth was so dry he couldn't even spit.

During the fighting he'd been afraid, especially when the Apaches charged and he knew he was about to die. He wanted to run away, but instead he pointed his rifle and fired, the bullet from his rifle splattering an Indian's face into a gruesome mess. The dead Indian was out there lying in a heap, while he was still frozen in place on his belly in the arroyo, staring at it. He was alive, although he wasn't sure if he ever wanted to kill another man. He rolled over on his back and gazed at the stars in the darkening sky. There would be no moon until after midnight. He listened to the clatter of hooves as a courier rode off to report on the skirmish and wondered how the men around him, now talking in low voices, could sound so calm.

"Is Conline gonna keep us here all night with no water?" Kerney asked, after the lieutenant ordered sentries posted.

"That man has put us in a guaranteed hell of a fix," Cal said. He sat up and took a swallow from a canteen. "Did you know the army put him in an insane asylum in Washington, DC? I swear on my mother's grave it's true. One of Conline's fellow officers told me."

Ignacio wondered what an insane asylum was as he greedily watched Cal hand the canteen to Kerney.

"Then we best say our prayers," Kerney said. He paused and took a drink. "We should vamoose out of here before Carroll rides in rattling his saber and gets us all killed."

Cal chuckled. "If I recall rightly, the good captain said reinforcements are coming."

Kerney grunted and passed the canteen to Ignacio.

Ignacio took a long drink of water and licked his cracked lips.

"How are you doing, Ignacio?" Kerney asked.

"*Bueno, jefe,*" Ignacio replied, his voice thin and wobbly. He coughed to cover his shakiness.

"Are you sure?"

"*Sí,* good." He cleared his throat. "We have more fighting *mañana?*"

"You can bet your boots on that, amigo," Cal answered.

"You did good today, Ignacio," Kerney said. "You showed grit."

Ignacio wasn't sure what *grit* meant but was glad he had some of it. "*Gracias.*"

Cal rolled three cigarettes and the men smoked in silence. It made Ignacio sick and dizzy.

"You'll get to liking it," Cal predicted just before Ignacio threw up.

Lieutenant Conline decided spending the night in a cold camp without water with several hundred Apaches nearby wasn't a good idea after all, so he ordered a march to rejoin Carroll's column.

"Well, maybe he ain't completely loco," Cal said as they headed out, the troopers riding two abreast behind them. "Least he don't want us to die of thirst."

Kerney laughed as he spurred his horse into a trot. "I reckon that dying of thirst can wait until tomorrow, then, because unless we trail back to Malpais Spring, the only good water within a day's ride is smack in the middle of Victorio's camp at Hembrillo Basin."

"What a comfort you are to a body," Cal replied over the braying of a thirsty pack mule from the back of the column.

* * *

The report on the skirmish with Victorio convinced Captain Carroll the Apaches were boxed in by the converging forces. In the predawn light with a harsh wind whipping up the Tularosa from the south, he led his Ninth Cavalry Buffalo Soldiers toward Hembrillo Basin.

Sunrise brought a blustery gale that kicked up a sandstorm, turned the sky yellow, and forced the column to halt for an hour, hunkered down in stinging gusts that rolled across the basin. When the storm abated, the march resumed and Carroll divided his troops, sending Lieutenant Conline ahead on a different trail to Hembrillo with orders to choke off any escape routes he might find through the narrow southerly mountain canyons.

By noon, men and animals were parched, but with water severely rationed, all drank sparingly from their canteens. One pack animal collapsed, never to rise again, and some troopers paused only long enough to load its supplies onto another mule and move the dead beast off the trail. If the column survived to return to Fort Stanton, there would be nothing left of the critter but picked-over bones bleaching in the sun.

Sand and dust from the storm had caked everything a dull alkali gray, and the column of troopers looked vaporous and ghostlike as it plodded toward Sulphur Canyon. Above, a hot sun burned through the yellow haze, and the only sounds on the trail were the squeak of leather, the clink of metal, and the steady, repetitious thump of hoofs in the thick dust carpet left behind by the sand-storm. Not a man spoke until Carroll called a halt and peered through his field glasses to scan the San Andres uplift in front of the column. Talk was hushed among the troopers as they warily faced the gap that marked the funnel pass to Sulphur Canyon.

After a short water break, the troopers, weary and slumped in their saddles, pushed on without complaint. Up ahead, John Kerney, Cal Doran, and Ignacio Chávez rode point, past the shallow arroyo where they had made a stand last night with Conline and his troopers. Windblown sand covered the tracks and footprints, leaving only the rotting partially eaten carcasses of the dead animals and spent cartridges that littered the ground.

They moved ahead cautiously, scanning the mountain guarding the entrance to Hembrillo Basin, looking for any telltale movement, alert to any puffs of black powder smoke, listening for the sound of the pounding hoofs of charging horses. All was quiet.

Accompanied by Sergeant Fletcher, Captain Henry Carroll came abreast of his two American scouts and the Mexican volunteer. "Gentlemen, it appears Victorio has fallen back to Hembrillo after yesterday's skirmish," he said, sounding pleased. "If so, we have him fixed in place. I'm recalling Lieutenant Conline to join us to bolster our forces."

"You may have him fixed in place all right," Cal replied, "but he's got fresh water and we ain't."

Carroll's back stiffened. "I'm aware of that, Mr. Doran. However, Colonel Hatch's plan is an excellent one. Rest assured that we will surround Victorio, close his escape routes, and quickly bring him down." He pointed ahead. "I mean to enter the basin at once."

"You might want to wait for Lieutenant Conline," John Kerney said, glancing at Sergeant Fletcher, who quickly looked away.

Carroll turned in his saddle and motioned for the troopers to move out. "We will not engage the Apaches until Lieutenant Conline arrives."

"Whatever you say, Captain," Kerney said. "But don't drink from the spring up ahead. The water's no good."

He spurred his horse forward in a fast trot. Cal and Ignacio quickly joined him.

"Do you think Victorio knows he's not supposed to attack first?" Cal asked.

John Kerney laughed in spite of himself. "Hell no."

"Madre de Dios," Ignacio said, crossing himself.

* * *

In spite of Carroll's warning, some of his troopers filled their canteens at the spring in Sulphur Canyon. About thirty men were soon so sick they fell behind the column as it entered Hembrillo Basin. Carroll pushed on without them.

At the neck of the basin, Kerney paused to let Carroll take a good look at the broad expanse of land that fell off into a series of crumbled ridges to bowl-shaped tumbled grasslands below. All looked serene in the pale yellow shafts of afternoon light illuminating the sheer, rock-strewn peaks and the web of arroyos that cut around knolls and wrinkled folds.

Kerney pointed out to Carroll some distant breastworks and the far-off rise of the twisted ridge that hid the Apache campground from sight. Carroll nodded and signaled the column to continue. As the troopers began their descent, Victorio and his Apaches attacked from fixed positions. Several soldiers went down immediately and Captain Carroll took a bullet in his arm. With the column in disarray, Kerney and his compadres led the soldiers at a gallop to a rocky ridge near the basin floor that provided the closest possibility for cover. A dozen or more horses and pack mules were shot during the dash, and those soldiers who lost their mounts scrambled on foot to reach the relative safety of the ridge.

At the ridge, men dismounted and dived for cover as company sharpshooters kept the Apaches busy. Squads of troopers hurriedly threw up makeshift earthworks for protection. Before he could dismount, Carroll was shot a second time. Cal and Kerney pulled him to safety behind a large rock where his wounds could be dressed.

Another officer took command and ordered concentrated fire on three entrenched Apache positions to the south and west. At first, the Apaches appeared to retire under the barrage, but it soon became clear that Victorio had simply moved some of his warriors closer and augmented the number of braves directly above the ridge in order to pour scorching fire on the soldiers. A squad tried to move against one of the Apache positions, only to be driven back dragging two wounded soldiers.

"Did you see that collection of squaws and old men over yonder come to watch our destruction?" Cal asked as he reloaded his rifle, his chin pressed against the ground.

"Yep," Kerney replied as he fired at the spot where he'd seen movement. On the crest that sheltered Victorio's camp and the clear waters of the spring-fed stream, a cluster of Indians looked down on the battle.

"On top of that, we're surrounded," Cal added.

"Think we're done for?" Kerney called out. All around him troopers were firing blindly at Apache strong points and flinching under the return volley that rained down. The unearthly sound of gunfire reminded Kerney of Chancellorsville, where he'd been convinced he would never see another sunrise. He wondered if this morning had been his last. It sure felt that way.

"We're finished," Cal yelled back. A young trooper belly crawled to a dead pack mule for ammunition, and when an Apache rose to drill him, Cal shot him dead. The trooper scrambled back to cover, unharmed, with ammunition he passed down the line.

"Let's go get some of these sons o' bitches," Cal said.

Kerney shook his head. "Not yet, and not just the three of us."

"First water," Ignacio said. He was on his belly behind a shrub next to Kerney, dirty from head to toe.

Kerney smacked his lips at the thought. His canteen was bone-dry. "How? Where?"

Ignacio pointed to an arroyo at the bottom of the ridge. "We dig and we find water."

Kerney nodded. It was a damn good idea. Daylight was fading and already everybody was suffering mightily from lack of water. Without it they'd be useless come sunup when Victorio attacked to wipe them out.

A steep gully of scrub oak dropped down into the sandy arroyo, where a low, slender overhang would give them some cover. After nightfall it would be safe to dig there for water if they could get down without getting shot.

Kerney looked at Cal. "Are you game?"

"Yep."

Kerney passed the word of Ignacio's plan down the line. Within minutes two dozen empty tin canteens covered in kersey cloth and three shovels were stacked in front of him. If they found water, troopers would lower the canteens on a rope one by one to be filled and hoisted up.

Night settled over the ridge with no improvement in the battle, other than a few more casualties. Some Apaches moved to within a hundred feet of the ridge and were firing at any sound troopers or animals made. Another eight horses and two more pack mules were hit, and the pitiful nickers of the dying animals were dreadful to hear.

Sharpshooters kept the Apaches above occupied as Kerney, Cal, and Ignacio rolled into the gully and belly crawled to the arroyo. They kept low to the base of the ridge, scooted to the narrow overhang, and started digging. The sound of their shoveling brought a fury of gunfire in their direction, bullets ricocheting off the rock face inches above their heads.

At two feet down the sand became moist. Another foot yielded a trickle of water. They dug deeper, until water pooled in a small pocket no more than six inches deep. Kerney filled a canteen and took a swallow. The muddy water was gritty with sand and tasted like dirt, but it didn't matter; it was wet. He passed the canteen along to Cal and Ignacio and called for another to be lowered.

Using Cal's bandanna as a filter, they strained the muddy water into the canteens and were able to fill twenty of them with drinkable water before the pocket ran dry. The troopers on top whispered down their thanks as each canteen was hoisted up.

In the thin night air, the chants and songs of the Apaches carried from every direction, and high up where the squaws and old men had gathered to watch the fight during daylight, a bonfire now burned brightly.

After digging a dry hole in a search for more water, Cal threw his shovel down in disgust and leaned back against the ridge wall. An Apache bullet dug into the rock above the overhang.

"Those damn Apaches will wipe us out if we try to climb up out of here. We're trapped for the rest of the night."

"It's not much longer to daybreak," Kerney said, "and at least we've got some water."

"Now, ain't we the lucky wretches," Cal replied.

Up above, gunfire had slackened. The moon was high in the night sky, which meant Victorio probably had his bucks moving in for the kill at first light. For certain they'd use the arroyo; it was a natural pathway for a charge up the ridge, and they would likely come in from both sides.

John Kerney unbuckled his cartridge belt, put it within easy reach, and held his six-shooter in his lap. They had crawled down the gully with only their pistols, and once the Apaches were upon them and their bullets were gone, that would be the end of it. But they'd take a few bucks with them before they went.

He'd not slept more than six hours since leaving Tularosa with Captain Carroll's column, and he was light-headed with fatigue. He knew Cal and Ignacio were in the same fix, but nobody complained. Close beside him, Ignacio sat mumbling a prayer to himself in Spanish.

The night was cold, but the chill didn't keep him from feeling a bone-weary drowsiness. He wondered where the reinforcements were. Those hundreds of troopers Captain Carroll had bragged on. Hadn't they heard the fighting? Or were they lost out in the hell-and-gone, as Cal had called it? Conline should have arrived hours ago. He couldn't be that far away.

He closed his eyes for an instant and his head dropped to his chest, startling him back to wakefulness. As morning washed over the battlefield, silence descended. No shooting, no chanting, echoed through the basin. He clutched his six-shooter and waited for the onslaught. It arrived almost immediately.

They beat back the first probe with the bark of guns ringing in their ears. They stopped the second assault ten yards from their position. From two sides, gunfire shattered the air and muzzles spat flames.

Kerney heard a gasp as Ignacio crumpled to the ground. He stooped down, picked up the boy's pistol, and fired both six-shooters at the withdrawing Apaches until the weapons were empty. Beside him, Cal threw lead at another retreating party.

Lying on his side, Ignacio stared skyward, thinking he might be blind. A flash of light had hit him with a shock so strong, his whole body had quivered uncontrollably. He knew he was shot but felt no pain. He thought about Teresa, wondered if he was dying, wanted to see his parents again, and got suddenly angry at a God that hadn't listened to his prayers.

He felt a hand on his cheek. "*Jefe*, am I dying?"

"You're too tough for that, compadre," Kerney replied.

"I can't feel my arm."

Ignacio struggled to sit up. Kerney held him down. A bullet had shattered the boy's left elbow, and he could see part of the bone jutting through the blood-soaked fabric of his shirt. The wound bled, but not much. He took off his bandanna and wrapped Ignacio's arm tight against his chest as a temporary splint.

"Don't move," he said. "We'll get you out of here."

"I need my *pistola*."

"You just lie still, amigo." Kerney was out of bullets and Ignacio's pistol was empty. He picked up a shovel to use when the Apache returned and watched Cal load his last three cartridges into his six-gun.

"I'm gonna charge those damn redskins when they come at us this time," Cal said with a tight smile.

"That'll put a hell of a scare in them," Kerney replied.

Cal eyed the shovel in Kerney's hand. "Just beat to death the buck who kills me."

"I will if I'm alive," Kerney promised.

They waited nervously for the chorus of war cries that signaled the Apache advance and the barrage of bullets that would lay them low. Instead, a great shout rose from the troopers on the ridgetop, quickly followed by the sound of army carbines in the distance from the north and west.

A fresh burst of gunfire broke out from the troopers above. It went unanswered, and a long minute passed before the possibility of survival sank in. Up top they heard men moving about, orders being shouted, horses being saddled. Victorio's siege had ended.

Kerney tossed the shovel aside and looked down at Ignacio, who was pale and sweating profusely. "Let's hoist him out of here," he said to Cal.

14

Kerney and Cal carried Ignacio out of the arroyo while the arriving reinforcements battled Victorio in a series of skirmishes, forcing the Apaches to fight a rearguard action from ridge to ridge as they pulled back. They were finally driven from their campground by a flanking attack and retreated south, leaving behind three dead warriors.

When the fighting ended, Kerney and Cal put Ignacio on a cavalry pony and led him to Victorio's abandoned campsite, where a post surgeon had set up a hospital tent. Three Buffalo Soldiers with mortal wounds lay on stretchers outside the tent while Dr. Appel, one of the post surgeons from Fort Stanton, worked on Captain Carroll. Four soldiers with light wounds sat watching, waiting to be treated.

Nearby, exhausted, filthy, desperately thirsty soldiers were drinking from the Hembrillo spring. Horses were whinnying and mules braying in excitement as troopers led them four at a time to the water. The ground was littered with rifles, bayonets, and gear the soldiers had dropped after the fighting stopped.

They put Ignacio on a stretcher, gave him water, wiped his face, and waited for Dr. Appel to finish up with Captain Carroll and the soldiers. Last to be seen, Ignacio was unconscious when Kerney and Cal carried him into the tent. Dr. Appel removed the bandanna Kerney had used to immobilize Ignacio's arm, cut away his shirtsleeve, took one look at the shattered elbow, and said the arm would have to come off.

"But not here," Appel added. "An ambulance will take him with the other wounded to Fort Selden."

"We'll follow along," Kerney said. In the war he'd seen piles of bloody amputated limbs outside hospital tents and watched men endure the terrible pain of the surgeon's saw only to die afterward. He wasn't about to let that happen to Ignacio.

"Suit yourselves." Appel removed loose pieces of bone and tissue from the wound, painted the smashed elbow with iodine, and wrapped it in wet bandages. When Ignacio woke up, he gave him two opium pills to blunt the pain.

"Is my arm okay?" he asked Kerney groggily in Spanish.

"The doctor at Fort Selden is going to fix it," Kerney answered. "You'll be good as new."

Ignacio smiled in relief. Kerney felt like a rogue for lying to him.

Outside the tent, two canvas-topped army ambulances with four-mule hitches arrived, accompanied by an escort of troopers. Kerney and Cal helped load the wounded and moved out with the escort, headed west through the Hembrillo toward the Rio Grande and Fort Selden. Two dozen or more dead army horses and mules lay strewn over the battlefield.

The caravan entered the Jornada del Muerto, turned south, and made good time on the camino to Las Peñuelas—the Big Rocks— a favorite Apache ambush site, where they encountered a company from Colonel Hatch's command searching for Victorio, who had escaped. After a brief water and rest stop, the party veered west again and soon raised Fort Selden, an adobe fort on a small plateau about a mile from the Rio Grande, where the river curved gently through a thick cottonwood bosque.

At the fort hospital, Ignacio had to wait again until all the soldiers had been treated before the post surgeon examined him. He was a thin man, getting on some in years, who wore spectacles that sat low on his pinched nose.

After a quick look at Ignacio's wound, he turned to Kerney and Cal. "You know this Mexican?" he asked brusquely.

"He's a friend," Kerney replied.

"Wounded at Hembrillo?"

"Serving as a scout," Cal elaborated.

The surgeon nodded. "I need to take his arm off at the elbow."

"I'd be grateful if you wouldn't do that," Kerney replied.

"That is not your decision to make."

Kerney pointed at Ignacio. "No, it's his."

The doctor glanced at Ignacio's elbow again. "He will not have much use of it."

"Maybe some?" Kerney asked.

"Possibly."

"Can you save it?" Kerney asked.

"Perhaps. Wait outside. I'll see what I can do."

"Thank you," Kerney said.

The doctor waved away the expression of gratitude and turned to a nearby table of surgical instruments. "Outside, please."

On the porch, Cal rolled two cigarettes and passed one to Kerney. The friends sat, smoked, and watched some troopers across the parade grounds working in the corrals.

"Think he'll save it?" Cal asked.

"It'll be a ruination if that boy has only one arm," Kerney replied.

"Not your fault," Cal said.

"I should have looked after him better."

The young second lieutenant who had commanded the ambulance escort emerged from officers quarters at the far end of the parade grounds and approached.

"Is Dr. Lyon operating on the Mexican?" he asked.

"Who?" Kerney asked.

"Our post surgeon, Dr. Lyon."

Kerney jumped to his feet. "What's his first name?"

"William."

"Is his wife's name Polly?" Kerney demanded.

"Why, yes, it is," the lieutenant replied, eyeing Kerney cautiously. "Do you know her?"

Kerney shook his head. "She has my son, Patrick, in her care. Where can I find her?"

Startled by Kerney's intensity, the lieutenant took a step back. "I think you should speak to my commanding officer."

"Take me to him," Kerney growled.

* * *

After a hurried explanation of who he was and why he was there, John Kerney convinced Major Nathaniel Griffin, the commanding officer, to ask Dr. Lyon and his wife to come to his office. Griffin agreed, but only if the doctor and his wife were told the reason for the meeting. Anxious to see his son, Kerney readily agreed.

After a long delay, the couple arrived and stood hesitantly in the doorway. Dr. Lyon gave Kerney a nervous look as he adjusted his spectacles, and his wife, a much younger, slight, plain-looking woman, stared at him defiantly. Patrick, wedged between them, gazed wide-eyed at John Kerney.

He could see Mary Alice's features in the boy's face, especially his eyes and the shape of mouth, and he had the square shoulders and high forehead of all the Kerney men.

Kerney cleared his throat, uncertain what to say, almost disbelieving that his son stood before him.

"We were told you were dead," Dr. Lyon said in a mumble.

Kerney kept his eyes on Patrick. "I'm not."

"Do you have proof of who you are?" Polly Lyon demanded, her voice quivering.

Kerney looked at her. "There's a man outside who knows me and what I've been through looking for my boy. And I wrote you plenty of letters in care of the War Department and never heard back. Did you get any of them?"

"We received no letters," Polly Lyon said.

"At Fort Union," Dr. Lyon said, clearing his throat, "the boy was in such a sorry state, we thought he would be better off with us."

"As my husband told you," Polly Lyon added, "Virgil Peters told us you were dead."

Kerney didn't believe either of them, especially the woman. He clenched his jaw to keep from exploding. "I appreciate you looking after my boy and all, but now he needs to be with me."

He turned back to Patrick. "I'm your father, Patrick. A long time ago I had to send you away with your aunt Ida, and I've been trying to find you ever since. I want you to come home with me."

Patrick shook his head and stepped back behind Dr. Lyon. The man who said he was his father was dirty and ragged looking, just like all the men in the mining camps where he'd lived before the doctor and his wife took him in. He didn't like the doctor and his wife but was scared to leave them and go someplace worse.

"You're not my pa," he sputtered.

"I am your pa," Kerney replied, looking from the major to the doctor and his wife, "and you all will hear me out and get this settled now."

Major Griffin nodded grimly, Dr. Lyon sighed sorrowfully, and his wife burst into tears.

They sat and listened to John Kerney's story well past dinnertime. Patrick hid behind Major Griffin's desk, occasionally peeking out to look at Kerney with wide-eyed apprehension.

When Kerney finished, the room was silent until Major Griffin spoke. "Do you believe him?" he asked Dr. Lyon.

"I do," Lyon replied.

"And you, Polly?" he asked.

Her face tear streaked and red, Polly Lyon nodded.

Griffin stood. "Have the boy ready to leave with Mister Kerney in the morning."

"No," Patrick wailed as he scampered from behind the desk and out the door.

"You will not have an easy time of it with him, sir," Dr. Lyon said sternly as Kerney started after Patrick.

"I expect not," Kerney replied.

15

A year to the day after the doctor at Fort Selden saved his left arm and John Kerney found his son, Ignacio was about to marry Teresa Magdalena Armijo. His parents, grandparents, and siblings along with many of his aunts, uncles, and cousins, some who had come from as far away as El Paso, had all gathered to attend the ceremony. At Ignacio's request, John Kerney and Cal Doran were to sit with his family in the front pews of the church, along with Kerney's son, Patrick. They were the only *americanos* invited to the wedding.

With all the Mexican villagers attending the ceremony and the pews full, the aisles would be crowded with people standing along the wall under frescos of the Stations of the Cross.

An hour earlier Ignacio had seen Teresa in her wedding dress. She looked beautiful to his eyes. Under a creamy white veil, her long, curly hair brushed her shoulders, and her dress, with a high collar and lace border, made her look like a regal lady. He was amazed at how womanly she seemed, as if she'd grown up overnight. She had a silk sash around her tiny waist and wore her mother's small silver cross on a chain around her neck. She smiled serenely at him, while her mother and sisters bustled about making last-minute adjustments to their dresses and the younger children's clothing.

In a few minutes the wedding party would leave the Armijo hacienda for the processional walk to the church, and Ignacio was nervous and uncomfortably hot in his new suit as he waited under a courtyard tree. He knew very little about married life other than the small familiarities and occasional fiery disagreements he'd witnessed between his parents, and he had no idea what kind of husband Teresa expected him to be. She was strong-willed just like his mother, but all she'd asked of him so far was that he not come drunk to their marriage bed on their wedding night. To that he had readily agreed.

In turn, he'd asked her to leave Tularosa and live with him at John Kerney's ranch for the first year of their married life. He knew she would not refuse him, for John Kerney had saved his life and many times she had witnessed his kindness and generosity first-hand.

Any other *jefe* would have let go a man with only one good arm. But once he'd recovered, John Kerney put him back to work drawing full wages, helping to build the ranch house.

He quickly learned to do most of his chores with only one good arm. Although he could use both hands, his frozen elbow didn't bend at all, making it difficult for Ignacio to lift a lot of weight. Still, he usually managed to figure out a way to get his work done without needing to ask for help, which was a great source of satisfaction to him.

As he waited for Teresa and the rest of the wedding party, Ignacio remembered how sick he'd been after his surgery. A bad fever lingered for more than a month after his return home from Fort

Selden, slowing his recovery. When it broke, an infection in his lungs kept him weak, wheezing, and in bed for two more weeks.

Throughout his confinement Teresa kept him company every day. As his condition improved and his mind cleared, he read to her from the dime novels Kerney brought as gifts whenever he visited.

Some of the books Kerney gave him were free with coupons that came in sacks of Bull Durham smoking tobacco. A few of them were hard for Ignacio to understand, especially the ones by a William Shakespeare who wrote in a funny kind of English. Other novels were much less of a problem for Ignacio, and with great delight he read to Teresa tales about seafaring pirates, bandits and rogues in the gold fields of California, intrepid explorers on the frontier, and daring young men in big eastern cities. Teresa liked the big-city novels best, whereas Ignacio favored the seafaring pirate stories.

His English got better the more he read to Teresa, and he encouraged her to practice new words with him. Slowly, she, too, began to learn the *americanos*' language, although she found it harsh on her tongue compared to Spanish.

Only when he was back on his feet did he realize that many in the village considered him a hero. While he'd not been named in the newspaper stories, it had been mentioned that a Mexican scout had been wounded in the Hembrillo battle. Also, some of the troopers who had fought at Hembrillo spread the word throughout the village that Ignacio and his bosses had risked their lives to get water for the trapped, desperately thirsty soldiers.

During long walks he took while regaining his strength, the men of the village, both young and old, pestered him to tell the story of Victorio's ambush. At the dinner table, his brothers and sisters asked to hear about it repeatedly. Soon, Ignacio tired of it all and, whenever possible, politely declined to recount his adventures. But it made no difference; others in the village gladly stepped forward to recite his bravery and daring.

In the latter stages of his recovery, Teresa made it clear that she would welcome Ignacio's petition to her father to ask for her hand, and his heart raced with joy. But even with his newfound standing in the village, he half expected to be sent away by Perfecto as an unworthy cripple. To his great delight, Perfecto not only agreed to the union; he also added to his daughter's dowry a lovely, tree-shaded lot along the river where one day Ignacio and Teresa could build an adobe casita. It was a prize piece of land, and Ignacio had been made momentarily speechless by Perfecto's generosity.

A breeze stirred through the leaves of the courtyard tree as Ignacio nervously awaited the appearance of Teresa and all their many relatives. He stiffened when the door opened and his father stepped out alone.

Cesario walked to him and clapped a hand on his shoulder.

"Are you ready, my *hijo*?" he asked.

His mouth suddenly dry, Ignacio swallowed and nodded.

"You must give your mother many grandchildren to comfort her in her old age," Cesario said.

"How many is that?" Ignacio asked.

Cesario chuckled, shrugged, and squeezed his son's good arm. "Only God can decide how many. Just do your best."

The door opened again and Teresa appeared, clutching a bouquet of spring flowers. She seemed somehow different to him, almost a stranger. He smiled shyly, wondering if she truly was the same girl he'd known all his life.

Up ahead at the side of the road, Cal Doran, John Kerney, and Patrick waited. He'd never seen the trio looking so clean and neat. He waved and the two men grinned and waved back.

"Let's go," Cesario whispered with a push. "The priest is waiting."

With his parents at his side and his brothers and sisters just behind, he joined Teresa and her family. He took her hand, and leading the procession, they walked up the dusty road to the hillside church.

* * *

Three days later, after the last of the wedding festivities, Teresa tried to keep her spirits up as the wagon bumped along the faint trail that served as a road across the basin to Kerney's ranch. Since they'd left Tularosa that morning, she'd felt less and less sure she was going to like life in the remote wilds of the San Andres Mountains.

If Ignacio were driving the wagon, she could pepper him with questions about her new home. But John Kerney sat next to her handling the reins because Ignacio's bad arm made it difficult for him to control the team of horses over rough terrain.

Kerney's son, Patrick, sat in the back of the wagon, squeezed in among the trunks, boxes, and barrels that held her wardrobe and all that she needed to set up housekeeping, including a crate of clucking chickens, a crowing rooster in a separate cage, and her precious packets of herb and vegetable seeds.

She had spent only a few hours in Patrick's company and found him to be like no other child she'd known. He said very little, seemed happy to be left alone, and whispered to himself a great deal. He hummed a tune she wasn't familiar with over and over again to the point of distraction.

She turned her head and looked back at the boy, who quickly glanced away. She'd caught him watching her several times and wondered if in time he would warm to her. From what she'd heard, until his father found him there had been mostly misery in his young life.

John Kerney slowed the heavily laden wagon to a stop at the approach to a steep hill and told Teresa and Patrick to get down and wait there. Ignacio and Cal Doran rode up on their horses, tied their lariats to the long wagon tongues, wrapped the ropes around their saddle horns, and used their ponies to help haul the wagon up the hill as Kerney urged the team forward. Once safely at the top, Kerney called for Teresa and Patrick to join them.

Patrick scooted ahead. As Teresa picked up her skirt and carefully made her way around the rocks in the trail, she wondered once more about what lay in store for her at the ranch. Why had John Kerney told her to come to him if she ever felt lonely or unhappy at the ranch? Would it be that miserable for her? Or did he think her unsuited for the primitive conditions she might face?

During much of their yearlong engagement, Ignacio had been gone, working for John Kerney and Cal Doran at the ranch. When he came to town briefly every month or so, he replied to her questions about how they would live at the ranch vaguely or with sweeping generalities. All she knew was that the valley was well watered, with good grass, the views of the basin were a marvel to behold, the ranch house was finished, corrals and a saddle shed had been built, and Cal Doran had bought some Mexican horses that he and Kerney had trailed north to the ranch a month ago. It was mystifying because Ignacio usually described things in much greater detail.

Since the start of the journey, she had twice tried to get John Kerney to tell her more about the ranch, but he only smiled and said it was coming along just fine. She wondered if she'd be living in a tent, sleeping on the ground surrounded by rattlesnakes and centipedes, and cooking meals over a campfire while the *americanos* slept safe and secure in the big house her husband had helped them build. Or would she be forced to live in a cramped cabin with three men, a boy, and absolutely no privacy? She had no idea what to expect, and it preyed on her mind.

She reached the hilltop to find the land beyond mostly a long stretch of flats with the San Andres Mountains filling a horizon lit up by the late afternoon sun. Ignacio smiled at her as he untied his rope from the wagon. Over the past two years, his body had become more muscular. He was taller now, filled out in the chest, and the mustache he'd grown made him look less boyish.

"Soon, we will camp for the night," Ignacio said to her in Spanish, "and tomorrow we will be at the ranch."

She glared at him with her hands on her hips. "I will not go anywhere tomorrow unless you tell me exactly how I am to live at this ranch you love so much. If you do not tell me, I will ask Señor Kerney to turn this wagon around and take me back to my family in Tularosa."

On the wagon seat, John Kerney shook his head and grinned at Ignacio. "You'd better tell her right now. Otherwise you're in a heap of trouble."

"Better get to it, amigo," Cal echoed as he coiled his lariat and mounted up. He looked at Kerney. "I'll mosey on ahead to the ranch. See you there *mañana*."

"*Mañana*," Kerney said.

Cal touched his spurs to Patches and trotted off.

Patrick scrambled to his pony, hitched at the back of the wagon. "Take me!" he called to Cal.

Cal backtracked and smiled down at the boy. "I can always use another hand, partner, but ask your pa."

"Can I?" Patrick asked with his chin stuck out defiantly.

Kerney paused. Patrick favored Cal over him, and there didn't seem to be much he could do about it. He was happiest when Cal was around and downright grumpy otherwise.

"Get your pony and go," John Kerney said.

Patrick climbed on his pony, and soon the two riders were lost in a haze of rippling heat waves rising from the desert floor.

Ignacio and Teresa were off behind the wagon, deep in conversation, with Ignacio doing most of the talking in rapid-fire Spanish while Teresa held him under a steady gaze.

"We'll camp here," Kerney said mostly to himself, thinking he needed to find a spot a good bit away from the wagon to bed down for the night.

* * *

The big secret Ignacio had kept from Teresa was the small casita he'd built for her behind the ranch house. It had adobe walls more than two feet thick, a small sitting room with a fireplace, and a bedroom with a small corner fireplace, just big enough for a bed and a dresser.

As Ignacio showed her the casita, her eyes filled with tears. It was far more than she'd expected. He'd plastered the inside walls with mud and finished them with a coat of yeso, a form of white lime. The dirt floor had been sealed with ox blood, and on one wall hung an image of the Virgin of Guadalupe in a frame he'd carved by hand.

He had furnished the casita with two surplus army barrack chairs and a table brought from the quartermaster at Fort Selden, a used bed frame purchased from the newly refurnished Rio Grande Hotel in Las Cruces, and a mattress ordered from Chicago, freighted in by train to the railroad siding at Engle, on the Jornada, west of the ranch. Everything was spotless.

"Do you like it?" he asked. "I can build another room if it's too small."

Teresa spun around. "It's perfect."

As she marveled at his thoughtfulness, she remembered her mother's words on a day long ago when they had argued about Charlie Gambel. *The gringo will bring you nothing but heartbreak. Ignacio will give you a home.* Her mother's prophesy had come true.

"Are you crying?" Ignacio asked.

"A little bit," Teresa replied with a smile. "Happy tears."

She caressed his cheek and kissed him. She'd been headstrong back then, unwilling to see all the qualities that made her best childhood friend such a good man. "I know married women from our village," she added, "who can only dream of having such a wonderful husband as you."

Ignacio beamed. "Let me show you the ranch house."

A few steps away stood the larger ranch house, where John Kerney, Patrick, and Cal Doran lived and where Teresa would do the cooking. There was a brand-new cast-iron wood cookstove in the large kitchen that was an absolute delight. She stopped and inspected it carefully before Ignacio dragged her away to see the rest

of the house. It meant no more bending over a scorching hearth
to stir pots and boil coffee.

Like the casita, the house was built with double adobe walls to
stay warm in winter and cool in summer. The roof was pitched, the
floors were wood rather than dirt sealed with ox blood, and it had
a long veranda that provided a grand view across the basin. On
very clear days, Teresa was quite sure she would see wisps of chimney smoke from the haciendas and farms in her village.

Two bedrooms and a large parlor were at the front of the house,
with the kitchen at the back. In the enclosed courtyard between
the two houses, a well had been dug so that water was close by, and
Ignacio had built an *horno* so she could cook outside when the
weather permitted.

"Can I keep my chickens and rooster here?" she asked John
Kerney.

"Yes."

"Thank you for the casita," she said.

"Don't thank me," John Kerney replied. "Your husband did it
all by himself. In the evenings when most men wouldn't care to do
another lick of work, he put up the adobe walls. He harvested, cut,
and dressed the vigas that span the ceilings. The only help he got
from us was raising the vigas and finishing the roof."

"But you let him build it on your ranch," Teresa said.

"Let him," John Kerney replied with a chuckle. "We couldn't
hold him back once you agreed to marry him."

She looked over the courtyard wall to the corrals near the pond
and saddle shed. They were entered through ax-dressed gates, and
between the timber fence posts, stands of dressed cedar poles were
tamped into the ground, braced with long horizontal saplings, and
laced together with strips of green rawhide that shrank and pulled

the poles tight together. In the horse corral there was a *bramadero*, or snubbing post, in the center, used for breaking horses to the saddle.

"I hope you like it here," John Kerney said.

"I know I will," she replied, wanting her words to come true.

16

Teresa's initial misgivings about living away from her family lingered for a time. It was pleasant enough in the valley, far nicer than she had imagined, and unusually heavy spring rains had turned the land green with tall grasses and wildflowers. Birds nested in the cattails and reeds around the pond, the stream through the valley ran crystal clear, the livestock looked sleek and healthy, and her herb and vegetable garden flourished.

But in spite of how nice it was, she missed her family, especially her sisters, as well as her friends, neighbors, and close relatives she'd known all her life. And while she appreciated the company of John Kerney and Cal Doran—when they had time for it—she yearned for the companionship and closeness of women.

Señor Kerney sensed her longings for home and frequently asked in his halting Spanish if she was content.

"You worry too much about me," she finally said.

"I know how lonely it can get for a woman," he replied.

"There is too much for me to do to be lonely."

"Work doesn't fix loneliness," he replied with a tight-lipped smile, "especially in a place pretty much empty of people."

It wasn't until Señor Cal told her the heartbreaking story of how Kerney's wife had died that she understood his concern for her well-being. It made her think even more kindly of him.

The rains continued throughout the spring, and by early summer the entire basin was in bloom. Clusters of brilliant red desert paintbrush, scarlet penstemon, pale blue gilia, and bright yellow Mexican poppies grew in profusion along arroyos. Beargrass and yucca flowered, and the soaptree yuccas grew tall, slender stems fifteen feet tall. Cholla and prickly pear cactus put out clusters of wine red and golden yellow blossoms.

Victorio and his warriors had been killed late the last year in a battle across the border with Mexican troops at Tres Castillos, and except for some Apache raids in the mountains of western New Mexico and the northern Sierra Madres of Mexico, most of the territory had remained peaceful. But in July, a band led by Nana, an old Apache chief who had been with Victorio at Tres Castillo, ambushed a pack train in Alamo Canyon south of the Mescalero Apache Reservation, wounding the chief packer and stealing three mules. The army tracked the Apaches into the basin, and at Laguna Springs they found the murdered and mutilated bodies of Victoriano Albillar from Tularosa and a man and a woman from the village of Mesilla. Suddenly, war with the Indians had erupted again.

At the ranch, the men stayed close by and kept their rifles at hand, but the Apaches skirted north, where they clashed with Buffalo Soldiers in a gap between the San Andres and Oscura mountains and then fled across the Jornada to their home range high in the San Mateo Mountains, raiding and killing for provisions along the way.

News of fresh depredations came to the ranch by way of a small detachment of soldiers patrolling the San Andres. A posse of miners had been attacked outside of the boomtowns of Winston and Chloride, a railroad work crew had been shot up in Rincon, and four Mexican sheepherders had been murdered at a stage stop on the Rio Grande.

Over the next few weeks, the skirmishes and battles continued far to the west and south of the ranch, with the army flooding the region with companies of soldiers while old Chief Nana and his warriors continued to elude capture.

On a late afternoon, after a light shower, with billowing clouds thick in the sky promising more rain, Teresa stepped into the courtyard to pick squash from her garden and water her chickens. She counted the hens, found one missing, and looked for it over the courtyard wall. It was nowhere to be seen. She returned to the casa, got the pistol Ignacio had given her for protection, and searched around the ranch house. Still there was no chicken to be found.

She looked out over the valley for any sign of the hen. At the dirt water tank Cal Doran and Patrick were moving some cattle back to the high pasture. In the horse corral, John Kerney and Ignacio were working two of the Mexican ponies that had recently been saddle broke. Soon the three men and Patrick would come stomping into the house over the hardwood floors, spurs jingling, wanting their supper.

Calling for the chicken, Teresa circled the ranch house and froze when she spotted a fresh moccasin footprint in the dirt and another one close to the courtyard wall near several hen feathers. Frightened, she returned quickly to the house, rang the bell on the veranda to summon help, and hurried inside. Ignacio and John Kerney arrived first, and Teresa told them of her discovery.

"A small footprint," she added. "Perhaps a child. I think they steal a chicken."

"Apaches don't travel alone," John Kerney said. "Stay inside with Ignacio while I take a look around."

He returned to the house just as Cal and Patrick rode up. "We got us an Apache visitor somewhere hereabouts," he said. "Maybe more than one, I'm guessing, but all I've spotted so far are the same footprints Teresa found. Looks like they stole one of her hens from the courtyard."

"Can we track him?" Cal asked.

Kerney nodded. "I think so. It could be a child. The prints are mighty small." He looked at Patrick. "You go inside with Teresa and Ignacio."

Patrick shook his head. "I want to go with you and Cal."

"Do as I say," Kerney ordered.

Patrick slumped in the saddle and didn't move.

"Mind your pa," Cal said.

Patrick slipped off his pony, tied it to the veranda railing, and stomped inside.

Kerney threw a leg over his horse and put his rifle in the scabbard. "I swear that boy acts more like you're his pa than me."

"Nothing I can do about it except chase him away," Cal replied. "Which way?"

"West up the canyon," Kerney answered. "Don't chase Patrick away. Best he has someone he likes."

"Even the longest road has an end," Cal said. "He'll come around."

* * *

They lost the tracks twice on rock ledges and had to ride in ever-widening circles to pick up the trail again. It was getting on to dusk as they followed the footprints north over a juniper-studded hill. High up on the next ridgeline, behind a towering rock outcropping, they spotted telltale campfire smoke. They left their horses out of sight, picket staked near a tree, pulled their rifles, and started climbing at an angle toward the outcropping. Halfway up, they caught the scent of roasting chicken.

John Kerney pointed left and then right to signal they should split up and come in on both sides of the outcropping, and began working his way carefully up the southerly slope. Cal cut back in the opposite direction and began climbing. Before he reached the top, an Apache yell broke the silence, followed by a string of John Kerney curses. He scrambled up the last ten yards to find Kerney with blood running down his face, holding down an Apache boy no more than twelve years old who was kicking to get free. Behind him on the ground was a pregnant Apache squaw struggling to get up. She collapsed on her back and started moaning.

"This little savage tried to kill me with a rock," Kerney said. "Almost put my eye out."

Cal peered at the gash. "You'll live. Let me check the squaw; then I'll tend to you."

"She's pregnant and not doing too good," Kerney said.

"I can see that," Cal said as he approached the sweat-drenched woman. She was a girl, really, probably not even Teresa's age. She hissed at him with angry eyes but was too weak to do any harm.

"She's got a broken leg," he said. "Looks recent."

"I know it," Kerney said as he pulled the kicking Apache boy upright and wrapped him in a bear hug. "Think you could climb down the hill and get your lariat so I can hog-tie this critter before he cracks my shins?"

"I'd be glad to oblige," Cal replied.

He scrambled down the hill, came back with the horses, handed over his lasso, and watched as Kerney wrestled to get the squirming boy hog-tied.

Finally finished, Kerney stood, brushed the dirt off his hands, and gave Cal a pointed look. "Thanks for all your help, partner."

Cal grinned as he watched the boy wriggling on the ground like a trussed-up lizard. "That was a tidy piece of work," he allowed as he placed a boot on the boy's back to hold him down while he inspected the dent in Kerney's forehead. "Looks like you'll survive. Keep an eye on the squirt while I get something to doctor you with."

He found some liniment in his saddlebags, cleaned the wound with his bandanna, and covered it with salve. "I think we should build a travois and get this squaw to the ranch pronto."

The squaw had stopped moaning and moving. Kerney bent down on one knee and lifted her buckskin skirt. Blood saturated the ground, and she was bleeding heavily. "There's no time," he said. "She's dropping the baby right now."

Although many times in the past he'd helped cows and mares during a difficult birth, he wanted nothing to do with this pregnant squaw. The damn Apache with her big belly was like a punishment from on high, a harsh reminder that he hadn't been there for Mary Alice. The image of his dead wife on the West Texas prairie outside their cabin welled up in his mind.

"Give me a hand with her," he said, trying to shake off that eerie feeling. She kicked with her good leg and tried to scratch him. Pressing her chest, he forced her to lie still as Cal gently spread her legs. Kerney probed gently with a finger until he touched something in the birth canal.

"Push!" he shouted.

The girl looked at him with frightened, confused eyes.

He made a shoving gesture with his free hand. "Push!"

With her face contorted in pain, the girl began pushing.

"Harder, dammit!" he yelled, willing her to get it done.

She screamed and pushed until Kerney was able to gently wrap his forefinger and thumb around the baby's head and carefully begin to tug it free. . . . With one last push by the girl, the baby and the afterbirth gushed out.

The infant, a boy, was small, silent, and blue. The umbilical cord was wrapped around his neck. Kerney's heart sank. He pulled the cord free and slapped the baby hard on the rump. Nothing. He did it again, hoping to hear a cry. Nothing.

"Baby's dead," Cal said in a whisper.

Kerney looked at the girl and shook his head.

She took a deep breath, turned away, and wailed.

"Untie the boy," Kerney said. He put the lifeless baby on the ground next to the girl and cleaned her up some before adjusting her skirt.

Cal looked over at the boy. He'd flipped over on his side and was watching them intently. "You sure?"

"Yep. Feed him some of that chicken he stole while I scoop out a hole for this little one."

"We're gonna have a gully washer of a storm before we can get these two back to the ranch," Cal said as he loosened the rope.

Kerney looked up. Heavy gray clouds filled the night sky. Miles away, lightning flashed and thunder rumbled, moving fast in their direction. "If she'll eat, give the girl some chicken too," he said.

The storm came pounding down as Kerney finished digging the grave with his bare hands for the dead baby. He laid the tiny body gently in the hole, covered it with dirt, and put a big rock on top to discourage wolves and coyotes. Somewhere, someday, an Apache family would mourn if they weren't all dead already.

Near the drowned campfire, Cal had built a travois using juniper saplings and his slicker, while the Apache boy sat at the side of the girl, silently watching.

Kerney gathered some branches, fashioned a temporary splint on the girl's leg, and carefully secured it with rawhide.

"Did they eat?" he asked Cal as they carried the girl to the travois.

"The boy did."

"Let's get them home," Kerney said, wrapping his slick over the boy's shoulders.

"Then what do we do with them?"

"After the squaw heals up a bit, I'll carry them to the reservation."

"If they don't kill us in our beds first," Cal said.

"We can lock them in the saddle shed if you like."

"That's not neighborly," Cal replied. "I'll keep an eye on them." Soaked to the bone, he got in the saddle and started down the hill, the travois dragging behind Patches.

With rain splashing over the brim of his hat, splattering his shoulders, Kerney offered a hand up on his horse to the boy, who shook his head wordlessly and hurried ahead to walk next to the girl on the travois.

Kerney followed along, wondering what had put those two out here on their own. All he could figure was they might have been part of Nana's band that had clashed with the Buffalo Soldiers farther north in the mountains. When retreating from their enemies, warring Apaches were sometimes forced to leave behind the old, the sick and the wounded to fend for themselves. If they survived, they'd trek many miles back to the reservation or to their remote Apache sanctuaries in the western mountains. The girl's broken leg was recent, so he figured her pregnancy must have slowed them down in the rugged high-country terrain. He wished he could talk Apache so he could find out what had happened. Maybe he'd learn more once he got them to Fort Stanton.

Every dry arroyo they'd crossed tracking the Apache boy from the ranch was now a torrent of angry water, and getting across ate up considerable time on the way home. It was well past midnight when they reached the ranch house. Teresa had all the kerosene lamps lit and placed on the veranda, while Ignacio stood waiting, long gun and pistol in hand, with Patrick at his side.

Kerney slid wearily out of his saddle and smiled at his son, who didn't even look at him as he jumped down to grab the reins of Cal's horse.

17

For several days after the Apaches arrived at the ranch, Patrick watched the boy like a hawk. The Indian refused to go into the ranch house and slept outside on hard ground. He refused to touch the blankets Teresa put out for him, and the only thing he accepted was a plate of food at mealtimes. He ate on the veranda under the window of the bedroom where the squaw with the broken leg had been put up.

He stayed there all day long, hardly moving. Once in a while he said something to the squaw in Apache through the window, but that was the only talking he did. Patrick threw pebbles at him to see what he'd do, but he didn't even flinch. He just stared at Patrick with empty eyes.

He was skinny but strong looking, with long dark hair that hung loose over his shoulders, dark skin, and a round face. His fierce eyes showed nothing, and he didn't seem to care if Patrick watched him for hours and hours.

The more Patrick watched, the more intrigued he became. He'd never seen anybody be so silent and motionless for so long. The squaw in the house was the same way: quiet and still. He'd wondered aloud if the squaw was the boy's mother, but Cal said she was too young.

Patrick had no use for mothers. Ida had told him over and over again that she was his mother, but sometimes when she got drunk she'd say he was an orphan and cry about a boy called Timmy. John Kerney told him his real mother had died on the prairie giving birth to him and that Timmy had been Ida's son and would've been Patrick's cousin if he hadn't got killed by outlaws.

Ignacio's wife, Teresa, who was nice, would sometimes try to give him a hug, rub his hair, or kiss his cheek—which he didn't cotton to at all. She had been teaching him the Mexican lingo and once he overheard her tell Ignacio in Spanish that he needed a mother. He didn't speak to her all day because of it. He *never* wanted to have a mother ever again.

Worst of all had been Dr. Lyon's wife, who told him he was bad and sinful and took a strap to him almost every day for misbehaving. She whipped him for not minding, for being lazy, for not remembering to say his prayers correctly. She kept him away from other children, locked him up when visitors came, and threatened him with more thrashings if he ever told the doctor about getting switched. Except for the good food she fixed him and the clean clothes she gave him to wear, he hated her.

Patrick was equally disinterested in having a father. Ida had told him Virgil was his pa and made him call him that or she would smack him. But when Virgil hit her and took her money, she said John Kerney was his real pa and no good to boot. When he lived with Dr. Lyon, he'd been forced to call *him* pa or get another hiding from his wife when he wouldn't do it.

Slowly Patrick had come to believe John Kerney was his true pa, but it didn't mean much because he didn't trust grown-ups no matter who they were. He'd been handed off from one to another, with no one wanting to keep him permanent like. And while he was glad to be rid of Dr. Lyon and his wife, didn't miss Ida and her crazy ways, or drunk Virgil, and the year at John Kerney's ranch had been the best of his life, he didn't think it would last. For now, he slept warm in a bed at night, hadn't gone hungry once, and hadn't been whipped or hit. Still, he kept watching and waiting for it to go bad again, to be told he was a devil's child, to be slapped and punished, and to get sent away with some stranger.

The next time it happened, Patrick decided he would run away and live like an Apache.

Since coming to the ranch, Patrick had heard the story several times about how his real mother had died in Texas, how bad men had killed his uncle and cousin, how John Kerney had sold everything to give Ida money to take him to Dodge City and care for him there, and how after learning Ida had died he'd searched for months to find him. Cal swore to him that it was fact, but the story didn't make Patrick either happy or sad. It was just a story.

He didn't remember much about Dodge City. But he had vague memories of living with Ida in a tiny room at the back of a general store, being hungry and dirty, wearing clothes too big or too small, going barefoot, and being sent away when Ida was busy with a man. After Virgil moved in with Ida, they both started drinking a lot, leaving Patrick to play in the muddy Dodge City streets with other ragamuffins and come home hungry to the stink of sweat and whiskey. He hated that smell. When Ida died at the mining camp, he often waited for hours in a cold tent with nothing to eat. When Virgil didn't come and didn't come, he went begging for food or money from the other miners or drunks in the tent saloons, who sometimes gave him two or three cents.

Patrick trusted nobody: not Cal, the person he liked best of anybody he'd met in the whole world, not Teresa, the nicest lady he'd known, not Ignacio, who called him the little *jefe* and also taught him Spanish words, and most of all not John Kerney, who had saved him from Mrs. Lyon's whippings.

On the third day after the Apaches came to the ranch, Patrick screwed up his courage, walked across the veranda to the Indian boy, and sat next to him. The Apache didn't move, didn't look at him, and didn't say a word. Patrick adjusted himself against the wall, crossed his legs, and remained motionless until he couldn't stand it anymore; then he jumped up and went to see what Cal was doing.

The next morning, he decided to try it again to figure out how the Apache could stay so still for so long. After his morning chores and again after lunch and supper, he went back and sat with the Apache, each time waiting it out a little while longer, until his muscles started twitching and he had to get up and move. Not once did the Apache say anything or even look his way.

Finally, Patrick got bored. It was dumb to sit and do nothing, dumb not to talk, dumb to sleep on the hard ground for no good reason, dumb to be a stupid Apache. He figured Apaches were just plain crazy. "Savages" were what they were called, and Cal said the word meant wild and inhuman.

Patrick stood up and saw John Kerney watching him from the end of the veranda. He was about to turn away when John Kerney motioned for him to approach. He screwed on a sour face and walked over to him very slowly.

John Kerney smiled at his son. "Do you think you'd like to see where the Apaches live?" He pointed at the faraway mountains to the east.

"Maybe," Patrick said, hiding his enthusiasm for the idea. "Am I going to live there?"

"No, your home is here. This is your ranch. I keep telling you that."

"Are there army soldiers where the Apaches live?" Patrick asked.

Kerney nodded. "There's a fort there. It's a nice one."

"Will you leave me with the Apaches?"

Kerney shook his head. "Why would I do that?"

"Because."

"I won't, promise."

Patrick looked him squarely in the eye without blinking. "Can I go now, John Kerney?"

Kerney suppressed a wince. Having Patrick call him by name always hurt. "I keep asking you to call me Pa. It's more natural."

Patrick shook his head. "You can whip me if you want."

"It's no cause for a whipping."

"Can I go?"

Kerney nodded. "Get along."

Watching Patrick run off toward the corral, where Cal was shoeing a pony, he wondered if he'd ever get through to the boy.

A week passed, and at supper one night Teresa told Kerney that the Apache girl was healed up enough to take back to the reservation.

Except for Cal, they would leave in the morning. In Tularosa, Teresa would visit her family, while Ignacio, Patrick, and Kerney pushed on to the reservation. On their way back, they'd pick up a load of lumber from the sawmill, which Kerney needed for the barn he planned to raise, collect Teresa away from her parents, and head home.

The trip caused great excitement and talk around the table. Even Patrick was eager to go, for he wanted to see how savage Apaches lived. That night, he dreamt about the morning he woke up to find Ida lying dead in bed beside him.

18

The news that John Kerney was bringing two Apache children to Fort Stanton caused quite a commotion when he appeared outside the fort. More than three dozen Mescaleros met the little party as it crossed the river, and they trotted alongside the wagon until it stopped in front of the post headquarters, where the Indian agent, Mr. Llewellyn, and Captain Carroll waited.

Llewellyn had orderlies carry the girl on a stretcher to the hospital under the watchful eye of an Apache scout and put the boy in the custody of an army sergeant. When Kerney asked why all the precautions, Carroll told him the two were brother and sister of Nana's second in command, Kaytennae, and needed to be questioned.

Llewellyn hoped having them back on the reservation might entice Nana and his band to leave the warpath and return to Fort Stanton. Captain Carroll didn't think their safe return would make one bit of difference to the old chief. Kerney pretty much agreed with him.

He left Ignacio at the wagon with Patrick, who watched the milling Mescaleros with wide eyes, and crossed the quadrangle to the hospital, where the post surgeon, Dr. Newton, met him on the front porch. Newton told him the girl would walk, but with a limp, once she recovered, and asked about the baby. Kerney said the baby had died, and Newton nodded, saying he figured as much.

Kerney thanked the doctor for the information and hurried next door to the quartermaster's store, anxious to know if the proposal he'd delivered two months ago to provide fifty saddle-ready cavalry horses to the army in six months had been approved. He was bidding against the Coghlan outfit, which had pretty much monopolized livestock contracts at the fort for the past five years, and didn't think he had much of a chance. All he could hope for was a small slice of the pie.

The quartermaster, Lieutenant Dawson, greeted Kerney with a firm handshake, escorted him into his office, and handed him a printed document that read:

QUARTERMASTER GENERAL SPECIFICATIONS
GOVERNING THE PURCHASE OF HORSES
FOR ISSUE TO CAVALRY REGIMENTS

Cavalry Horses: To be geldings of hardy colors, sound in
all particulars, in good condition, well broken to the saddle,
from 15 to 16 hands high, not less than 5 nor more than 9
years old, and suitable in every respect for cavalry service.

"Would you be able to fulfill all those specifications?" Dawson asked as he settled in behind his desk.

"I surely can," John Kerney replied, his voice catching in his throat.

Dawson smiled. "Our post commander feels strongly that your service to the regiment at Hembrillo Canyon deserves to be rewarded. Therefore, I am authorized to contract with you for fifty cavalry horses to be delivered here six months hence."

"That's mighty generous," Kerney said, trying not to gulp. As soon as they got back to the ranch, he and Cal would have to hive off in a hurry down to Mexico and buy at least sixty or more horses, trail them home, and get busy breaking them. There wasn't a moment to lose.

Dawson slid a paper across his desk, handed Kerney a pen, and indicated where to sign.

Kerney scrawled his name, stood, and shook Dawson's hand.

"I'll see you in six months, Mr. Kerney," Dawson said, "with fifty horses ready for inspection."

"You have my word on it, sir," John Kerney replied.

He left the lieutenant and crossed the quadrangle with his mind racing ahead to all that needed doing. If the day wasn't already more than half gone, he'd start for the sawmill immediately, load up the lumber for the barn, and set off for the ranch at first light.

At the wagon, he told Ignacio and Patrick the good news about the contract and what needed to get done pronto. Ignacio grinned from ear to ear, and Patrick asked if he could go along with him and Cal to Mexico.

"Please," he begged.

"Why not?" Kerney said, feeling charitable to all that might be asked of him as he climbed on the wagon and started the team.

"You mean it?" Patrick asked as he climbed on his pony.

"I do," Kerney replied.

They set up camp on a small hill behind the quadrangle, and

Ignacio made a meal of beans, chili, and tortillas his mother-in-law had given him.

Over a cup of coffee after supper, Kerney pondered what Coghlan might do once he learned he'd lost the contract. He was the richest man on the Tularosa, but that didn't stop him from wanting more. He hired no-accounts and outlaws, sold stolen livestock to the army whenever he could get away with it, and was known to use gunslingers to scare away any competition. Coghlan would try something—of that Kerney was certain—so he would need to be ready for whatever play the man made.

He slept poorly, his mind busy with plan making. If they could get to Mexico and trail the horses back within a month, they'd have to work mighty hard to get them well broke for the army in time. The small cattle herd could range free and putting the barn up would just have to wait. But there was no sense not hauling the lumber to the ranch so they could start building it as soon as time allowed.

Kerney roused Ignacio and Patrick out of their bedrolls an hour before first light, told them to have some hardtack and jerky for breakfast, get saddled up, and start moving. By evening they were at the sawmill, where Kerney decided to load the lumber and keep traveling under a full moon.

The heavy wagon moved slowly down the road to Tularosa. On several steep-side hills, Ignacio had to tie his rope to the top of the load and use his horse to pull back to prevent a slip to certain disaster down a descent.

They reached Tularosa exhausted and slept in the courtyard of the Chávez hacienda until they woke up hungry at dawn. Over breakfast, Ignacio's father, Cesario, suggested they stay and rest up for a day, but John Kerney was having none of it.

"There's too much work to be done," he said.

Cesario had inspected the wagon earlier and found it to be overloaded. He turned to Ignacio and said in Spanish, "If we use two wagons to cart the lumber, it will be much safer. Tell him I will gladly take half of the lumber to his ranch in one of my wagons."

Ignacio translated for Kerney, who nodded, smiled, and thanked Cesario for his willingness to help.

The small caravan left as soon as the load was divided between the two wagons, tied down, and provisions for the journey to the ranch had been laid in. Ignacio and Patrick on horseback led the way, followed by John Kerney in the front wagon and Cesario in the rear. Teresa rode with Cesario, and over the creak of the wheels Kerney could hear the two chatting in Spanish. They spoke rapidly, and his grasp of the lingo wasn't good enough to make out much of what they were saying.

That night at camp, Ignacio, Teresa, and Cesario gathered around the fire, deep in conversation until it was time to turn in. Patrick sat quietly listening to them for a spell, which wasn't his normal whirlwind behavior, so in the morning Kerney asked him if he'd like to learn Spanish.

Patrick nodded his head vigorously.

"I'll ask Teresa to teach you," he said.

"She already is," Patrick replied matter-of-factly. "So is Ignacio."

They made good time across the tableland and through the alkali flats on a partially cloudy day that kept the temperature from soaring, and with the San Andres looming ahead they were no more than five hours from raising the ranch when they entered the last stretch of steep hills. They moved the two wagons up the trail one by one, Ignacio's lasso taut between the wagon and his saddle horn on the downslope, his pony pulling back with all its might to keep the wagons upright. On the upslope his pony scratched gravel with the teams, pulling to get the wagons to the crest. At each hill, Teresa followed on foot and Patrick on his pony at a safe distance behind the wagons.

Only a few more rock-strewn hills remained where the trail had been severely eroded by the drenching rains of spring and summer. Because of the steepness, Ignacio tied his rope to the rear axle, twined it around a huge boulder, and slowly played it out as Kerney's team entered the downside of the last hill. The axle broke, the load shifted, and the wagon tumbled to the bottom of the decline, throwing Kerney from the seat. The last thing he saw was a shower of heavy, milled plank boards raining down on him as the panicked team dragged the overturned wagon away.

"Madre de Dios," Ignacio cried as he jumped from his horse, ran to where Kerney was buried, and started feverishly pulling the lumber away from Kerney's body with his one good hand. Cesario, Teresa, and Patrick quickly joined him. Patrick watched as Cesario and Ignacio heaved aside a shattered, heavy plank to reveal Kerney's body. A long wooden splinter had penetrated his skull.

There was silence for a second until Cesario said, "*Muerto.*"

"That means dead," Patrick said emotionlessly, staring at John Kerney's bloody face.

"*Sí,*" Ignacio said softly.

Patrick turned on his heel, ran to his pony, and rode away in the direction of the ranch.

"Go after him and bring him back with Señor Cal," Teresa said. "We will wait here for you."

"*Sí,*" Ignacio said, his heart almost breaking.

❋ TWO ❋

Patrick Kerney

19

They buried John Kerney, aged thirty-seven years, at the ranch, high on a hilltop, and marked his grave with a cross made by Ignacio. It was the same summer Sheriff Pat Garrett gunned down Billy the Kid inside Pete Maxwell's house in Fort Sumner and old Nana's raids, the last true Apache uprising east of the Rio Grande, ended.

The task of raising six-year-old Patrick Kerney fell to Cal Doran, who took on the job with the help of Ignacio and Teresa Chávez. It didn't amount to much of a chore, as the boy didn't appear at all bothered by the death of his pa. In fact, he showed scant emotion about anything.

Cal figured the button had lost so many people in his short life that he was numb to it all. There seemed to be no softness to him, and he didn't take kindly to sentimental feelings from others. Not even Teresa's sweet disposition cracked his shell. No matter how agreeable and evenhanded Cal tried to be with the boy in those first days, he always felt Patrick stayed on the lookout for treachery and betrayal.

After the burial, the men salvaged what they could of the milled lumber and stacked it next to the saddle shed. They dragged the shattered wagon to the ranch and parked it next to the lumber. The barn would be built and the wagon repaired when time allowed.

Cal chased down the wagon team that had bolted after the accident, doctored some minor scrapes and cuts to the animals, turned them loose in the west pasture, and after a few days closed up the ranch and took everyone to Tularosa, where they stayed with the Chávez family while he set about hiring hands to hit the trail to Mexico in search of ponies to buy. He wasn't about to let John Kerney's quartermaster contract go unfulfilled.

At the saloon, Pat Coghlan tried to buy him out of the horse contract at a dime on the dollar, and Cal told him where he could shove the idea. His reputation with a gun made Coghlan back off, but not quickly enough to convince Cal the man would let matters end there.

He hired three Texas waddies, told Ignacio to look after the ranch and Patrick until he returned, and made tracks with his small outfit to Mexico. A month later he was back with sixty-five half-wild Mexican ponies, each handpicked to meet the quartermaster's requirements. He let two of the cowboys go and kept George Rose on the payroll.

George had been part of the posse that battled Billy the Kid and the Regulators for five days in Lincoln during the summer of '78 and had worked in the Seven Rivers area of the Staked Plains east of the Sacramentos before drifting to the Tularosa.

A short, stocky waddie with a broken nose and a toothy grin, George pulled his weight in the saddle, knew how to treat horseflesh, and was good with a gun, which was exactly what Cal needed if Pat Coghlan decided send his *pistoleros* to cause trouble.

Through a wet fall and a cold winter, Cal and George broke horses in driving rainstorms and heavy snow. In early February they trailed the ponies east to Fort Stanton, where it took the army boys three days to inspect the horses, put them through their paces, and make payment. Cal left the fort with another contract in his pocket for fifty more ponies due in six months.

On the way back to the spread, the two cowboys planned a stop in Tularosa to celebrate at Coghlan's saloon and pick up Patrick, who'd been living with Teresa and the Chávez family since before Christmas. Teresa was about to have her first baby, and Cal figured she would soon hold Ignacio to his promise to quit the outfit and return to his village. He didn't cotton at all to the idea of losing Ignacio.

They rode into Tularosa on a clear, mild winter's day. The town had changed again. Land was cleared for crops farther away from the river, and some nester shacks and homesteads fronted the wagon road that climbed the hills to the high country, where the Apaches had more or less settled down since the troublemakers had been shipped by train to Florida.

Railroad tracks now ran the length of the territory from the Colorado border to the dusty streets of Las Cruces and down to El Paso. Easterners and flatlanders had been trickling into the fringes of the basin for the past year, and there was talk of building another railroad up the Tularosa from El Paso.

Dryland farmers were proving up land away from reliable water sources, syndicates of big-city bankers were buying and combining small spreads and putting large herds on their empires, and prospectors were searching the San Andres Mountains for signs of precious ore. It was getting downright crowded in places.

They pulled up in Cesario Chávez's courtyard and Teresa

stepped outside to greet them, smiling and holding a bundle in her arms.

"By golly," Cal said with a laugh as he slid out of his saddle. "Have you gone and done it?"

"*Sí*, a boy." She pulled back the blanket to reveal the baby's face. "Juan Cesario Chávez. He is named for John Kerney and Ignacio's father. He's one week old."

"That's a mighty fine name." Cal peered down at the rosy-cheeked baby. Juan Cesario had a full head of curly dark hair, Ignacio's chin, and Teresa's eyes. "Has his daddy come in from the ranch?"

Teresa laughed. "*Sí*, and I sent him away again. He left early this morning to go back. He took Patrick with him. They were both being pests."

Cal laughed. "Come take a look at this little button," he called to George.

George dismounted and gave the baby a quick look. "He's cunning; that's for certain."

Teresa looked perplexed.

"It means cute," Cal explained. "Good-looking."

Teresa nodded. "Good-looking, yes." She opened the door and gestured for the men to enter. "Come. I don't want Juan to catch cold. Food is on the table, and you must eat."

"We could use some home cooking," Cal said.

The large room that served as the kitchen and the parlor was filled with family. Teresa's parents, brothers, and sisters were there, as well as all of the Chávez family, minus Ignacio.

Several children made room at the long table for Cal and George, and they were soon spooning down mouthfuls of beef stew cooked with green chili and wiping their bowls clean with fresh, warm tortillas.

"Now that little Juan is here, I suppose you'll be wanting Ignacio closer to home," Cal said to Teresa.

"He loves the ranchero more than anything, but with a baby now and so far from our families . . ." Teresa shrugged.

Cal nodded sympathetically. "I'll talk to him."

Cesario clamped a hand on Cal's shoulder. "He must come home. We plant soon, and we must build their casa on the land Perfecto gave him. *Más importante.*"

Across the table, Perfecto smiled and nodded in agreement while Cesario's wife ladled more stew into Cal's empty bowl.

"I'll send him home in two weeks," Cal said.

"*Gracias,*" Cesario said.

After a second helping and another cup of coffee, Cal and George said adios and rode to Coghlan's store, where Cal picked up a letter from a lawyer in Mesilla. At the saloon, Cal spun some silver on the bar and ordered a shot of rye, while George slipped away with a hurdy-gurdy girl and a bottle of whiskey under his arm in the direction of the rooms behind the wagon yard.

He read the lawyer's letter and was about to invite a pretty little redhead to join him for a drink at the bar when Dick Turknet sidled up and gave him a hard look.

"Got something stuck in your craw, Turknet?" Cal asked.

"Coghlan doesn't want your business anymore," Turknet said tersely, "here or at his store."

Cal downed his whiskey and called for another one. "Haul in your horns, hombre." He ignored the gunslinger while the bartender filled his glass. "I'm guessing your boss heard I got another contract for army ponies."

"That's the gist of it."

Cal sipped his whiskey slowly, put the glass gently on the bar, and turned to face Turknet. "Are you willing to get yourself killed trying to run me out of here?"

Turknet responded with a toothy smile. "I ain't that short of brains. I'm just the messenger boy."

Cal smiled back. "Fair enough."

Turknet nodded and left with two young *pistoleros* trailing behind him. Cal figured waiting on Coghlan's next move would just be too aggravating. Why not counter his warning with a play of his own?

He finished his drink and asked the bartender to have George wait on him once he was done with his poke. There was no sign of Dick Turknet and his sidekicks on the street. He rode Patches to Coghlan's big house and knocked on the door. Alice, Coghlan's wife, answered.

Cal flashed a courtly smile. "Good day, Mrs. Coghlan. It's a pleasure to see you again, ma'am, and I surely do hate to impose on you at home, but if Mr. Coghlan is available, I do need a minute of his time."

She was a tall woman who masked her plainness with fancy clothes and expensive jewelry. The Mexicans called her *La Madama* because she liked to lord it over them, acting like royalty and not some blackguard's wife.

She swung the door wide open. "Come in, Cal. He's in the study."

Cal followed her through the front parlor, which was filled with furniture, paintings, and statuary Coghlan had bought on trips back east and voyages to the old country. The door to the study was open, and behind a huge desk, studying some papers, sat Patrick Coghlan, big in the chest, red faced, with thick eyebrows that ran together and hands twice the size of an average man's. Across from him sat Morris Wohlgemuth, his manager.

"Cal needs a word with you," Alice said from the open door.

Coghlan looked up, leaned back in his chair, and smiled broadly. "Certainly, my dear."

Cal stepped in and Alice closed the door behind him. Coghlan's smiled faded. "Why are you here?"

"Dick Turknet said you wanted to palaver."

"Is that what he said?" Coghlan replied.

"That's what I took him to mean. I don't appreciate getting messages from your hired help. Thought I'd hear what you had to say direct."

"Maybe Turknet didn't make my message clear," Coghlan said, "so I'll explain it. Stay out of my store and saloon. Come around again and I'll take it you're looking for trouble."

Wohlgemuth sat as still as a mouse, staring at the papers in his lap.

"That's clear enough," Cal said, "although it strikes me peculiar that a big man like you can be so piddling about losing another army contract to a small outfit like mine. So I've got a caution for you. If anything unnaturally worrisome happens out at my ranch or trouble befalls any of my friends, you'll see me again and I won't be cordial."

"'Tis a brave one you are," Coghlan replied, his color deepening, his brogue thickening.

"Keep your riders reined in, Coghlan."

Coghlan rolled his tongue over his lips. "I'll give your proposition some thought."

Cal touched the brim of his hat. "*Buenas noches.*"

Back at the saloon, George's horse, a dapple gray named Alibi, was still hitched outside. Cal led the pony into the wagon yard, called out to George, and told him it was time to jingle his spurs. Soon a door flew open and George came out, hat jammed down over his ears, a half-empty bottle of whiskey showing in a coat pocket.

"You sober enough to ride?" Cal asked.

"Many a times old Alibi has carried me home after I've had a bottle or two," George said as he threw a leg over his horse.

"And a few times he got you lost," Cal replied. "Are you too liquored up to listen to what I want to tell you?"

"My ears ain't drunk."

"I want you to get back to the ranch and keep an eye on things," Cal said. "Look after Ignacio and Patrick. Don't leave them alone."

"What's got you spooked?"

He gave George the lowdown on his visits with Dick Turknet and Pat Coghlan and told him he was heading to Mesilla on some legal business.

"You ain't been charged with a crime, have you?" George asked.

"Not yet," Cal answered as he turned Patches down the wagon road that led across White Sands to Las Cruces. "*Hasta la vista.*"

* * *

The railroad had bypassed Mesilla, the largest town in the valley and the Doña Ana County seat, in favor of Las Cruces, turning it into a boomtown. What had been a sleepy village of small homes, several hotels and saloons, a trading post, and a general store now sported streetlamps in front of the Montezuma Hotel, a drugstore, a photography studio, a row of trees planted on the town plaza, and a population that had almost doubled in a year. Merchants newly arrived in town were busy putting up brick-and-mortar buildings on Main and Church streets. One such structure had high windows covered with ornate iron grills. The sign in front proclaimed it to be a bank.

Land around the train depot and the switching yards had been divided into lots, and homes were being built with inexpensive milled lumber delivered by rail. Just beyond the depot stood a new general store that took up a block. With a brick facade, a long freight platform wagon high for easy loading, fancy iron hitching rings for horses, and a covered porch with chairs suitable for lounging, it was a modern marvel.

To the east of the town, the Organ Mountains rose like an array of tall, rugged spires that cast long early morning shadows down the uneven, shrub-covered foothills to the valley. To the west, the land climbed more gradually, with solitary peaks off in the distance and a sheer, barren uplift range close by that kept the Rio Grande from wandering into the desert.

Cal rode through Las Cruces without stopping, crossed the Rio Grande, and arrived in Mesilla just in time to join the Mexicans filling the streets after their siestas. It was Sunday, and government buildings, including the territorial court, the land office, and the county offices, were closed for the day. But the saloons were doing good business. Cal rewarded himself with a whiskey in one of the dozen or more saloons that served the two thousand residents of the village and the folks who streamed into town for business or pleasure. It was twelve and a half cents a shot, half of what Coghlan charged at his saloon, so he decided to have another before seeking lodging for the night.

Mesilla was mostly Mexican. In fact, it felt and looked Mexican, the way Tularosa had a few years back. The village had been started after the Mexican-American War by families who wanted no part of the United States. They wound up citizens anyway, after the federal government bought almost thirty thousand square miles of land from Mexico for ten million dollars.

The tiny plaza had a church, several large haciendas, a general store, and a couple of saloons. The rest of the drinking establishments were on side streets. Brown and whitewashed adobe houses spread out from the plaza, and rich bottomland farms lined the river. Many of the folks out on the street were Mexican women hurrying on their way to church for vespers.

Cal put Patches in a livery for the night and found a room in a casa on a narrow lane just off the plaza that offered a meal and a bath with clean water for two dollars more.

Two months after John Kerney's death, Cal had sent a letter to Albert Fountain, a lawyer in Mesilla, with a list of instructions and a bank draft to cover legal fees and expenses. In the morning, he would meet with Fountain, who had papers drawn up to make him Patrick's legal guardian and Patrick his sole heir, a title deed application at the land office to buy an additional six thousand acres adjacent to the ranch, and a document conveying the original title to the ranch from Calvin Doran and John Kerney, deceased, to Calvin Doran and Patrick Kerney, a minor.

Kerney had registered his brand as the Double K in memory of the family he'd buried on the West Texas plains, and Cal saw no reason to change it.

As he soaked in the tub he thought about Patrick. In spite of his stubbornness and suspicious nature, the boy had come a ways since John Kerney's death. Once he realized he wasn't going to be sent away, he started acting like he had a home, or at least a place where he could stay. He now spoke Spanish like a native and had taken to reading books borrowed from Ignacio. With no public schools in the territory, much less on the basin, Patrick's only chance for learning was at home. So before heading back to the ranch, Cal would load up on some books for the boy that could teach him numbers, penmanship, and maybe some history.

Patrick had the makings of a hand. He'd sprouted two inches in the last six months, sat a horse as well as any cowboy, had learned to rope, and seemed to thrive on hard work like his daddy before him. If he stuck with ranching, he'd be a cowman from his boot heels up.

As for Ignacio, that one-armed Mexican had become about as good a ranch foreman as Cal had ever known. Maybe he could talk Ignacio into hiring on every now and then when he needed an extra hand.

Cal soaked the washcloth in the water and draped it over his head. John Kerney's death had turned him into a responsible, upstanding citizen, something he'd never imagined for himself some years back. The notion of it tickled him. It would have likely tickled John Kerney too.

The hot water eased the pain in his bones from the long journey. But heading home when his business was done would be as easy as roping a newborn calf. He'd load Patches on a livestock car, take the train from Las Cruces to Engle, and ride over the pass through Bear Den Canyon to the ranch. It would take two days off the trip.

The six thousand acres he was fixing to buy had cured grass on it that hadn't been grazed. When he got home, he'd turn the stock out to fatten them up a bit and cut the remaining grass for hay to use in the winter.

The time was coming when he'd have to think about doing some fencing. The days of open range were passing, but not quite yet.

He climbed out of the tub, rubbed himself dry, and got dressed. He had a hankering for some female company, and not all the pretty señoritas he'd seen on the street earlier were going to evening vespers.

20

D rought hit the Tularosa in 1889 and settled relentlessly over the basin. The following spring brought blistering winds that were oven hot and spawned dust devils coiled a mile high, six or more swirling across the parched valley almost every day. When the winds settled, the sky was turquoise blue but the mountains were invisible behind the thick haze of dust and debris that had blasted through the mesquite and cactus. Weeks passed without a cloud in the sky.

Where a hundred thousand cows had roamed on great pastures of black grama and buffalo grass, only leafless plants survived. Even the tough sacaton grasses that fringed the alkali flats withered away. Mesquite, barrel cactus, century plants, and slender ocotillos dotted the grim landscape, while the carcasses of dead animals fouled what few shallow water holes remained out on the flats. At Three Rivers, maggots floated downstream from the springs above into the Tularosa River.

Over the winter most of the Double K stock had survived on cured grass in two pastures Cal had purposely left ungrazed in hopes the drought would break come spring. But it had only worsened, and with the grass eaten down to the roots, the cattle had scattered in search of any browse.

At the ranch house, the stream through the valley was bone-dry and the cistern and dirt tanks were empty. The pond and the well still produced water, although the flow had slowed.

Throughout the winter they'd kept the horses corralled by the ranch house, getting them saddle ready for the army. The Double K still had a quartermaster contract for twenty horses, but with money short, George, the hired hand, had been let go. The task of gentling and training the ponies fell mostly to Patrick, who quickly proved himself to be about the best bronc rider Cal had seen in a long spell. With Patrick busy with the ponies, Cal spent his time day-herding cattle over twenty square miles of pastures, valleys, and high country, trying to keep them alive.

With the coming of spring, Cal and Patrick were out every day looking for strays. Most of the profits they had been banking on from the army contract had already been eaten up by wagonloads of horse feed purchased on credit in Tularosa and brought to the ranch by Ignacio and Cesario. Once they settled their accounts for the feed and other bills, Cal figured they'd be lucky if they came away with a twenty-dollar gold piece. And he wasn't counting on any more quartermaster contracts. Talk in Tularosa was that the army planned to shut down Fort Stanton now that Geronimo and his bucks had been shipped off to Florida and the Apache menace had ended.

At the southernmost pasture, the cow tracks wandered off in the direction of Hinman Rhodes's homestead. A Civil War veteran, Rhodes had been a colonel in a volunteer infantry regiment out of Illinois. His oldest son, Eugene Manlove Rhodes, a young cowboy six years older than Patrick, had worked for a time at the Bar Cross, the biggest outfit on the Jornada, before leaving for California to go to college.

"That's where they're headed," Patrick said, his head bent low, reading the trail.

"Reckon so," Cal said.

Patrick jigged his horse and loped ahead under a brilliant, cloudless sky. During the winter, he'd sprouted to five-ten, gained muscle, and filled out in the chest. His square shoulders, blue eyes, thick eyebrows, and long legs reminded Cal of John Kerney. From a distance, he looked like a fully grown man. Only up close did his boyish features give him away as a fifteen-year-old.

Like his pa, Patrick was quiet by nature, but he lacked John Kerney's sense of humor. Most found him standoffish; others thought him downright disagreeable. Either way, it didn't seem to matter much to the lad.

Cal smiled at Patrick's eagerness to raise the Rhodes homestead. The lad loved to read, and Colonel Rhodes had shelves of books that he let Patrick borrow two at a time. Reading by lamplight at night, Patrick raced through tomes by Dickens, Scott, Cooper, Longfellow, Byron, and the like. When he was done with the books, Cal would read them. Sometimes, they read aloud to each other.

They entered the mouth of the canyon, rounded a curve, and slowed to a stop when they spotted smoke rising from the cabin chimney. Colonel Rhodes, his wife, Julia, and their two younger children, Helen and Clarence, had spent the winter in Mesilla and weren't due back at the homestead until summer.

"Trouble?" Patrick asked. During the Rhodes's absence, the remote two-room cabin had become a convenient way station for rustlers and outlaws looking to slip the law. They had come upon some tough hombres in the past.

"Maybe," Cal said as he scanned the horse shelter, the cowshed, and the plot of fenced pasture close to the spring in the narrow canyon. The small herd of cows they'd tracked milled around the spring, and a saddled horse lazed in the pasture, ready to make tracks for his rider at a moment's notice. A fresh, uncured cowhide draped over a cedar rail. Not signs of someone with a law-abiding nature.

But it wasn't always easy to tell fine, upstanding citizens from hardened *pistoleros*. It was common practice on the open range to butcher an unbranded stray or a maverick for beef. A broke, hungry cowboy without a job didn't think twice about it. Mavericking went on all the time during brandings and roundups, and most ranchers bragged about never eating their own beef at the table. But with the drought taking its toll and leaving so many dead cattle on the range, every cow mattered.

"Let's act neighborly so as not to rile anyone inside," Cal cautioned as they approached.

They stopped well short of the cabin, and Cal called out to announce their presence. Quickly the cabin door opened and a bow-legged, bearded, one-eyed cowboy with a gap between his two front teeth and a six-gun low on his hip stepped out.

Cal recognized him instantly. "Howdy, Bud."

"Is that you, Cal?" Bud McPherson asked, squinting with his one good eye.

"I reckon," Cal replied. "It's been a long time. I heard you were up Montana way."

"Drifted back sometime ago," McPherson replied, giving Patrick a quick, wary glance. "Who's your pard?"

"This here lad is Pat," Cal said.

Being called a lad didn't sit well with Patrick, and he shot Cal a prickly look before touching the brim of his hat in a greeting.

"Those are our cows yonder at the spring," Cal added, ignoring Patrick's sulkiness. "We rode sign to find them. We'll collect them and be on our way."

McPherson relaxed a bit. "You turned to ranching?"

Cal shrugged. "Keeps the law from worrying over me."

McPherson chuckled. "Climb down and have some coffee. I'm just camped here for a few days. Found the place empty."

"I could use a cup," Cal said, turning to Patrick. "Start those cows up range. I'll be along shortly."

Patrick balked. "I need books."

"Not this time," Cal replied sternly as he swung out of the saddle. "Get those cows moving so we can raise the ranch pasture by sundown."

Patrick stared hard at Cal before turning his pony and trotting away.

"Lad's a book reader, is he?" McPherson said as he stepped inside the cabin.

"That he is," Cal said.

"Well, I ain't ever seen so many books in a homesteader's cabin before," McPherson said as he walked to the big stone fireplace and reached for the coffeepot. "Those folks must plumb not have enough to do."

"The owner is an educated man," Cal said, looking around. Everything seemed to be in its place: the tall bookshelf, the piano, the pots by the hearth, the furniture the colonel had made himself. There were some dirty dishes on the table and some clothes soaking in a pot of water, but Bud hadn't caused any damage to the place as far as Cal could see.

McPherson handed Cal a tin cup, filled it with coffee, and poured one for himself. "Sit a spell," he said as he kicked a chair back from the table.

Cal pulled up a chair across from McPherson.

"Is that your boy riding with you?" Bud asked.

Cal took a sip and shook his head. "His pa is dead. I look after him. He fights the bit once in a while, but mostly he's a good lad if you can put up with his sullen moods. You may have met some of his other kinfolks sometime back."

"Not around here, I reckon."

"Nope, up on the panhandle when you and your boys were none too careful about what you threw a rope at."

Bud laughed. "Hell, that was a long time ago, and I admit we didn't stop to tip our hats and say howdy. Doubtful I'd remember his kin."

"Dick Turknet brags he paid half what your horses were worth before you lit out for Montana."

"Them ponies were some fine horseflesh. Old Dick caught me with empty pockets and a sheriff on my trail looking to hang me."

Cal pushed the tin cup to one side. "For horse thieving or murder?"

"From his point of view, a little bit of both, I reckon." Bud squinted at him with his one good eye. "Why the all-fired interest in what happened in Texas?"

"Because you killed that lad's kin in Texas," Cal replied. "And from what I gather, you haven't stopped your murdering ways."

McPherson dug for his six-shooter, and Cal shot him between the eyes before he could clear leather. His head snapped back and he slumped forward in the chair.

Cal didn't feel the least bit bad about shooting McPherson. The man's habit of killing people had made a mess of Patrick's young life. And if Colonel Rhodes and his family had been at the cabin when McPherson showed up, they'd likely all be dead.

At the Doña Ana County courthouse there was a wanted poster out of Arizona for McPherson with a reward of five hundred dollars, dead or alive. He'd gunned down a deputy sheriff in Tucson.

In better times, Cal would have planted McPherson in a shallow grave, turned his horse loose in Cottonwood Canyon to find its way, and forgotten about it. But five hundred dollars would keep the Double K afloat for another year without going hat in hand to the bank.

He got McPherson's horse from the corral, tied his body across the saddle, packed up his bedroll, cleaned up the blood inside the cabin as best he could, and put out the fire. Before starting out, he looked for books Patrick hadn't read and settled on one about the Revolutionary War hero John Paul Jones and a worn copy of Robinson Crusoe.

He stuffed them in his saddlebags and set out at a lope. He should have no trouble catching up to Patrick trailing those slow-moving cows. The lad would have to get them to the ranch by himself, but he was enough of a hand to do it.

Patrick would surely be curious why Bud McPherson was suddenly deceased. Cal pondered the best way to explain it. He settled on the notion that John Kerney's son deserved to know that some justice had finally been served.

He caught up to Patrick trailing behind the tiny herd in a long valley that snaked between two bleak ridgetops and gave him the lowdown on Bud McPherson.

Patrick gazed at the body draped across the saddle. "How do you know he was one of the killers?" he asked.

"Your pappy learned of it years ago. He just didn't see a reason to go chasing after McPherson up Montana way. Not with a boy to find and raise."

"Well, then I guess it's a good thing you shot him for what he did," Patrick said. "But there was no need to send me away before the gunplay."

"There's no sport in seeing a man shot down," Cal replied.

"I don't need to be mollycoddled."

"I'll decide what you need until you're full grown. I'll be gone for a day or two getting this straightened out with the sheriff. You head home and stay close by."

Patrick nodded abruptly and spurred his horse in the direction of the cattle. He didn't turn to look back until Cal was well out of earshot. For years, he'd heard about the murder of John Kerney's kin on the Texas panhandle, but he had no strong feelings one way or the other about McPherson or his gang. Those folks who'd been killed long ago had never been real to him. He felt no binding ties to them. McPherson's death meant nothing to him one way or the other. The five-hundred-dollar reward Cal had mentioned sure was good news in hard times, though.

Still miffed at missing the gunplay at the cabin, Patrick watched Cal disappear up a rocky draw. He sure would like to have seen that, and who was to say what he needed?

He moved the small herd along at a good pace, chasing a few strays now and then, and raised the ranch at dusk. He put the cattle in the pasture next to the horse corral, fed the ponies some hay, and fixed a dinner of beefsteak, boiled potatoes, and canned peaches. He sat at the kitchen table with his food and looked over the two books Cal had brought him from the colonel's library. The Robinson Crusoe one looked interesting, and he was soon engrossed in the story, until he got too drowsy to continue.

A clear sky had let the night cool down nicely, and he was tired from a long day. Tomorrow, he'd ride to the far north canyon where two years ago Cal had hired a crew to dig a well and put up a windmill. The windmill fed a big dirt-and-rock stock tank that held three hundred gallons of water, and to keep every critter on the basin from drinking it dry, they'd fenced off the narrow entrance to the high-walled canyon.

The steep cliffs of the canyon looked like huge building blocks quarried by giants and stacked neatly on top of one another. The canyon walls were sheer enough to keep stock from straying in or out, the grass hadn't been overgrazed and there were stands of four-wing saltbush cattle liked to munch on in early spring.

He'd grease and adjust the windmill, a chore that needed doing on a regular basis, water any strays he rounded up along the way, and let them graze for a time in the pasture.

The last time he'd been up there, he got stung several times by wasps from a nest beneath the platform at the top of the wooden tower, and it had made him as sick as a pup. He'd knocked the nest down and burned it, and sure hoped the wasps hadn't come back.

He rolled on his side and drifted to sleep listening to the far-off whistle of a female mountain lion calling her cubs.

21

At sunup, Patrick was tending to the horses when two riders appeared on the flats. He left the corral, mounted his pony, and loped in their direction, wondering who would be calling so early in the day. He didn't recognize the riders or their horses, and the closest neighbors were thirty miles away and not prone to visiting at first light. If they were rustlers or outlaws, it would be certain trouble if they found out he was alone at the ranch. He had to stop them before they got too close.

He reined in fifty yards shy of the men, yanked his rifle from the scabbard, and called for them to state their business.

The riders pulled up.

"No need for that rifle," one of the riders replied. "I'm Oliver Lee from Dog Canyon, and I'm looking to speak to Cal Doran. This here with me is my brother, Perry Altman."

Patrick put his rifle away. He'd met Lee and Altman in town several times. They were Texans who'd arrived in '84 and now ranched on the east side of the Tularosa. They each had their own spread, and both were considered excellent horsemen.

Patrick jigged his horse forward to the men. "You can talk to me," he said when he arrived.

Oliver Lee smiled. "Best we speak to Cal."

Patrick held his tongue and stared at Lee. He had dark black eyes, a square jaw, and the reputation of being a wizard with both a rifle and a six-gun. According to those who knew him well, he neither drank nor smoked.

"Is Cal up yonder?" Perry Altman asked with a nod toward the ranch house. Lanky and sandy haired, Altman was Lee's older half brother.

Patrick shook his head. "But you fellas are welcome to light, sit a spell, and have a cup of coffee."

Lee nudged his horse closer to Patrick. "Appreciate the invitation, but we're short on time. We cut sign on some cattle a ways back that were stolen off my ranch, and we mean to catch up with the rustlers that took them."

"I brought some strays in from Cottonwood Canyon last night, but none were yours," Patrick replied.

"Figured as much," Altman said, eyeing the cows up in the pasture. "Did anybody ride through while you were gone?"

"Can't say as they did," Patrick replied. "I didn't see any fresh sign."

"They probably skirted north to avoid the Double K," Altman said to Lee.

Lee nodded and touched the brim of his hat. "We won't take any more of your time. Let Cal know we need to parley with him."

"I'll do it," Patrick said, wondering what was so all get-out important. Whatever it was, he darn sure wouldn't be excluded from it.

The men turned back toward the flats, their horses kicking up dust that glittered like flakes of gold in the early morning sunlight. Already hot, it would be a scorcher when the winds picked up. Patrick shoed two of the saddle horses he'd gentled for the army, packed a lunch of hardtack and jerked beef, put tools and a grease can in a saddlebag, and left a note for Cal telling him where he'd gone. Then he closed up the house and headed for the windmill.

Setting a steady pace, he made good time into the mountains, where the piñon pine and juniper trees clung to the higher slopes and desert willows nestled in narrow draws. On a mound of tailings near an old mine shaft, a buck mule deer watched cautiously, its big ears twitching, before bolting away. The buck would be fun to hunt come fall if the drought or a mountain lion didn't get it first.

A couple of miles out from the canyon, Patrick expected to pick up some strays ranging close to the scent of water from the windmill, but this time there wasn't a critter in sight, and no fresh sign.

He turned his pony up a dogleg arroyo through a narrow cleft into an adjoining valley that paralleled the granite mountaintops and stopped short when he saw dozens of cow tracks heading smack-dab toward the canyon windmill. Horseshoe prints showed three riders pushing the cows along. His pulse quickened as he pulled his rifle and spurred his horse into a gallop. At the fence line, he reined to a stop. The wire had been cut, the cow tracks ran straight toward the water tank, and several acres of grass had been grazed to a nub. There wasn't a man or beast within sight.

Patrick put his rifle away, climbed off his horse, and walked to the north edge of the mouth of the canyon, where a partial roll of wire was stashed in case fence repairs were needed. He carried it back to the posts where the wire had been cut, rolled out two strands, and started splicing, cursing under his breath as he worked. There was no lock on the gate to the canyon, so cutting the wire had been done out of pure orneriness. Or maybe the rustlers knew any hand worth his salt would repair a fenced water source before taking up the chase.

He tightened each wire, opened the gate, and rode to the windmill. A flock of crows flew up from behind the water tank as he approached, lighting on the windmill. They had been feeding on a scrawny dead cow carrying Oliver Lee's brand. Still warm to the touch, it hadn't been pecked at much by the crows. He tied a rope to its hind legs, wrapped the rope around his saddle horn, and dragged the carcass to the far end of the canyon, the crows circling above, cawing in complaint.

Back at the windmill, he threw a saddlebag over his shoulder and started up the tower, looking for wasps as he went. He reached the platform without getting stung, let out a sigh of relief, set the brake, and started greasing the gears. He finished up by checking the bolts on the wind vane and then scanned the canyon for strays. Except for the crows hopping around and screeching at each other near the dead cow, the canyon was empty.

Cal had told him to stay close to home, and he'd stretched it by riding out to the windmill. He climbed off the tower, threw a leg over his pony, and decided to track the rustlers for a while. It was what Cal would have done, so why not? Besides, the trail was too fresh not to.

With the sun at noon, he closed the gate and started his pony in a slow trot, following the tracks heading eastward toward the basin. Again, there were the same three sets of horseshoe prints, one with a distinctive crack near the toe, on the right foreleg.

From the tracks, he could tell the rustlers were driving about fifty cows. Were they looking to reach the high country of the

Sacramento Mountains and sell the animals to the Mescaleros or the army at the fort? Or cross the mountains and trail them down to Mexico on the Staked Plains, rustling more stock along the way?

The tracks passed through crooked draws, over bare, gravelly, shallow saucers, and up flinty hills, always bearing east. Patrick topped out on a nameless rise, and off in the distance about ten miles away he could see a sizable dust cloud on the trail to Malpais Spring. A few miles behind, a smaller dust cloud drifted off into the sky.

Patrick paused. He figured Oliver Lee and Perry Altman were closing in on the rustlers, but his way home lay south, not east. He could turn back a half mile to a gap that would take him down to the flats and on to the ranch, or he could ride ahead and see what was going to happen at Malpais Spring.

He grinned and spurred his pony forward.

* * *

Oliver Lee used his boot to turn over one of the dead rustlers. It wasn't somebody he knew. He did the same with the second body and recognized a Mexican named Francisco Olivares. Lee had shot both men out of their saddles. The third thief had turned tail before Oliver could get a bead on him and was halfway to Tularosa if his horse hadn't dropped dead under him.

Perry Altman rode up from the milling cows to point out a rider coming at a fast clip from the west.

"Saw him," Oliver replied.

"I count fifty-six bovines," Perry said. "Forty-two yours, six are mine, five from the Double K, and the rest mavericks."

Lee climbed into his saddle. "Start them for water at Malpais Spring. I'll go and meet our company."

He pulled his rifle, trotted down the road, and put the long gun away when he recognized young Patrick Kerney.

"I've got five of your cows up ahead," Lee said when Patrick came close. "You can cut them out if you like, or you can help us trail them to Tularosa, where we can sell them along with mine to the Indian agent. I hear he's looking to buy some replacement cattle for the Mescaleros."

"I reckon that would be best," Patrick said, looking past Lee at two riderless saddle horses ahead. "Did you get all three?"

Lee shook his head. "One skedaddled. I mean to write my lawyer, Albert Fall, in Mesilla about this little war I had today and ask him to send the sheriff so I can turn myself in. I'd be obliged if you'd vouch for what you know about it. I can take down your words if you don't know how to write."

Patrick stuck his chin out. "I can write my own words."

"I meant no offense," Lee said in a soft Texas drawl. "Still want to ride with us? If we push those cows along, we should raise Tularosa by tomorrow afternoon."

"I'm in," Patrick replied as he scanned the ground. The rustler who'd skedaddled was riding the horse with the cracked shoe on the right foreleg. He sure hoped for a chance to meet up with that hombre so he could prove himself a man to Cal and anyone else who might doubt it.

22

The railroad siding and watering stop at Engle had grown into a thriving town with a station, hotel, stores, saloons, post office, and houses that stretched along both sides of the tracks. A mining boom in the Black Hills and mountains west of the Rio Grande had spurred growth, and it was now a convenient trading and shipping center for the big cattle ranches on the Jornada and settlements along the river.

Cal had arrived in town the previous evening and immediately telegraphed the sheriff in Doña Ana County, who sent Deputy Filipe Lucero up by train to verify the death of Bud McPherson and fill out the papers for the five-hundred-dollar reward, to be paid by the sheriff of Pima County, Arizona Territory.

Lucero hired a carpenter to make a casket, and by early morning McPherson had been buried in the local cemetery and Cal was on his way home. He pushed Patches hard, raised the ranch by late night, and found Patrick's note. The lad was way overdue from his chore at the windmill. It seemed like Patrick's notion of sticking close to the ranch needed some correction.

Cal fed and watered Patches, turned him out in the horse corral, saddled another pony, filled a canteen, packed hardtack and some canned fruit in a saddlebag, and struck out by moonlight to find the boy. He moved slow, looking for any sign the lad might have suffered a bad fall or some wrongdoing. When he came upon the cow tracks and the hoofprints, his pulse quickened and he spurred his horse into a fast trot.

At the mouth of the canyon, Cal found the patched barbwire fence and the fresh tracks of Patrick's pony heading east, trailing the cattle. He didn't even bother to enter the canyon; the signs told him all he needed to know. Patrick was following the rustlers.

Daybreak brought him to two bodies laid out facedown at the side of the road west of Malpais Spring. He dropped out of his saddle, half expecting to see Patrick dead on the ground. He turned the bodies over, happy to see that Patrick hadn't gotten killed, leastways not here, not yet. He recognized Francisco Olivares and figured him and his partner to be two of the rustlers.

Cal walked in an expanding circle and read sign. The gunplay had happened before Patrick arrived. Two riders had thrown lead at the three outlaws, and one had gotten away riding a pony with a cracked shoe. Patrick had joined up with the two riders heading east toward Malpais Spring.

Cal ate a can of peaches, drank the sweet nectar from the bottom of the can, tossed it away, and got back in the saddle. With the sun full in his eyes above the Sacramentos, he started out at a trot. Although cattle and the men driving them moved slow, he doubted he could catch them before they reached Tularosa, but he wouldn't be far behind.

* * *

Eating dust, Patrick rode at the rear of the small herd as it passed by the green fields of Tularosa. In spite of the drought, water from the river still flowed in the acequias that irrigated the fields, family wells continued to supply clean drinking water, grasses in the pastures near the river flourished, and the cottonwood trees the Mexican families had planted years ago towered over the casitas and the narrow lanes of the original settlement. Coming from the dry, cracked, glaring desert basin was like entering a peaceful, lush oasis.

In one of the fields Patrick thought he spotted Ignacio in among some sheep, but he couldn't be sure. The hacienda he'd built for Teresa and their three children hugged a bend in the river, steps away from the house where Ignacio's father, Cesario, now a widower, lived. Patrick decided to visit the Chávezes once he finished up business with Oliver Lee.

The Chávez family, with all its children, relatives, and friends, was a mystery to Patrick. He'd watched them over the years and never understood how they all got along so well. He kept waiting for some big fracas or disaster to rip apart the family, but even in hard times they seemed happy. He settled on figuring it had something to do with their being Mexicans.

In the low foothills above the village, on the wagon road to Fort Stanton, they put the cows in a fenced dirt pasture at an abandoned farmhouse. A few years back, rumors of a railroad coming to town had doubled the population, and when the story went belly-up and the drought settled in, a good many of the newcomers moved on. The abandoned farm was just one of dozens that bordered the outskirts of Tularosa.

In town at Coghlan's store, Patrick wrote out what he knew about the rustled cattle and gave it to Oliver Lee, who read it through and nodded his thanks.

"You make a hand," Lee said, tucking Patrick's note in the envelope he'd addressed to Albert Fall. "I appreciate your help trailing those cows."

"I'm more than a hand," Patrick replied. "The Double K is half mine. If you're figuring on palavering with Cal, you're gonna be talking to me anyhow, so what's on your mind?"

Oliver Lee tipped back his hat and gave Patrick a long, serious look. "I suppose you're right," he finally said. "I heard tell that the Double K has had business dealings with Albert Fountain, and since I'm gonna be having a real set-to with the man, I wanted to know if that would put us on opposite sides of the fence."

"What kind of set-to?" Patrick asked.

Lee sealed the envelope and handed it to the clerk. "I told you what's on my mind. Now I'd be obliged if you'd tell Cal that if we ain't at odds with each other to come visit. Fair enough?"

"Fair enough," Patrick replied.

He left Oliver Lee and walked his horse over to Ignacio's house, where he found Teresa and her three children, Juan, Sofia, and Bernardo, at home. Juan, the oldest son, was leading Sofia, age five, and Bernardo, age four, around the courtyard on the back of an old burro. Teresa knelt at the *horno* with her back to him, cooking fresh tortillas over the embers. The smell made his stomach grumble.

He called out "*Buenas tardes*" at the open gate, and the children stopped and looked at him without saying a word. That was all right with him. He never had much for young'uns anyway, not even when he was one himself.

Teresa rose from the *horno* and turned to greet him, showing her swollen belly. "Patricio, *entra*."

Teresa had lost her last two babies at childbirth and once had been near death herself.

"Ain't that baby about due?" Patrick asked.

"*Sí*, very soon." She turned to her oldest son. "Juan, go to your father and tell him Patricio is here."

Juan pulled brother and sister off the burro, jumped on its back, and trotted through the gate.

"And tell him enchiladas will be waiting when he arrives," Teresa called. She smiled at Patrick. "You will eat with us."

"*Con mucho gusto,*" Patrick replied.

* * *

Cal rode up just as Patrick sat down with Ignacio, Teresa, and the family to eat. He looked drug out and worn down and shot Patrick a long, stern look before digging into a plate of enchiladas Teresa quickly fixed for him. Patrick used the opportunity to avoid a tongue-lashing by explaining the events that had brought him to Tularosa, starting with Oliver Lee's early morning visit to the ranch two days ago. He finished up by mentioning Lee's plans to settle Albert Fountain's hash.

"The feud is turning into a war," Cal said with a shake of his head.

"About what, amigo?" Ignacio asked.

"Who's gonna rule the Tularosa and beyond," Cal answered. "Right now it's up for grabs. The big spreads are suing to get water rights from the small outfits. Fountain is representing them in court. It would put a lot of us under if he wins. Seems Oliver wants to fight back."

"Who are we siding with?" Patrick asked as he finished mopping up the last of the sauce on his plate with a tortilla. He favored Oliver Lee over any lawyer.

Cal pushed his empty plate aside. "Depends on what Oliver plans to do. I'll hear him out."

"I want in on that powwow," Patrick said.

Cal looked at his young ward, who met his gaze without flinching. Finally, he nodded. "I guess it's time for you to have a full say in this partnership."

Patrick nodded to keep from grinning. "One more thing: Lee said we had five cows in that herd we trailed to town and put to pasture. I counted seven."

"Did you say anything to him?" Cal asked.

Patrick shook his head. "I'll tally up with him tomorrow."

"Good enough," Cal said.

Ignacio slapped Patrick on the back. "We must celebrate your good work. I'll buy drinks at the cantina. Come."

Teresa glanced pointedly from Ignacio to Cal to Patrick. "Do not come back into my house *borracho*," she cautioned.

All three men nodded solemnly as they pushed back from the table. Ignacio kissed Teresa, hugged Bernardo and Sofia, and rubbed Juan's head before following Cal and Patrick outside.

Sand hung in the evening air, the remains of a brief windstorm that had rolled across the basin and drifted eastward into town. It had cooled some but was too dry to make much difference. Every track their ponies laid down raised puffs of dust, the leaves on the cottonwood trees were caked with grit, and the horses hitched outside the cantina were listless from the heat.

The cantina was on the outskirts of town along the White Sands road. It was nothing more than the front room of a small house, crammed with tables and chairs occupied by villagers, cowboys, teamsters, Buffalo Soldiers from the fort, and a sin-busting preacher who had passed out on his Bible at a table near the front door, an empty whiskey glass close at hand. At the back of the room the owner stood behind a waist-high counter pouring straight shots of whiskey carefully delivered to customers by an old woman. A sign nailed to the wall behind the counter listed the house drinks. The cantina served rye and bourbon whiskey, nothing more.

While Ignacio ordered drinks from the owner, Patrick sat with Cal at a table and studied all the cowboys in the room.

"You looking for someone?" Cal asked.

Patrick nodded. "Whoever rides the sorrel gelding outside is the rustler who got away from Oliver Lee and his brother. It has a cracked shoe near the toe on its right foreleg. I noticed its horse tracks as we came in."

Cal scanned the customers. Two cowboys at a table at the back of the room caught his attention. The gringo cowboy wore his six-gun low and tied down, and he'd seen the Mexican vaquero a time or two with Francisco Olivares, one of the cattle thieves Lee had shot dead.

Ignacio came back carrying a full glass, which he put down in front of Patrick. "Just one, my friend. Drink it straight down and try not to make a face."

The old woman came along behind him with two more drinks, plunked them down, and waddled away.

Ignacio sat, smiled, and raised his glass. "*Salud!*"

Patrick drained the glass and choked back a gasp.

Ignacio kept a straight face and smiled approvingly at his young friend. "*Bueno.*"

Cal put his empty glass on the table and nodded at the two cowboys. "You know those fellas, Ignacio?"

Ignacio studied the two men. The gringo looked vaguely familiar but he couldn't remember from where, and the vaquero he'd seen in the village once or twice but didn't know. He shook his head. "Why do you ask?"

"They may be rustlers," Cal replied. "One of them, at least. Stay here while I find out who they are." He walked over to the owner and spoke to him before moving on to the cowboys.

Patrick tensed up. Over the din, he couldn't make out what was being said, but it looked tame enough, with everybody smiling. Although he didn't want to be left out of any play Cal made, he suddenly wasn't sure if he had the grit for a gunfight. After a minute or two, Cal returned.

"Those old boys are loyal and industrious employees of Pat Coghlan," he said as he sat. "Both work at Coghlan's Three Rivers spread."

"That's where they were driving those cows, I bet ya," Patrick said. "Who rides the sorrel?"

"The fella with the scar on his cheek. Goes by the name Sam Nash."

Ignacio sat bolt upright in his chair. Sam Nash was the man who'd robbed and beaten him in La Luz after he'd left his father's house to strike out on his own. John Kerney had caught Nash trying to sell the old Colt Dragoon *pistola* Ignacio's father had given him and had raked it across Nash's face to teach him a lesson.

Ignacio always felt that he, not John Kerney, should have stood up to Sam Nash and felt shame for not doing so. Now he could do something about it. "*A la bueno de Dios,*" he said.

"Why is that good luck?" Patrick asked, trying hard not to show his nervousness.

"Sam Nash beat and robbed me. In return, John Kerney gave him that scar on his face." Ignacio studied the cowboy intently. "*Sí,* that is him, I'm sure. Now I will pay him back myself for his crime."

"Best you let me handle this," Cal said.

Ignacio grabbed Cal's arm before he could rise. "It's not your fight, amigo."

"Like hell it's not," Cal said. "He cut our fence and stole our cattle."

"First me," Ignacio replied hotly. "Then you can have him."

"You sure you want to do this?" Cal asked. He'd never seen Ignacio so riled.

Ignacio nodded.

"Then let's make it an even fight."

At Nash's table, Cal pulled up an empty chair and leaned close. "My friend over there wants to fight you, fair and square," he said. "Fisticuffs only."

"Which one?" Nash asked cockily, glancing from the tense-looking young cowboy to the Mexican glaring at him across the room.

"Ignacio Chávez."

Nash laughed as he studied Ignacio. "You're funning with me now, right? I've seen this busted-up Mexican around. He doesn't even have two good hands. What does he want to fight me for?"

"I'll leave that for him to explain once he clips your horns," Cal replied, looking Nash over. He was about the same size as Ignacio, a mite heavier, and looked sturdy. With two good hands, Ignacio would have been his match. But with only one, Cal wasn't so sure. But Ignacio's right arm was mighty powerful, so maybe it would even out.

"Before you get started, you and your pard put your lead chuckers on the table," Cal added.

Nash smiled, stood, and put his six-gun on the table. The vaquero did the same.

"I'll keep score," Cal said as he turned to the vaquero. "You stay here with me."

The man gave Cal a toothy smile, shrugged, and stayed seated.

Nash didn't wait for another invitation to start brawling. He rushed and butted Ignacio in the gut as he started to rise. Ignacio and the chair skidded into a table of men, who scattered out of the way. As Ignacio got up, Nash threw a fist under Ignacio's eye and slammed another into his nose. Cal winced when he heard the bone crack. The blow knocked Ignacio to the floor.

Every man in the room was on his feet, giving way to the fighters, hooting and hollering for more.

Ignacio scrambled upright, blood pouring from his nose, as Nash moved close and swung a haymaker. Ignacio leaned back and took the blow on his shoulder. He hit back with a pounding right to Nash's head, missed with another punch that Nash ducked, and took a blow to his groin that put him on his knees.

The vaquero laughed. Cal told him to shut up.

Nash moved in for the kill, bent down, and cocked a hard left hand at Ignacio's jaw. Ignacio caught it in midair with his good hand, squeezed, and twisted. Nash screamed as his wrist snapped. Holding it tight, Ignacio rose slowly from his knees, yanked Nash by the arm, and slammed him against the wall. Before Nash could turn, Ignacio pounded his face into the wall, once, twice, and again for good measure. Nash went limp and sank to the floor like a rag doll.

Rocking unsteadily back and forth on his feet, Ignacio dropped with a thud, grabbed his private parts, looked at Patrick, and grimaced. "*Madre*, it hurts."

"You whipped him good," Patrick said as he wiped blood off Ignacio's face with his bandanna. "Can you stand?"

"*Un momento.*"

Secretly glad he hadn't gone up against Nash, who surely would have whipped him bad, Patrick reached under Ignacio's arms to lift him. "Come on, we'll get you home."

"Teresa," Ignacio sighed. "She won't be happy."

"Leastways, you aren't *borracho*," Cal said with a laugh as he stepped in to help.

Ignacio groaned as he stood unsteadily on his feet. "I better have one more drink," he said.

Cal laughed again, steered him to an unoccupied table, bought a round from the owner, and paid for the damages. With drinks in hand, the trio sat and watched Sam Nash come around. Moaning and clutching his broken wrist, he looked like he'd been kicked in the face by a mule. His vaquero drinking partner was nowhere to be seen.

The town constable arrived and Patrick told him about the stolen cattle and Nash's part in the crime. The constable asked Patrick to sign papers against Nash in the morning and set about organizing several men to help get his prisoner tied to the sorrel horse and carted off to the hoosegow.

On his way out, Nash asked Ignacio what had set him off.

"Years ago, you beat and robbed me at my camp in La Luz," Ignacio said. "You took my *pistola* and my *dinero.*"

Nash shook off some cobwebs. "That was you?"

"*Sí,*" Ignacio replied.

"I'll be damned. You were just a skinny Mexican kid back then."

"Now we're even," Ignacio said.

With Nash safely on his way to jail, the three men celebrated with another drink before leaving. Ignacio took one look at his horse and decided it would be less painful to walk home. The trio slowly made their way up the road leading their ponies, Ignacio shuffling along.

Patrick's head buzzed from the whiskey and he didn't feel all that steady himself. "I bet that old boy never thought he'd get whipped by a Mexican," he said.

Ignacio stopped and glared at Patrick. "Sometimes I think you're not so smart."

"What are you getting all riled about?" Patrick asked.

"The man thinks you have poor manners," Cal explained.

"That ain't so," Patrick replied.

"Best you stop talking," Cal said as he led Ignacio down the road, "before Ignacio decides to take you on."

On a cool, cloudless night with stars filling the sky and the occasional bark of a lonesome dog on the other side of town, they unsaddled their horses in the pasture near Ignacio's house, rubbed them down, and carried their tack to the courtyard.

As they approached the door, Juan came bursting out. "Papa, come quick," he said. "Mama's having the baby."

23

In 1893 the drought eased just as the cattle market collapsed. According to the newspapers, it wasn't just about cattle selling for less than a penny on the pound and stockmen going under. Across the land, banks closed, railroads went broke, and big companies shut down, throwing people into a fright. In New Mexico, most folks were already back on their heels, so the money panic spreading across the land was just another ripple of hard times in a hard country.

Even with a welcome string of spring showers, Cal didn't trust the good weather to hold. Over the last three years, he'd seen too many stormy skies and soaring thunderheads drift over the basin without dropping a lick of rain to hope for a really wet season. Besides, a little rain wouldn't do the grass any good because there wasn't much of it left. The thick pastures that had grasses shoulder high to a horse when he first came to the Tularosa were long gone, eaten to the roots by starving animals or burned to a crisp by three years of unrelenting sun. In places, especially out on the flats, the ground was bare and barren. Still, with the drought slackened a bit, it was good to see some greening up of the land, even if it was mostly mesquite and greasewood.

In the ranch-house kitchen, Cal poured another cup of coffee and walked out on the veranda. First light was breaking over Sierra Blanca, and the sun's rays touched the wispy clouds at the peak and for a brief moment lit them up like a halo. He took it as a good omen for the day. Below, near the barn, he heard Patrick's horse snort and whinny. He looked down and saw Patrick saddling horses. Old Patches, the pony he'd ridden into New Mexico many years ago, had died during the winter, and Cal had buried him on the hilltop near John Kerney's grave. His new horse, a red roan gelding fifteen hands high, was a fine animal he'd yet to name. He was thinking of calling it Bandit but hadn't settled on it yet.

Patrick had cut out six more ponies they would need in the mountains and put them in the corral. Working in rugged, steep terrain taxed both horse and rider, and they would have to change horses frequently to gather the half-wild steers, a few mean old bulls, about three dozen dry cows, and six or so scrawny yearlings. Cal guessed there were no more than fifty or sixty head to be gathered. The rest had been sold off because of the drought. What remained he'd agreed to ship to a wealthy rancher in Juárez who would pay live weight, cash on delivery.

The Double K high-country pastures still had some grass but wouldn't for long unless the cattle were moved and the land rested. With reliable water from the mountain springs and the canyon windmill, along with a few good seasons of rain, they'd be able to restock. And if the cattle market revived, the outfit just might survive.

Working a small bunch of cattle out on the flats wasn't a big challenge, but mountain country required a whole different approach to gathering. It meant spending hours looking for fresh tracks, chasing the critters down after they had been spotted, and bunching and holding the gathered cows together while they scouted for more. Once all the critters were gathered, they'd push them along to the ranch and rest them for a few days before driving them to Engle for shipment to Mexico.

Cal sacked the grub and carried it outside, where Patrick waited with the pack animals. He tugged the breast collar on each packhorse before checking the breeching at the animal's haunches. Patrick had also put breast collars on their horses to keep the saddles from slipping back on steep climbs. Cal checked those too, knowing full well Patrick didn't appreciate the inspection. He rankled easily if he thought his abilities were being questioned, especially now that he'd reached full manhood.

"I don't want you losing your saddle on some steep trail and breaking your neck," Cal said. "We lost your pa to a bad wreck. Don't need a repeat."

"Don't worry about me," Patrick replied testily.

They loaded grub and supplies on one pack animal and horse feed and camp gear on the other, secured their long guns in scabbards, tied off their bedrolls, and mounted up.

Cal looked skyward. There were a fair number of clouds above. "I sure wouldn't mind getting rained on," he said.

Patrick nodded. "Me neither. This sure beats driving a Winona wagon for the Bar Cross."

"It beats sheriffing too," Cal said as he gave one last look around the ranch and the basin beyond. He never tired of the view.

Both men had hired out during the lean years, Patrick hauling supplies from Engle to the Bar Cross headquarters, Cal working as a deputy sheriff first in Lincoln County and for a time in Doña Ana. Their wages had kept the Double K afloat.

"You got a name for that pony yet?" Patrick asked.

"I'm thinking Bandit," Cal replied.

Patrick nodded. "I like it."

Bandit snorted and nodded his head.

"So does he, I reckon," Cal replied. "Bandit it is, then." He turned Bandit down the hill to the corral, where the string of horses waited. "Now, if you'll get that old *caballo* of yours to move, we can start riding sign and corralling some critters. Day will be half gone before we get to chasing steers off their getaway trails."

Experience had taught them the best way to work the gathering. They circled the rock-strewn mountainsides of each pasture, crossed the side canyons, and moved up and down the draws and arroyos until they busted the cows into the open. What they gathered each day they trailed to the fenced windmill canyon, where there was grass and water.

For five days they went from sunup to sundown, stopping only at noon for dinner or to switch horses. Each day they had to neck an outlaw steer or two to a tree with tie-down ropes while they popped cattle out of the brush and backcountry. When they returned and untied it, the reluctant critter tried to hook them with its horns and get away. But there was none better than Cal at getting an angry steer to come along. He necked each of the old outlaws to a docile cow and led the two along until the old steer calmed down enough to be cut free. Then he led it with a slack rope and put it with the bunch already in the pasture, where it stayed.

At dusk, with the cattle fenced, they unsaddled, checked the horses for sore backs and cuts, and watered them at the tank before fixing supper. Come morning on the last day, they rested the pony string, did one final scout high above the windmill canyon pasture, and brought in two cows they scared up on the getaway trails before heading the bunch home for the ranch.

Patrick led, keeping the cattle close, while Cal worked both wings to stop the outlaws from breaking away to freedom. Bandit kept all but one from escaping, and they got to the ranch after a waterless trek with eighty-seven critters, more than Cal had reckoned. Some were mavericks and a few he recognized as Bar Cross cows. But they were unbranded and Cal had no compunction about putting his iron on them.

After two days of rest in the cow pasture, they branded the cattle with the back-to-back Double K iron, fed them hay from the barn, and got ready for the trail drive to Engle. It would be a long journey with the slow-moving critters.

"I don't like the notion of no cattle on the ranch," Patrick said over supper. "Makes me feel downright useless."

He'd been quiet all day, almost sulky. "Can't be helped for now," Cal replied.

"Maybe I should sell out my share of the outfit and move on."

Cal studied Patrick carefully and said nothing.

"See something of the world," Patrick continued. "Find a piece of land that isn't all dust, sand, wind, and greasewood."

Cal cut into his beefsteak, forked a bite, and chewed.

"Head north were they get rain more than twice a year," Patrick added. "Do something else for a change. Maybe get some schooling like Gene Rhodes did when he went off to college in California."

Patrick sounded more and more earnest as he gathered steam. It wasn't unreasonable for a young man of eighteen to want to strike out on his own. Cal had left home even younger, leaving behind his parents, a kid brother, and a baby sister in East Texas, where his father preached the holy word and his mother taught school.

He decided to take Patrick seriously. "I'd like a say in who you decide to sell your half of the Double K to," he said.

Patrick laughed. "I mean to sell it to you, if I do."

Cal put his fork down. "You know darn well how much money I've got."

"You can borrow. We own this outfit free and clear."

"What a bank would give me for half of this place right now isn't enough to spit at. Besides, I'm not looking to lose you as a partner."

"I'm pretty much fixing to move on for a spell. I just need a stake to get started. I sure ain't going back to driving a wagon for wages. Not this cowboy."

Patrick's jaw was set, a sure sign he wasn't joking.

"Let me think on it for a while," Cal replied.

"Until when?"

"Until we settle up for the cattle in Mexico."

Patrick stood. "Fair enough. We need to shoe some horses before we start for Engle with those critters."

"I know it. We'll get it done tomorrow and hit the trail the day after. Think you'll miss the old place once you're gone?"

Patrick looked pensive for a moment. "Don't know. I guess I've sort of got settled here since John Kerney fetched me to it, but I've never figured to stay forever." He picked up his plate and put it in the sink. "See you *mañana*."

"*Mañana*," Cal replied.

He watched Patrick leave the room. He had John Kerney's same square shoulders and carried himself just like his pa, but there was no humor to the lad, and he showed no gratitude for the kindnesses of others. Never once had Patrick uttered a word of thanks to Cal for taking him under his wing, making him a full partner, raising him up, teaching him to cowboy—nothing. For that matter, he'd never seen him show a lick of appreciation to Ignacio and

Teresa for all of their kindnesses. It just wasn't in him to be grateful or easy in his manners.

Once they left the ranch, Cal planned on being gone for no more than two weeks. He wondered if he'd really be trailing back to the Double K alone.

24

Pushing hungry, thirsty cattle to Engle wore down the men and critters alike. Cal and Patrick spent thirty nonstop hours in the saddle driving the sore-footed animals through rocky canyons, over steep hills, and around wagon-size boulders. They lost two along the way, a sickly yearling and a weak old cow. In Engle, they herded the bawling, thirsty animals into the huge Bar Cross stock pen at the railroad siding, watered them down, and went to the station to hire cattle cars to ship the stock to El Paso. The stationmaster scheduled them for a southbound train leaving in six hours. After Cal paid the freight charges, the two men walked across the street for a meal at the hotel.

Over plates of eggs, bacon, and sourdough biscuits, they talked about what the cattle would bring upon delivery.

"I allow they're scrawny critters," Cal said, "but eyeballing them I figure I can put three hundred dollars in your pocket once we get paid, if you still want to hit the trail and shake off some Tularosa dust for a while."

"By a long stretch, three hundred ain't gonna buy my half of the outfit," Patrick said.

"Didn't say it would. But it might do until we can settle up."

"Three hundred will suit until then," Patrick said. "Once I settle, I'll let you know where to send the rest of the money."

Cal nodded at a couple of Bar Cross hands who'd entered the dining room. "Where do you plan to head first?" he asked.

"Maybe up to Santa Fe," Patrick answered, ignoring the cowboys. "I've got a hankering to see that town. Then maybe into Colorado. Denver. Cheyenne. I'll see how far the itch takes me."

Cal pushed back from the table. "We'll shake on it in Mexico."

"In Mexico," Patrick echoed as he rose to his feet. The last two times Cal had gone to buy ponies in Mexico, Patrick had stayed home. This time he'd get to go, and he was eager to see the country.

At the Bar Cross corral, they loaded the animals in the livestock cars at the siding and stretched out on their bedrolls in the shade. When the clanking and puffing of an approaching engine woke them, they put their horses in an empty stock car and rode with them all the way to El Paso, the sound of the wheels on the rails lulling them back to sleep.

In El Paso, Cal left Patrick with the cattle in a holding pen at the rail yards and went across the border to Juárez looking for their Mexican buyer, Emiliano Díaz, a Chihuahua cattleman. He found him in the bar of an old hacienda on a plaza across from a white-washed church with a bell tower topped by a cross. Encircled by trees, the hacienda had three-foot-thick adobe walls and a dining room filled with men with long Spanish faces. The gaming rooms were alive with action at the tables, the gamblers surrounded by lovely señoritas who had private rooms along a long hallway that they used to entertain their guests.

"Ah, my old amigo," Díaz said with a smile as Cal joined him at his corner table. "This time I buy, you sell."

"That's the way of it," Cal said as he sat and shook Díaz's hand. Twice he'd bought Mexican ponies from Emiliano to break to the saddle and sell as cavalry mounts to the army. He was a fair man to do business with.

A big man with a full mustache under a narrow nose, Díaz had thick eyebrows and blue-green eyes. He was pure Spanish, a descendant of the conquistadors, and proud of it.

"How many cows do you have for me?" Díaz asked.

Emiliano's ranch manager, Makiah Whetten, a Mormon with three wives and nine kids who also ran his own small outfit adjacent to Díaz's ranchero, had taught him English. Díaz spoke it well.

"Eighty-five," Cal replied. "They're mighty scrawny but should fatten up on the range."

"No matter. Finally we have the grass. You'll bring them across tomorrow."

"I could use a hand," Cal said. "There are only two of us."

Díaz nodded. "Whetten is here with me. He'll help you and tell me how much I paid. Not too much, I hope." Díaz grinned. "You and your partner will stay here as my guests, no?"

Emiliano owned the hacienda. It had been in his family for two hundred years.

"*Gracias,* but not tonight," Cal said. Unguarded, the cows might easily disappear across the border before he could deliver them to Díaz's manager. He couldn't risk it. "We'll stay with the stock."

"*Mañana* then. We will eat together and perhaps I will win some of my money back at the tables."

"Not from me," Cal said.

Díaz laughed. "From the señoritas, then."

Cal smiled. "Could be. *Buenas noches.*"

* * *

Makiah Whetten came at daybreak and sized up the stock. Rested, fed, and watered, the critters looked better than they had in days but were still pretty puny.

A slender man originally out of Utah, Makiah had a calm and easy way about him. He tallied the animals, estimated the total weight, and told Cal and Patrick what he'd pay. It was about what Cal had expected, plus fifty dollars.

"He needs these critters," Makiah said. "He let about eighty percent of his stock die during the drought. I couldn't get him to pay a penny for feed. Said he'd just as soon get some new blood-lines. He's got Oliver Lee coming down next month with two hundred head."

"I wish I had more to sell him," Cal said.

Makiah smiled. "He still might be buying in a year or two. The Díaz ranch covers over half a million acres."

They left the rail yard and pushed the cattle over some low hills with the stark Franklin Mountains at their backs and the town of El Paso nestled along the Rio Grande. Makiah took them along the riverbank to a spot where some cow tracks wound down to the water.

"No quicksand here," he said as he signaled Cal and Patrick to start the cows across.

The mountain cows had never seen so much running water in their lives. They balked at the bank, mooing and backtracking at the frightening sound and sight of the river. Cal and Patrick roped a bull and a steer and drug them across, hoping the others would follow, but it was wasted effort. Let loose, the critters just splashed back across to the other side and rejoined the bunch.

"What are we gonna do?" Patrick asked, looking at the snorting, bellowing cattle on the riverbank.

"With the river running low and sluggish, we can mill them across," Cal said. "I'll prod the lead steer and start them turning. You and Makiah tighten the circle. Once they get their feet wet, it should be all right."

Patrick gave Cal a dubious look. "If they stampede in the water you'll be stove up or worse."

"Then I reckon we'd better do it nice and slow," Cal said as he pointed Bandit at the lead steer.

He got the lead steer in the middle of the river with a few of the cows trailing behind and started moving them in a slow circle while Patrick and Makiah prodded the rest of them into the water. They milled around Cal and pressed tight against Bandit as he moved them through the brown stream into Mexico.

Once the bunch was settled on the other side, Cal quickly turned them south, eager to avoid any customs agents wanting to see proof that duty had been paid on the critters. Makiah took the lead and they raised dust for five hours, pushing the slow-moving cows along, until they reached a fenced pasture in some low hills along a mountain range where three vaqueros waited. The grasslands looked better than the Tularosa flats, but not by much, and Cal wondered if Díaz was doing the right thing stocking so soon after the drought.

After they had the cattle in the pasture under the care of Díaz's vaqueros, Makiah paid Cal in greenbacks and the three riders turned their horses toward Juárez.

As they loped along, Makiah urged Patrick to stay away from the sinful temptations at Díaz's hacienda. All it did was whet his appetite. When they parted outside of town, Cal watched Makiah ride off and wondered what kept a scripture-quoting Mormon working for a sly old sinner like Díaz.

"Was he serious about the hacienda?" Patrick asked.

"Sure as shooting he was," Cal replied. "You ain't seen nothing like it. It's one fancy place. So fancy, no leg irons are allowed. Best we stop for a bath, shave, and a fresh set of duds before we show up for supper."

Patrick grinned. "That'll be all right with me."

On a side street in Juárez, not far from Díaz's hacienda, they put their horses in a livery, bought some new duds at a dry-goods store and had a bath and a shave at a barbershop next to a small hotel. Over coffee in the hotel dining room, Patrick asked Cal to settle up.

"Am I buying you out?" Cal asked.

"Yep," Patrick replied.

"Then I need a paper from you saying so," Cal said.

"A handshake ain't enough between us?"

"Not when it comes to owning land. See if the hotel proprietor has paper and ink, and we'll study on what to write."

When Patrick left, Cal calculated how much money he could give as a partial payment to buy out their partnership. He decided on four hundred, which would leave enough to get home and tide him over for a spell.

Patrick came back with an inkwell, pen, and paper. "Who's gonna write it?" he asked.

"You're selling, so you do it. Put down for the sum of four hundred dollars as part payment, you agree to sell your half of the Double K ranch to me, Calvin Doran."

Patrick began to write. When he finished, he looked up. "What else?"

"The final payment will be half the money loaned by a bank on the Double K ranch less four hundred dollars, making me, Calvin Doran, sole owner. You give up all claims to the Double K."

"If I give up all claims, how will I know how much money is half?"

"Put it down that you have the right to examine all the bank papers."

Patrick wrote it down. "Done."

"Sign your name and put in the date."

"Maybe I should look for someone who'll pay more for my half," Patrick said.

"You can do that if you want," Cal replied.

Patrick shook his head. "Nope, this will do." He signed with a flourish and gave the paper to Cal.

Cal put it in his pocket and slid the greenbacks across the table to Patrick. "You can roam fancy-free now, amigo."

Patrick grinned. "Let's head on over to the hacienda and celebrate."

Cal sipped his coffee and smiled at the eager young cowboy, all cleaned, wearing new duds, smelling like lavender, with money in his pocket and raring to go. He'd brought him up the best way he knew how, and now it was up to Patrick to pick the trail he wanted to follow.

"Put some of that *dinero* in your boot before we leave," Cal cautioned.

"Good idea." Patrick stuffed money down his boot and stood up. "Is the food any good? I could eat a bear."

"Best food in Juárez," Cal replied, "and the women ain't bad either. But old Makiah Whetten warned you off them."

Patrick laughed. "That won't stop me."

"Didn't think so," Cal said as he adjusted his hat and headed for the door.

25

Martin Cardenas, the man who ran the hacienda for Díaz, greeted them when they entered the bar and said Don Emiliano would be with them shortly. Built low to the ground, Cardenas was a bull of a man with a thick neck and arms that bulged against the sleeves of his coat. Cal whispered something to Cardenas as he escorted them to Díaz's table. After the bartender brought glasses and a bottle of tequila, Cardenas excused himself and left the room.

"What did you say to him?" Patrick asked.

"I asked about a certain girl," Cal said.

"Why, you old bull," Patrick said with a laugh.

Cal smiled. "Don't you 'old bull' me, youngster."

Patrick chuckled. "That Cardenas is a tough-looking hombre."

"He keeps the peace," Cal said as he poured shots of tequila and raised his glass. "*Salud.*"

"*Salud,*" Patrick replied. He knocked back the shot, felt the fiery liquid sear his throat, and took a good look around the room. The adobe walls were whitewashed and the bar was made out of solid wood, with a brass foot rail. All the tables and chairs matched, and the place was as neat as a pin. The girls with the customers were all young and pretty, and none of the men looked rowdy.

He poured a second round just as Díaz entered the room and joined them at the table. Cal introduced Patrick to Díaz and the men shook hands.

"The señoritas will be fighting to oblige this young man once they meet him," Díaz said with a laugh. "You may have to stay for a week to please them all, if you can afford it."

"He can't," Cal said.

"How sad. Many hearts will be broken. Come, let us have a drink and then eat. Afterward, you are my guests for the night and Martin has a room ready for you." Díaz poured a shot.

"You are a generous man, Emiliano," Cal said.

"My enemies do not think so," Díaz replied. "*Salud.*"

Two drinks later they were seated in the dining room at Díaz's private table. Bread and tortillas were brought to the table along with wine and a vegetable soup. Roasted chicken stuffed with onions came next, followed by chili peppers stuffed with minced meat smothered in sauce.

The cups were silver, and according to Díaz the serving plates were blue-and-white Spanish porcelain. The wine, he said, was from El Paso.

Patrick ate until he could hold no more. Never had he had such a good meal in such a fine place. He leaned back in his chair, sipped wine, and took a good look around the room. The men, Mexican and American, all looked prosperous and old. Probably in their forties and fifties, Patrick guessed, which was about Cal's age. There wasn't a dirty, smelly waddie in the whole bunch. The only American he recognized was Pat Garrett, who had a red-headed señorita sitting on his lap. As sheriff, Garrett had visited the Double K several times looking for outlaws, and stayed overnight at the ranch more than once.

Patrick reminded himself that the fancy ladies in the room were just a bunch of gussied-up, sweet-smelling soiled doves, no different from the saloon and dance-hall strumpets he'd known as a young boy. No different from Ida.

The sight of Virgil Peters ushering a stumbling drunk to their tent in the mining camp and Ida shooing him outside came into his head. Many a night he'd sat out in the cold, waiting to be let back in, listening to the grunts and groans while Virgil stood guard in front of the closed tent flaps. He pushed the thought out of his mind.

Díaz passed around cigars and a waiter lit them. Patrick didn't like tobacco much, but he puffed on his as Cal and Díaz talked about improved ice-cooled railroad cars that could cart dressed beef for a thousand miles with no spoilage. They were in wide use back in Chicago, Boston, and New York City, but they wouldn't work in the desert country, where there was little to no ice to be had.

The señoritas in the room were much more interesting than talk about dressed beef, ice, and railroad cars. A small, dark-haired girl particularly drew Patrick's eye, but he didn't know how to go about arranging a poke. Back in Tularosa at Coghlan's saloon, all a man had to do was look at one of the women and she was ready to take him to a room and lift her skirt.

He'd done it only a couple of times with Coghlan's hurdy-gurdy girls when Cal was away on sheriff business, and it hadn't gone so good. He blew the plug and got bucked off sooner than he should have, and it mortified him greatly.

He stopped staring at the dark-haired girl and glanced at Díaz, who grinned at him.

"The señoritas in the room are already engaged for the evening," he said, reading Patrick's mind. "However, as you walk down the hall to your room, you may see one you like through an open doorway."

Patrick nodded as if to signal that he knew exactly how to behave and kept puffing on his cigar. He waited until Díaz and Cal returned to their conversation before pushing back from the table and leaving the dining room. In the hallway, Martin Cardenas gestured at the several open doors.

"Any one, señor," he said softly. "Your room is through the passageway at the end of the hall. Señor Cal has already paid for your señorita."

"*Gracias*," Patrick replied as he headed for the hallway, eager to see if there was a tiny, dark-haired whore in any of the rooms with open doors. He wanted a tiny one.

Cal watched him go, and after a few minutes of jawboning, Díaz excused himself and left Cal alone at the table. He was about to get up and say howdy to Pat Garrett, who'd hired him as one of his deputies during the Lincoln County War, when he heard a woman's high-pitched cry and saw Martin Cardenas barrel down the hallway past the open dining room door.

Curious about the commotion, Cal stepped into the hallway in time to see Cardenas fling Patrick out of one of the rooms, pound him with his fists, and drag him past the barroom into the courtyard. The patrons emptied the bar to watch the fight, and Cal pushed his way through in time to see Patrick take a powerful body blow that doubled him over. He dropped his guard, and Cardenas quickly drove a combination of punches into Patrick's face, raked his knuckles across his cheeks, and hammered a hard left hook into his left ear. Patrick tried to backtrack. Cardenas grabbed a handful of Patrick's shirt and drove a fist into his mouth that buck-led his knees. He gave him a hard push, and Patrick fell, his head bouncing on the ground. Someone in the crowd hollered bravo. Cal had to admit that Martin had put on one hell of an exhibition. He wasn't even breathing heavy.

"You have no part of this, señor," he warned Cal. "Take him out of here and do not bring him back."

"I'll surely do that if you tell me what caused the whipping you just dished out," Cal said evenly, inspecting Patrick's face. One ear was slightly torn, his face was skinned, both eyes were swollen, and his lower lip was mangled.

"He beat the señorita, so I beat him," Cardenas replied.

"Fair enough. Do you know why he hit the señorita?"

"Does it matter, señor?"

"I guess not." The courtyard had emptied. "When he comes around, I'll walk him out the courtyard gate."

"*Bueno.* Tell him never to come here again."

Cardenas left and returned quickly with Patrick's hat, boots, and money. Cal hunkered down next to Patrick and waited. When the young man woke up, Cal lifted Patrick to his feet, stuck his hat on his head, and walked him slowly out to the street toward the little hotel.

"What happened with the girl?" Cal asked.

"It's none of your business," Patrick slurred through his busted mouth.

"Was she trying to kill you, steal your money?"

"No."

"Then you had no cause to hit her."

"When is hitting a whore bad?"

"No woman deserves a beating because of what she does for a

living." Cal stopped in front of the hotel. "Martin Cardenas will kill you if you go back to the hacienda. You savvy?"

Patrick nodded.

Cal handed him his boots. "Your money is in your boots. Get a room."

Patrick rocked, unsteady, on his heels. One eye was closed and he could barely see out of the other. "I'll see you *mañana*."

Cal sadly shook his head. "Nope, we're quits."

He turned back toward the hacienda. He needed another drink to help him get over the anger he felt toward Patrick. Had he really failed him that badly?

26

Patrick woke up with a splitting headache, his mouth dry with caked blood. He forced one eye open. He was on a bed jammed up against the wall of a tiny room. His hat hung on a wall peg and his clothes were on the floor next to a washstand with a water pitcher and a basin. His face felt like a bull had stomped on it. The memory of the beating coursed through his aching head.

At the washstand, he filled the basin, splashed water on his face, and squinted into the mirror. He had two black eyes, red welts on his cheeks, puffy lips, a loose tooth, and a gash above his right eye. A small chunk of his left earlobe dangled like a glob of fat.

Had Cardenas done all that damage with just his fists? He hadn't even thrown a punch at the hombre. He must have looked like a sissy getting whipped like that.

He sank back on the bed and glanced out the narrow window. It was light outside, but he didn't know what day it was. His head wasn't working too good, but he recalled Cal walking him down the street to the hotel, handing him his boots, and saying something about his money. He sat up and looked at his pile of clothes. His boots weren't there. On his hands and knees he searched under the bed and pulled out the boots. In one of them he found his money jammed against the toe. He got dressed, stuffing his blood-stained, torn shirt into his pants and his greenbacks into a pocket. He pulled his hat down low and left the hotel, hoping not to be seen. Fortunately there was no one in the lobby. He stepped outside and looked skyward. Best he could tell with his fuzzy vision, it was getting on to midday. He walked to the livery stable, where the old man who looked after the horses glanced at him and pointed to a stall. There he found his horse, along with his saddle, rifle, six-gun, and all his gear.

"The *americano* you came with gave me money to keep an eye on your things," the old man said.

"When was that?"

"Last night, very late. He woke me up."

"Is his horse here?"

The old man shook his head. "He left real early."

"*Gracias.*"

"*De nada.*"

He saddled his pony and rode out of Juárez, glad to be rid of the town, Cal Doran, and the Double K. He saw no need to return to the Tularosa ever again. The last dozen years had just been a wreck waiting to happen, and he'd been smart enough not to get trapped into believing it would last. He'd always figured that when push came to shove, no one would stand by him.

He crossed into El Paso, stopped at a drugstore, and had the proprietor apply a poultice to his eyes, cut off the dangling bit of his earlobe, and put iodine on his cuts. He bought some patent medicine, stocked his saddlebags with grub at a general store, and headed west toward Arizona Territory, not north to Santa Fe.

He didn't want to get anywhere near the Double K. He had

enough money to drift for a spell, and there would be more coming soon. He jigged his horse into a trot and followed the afternoon sun across a wide stretch of land, with mirage-like mountains shimmering on the horizon. Come nightfall, he hadn't seen a homestead or a ranch all day, so he staked his horse, drank some elixir, bedded down under the stars, and fell asleep to the sound of a faraway passing train.

An hour before dawn, he woke feeling much improved, and by first light he was drifting south and west along the Mexican border. He kept to that course for several days, stopping one night at an abandoned border-crossing station, where he stayed in an empty shack, and the next night in some hills that looked down on a wide, long valley that ran into southerly mountains.

He hadn't seen anyone since leaving El Paso and didn't mind the lack of company, although he thought about Cal now and again. The old man had quit him for hitting a whore as if he had no respect for women, which wasn't true. Except for Teresa, the women in her family, and Ignacio's dead mother, he just hadn't met a decent one yet, leastways not a decent unmarried white woman.

As his scrapes and bruises healed, his spirits rose, and he took more careful notice of the land. He'd been passing through a chain of mountains separated by wide valleys, and from every crest he could see more mountains beyond. In the valleys there were shallow lakes the Mexicans called playas, live streams in the high country, and numerous springs in swales by the low hills and in seeps where cottonwoods thrived. There was deer, bear, coyote, and wolf sign around watering spots, and the cattle on the land carried the Diamond A brand. While the grass wasn't stirrup high in the pastures of the vast valleys, it hadn't been eaten to a nub and was plentiful around the hilly *ciénagas* where cattle gathered.

It reminded him of the Tularosa in a way: a whole string of Tularosa Valleys, each stretch of basin and hill country bounded by mountains. Except the mountains weren't as grueling to cross and the flats were less hostile to man and beast. Patrick reckoned the country made tending cattle a whole lot easier.

A bare grub bag and an empty stomach tempted him to shoot and slaughter a yearling. He was about to cut a critter out of a nearby bunch when he spied a distant horseman leading a pack animal entering the valley from the westerly mountains.

On the Tularosa, outlaws sought remote places to hide or seek refuge from the law, and Patrick figured it was no different here. Some of them were lone wolves; others ran in small bands. Most all of them traveled well heeled and well supplied to outlast and outrun the law.

Patrick dismounted, staked his pony to keep it from running, pulled his long gun, and waited. The rider headed straight for him at a leisurely pace. When he got within rifle range, Patrick put a bead on him. The rider stopped and raised his hands.

"There's no call for that rifle," the man hollered.

"Maybe so," Patrick replied.

The rider had scabbards strapped on either side of his saddle, one for a shotgun and the other for a repeating rifle. On his hip was a Colt .45, low and tied down, and he carried a sheathed knife on his belt. When Cal took to working as a deputy, he rode out of the Double K equipped the same way.

"Are you the law?" Patrick asked.

The cowboy grinned. "That line of work wouldn't suit this old boy. I work for the Diamond A. I'm on my way to a cow camp. Can I light?"

"Go ahead." Patrick lowered the rifle but kept it cradled in his arm. He'd never seen a working hand packing so much hardware, and it made him suspicious.

The cowboy slid out of the saddle.

"You're toting a lot of iron," Patrick said.

"Desperados have been raiding up from Mexico, renegade Apaches too. I'm not about to lose my hide or my scalp. Looks like you had a run in with a wildcat."

"Where's the cow camp?" Patrick asked.

"South a ways, right on the border at the old Lang ranch. You're welcome to ride along."

Patrick nodded toward the mountains. "I'm heading west."

The cowboy shrugged and swung into his saddle. "Suit yourself."

"Any ranches nearby?"

"Another day's ride and you'll reach the Fitzpatrick spread if you drift northwest from here."

"Thanks."

"Adios."

"Adios."

Patrick watched the horseman for a time before riding into the valley. On the off chance the waddie did work for the Diamond A, he decided not to shoot a yearling. Instead he stopped at a seep on the far side of the valley, shot a rabbit, and cooked it for his supper.

Night had fallen by the time he finished eating, and the moon wouldn't rise for hours. His campfire was a beacon that could draw the attention of anyone bent on banditry, and he still carried misgivings about the horseman who had passed by.

Cal had taught him to be vigilant and cautious. He moved his saddle and bedroll out of the light, staked his pony in a grassy area where it could rest and graze, took his rifle, and moved to an old cottonwood tree at the edge of the seep. There he waited, listening to the night sounds and watching the fire burn down, his hands sweating as he clutched his rifle.

Many times, Ignacio had told him how John Kerney saved his life by bushwhacking Charlie Gambel in Hembrillo Canyon. Patrick wasn't sure if he could do the same and was almost convinced he wouldn't have to when he heard soft footsteps approaching. The fire had died down to embers, casting a pale glow. He raised his rifle, held his breath, watched, and waited. A shadowy figure came out of the darkness, and Patrick fired. He heard the man grunt and saw him drop, but he didn't move. There was a rustling of grass and the sound of receding footsteps, followed by horses cantering away. He waited a little longer before approaching the man on the ground. It was the rider he'd met earlier in the day. He was still alive.

Patrick pointed his rifle barrel at the cowboy's head and took the six-gun from his hand.

"You sure are a sly one," the cowboy wheezed.

"Where did I hit you?" Patrick asked.

"In the lung. I'm sure to die."

"What's your name?"

The cowboy coughed. "Matt Donavan. Bury me."

"I'll leave that for your partner."

By the time Patrick doused the embers, saddled his horse, and rode off, Matt Donavan was dead.

2 7

Back at the Double K, Cal shook off feeling lonesome by keeping busy. Looking forward to the day when he could restock, he rebuilt some traps in the high-country pastures. Around the ranch house, he replaced rotting corral posts, cleaned accumulated gear out of the casita Ignacio had built for Teresa, and mended bridles, saddles, and his favorite pair of chaps. He patched the barn roof, hauled in enough firewood to last for two years, and made a new gate for the horse corral. He had half a mind to clean out Patrick's room but decided to let it be.

Half a dozen ponies and a few outlaw steers were the only livestock on the ranch. No cattle to tend gave Cal too much idle time. He turned his attention to the bits and pieces of the wagon John Kerney had been driving the day he died. For years, it had sat in a pile, untouched, weathering, rusting, and rotting. All along, Cal had wanted to fix it up into a hay wagon, but Patrick had resisted, although he never said why.

He spread out all the unbroken parts and decided it would take two new wheels, a tongue, a rear axle, ribs, slats, and a hell of a lot more skill than he had to rebuild it. He gave the whole caboodle to Ignacio, who hauled it away after spending the night at the ranch with Cal, drinking, reminiscing, and fretting about Patrick. Cal said nothing about Patrick quitting the partnership or what had happened in Juárez.

After Cal went back to the hacienda that night in Juárez, the whore had told him Patrick started hitting her when she coyly said she was a virgin, something many of her other customers liked to hear. Why it set him off made no sense to either Cal or the girl.

Each month he made a trip to Tularosa, expecting a letter from Patrick, but none came. A banker in Las Cruces had agreed to make a loan against the ranch, but Cal wouldn't sign the mortgage papers until Patrick asked for the money.

He got back from a trip to town to find George Rose's pony in the corral and George sitting on the veranda admiring the view, his bedroll spread out on the floor. Cal could smell beans cooking in the kitchen.

"How long have you been here?" Cal asked as he rested his bones in a chair next to George.

"Got here yesterday," George replied.

"Are you fixing supper?" Cal asked.

"The bean pot is simmering and I've got a couple of beefsteaks ready to grill," George said.

The cowhide draped over the corral fence carried the Bar Cross brand. George had dressed the carcass, wrapped the meat in burlap, and hung it up high to dry in the barn.

"Did that little dogie you butchered follow you all the way from the Bar Cross range?" Cal asked.

"Now, ain't that something?" George said with a sly grin.

"It figures," Cal said. "I don't have a job for you, even if you did fix my supper."

"There ain't no jobs hereabouts, so I ain't asking. But I'll work for keep and browse for my pony if you don't mind the company."

Cal looked surprised. "I thought Oliver Lee was hiring guns."

"I'm feeling too peaceable in my old age for that kind of work. Where's young Patrick?"

"He struck out on his own some six months back."

"A bright lad needs to do that every now and then," George said. "When's he coming back?"

"Can't say."

"What about my proposition?"

"I could use a hand building a water tank next to a spring that hasn't dried up. I plan to run a pipe to it."

"The one up by Big Sheep?"

"Yep."

"I'm your man."

"You can bunk in Patrick's room," Cal said, glad for George's company. It had been too damn quiet at the ranch for too long.

28

The Yuma Territorial Prison sat on a bluff above the Colorado and Gila rivers in far western Arizona. Beyond the walls lay the town of Yuma and a thousand miles of bleak, sun-soaked desert and desolate mountains. The buildings were squat, surrounded by an adobe wall eight feet thick and eighteen feet high with guard towers on each corner. Inside, there were cell blocks, a mess hall, a recreation hall used for Sunday services, an exercise yard, a blacksmith shop, a tailor shop, stables, a library, a hospital ward, and a small ward to house women prisoners. Quarters for the superintendent and his assistant were outside the prison walls. So was the prisoners' graveyard.

Patrick Kerney arrived in the early summer of 1893, convicted of grand larceny in Cochise County for stealing a saddle from a livery in Tombstone. He had been sentenced to two years under the go-by name of Pat Floyd he'd given the law to hide his true identity.

He'd packed a heavy load of bad luck into Tombstone from New Mexico, losing all his greenbacks at cards within a month. With the money gone, he had soured on the deal Cal had made with him to buy out his half of the Double K. The more he thought about it, the more he decided Cal had been too eager to see him gone from the ranch. Hadn't Cal told him what to write down to make the sale legal, and now he had Patrick's signed paper to prove it? Hadn't Cal decided that four hundred dollars was enough money to give him? Had that been a fair shake? He sure would make it his business to find out from the bank how much he was owed come time to settle accounts.

Patrick fretted that he had been hornswoggled. The Double K wasn't a big outfit like the Bar Cross and the Diamond A, but it wasn't a small spread either. Even with the drought and the cattle market gone belly-up, the land with all the improvements had to be worth a pretty penny. He'd poured years of sweat into the Double K and damn sure wasn't gonna lose it by being stupid.

Maybe it had been thickheaded to give up on the Double K to begin with. After all, John Kerney had started it for him. Maybe Cal had always wanted it for himself.

Patrick took to working odd jobs trying to win back a stake so he could return to the Tularosa and set things right. He figured to pay Cal his four hundred dollars and get back to doing what he knew best. Instead, he kept putting his *dinero* into circulation at the gambling tables and wound up losing his saddle in a faro game. It was a double-rigged, hand-tooled stock saddle with wool-lined fenders and a nickel-plated horn Cal had given him for his fifteenth birthday.

He couldn't abide losing it, so he stole it back. When he tried to skedaddle from town on his pony, the town marshal caught him and locked him up. After the trial, the marshal sold Patrick's pony to pay for his keep in jail and he went to Yuma Prison with absolutely nothing to his name but the clothes on his back.

Within a month of his arrival at Yuma, a new cell mate named John Flynn arrived and had to sleep on the floor because of over-crowding. A hard case in for manslaughter, Flynn wanted Patrick's bunk. One evening after mealtime, he picked a fight with Patrick in the exercise yard. The guards broke it up quickly, but it cost Patrick his job in the kitchen. For the next two months, along with Flynn and other hard cases, he broke rock and made adobes on the Troublemaker Crew.

By the end of every day, six days a week, he was ready to drop. His body ached from his toes to his head. Hours after work ended he could still hear the sound of sledgehammers ringing in his ears.

He slept with seven other inmates in a stinky, dirty, eight-by-ten-foot cell, one of a double row of cells facing each other along a long corridor. The walls were granite, three feet thick, and an iron grate locked them in at night. Six narrow steel beds, eighteen inches wide, stacked three to a side were anchored to the walls. A bucket served as the crapper. Besides his cell mates, he lived with roaches, bedbugs, lice, fleas, and spiders. He had an upper berth, which made it easy for him to avoid conversation once the guards locked them in. Two men slept on the floor on straw-tick mattresses. Flynn wasn't one of them; he'd been knifed by another prisoner and was in the hospital dying.

Most nights during the summer, it didn't cool down enough to sleep until late, and he would lie awake thinking how much he hated being locked up.

During the day, he broke rock near the guards who watched over the crew to avoid any further trouble with the hard cases. The strategy worked. In the yard after dinner, he stayed to himself, avoiding the heat-stroked locos who lived in the mental wing, the lily-livered trustees who cowered together like a herd of sheep, and the toughs who roamed trying to get money from the men who sold their handcrafts to town folks on Sundays. The consumptives stayed pretty much isolated in their special ward. He never saw the three women prisoners, who were kept in the inner yard.

He spent his Sundays in the prison library, reading Mark Twain, Herman Melville, William Dean Howells, and James Fenimore Cooper. He liked tall tales and rousing adventures that made him yearn for his freedom. No matter what happened in the future, he vowed never to get locked up again.

On Sundays, the only day of rest, the library was the quietest place in the prison. The main yard filled up after church with town folks who came to gawk and buy the prisoners' handcrafts. Inmates could have family members visit on the Sabbath, and there were always a few men due to be released who got fresh duds to wear when they walked out the gate. Seeing folks walking around free to come and go as they pleased dejected Patrick no end, so he hid out in the library.

Every Sunday on his rounds, Superintendent Thomas Gates stuck his head in the library, glanced around, and disappeared across the yard. Gates had a shoot-to-kill order on prisoners trying to escape and had enforced it more than once, but he was harsh only with men who deserved it. For those on good behavior, there was an occasional concert to attend put on by townspeople and the freedom to use the library in the evenings after mealtime. As a troublemaker, Patrick could use the library only on Sunday.

One day Gates spied Patrick teaching Francisco Lopez and another Mexican prisoner some American words and called him outside.

"You speak Spanish?" Superintendent Gates asked.

He was a tall man with thin lips and a hawk-like nose. Patrick figured him to be old, maybe fifty.

"Yes, sir," Patrick replied.

"Do you read and write English?"

"Yes, sir."

"Do you believe in the good book?" Gates asked.

Patrick paused only slightly. If being religious would bring him good luck, he'd be a Holy Roller. "I surely do."

"What's your work detail?"

"I've been busting rock, but Officer Hartlee says I'm to go back to the kitchen soon."

Gates nodded and walked off without another word. On Monday, he had Patrick brought to his office and made him stand silently at attention while he thumbed through some papers on his desk.

Madora Ingalls, known to all as Dora, was the wife of Thomas Gates's friend Frank Ingalls, who had twice been superintendent at Yuma. Dora had started the prison library some years ago, and it had remained her favorite charitable undertaking. The most recent library trustee had died a while back, and Dora had been nagging Gates to appoint another. But this time, she wanted someone who could teach Mexican prisoners English. Dora believed that if the Mexicans learned English they would be less inclined to remain lawbreakers.

Thomas Gates wasn't convinced of her logic, but he wasn't about to argue with a woman as formidable as Dora Ingalls. He scanned Pat Floyd's record: one reported conviction for theft, one fight started by another prisoner, no other infractions.

He looked up at Pat Floyd. He seemed a bright enough lad, neither surly nor too submissive, with no record of incorrigibility or violence.

"You are fluent in both English and Spanish?" Gates asked.

"Yes, sir," Patrick replied.

"And can write in both languages."

"Yes, sir."

"I haven't seen you at Sunday services."

Patrick lowered his head. "No, sir."

Gates sighed. Sometimes prison moved men away from the Lord. "That must change."

"I'll be there next Sunday for sure," Patrick said.

"Good," Gates said as he wrote a note on the paper in front of him and slid it into a desk drawer. "Starting now, you're the library trustee. In addition to your normal duties, you will teach English to some Mexicans who will be selected by Mrs. Madora Ingalls."

"That would be my job?" Patrick asked.

Gates nodded. "Keeping the library in order and teaching Mexicans to read. Mrs. Ingalls will inform you of your duties and supervise your work with the Mexican prisoners."

"Yes, sir," he said, holding back a smile. Short of getting cut loose, he couldn't think of anything better than getting off the rock pile and into the library.

"I'll tolerate no informality on your part with Mrs. Ingalls. Also, do not fail to meet her expectations. One mistake and you'll be back on the rock pile, understood?"

"Yes, sir."

"That's all."

The guard who escorted Patrick away from Gates's office told him Mrs. Ingalls usually arrived after the start of morning work details to select and distribute books to the hospital patients. He unlocked the library and left him alone to wait for Mrs. Ingalls, who soon arrived with a stack of books in her arms, which she placed on the desk.

"Are you my new trustee?" Dora Ingalls asked. She was a comely woman with a tiny waist and a lively, intelligent face. A woman of breeding, Patrick figured, never having met one before in person, only in books.

"Yes, ma'am," he said. "Pat Floyd."

"Well, Mr. Floyd, these book have just been donated to the library by some good citizens of Yuma, and we need to catalog them. Let me show you how to do it."

"Yes, ma'am," Patrick replied.

"Are you familiar with our library?"

Patrick nodded.

She took a ledger out of the desk drawer, explained the cataloging process, and had Patrick enter the title of the book, the subject matter, and the author's name.

When he finished, Mrs. Ingalls smiled. "Excellent. You can read and your penmanship is very good." She handed him a Spanish Bible. "Pick any page and translate a section into English."

He thumbed through the Bible and translated three sentences from the Book of Matthew about Jesus sending his disciples out among the people.

"That will suffice," Dora Ingalls said cheerfully with an approving nod, taking the book from his hands. "We have much to do. I know there are several of the Mexican prisoners who read and use the library. They will be our first experiments. I'll guide you as to how to teach them."

She gestured at an empty chair as she sat at the table. "Sit. Let's not waste a moment."

* * *

During his first month as the library trustee, Dora Ingalls kept a close eye on Pat Floyd. She had been initially concerned about his youth. All of the previous trustees Thomas Gates had assigned to the library had been older men convicted of crimes such as embezzlement, forgery, or defrauding creditors. They were of a meek temperament and fell easily into the library routine.

Her worries were unfounded. Pat Floyd was bright—of that there was no doubt—and he did all that she asked of him without complaint. He was attentive to her but appropriately polite, and according to Reverend Parker he'd attended every Sunday service since his appointment as a trustee.

Often she would arrive at the library to find him with his head in a book, but she knew nothing about him. Not once had he said anything about his life before coming to the prison. All she knew was that he'd been caught stealing a saddle in Tombstone.

Only a few Mexican prisoners were interested in learning English, and it was here where Pat struggled, sometimes losing his temper with them as they stumbled over comprehension and pronunciation. He was not, Dora decided, cut out to be a teacher, and while the experiment wasn't working as well as she had hoped, it was a beginning. Thomas Gates, however, was pleased with the effort and had taken to bringing visiting dignitaries by to show it off.

After Patrick had served six months as the library trustee, Superintendent Gates met with Dora and asked if he was fit to be released.

"I am overrun with prisoners," he explained, "and the governor will grant pardons to those I recommend."

"Although I shall be sorry to lose him," Dora answered, "he shouldn't be kept here a moment longer."

Gates nodded. "I'll see to it by week's end."

"But you must replace him by then," Dora noted.

"Of course," Gates replied, wondering if any of the newly arrived prisoners would be suitable. After supper, he would carefully review the files.

2 9

Patrick left Yuma Prison through the whitewashed adobe sally port with a five-dollar gold piece Dora Ingalls had pressed into his hand and a pardon made out to Pat Floyd in his pocket. At her insistence, he had promised to get some schooling to advance himself, but he knew he was meant to ranch, not be a scholar. He was still a partner in the Double K, and he'd have it back if it took a year or more to get the money to do it.

He'd never known a woman like Madora Ingalls. For six months he'd fantasized about her. She was too good for him and that made him angry at times, but he always managed to hide it. He wondered what her husband was like and pictured him as a fat, old man who ate like a pig and always had bits of food in his beard. He imagined her undressing in front of him, seeing her breasts for the first time. He dreamt about her and woke up with the image of her in his mind, her blue eyes sparkling, her face lit up when she smiled.

He knew he'd never meet anyone like her in a gambling parlor, dance hall, or saloon. Maybe that was the way it was supposed to be. Women like Dora Ingalls were too damn pretty, too smart, and too highfalutin to be interested in the likes of him.

He walked to town and bought a ticket at the train station for Tucson. Although it was still late spring, it was likely the big outfits outside Tucson would be hiring soon for fall works. If he could get a start, he planned to work his way home to New Mexico. Once there, he'd figure out what to do next.

Starting right now he was Patrick Kerney, not Pat Floyd, and this time he'd live up to his name. He'd find a way to pay Cal back every cent of that four hundred dollars he'd squandered, even if it took years and he had to live poor to do it.

He sat on a bench at the station, waiting for the train, staring back hard at the people who passed him by with their noses in the air. They gave him a wide berth and cautious glances as they waited for the train at either end of the platform, far away from him. He felt like he was a different breed than all of them, and it didn't bother him a bit.

* * *

In Tucson, Patrick got a job mucking out stalls at a livery stable for fifty cents a day and a place to sleep. He knew that a cowboy without a saddle was as useless as a milch cow without teats. No self-respecting rancher would hire such a sorry sight. He ate one meal a day and finished up at the end of the month with enough money to buy a beat-up eight-dollar saddle. He patched the torn fenders with some rawhide as best he could, bought some cheap leather-covered steel stirrups, and got a train ticket to Benson. He'd heard that the Wilcox ranch, a huge spread along the San Pedro River, was hiring for fall works. At Benson, he hitched a ride with a supply wagon heading to the ranch. Fats, the old stove-up waddie driving it, told him the boss was fixing to gather from the Dragoon Mountains north to Cochise, a fuel stop on the Southern Pacific, and after that work northwest to the Galiuro Mountains. Fats reckoned the job would last at least a couple of months, maybe longer.

The Wilcox estancia sat in a valley hard against some pretty, grassy hills. A long house with a pitched roof, a wide veranda, and a chimney smack dab in the center of the building was enclosed by a low, white picket fence. There were haystacks and a grove of fruit trees behind the house, and down by the barn were two adobe bunkhouses and the ranch manager's cabin. A nearby big corral held a good eighty or so horses, the remuda for the roundup. Fats told him there were at least thirty cowboys already on the payroll. Patrick spotted a bunch of them working with some raw-looking broomtail broncs at another corral out by a pasture.

He grabbed his saddle and jumped off the wagon at the gate to the picket fence as Fats rattled away in the direction of the cookhouse. A man stepped out to meet him before he reached the veranda. He was rail thin, with a broad nose, deep wrinkles around his eyes, and the leathery skin of lifelong rancher. He was old, far older than Cal.

Patrick touched the brim of his hat. "Mr. Wilcox?"

Sam Wilcox nodded as he looked the young cowboy over. His clothes were past due for the rag bin and his saddle was about the sorriest he'd ever seen.

"I hear you're hiring," Patrick said.

"Could be," Wilcox said. "What's your name, son?"

"Patrick Kerney."

Wilcox eyed Patrick with greater interest. "Any kin to John Kerney?"

"He was my pa."

"He's passed on?"

"Yes, sir, sometime back, when I was just a button."

"Sorry to hear that; he was a good man."

"Yes, sir."

"He came west with me out of Texas. He was always looking to find you. I guess he did."

"Yes, sir, he did."

"You've forked cows some?"

"Yes, sir, most of my life, and I'm a fair hand with ponies."

Wilcox rubbed his nose. There was no reason not to believe the lad, but he wasn't about to give a job to someone who couldn't make a hand, no matter who his daddy was. A waddie looking for work on foot wasn't typical, and the saddle sure didn't show much pride.

"Go see my manager, Dan Burgess," he said. "He's working those mustangs at the corral in the pasture. If he thinks you're worth your salt, he'll take you on."

Patrick touched his hat. "I'm obliged."

Wilcox waved off the lad's gratitude. "You go see Dan."

* * *

Dan Burgess watched the young cowboy terrapin his way to the horse corral with a saddle slung over a shoulder. He draped it over a low railing and found space between two of the boys at the fence who were watching Jack Thorpe working a bronc.

The lad looked like he'd fallen on hard times and Dan wasn't one to throw bones to stray dogs. He wanted hard-riding hands who could work the brush, the flats, and the high country without being mollycoddled. He gave the cowboy a brief nod and returned his attention to the corral.

The corral had two gates, one opened to a fenced pasture for horses, the other to the outside range. Young ponies and wild mustangs were brought to the horse corral, where they were snubbed to the snubbing post, blindfolded, hackamored, saddled, and ridden for the first time. It was a long, drawn-out process. A year could pass before a cow pony was ready to work cattle.

Today, Dan had his best riders working with some top broncos brought in from the south range that Mr. Wilcox wanted saddle broke as cow ponies. Burgess had handpicked the broncos himself. Sound in body, quick of foot, spirited, and intelligent, they would be more valuable once trained than any other animals on the ranch. They had to be good at cutting cows in and out of bunches, running fast in spurts, stopping and turning quickly, and not shy of the rider's lariat.

Dan Burgess wasn't one for busting horses. He didn't believe in rough riding, quirting, lashing, or using spurs to tame a horse. Over the past two days, the ponies had been introduced to the hackamore and the saddle and walked riderless around the corral. None had yet been introduced to the bit.

Like all horses, they'd bucked the empty saddle both days before accepting it. Today, the horses were being mounted, and Dan had high hopes there would be very little bucking. He wanted no spoiled ponies. Only a few had jumped with an arched back and stiff legs when mounted before slowly settling down, trembling under the weight of the rider.

After each horse had been ridden around the corral for a while, it was unsaddled and returned to the fenced pasture. The next horse to be ridden was a three-year-old buckskin, fifteen hands high, with a white stripe from his forehead to his muzzle. It had proved to be the most ornery pony in the bunch, high rolling and pitching his rider off three times, and had yet to be successfully ridden.

Dan wanted it ridden before the end of the day. Why not give it to the raggedy young cowboy to try? He went into the fenced pasture, brought the buckskin into the corral, and looked at the lad.

"What's your name, son?" he asked.

"Patrick Kerney."

The boys lining the corral turned and stared at Patrick.

"Think you can ride this thrifty pony?"

"Yes, sir," Patrick said.

"He's all yours," Dan said.

The cowboy ducked under a railing, took the reins, and walked the horse to the far side of the corral, away from the hands, who had congregated by the gates.

Dan hitched himself up on a top railing and watched. Instead of reaching for the saddle blanket right away, the lad spent time talking to the buckskin, rubbing its back, withers, neck, and girth, keeping his hand away from its head. The buckskin snorted, shivered, and pranced a bit before settling down. Only then did the lad approach the pony's head, rubbing it as he attached a long line to the hackamore. He stepped back to the middle of the corral and tugged slightly on the rope, and the buckskin began to move in a slow, circular trot. After giving it a few turns around the corral, he stubbed the pony to the stubbing post, rubbed his forehead, and gently placed a saddle blanket on its back. The buckskin flared its nostrils and looked at the cowboy, who inched closer to its head. He stroked the pony's mane, talked to it low and slow, and rubbed the saddle blanket back toward the haunches. The pony twitched an ear and stood still.

He picked up the saddle next to the stubbing post, showed it to the buckskin, and gently hoisted it on its back. The pony arched its back, stiffened its legs, dropped his head, and bucked once. The lad pulled off the saddle and waited for the pony to calm down before trying again. It took three more tries before the buckskin accepted the saddle without complaint.

He cinched the saddle and used the long rope to canter the buckskin around the corral, keeping him close to the railing. After four turns, he stopped the horse and made him back up. He did it several more times, until the pony pawed the ground and stood still.

Dan waited for the lad to ride. After a long minute stroking the buckskin's forehead, he swung into the saddle. The pony froze, pitched, twisted sideways, came down on all four legs, and shook hard. The lad rode it out. Dan waited for the buckskin to go after his rider again, but it stood pat. The cowboy trotted the buckskin around the corral a few times, remounted the pony twice again, and then slid out of the saddle in front of Dan.

"He'll be a good one," Patrick said, handing over the reins.

"That he will," Dan Burgess said. "Welcome to the outfit. Pick a range pony for yourself out of the remuda. Jack Thorpe here will show you where to bunk."

The cowboy smiled. "I'm obliged."

* * *

Sam Wilcox sat in his office, which looked out on the veranda and the neat picket fence, working on numbers. Cattle had come back to a fair price, and this year looked slightly better. He planned to send Dan Burgess out with the hands to gather in three groups, each under a top hand. He was hoping to gather at least three to four thousand head. In two days, riders from other outfits would be at the ranch to join the roundup. They would cut out their stock to be thrown over to their home ranges after each gathering.

He heard the floor squeak and looked up to see Dan Burgess standing in the open door.

"That's some cowboy you sent to me," Dan said with a big smile and a shake of his head. He had deep-set eyes and chubby cheeks, which gave him a jovial air, but he was as hard as nails.

"Is he about useless?"

"I'd say he's a top hand with horses. I took him on and told him to pick out a pony. Did he come with anything but that sorry saddle?"

"Nary a thing," Wilcox replied. "Give him a decent saddle and some tack and have Fats put a bedroll together for him. That old boy has gear stowed away he'll never use again. If he gets ornery, tell him I'll pay him for it."

"I've got an old pair of chaps hanging on a peg at the cabin gathering dust," Dan said.

"That'll do. Get him some gloves too. He'll need them in the brush." Wilcox waited for Burgess to skedaddle, but he stayed put. "What is it?"

"I'm thinking the lad has been in Yuma."

"If so, he's not the only cowboy around here who forgot to be law-abiding one time or another," Wilcox replied as he picked up his pen. "Keep your eye on him for a spell. Let me know if he's not a square shooter."

30

The Wilcox ranch, known by its brand, the Flying W, covered nearly a half million acres on two separate ranges. Once the stray men from the other ranches joined up, more than fifty cowboys worked the gathering. On the southern grasslands and the flats it went smoothly, but the brush in the foothills of the rugged Galiuro Mountains was a different matter. Popping the cows out of the thickets took ingenuity. The boys divided up, half to one end of each big swath of dense undergrowth, half to the other end. Farther along, in the direction the cattle were hazed, more men waited on either side of the brush to turn the cows into the open. In places where the terrain was too steep for the cattle to get any higher, they chased the critters out of the wetlands and pastures in the lower canyons.

After all the cows were hunted out of the brush and gathered, the stray men from the other outfits trimmed the herd and threw their stock over to their home range as the Flying W boys pushed the beef along to the railhead in Benson.

Patrick didn't think he had a chance to be kept on as a steady hand over the fall and winter months. He figured to be paid and let go to ride the chuck line looking for work. Most ranchers wouldn't be hiring, but maybe he could find a job looking after stock at a remote winter line camp or driving a wagon. The dismal prospects disheartened him.

He hadn't spent a lick of the wages he'd already drawn. He needed every penny to buy a horse and a good saddle before moving on. He hoped Mr. Wilcox would sell him the spirited black pony he'd favored during the roundup.

With the cattle in the corrals at the rail yard, he lined up with the other boys and waited his turn for his wages. When it came, as Dan Burgess counted the greenbacks into his outstretched hand, he asked about buying the pony. Dan told him to see Mr. Wilcox over at the hotel.

In the hotel bar he found another cowboy, Richard Jacobi—called Jake by all who knew him—waiting to see Wilcox. Along with Jack Thorpe, Jake was one of the top riders in the outfit. Originally from Chicago, he'd enlisted in the navy when he was sixteen and served for five years before heading west to cowboy. He'd been on ships that took him to Asia and Brazil, and in the evenings at the cow camps and in the bunkhouse he told stories of his travels that had everyone wanting to hear more.

"Let me buy you a drink," Jake said, spinning a coin on the counter.

"No, thanks," Patrick replied.

Jake shrugged and ordered another beer for himself. "You hoping Wilcox will keep you on?"

"I'm hoping to buy that black I've been forking."

Jake nodded. "That's a fine pony."

"It is."

"What you gonna call it?" Jake asked.

"I don't know," Patrick replied. "I've never cared to give my ponies names."

"Not ever?" Jake asked, thinking that was mighty strange. On the range, a man's pony was often his only companion and best friend.

"Nope," Patrick said with a shake of his head, "but maybe I will this time. Where are you drifting next?" Riding the chuck line with a partner would be a lot more agreeable than doing it alone.

"I'm hoping to stay put for a spell," Jake said with a grin. "Wilcox is fixing to gather more broncs to train and sell for cow ponies. He's gonna need more than Jack Thorpe to fork them. It wouldn't sit right not to ask him to be kept on, seeing that he wants to talk to me anyhow."

"I wish you luck with it," Patrick said, feeling a stab of envy. A tough waddie with a broken nose from fist fighting for sport in the navy, Jake had worked four gatherings at the Flying W. He was a top hand and stood first if Wilcox planned to take on another steady man.

"I guess you'll be riding the chuck line," Jake said.

"If I can buy that black, I will," Patrick replied, straight-faced.

Jake laughed and finished his beer just as Sam Wilcox entered the bar and called the two men over to an empty table.

"Good, you're both here," he said as he motioned to the barkeep for a bottle and glasses, "so I won't have to work my jawbone twice. Now that the beef roundup is done, I can turn my mind to the ponies. You boys know I've got twenty-some cow ponies started back at the ranch. I want to triple that number and have most of them ready to sell before spring works. The best I'll keep for the Flying W."

He paused as the barkeep brought the glasses and whiskey bottle. "First we'll need to gather the wild broncs from the southern range and cut out the choice ones. My steady hands can do that, but Dan and Jack Thorpe will need a lot of help finishing those ponies. I'd like you two boys to stay on at top-hand wages to get the job done."

Patrick was stunned. Top-hand pay was ten dollars more than hired-hand wages. He opened his mouth, but nothing came out.

Jake Jacobi hooted and slapped Patrick on the back. "We're your boys, all right, Mr. Wilcox," he said, grinning from ear to ear.

Patrick nodded in agreement.

"Good," Wilcox said, raising his glass.

"I'd like to buy that black I've been riding, Mr. Wilcox," Patrick said, reaching for his money.

"Done, for twenty dollars. Tell Dan to take it out of your wages."

"That black is worth twice that," Patrick said.

Wilcox smiled as he finished his shot, put some coins down, and stood. "You're a man who knows good horseflesh. Tell Dan I said twenty-five dollars firm. I'll see you boys back at the ranch."

"Whoo-ee, what an ease to my mind," Jake said after Wilcox left. "Now I won't have to bed down in some empty line camp until spring works. Let's celebrate."

"Maybe later," Patrick replied as he tugged at the frayed shirt he'd put needle and thread to at least a dozen times. "I need to buy a saddle, new boots, and some gear."

Jake slapped his glass down on the table, picked up the whiskey bottle Wilcox had paid for, and tucked it under his arm. "Since I'm feeling flush, with a raise to come, I'll go with you. But I'll shy away if you're planning to do any more horse-trading with the boss. That's the first time I've seen a cowboy open his mouth to pay more for a pony."

"Maybe I'll call him Blackie," Patrick said as they walked out of the hotel.

"Plumb clever," Jake replied laconically.

Patrick laughed. "Not the best I can do, I reckon. How about Cuidado?"

"What's that mean?" Jake Jacobi asked.

"Watch out," Patrick replied.

"Cuidado," Jake said. "Now, that's a good one."

"Then Cuidado it is," Patrick said.

* * *

Throughout the fall, Patrick and Jake worked side by side with Jack Thorpe at the horse corral with the wild broncos gathered from the open range. They culled the top forty ponies, turned the rest back on the range, and got to it. By the week before Christmas, the horses were so well started and the ranch in such good shape for winter that Sam Wilcox gave all the boys Christmas Eve and Christmas Day off.

Except for Patrick and Fats, who'd stayed to do his daily ranch chores, all the hands were in town for a little fun and some shopping. They'd be back for the traditional Christmas dinner at the big house with the boss. This year, Wilcox's widowed daughter, Sallie, who had recently come from Texas with her three girls to live on the ranch, would be there. The oldest girl, Lucinda, was sixteen and a looker. From the talk around the bunkhouse, Patrick knew some of the boys were going to return with new duds so they would be rigged out decent on Christmas Day in hopes Lucinda would find them pleasing to the eye.

Alone in the bunkhouse, Patrick washed his only good pair of pants and a shirt, dried them near the woodstove, stitched up a rip on a sleeve, and pressed everything with an iron he'd borrowed from María, Wilcox's Mexican housekeeper. He knew the boys thought he was too stingy to spend his money, and some had even said outright that his duds were a disgrace to the outfit. He couldn't fault them for that, but he never said a word about why he was tightfisted with his money.

He'd spent most of his wages from the fall works on outfitting himself with a saddle, tarpaulin bedroll, yellow slicker, new chaps, rawhide gloves, a Colt .45 and a holster, boots, a hat, and the two sets of duds he'd bought. He was still toting the Winchester Mr. Wilcox had originally loaned him, buying it outright with money from his first pay as a top hand. Come next payday, Dan Burgess would give him a bill of sale for Cuidado, so he'd own his pony free and clear and have a hundred dollars set aside toward the money he owed Cal. Still, it would take a lot more time to save the rest.

He aimed to not be embarrassed at Christmas supper sitting with the gussied-up girls and fancy-dressed cowboys, but when the time came he was uncomfortable and self-conscious. The only time he'd felt worse was as a ragamuffin begging for food in the mining camps when Ida got too drunk and forgot to feed him.

They all sat at a long table loaded with platters of roasted beef, fried chicken, potatoes, and homemade pies. Sam Wilcox sat at the far end, his daughter and her girls surrounding him. Lucinda, her mother, and her sisters were in their holiday best, with ruffles at their collars and bows in their hair. The cowboys wore spanking-new shirts and flashy bandannas around their necks. Even Fats had spruced up in a white shirt and pair of red suspenders.

Lucinda's mother had placed Patrick as far away from the family as she could, at the other end of the table with Fats and a young, freckle-nose waddie who was riding the chuck line and had showed up for supper. After the food was passed around, Patrick concentrated on his supper and said little. Fats wasn't much of a talker to begin with, and the freckle-nose drifter was too busy packing away the victuals to have much to say. Patrick chewed his beef and felt like there wasn't one waddie in the room he'd call a true friend, not even Jake.

During the meal, Sam Wilcox kept eyeing him. He finally leaned over and said something to Dan Burgess. When the plates had been cleared, the last toast had been made, and the men were making their good nights and filing out, Dan told Patrick to wait for Mr. Wilcox in his office. A good ten minutes passed before Wilcox arrived, looking less than friendly.

"I asked Dan Burgess why one of my top hands would come to my table on Christmas looking like he doesn't have three cents to his name. He said you've been drawing your wages right along. I want to know what you've been doing with it. And I warn you, I was a good, plausible liar in my youth, so you better tell me the truth."

"I've been saving it, Mr. Wilcox."

"All of it?"

"Yes, sir, except for the money I still owe you for the pony you sold me."

"Saving it for what?"

"I've got my reasons, sir, and I don't mean to reflect badly on you or the brand."

"You need to do better than that, son." Wilcox lit a cigar.

"I need a stake to buy back a spread I let go on the Tularosa. It was plain dumb of me, and I mean to get it back."

"I hear the drought hit hard there."

Patrick nodded. "It did, and a lot of nesters have moved on. But the grass is coming back in the high country."

Wilcox nodded approvingly. "If you can get back your land, more power to you. Someday a lot of these boys at the Flying W will be busted-up old waddies with nothing to show for a life's work except stories nobody wants to hear."

"There's truth to that, sir," Patrick said.

"I wish you the best, but while you're working for me I expect you to dress like you're proud of the brand. Fats is going to town for supplies in the morning and you're going with him. Buy some new duds with a few of those greenbacks I've been paying you. It won't set you back that much."

Patrick stood, hat in hand. "Yes, sir. I'd be obliged if you'd keep my plans to yourself. I don't need a bunch of old boys joshing me about turning into a stockman."

Wilcox nodded. "I won't say a word."

"Thank you."

After Patrick left, Sam Wilcox sat and thought over what he'd been told. The cowboy seemed sincere enough and he'd spun a believable story, but Wilcox flat-out figured there was more to it than that. He shucked off thinking about the young cowboy and finished his cigar.

31

Patrick and Jake Jacobi stayed on at the Flying W for a short time after spring works to finish the cow ponies and put them through their paces for a rancher out of California who had a spread along the central coast. The rancher picked out thirty of the best ponies and even tried to buy Cuidado out from under Patrick at a hefty price. Patrick turned him down, so instead the rancher proposed to hire both cowboys to take the horses to his ranch by rail, promising steady work once there. Patrick turned him down again, but Jake jumped at the chance. Working on a ranch in sight of the ocean sounded like pure heaven to him.

At the rail siding in town, Jake and Patrick loaded the ponies on stock cars and said adios.

"Sure you don't want to come with me and see the ocean?" Jake asked with a grin.

"Wrong direction, amigo," Patrick replied as he picked up the rope to his packhorse, a sturdy gray, and climbed on Cuidado.

He waved good-bye and headed north out of town. Over the past few weeks, he'd studied hard about what to do when the job at the Flying W ran out. He had three hundred dollars tucked away, another thirty dollars in his pocket, and enough grub and supplies to get him back to New Mexico, but he was still shy of what he owed Cal. He decided to ride the chuck line north awhile before swinging east, in the hopes he might land a job along the way.

The first night he camped at an empty cabin in the hills protected by an old hound dog that flopped down in front of him and rolled on his back when he arrived. In the morning, he fed the hound a piece of bacon from his breakfast, and the old dog kept him company for a few miles along the trail before turning for home.

Over the next week, he had a few meals and a warm place to lay his head at several high-country ranches that bordered Apache lands, but nobody was hiring. He kept north, climbing steep, pine-covered plateaus, crossing mountain meadows thick with herds of elk, fording fast, clear-running streams shaded by willows, plunging down deep canyons only to raise distant mountains at the crest of an enormous rim. He rode under tall pines that dotted grassy pastures and stopped at small lakes tucked into tiny saucer valleys at the base of soaring peaks still dusted with snow above the timberline.

The untamed land was about the best piece of outdoors Patrick had ever seen, and the solitude that came with it was a balm to his mind. He spotted a grizzly bear ambling through the forest, and a wolf serenaded him at night. At dusk as he snaked wood for a campfire, he saw the flash of a cougar in a mountain meadow, and next morning before first light an owl woke him with its gentle call. Eagles and hawks hunted above on wind currents, woodpeckers beat tattoos that echoed through the woods, and wild turkeys gobbled out of sight in the underbrush. It was one of the best trail rides he'd ever made.

He crossed into New Mexico and passed through the mesa lands on the Zuni Pueblo without stopping. He pushed on to Ramah, a Mormon farm and ranching settlement in a pleasant, tree-shaded valley with thick bottom grass along a wide stream. He stabled his ponies at the livery and in a rickety bathhouse behind the general store he soaked in the tub until the water cooled. After a campfire dinner, he spread out his bedroll on soft hay in the livery and fell asleep before dusk turned to night.

The next day, in a hurry to reach the Tularosa, he moved on without trying to find work, riding through red rimrock country, where tall, thin, wind-carved spires and odd-shaped pinnacles hovered over juniper woodlands. At Inscription Rock he watered his horses at the pool at the base of the mesa and studied the names carved into the stone. For hundreds of years, Spanish explorers, scouts, Civil War soldiers, Catholic priests, army officers, cowboys, and travelers had stopped to chisel their names into the soft stone near the water hole. He added his initials before continuing east.

He followed a wagon road that skirted some northerly mountains and, with the sun low in the west, camped for the night at the edge of lava badlands that reminded him of the Tularosa malpais. To the southwest, a line of mountaintops peeked above the horizon as the setting sun lit them on fire. He went to sleep with the pull of home tugging at his memories.

The next day at Grant, a fueling stop on the railroad, he bought fresh grub for himself and feed for his ponies and camped for the night. Eager to keep moving, he slept poorly and rose early, and by noon he was back in the badlands trailing southeast toward the Rio Grande. Four long days of travel across a rough country of sharp ridges, narrow divides, and staircase mesas brought him at last to a scarp overlooking the twisting green bosque of the Rio

Grande. To the east the Fray Cristobal Mountains, dwarfed by sky and tier upon tier of desert tableland, tumbled across the horizon. On the other side of the cameo-clear mountains, a hundred miles or more from where Patrick sat on his weary pony, was the Tularosa and home. But he wouldn't go there yet.

Three days later he arrived in White Oaks, a mining town on the north end of the Tularosa. He made camp at an abandoned cabin on the outskirts of town, deposited three hundred dollars in the bank under the name of Pat Floyd, went looking for work at the Old Abe Mine, and got hired on as a laborer at two dollars and fifty cents a day.

He worked six ten-hour shifts a week and lived like a hermit at the cabin on fifty cents a day. To the townsfolk he was just another one of the faceless men who disappeared down a thirteen-hundred-foot shaft every morning and every night. He never hated a job more.

On Sundays, he took Cuidado out for a ride, good weather or bad. Leading the gray, he galloped them across the grasslands outside of town, scattering the few remaining antelope herds that hadn't been wiped out for fun by the town folk. There were bones and carcasses all over the flats.

When he got to feeling lonely, he walked to town and looked at the people. Although it was a fair size, with more than two thousand people, White Oaks wasn't much of a hell-raising place. It had only a couple of saloons, the most popular the Little Casino, but no hurdy-gurdy girls worked there. The Ozanne Hotel had a fine dining room, but Patrick had never eaten there because of the cost. He did his shopping on Fridays after work at the Ziegler Store, which stayed open to serve the miners, who'd been paid and needed to buy grub and sundries.

There was a fairly new stone schoolhouse and some fancy two-story homes with gables and latticework porches some mine owners and managers had built. Sometimes, the families were out on the porches when he passed by, but not once did anyone venture a howdy in his direction.

He quit the day he had enough to pay Cal what he owed. He got a shave, a haircut, and a bath, changed into fresh duds, and took his money from the bank. At the cabin he packed his gear on the gray pony and rode out of town feeling like a new man.

His pulse quickened as the Oscura Mountains came into view. There were mountains roundabout as the basin stretched out before him, flinty, dusty, encrusted with the black lava tubes that snaked over the gravelly, rolling land. There was nothing green or grassy about it, nothing comforting, yet it pleased Patrick to see it once again. Old, twisted alligator junipers poked out of deep lava holes, stands of mesquite meandered in shallow draws, sagebrush savannas waved on sacaton flats, and the rolling sugar white sand hills that brushed the shallow lake along the road to Las Cruces sparkled in the morning sun.

There were cattle on the range, but far fewer than before the drought. The land had come back some, but where once tall grasses had flourished, sandy cactus benches now prevailed.

He wanted to keep on riding through the night but pulled up at Malpais Spring instead. He fed the horses, made a cold camp, and slept fitfully, waking from a bad dream that had him seeing the Double K in ruins. Troubled in mind, he saddled up and rode under starlight, raising the Double K at midday. A windmill had been thrown up next to the saddle shed, but aside from that everything looked the same. There were cows and some horses in the pasture, and a saddled pony stood hitched to a corral post near the open barn door.

He reined Cuidado to a stop just as Cal stepped outside. He tipped his hat back, glanced at Patrick, and studied Cuidado.

"That's a thrifty-looking pony," he said, as if nothing bad had ever passed between them.

"He'll do," Patrick replied. There was gray at Cal's temples and a few more wrinkles around his eyes.

"What happened to your saddle?" Cal asked.

"It got stolen," Patrick said, twisting the truth.

"Too bad."

"Yep."

"You here for your money?" Cal asked.

Patrick shook his head. "Nope. I want back in as partner."

Cal smiled. "This hardscrabble place ain't worth the money I gave you."

"Maybe, but its half mine, and I'm here to claim it."

Cal studied Patrick. This wasn't the same man he'd last seen in Juárez. He looked harder and he talked tougher. "You got four hundred dollars?"

Patrick nodded. "I do." He pulled the greenbacks out of his pocket and handed the money to Cal.

Cal counted it. "Four hundred exactly. Light. George is up at the house rustling supper. He's been asking me regular when you'd be coming home. I guess now he'll have to come up with something else to worry me about."

Patrick slid out of his saddle. "I want that paper you made me sign."

"I didn't make you sign anything. But come up to the house and I'll get it for you."

"I'll be there after I take care of my ponies," Patrick said as he led Cuidado and the gray to the barn.

Cal watched Patrick walk away, wondering why he acted hard done by. He'd hoped for Patrick's return for a long time, but it sure wasn't the happy occasion he'd imagined. He decided it wasn't worth trying to read Patrick's mind. He was here, the ranch was half his, and that was that.

At the ranch house, Cal told George that Patrick was back and went to find the bill of sale.

32

onths before Patrick returned to the Double K, Cal had signed a contract with the Indian agent at the Mescalero Apache Reservation to deliver one hundred and fifty head of beef to a place called Pine Tree Canyon after the fall works. With a bank loan, he'd restocked the ranch with whiteface Herefords, running three hundred head of cows, yearlings, and a few newborn calves in the high-country pastures. Proceeds from the sale would pay off the loan and leave enough profit to carry the outfit to next spring.

In August, Cal rode out with Patrick and George to gather the cattle for the drive to the reservation.

"There's one loco longhorn bull up yonder we haven't been able to corral," Cal said as they entered the canyon above the west pasture, the ranch headquarters a far piece in the distance.

"Last of a breed, soon not to be seen hereabouts again," George added with a chuckle. "He's a mean old brindle bull."

"We should shoot it and mount the horns," Patrick said. The ponies and the pack animals slowed as they clambered over the rocky canyon bottom.

George cleared his throat and spit. "Can't say I agree with that. I'd miss the critter."

"He's eating Double K grass," Patrick replied. "I say shoot it."

"I like seeing that old-timer every now and then," Cal said. "I vote to let the brindle live."

George chuckled. "Two to one, the vote goes in favor of the bull."

"When did you become a partner in the Double K?" Patrick snapped.

"You know I ain't," George replied. He gave a yank on the rope to the packhorses trailing behind him and fell silent.

"George has got a voice in how things get run around here," Cal said quietly.

"Is that a fact?" Patrick asked.

"It is for me," Cal answered.

Patrick shrugged. "Have it your way." He loped ahead to where the canyon widened near an arroyo and curled up another draw.

"He ain't the same since he came back," George said grumpily once Patrick was out of earshot.

"He'll come around," Cal replied for the umpteenth time, although he was starting to believe his prediction was wishful thinking.

Patrick hadn't set foot off the ranch since his return. He worked hard, day herding the cattle in the mountain pastures and looking after the outfit's small remuda of cow ponies and pack animals, but he sure didn't make good company. Unless they were talking about ranch business, he had little to say.

Cal figured something bad had happened to Patrick but didn't see a way to ask about it. All he knew was Patrick had drifted into Arizona Territory and worked as a top hand for a big outfit east of

Tucson. There had to be more to it than that, but he'd never met a man with a secret to be kept who appreciated folks meddling in his business.

They reached the first pasture by midmorning, a stretch of land that wandered through gaps, draws, arroyos, and slot canyons in the middle of the mountains. The gathering went off without a hitch. At dusk they built a brush fence to keep the cattle contained in a small canyon and hunkered down over a Dutch-oven meal of beef and potatoes fixed by George.

"This has been about the easiest day gathering in these mountains I've known," Patrick said.

"Herefords are a mite more peaceful to manage," Cal said. "They're not half as cunning as longhorns."

"That's the truth of it," George said as he ladled more beef on Patrick's plate. "But that pony of yours sure makes forking cattle look easy. I've never seen a cow pony cut as good as that one."

"I trained Cuidado myself."

"Well, watch out for Cuidado, I say," George replied with a forced chuckle, "because he sure takes the cake."

"That's quite a moniker you gave him," Cal said as he reached for the coffeepot. "Is it a warning about the horse or the rider?"

Patrick smiled thinly. "Maybe both. How come you stopped raising horses?"

"When the army shut down, the market died."

"I'd like to start back up again," Patrick said, "this time finishing cow ponies. As long as there are cattle outfits, there's gonna be a need for top horses."

Cal refilled his coffee cup. Good cow ponies brought top dollar, and Patrick was right about ranchers always wanting to add some to their remudas. "How many ponies do you have in mind?" he asked.

"I figure twenty-five or thirty could be ready by next fall, if I can round up some good-looking stock after we're done trailing these cows to Mescalero."

"There are a couple of wild mustang herds on the south end of the basin nobody's laid claim to. Fifteen hands mostly, with some Spanish blood from what I can tell."

"You've seen them?"

"Last spring," Cal replied, "when we trimmed the last of our longhorn strays during Oliver Lee's works. I'd say those ponies would do."

Patrick's smile widened a bit. "Then, let's do it."

It took three more days to gather all the livestock and drive them to the west pasture near the ranch. There they cut out and corralled the cattle for the trail drive to Mescalero and spent the rest of the day preparing for an early start in the morning.

After George cleaned up the dinner dishes and jingled his way to the casita, where he now bunked, Patrick unexpectedly appeared in the front room. He sat in a chair next to the desk where Cal was doing some figuring in a ledger book and didn't say a word.

"Do we need to talk business?" Cal asked as he closed the book.

Patrick nodded. "Is my name on the ranch account at the bank?"

"It is," Cal replied.

"I can get money out under my name?"

"You can, if we have a balance and it's under five hundred dollars. Otherwise, it takes both of us to sign for it."

"Do we have money?"

"Some."

"How much?"

"Three hundred thirty-seven dollars, but that's loan money I'm hoping not to have to use."

"You're keeping the four hundred I gave you?"

"I am for now."

"Can I see all the papers the bank has about the spread?"

"Yep. But your name isn't on the loan I took to buy the Herefords."

Patrick shrugged. "That doesn't matter to me."

Cal pushed the ledger across the desk. "This shows all our costs and earnings for the year so far. Take a gander if you've a mind to. The books for earlier years are in the bottom drawer."

Patrick took the ledger. "I'm thinking we should let George go after he helps us trail the cattle to Mescalero."

"With ponies to train and cattle to watch over, that would stretch the two of us real thin."

"I'll pick up any part of the load you can't."

Cal raised an eyebrow. Maybe he'd lost a step, but he didn't cotton to the idea of Patrick calling him an old man. "I'll do my fair share and we'll keep George on."

Patrick opened the ledger, leaned forward, and paged through it under the lamplight. "What are we paying him?"

"Thirty a month. He's worth forty-five."

He looked up from the ledger. "We could use that money other ways."

Cal shook his head. "We can always use money other ways, but that old boy stays. For three months, he worked for his keep and didn't draw wages at all."

"Well, that was right charitable of him, but I say he goes."

Cal shook his head. "Nope, he stays. We've got rustlers roaming the basin and have lost eight cows already this year. I'm not about to let go a good hand who knows how to handle a gun and cares about our brand."

Patrick chewed his lip. "If you're that mule-headed about it, fine."

Cal patted the left side of the desk. "In this other bottom drawer you'll find the ranch deeds, land titles, government paperwork, and the legal documents about our partnership. Now that you're showing interest in the business end of things, it's best that you acquaint yourself with the details."

"I'll start right now if you'll give up your seat," Patrick said.

Cal pushed back the chair and stood. "If you have any questions, we can talk about them on the trail."

"*Bueno,*" Patrick said as he came around the desk.

Cal said good night and went to his room thinking Patrick's newfound interest in the operation of the ranch was something he needed to get used to and pronto.

33

On the first day of the trail drive, Cal expected Patrick to talk more about the business of running the ranch, but the subject never came up. Nor did he have anything to say about the legal papers, which included Cal's will naming him as his heir.

They reached Tularosa after resting the herd overnight at Malpais Spring and made camp outside of town on the road to Mescalero. George stayed with the herd while Cal and Patrick paid a visit to Ignacio. They found him in the courtyard of his hacienda sharpening axes and saws for his annual firewood trip to the mountains.

He put down a saw, grinned, and clasped Patrick's shoulder. "Tell me, did you see the ocean?"

Patrick shook his head. "Never got west of Arizona."

"Ah, how sad. I would like to see the ocean before I die. All that water, it must be *maravilloso,* and the sound of the waves. But tell me about Arizona."

"It's a lot like New Mexico, except hotter and not as pretty most places. Can't say I favored it."

"Where will you go next?"

"I'm sticking right here," Patrick said with a tight smile. "I had a touch of being dull brained for a time, but I wised up before old Cal could hornswoggle me out of the Double K."

Ignacio shot a questioning look at Cal, who showed no reaction.

"Let me go and get Teresa and the children," Ignacio said. "They will want to see you after so long a time."

"I'm hankering for a drink to wash down the dust," Patrick said. "Maybe later."

"Where are Teresa and the children?" Cal asked, ignoring Patrick's hurry to get away.

"At her mother's. All the aunts are together making clothes for the young ones. Stitching and talking, for days now."

"Isn't that the way of women?" Cal said with a laugh.

"Are you two gonna dawdle and jawbone?" Patrick asked impatiently.

"For a time," Cal replied softly.

"Then I'm gonna mosey to the cantina for that drink."

"But you must tell me more about Arizona," Ignacio pleaded.

"Nothing more to tell," Patrick replied as he gathered up the reins to Cuidado. "I hired out for a while, trained some cow ponies, and rode home."

Ignacio looked quizzical. "*No más?*"

"No more than that."

"What happened to your old pony?"

"I had to shoot him," Patrick said. "Adios."

"Adios." Ignacio turned to Cal as Patrick rode away. "I got coffee and some of Teresa's *bizcochitos* inside."

"I'm your man," Cal said.

In the big room where the family cooked and ate, and the two oldest children slept on the *bancos* near the fireplace, Ignacio and

Cal sat at the long table, drank coffee, and ate Teresa's sugar cookies.

"My cousin Edmundo saw Patrick in White Oaks," Ignacio said. "He said Patrick was working at the Old Abe Mine."

Cal raised an eyebrow. "Not just passing through?"

Ignacio shook his head. "He saw him on Sundays riding that black pony, or buying supplies at the general store on paydays."

"First I heard of it. He hasn't had a hankering to tell me much about his time away. Came back hell-bent to make a go of the ranch."

"That's good, no?" Ignacio said.

"I hope so, but he sure ain't good company. But then, he's never had an overly friendly way with people."

"Edmundo said he was using a different name in White Oaks."

Cal reached for another cookie. "A go-by name usually means a man is hiding something."

"*Qué?*"

"I don't know, except he lost everything he left home with, right down to his rain slick, bedroll, saddle, and guns. He said his saddle got stolen, but I don't know any cowboy worth his salt who'd let that happen. It sure wouldn't have happened around decent, honest folks. And for a man to lose his guns without so much as a fight makes no sense unless he had to give them over to the law."

"He became bandito perhaps," Ignacio speculated, "running from the law."

"Could be, but I'll fault no man for that without knowing the whys and wherefores."

"I used to think Patrick would be like his father, but not so much anymore."

"Well, he's a loner for sure, but that's no crime," Cal said. "Besides, who's to say he won't find his way to being a good man?"

"But maybe not an easy man," Ignacio said. "Teresa prays for him every night. She says he has a troubled soul."

"Well, that's a fact." Cal finished his coffee and stood. "I plumb forgot how good Teresa's coffee is."

"Maybe you'll come back for more."

"Count on it."

In the courtyard, Cal said good-bye to Ignacio. On his way to the cantina, he spotted Patrick's pony hitched outside Coghlan's saloon and stopped. Inside, Patrick was nowhere in sight, but Dick Turknet and four tough-looking hombres were at a table near the end of the bar. In spite of his agreement with Coghlan to stay out of his establishment, Cal wasn't about to turn his back on Dick Turknet and leave. He ambled to the bar and ordered a shot. It didn't take Turknet long to mosey over.

"Are you gonna pester me?" Cal asked.

Turknet shook his head. "You look dusty. Let me buy you a drink."

"That's mighty generous, but your boss might not appreciate such a friendly gesture."

"I ain't working for Coghlan no more." Turknet called the barkeep over and asked for glasses and a bottle.

Cal had heard the king of Tularosa now wore a shaky crown. Talk was his Three River Ranch was about to go into foreclosure.

"Did you quit or get let go?" he asked.

"Let go," Turknet answered as he poured. "Coghlan knows how to make money, but not how to keep it. He's selling off cows to pay his debts. Me and a bunch of the boys are gonna have to start riding the chuck line soon."

"That's a damn shame," Cal said as he raised his glass and downed his drink, thinking the idea of Turknet riding the chuck line was pretty far-fetched. "Have you seen my young pard?"

"He's getting a poke," Turknet said. "One of the new girls caught his eye."

Cal nodded. What had happened to the whore in Juárez ran through his mind, and it vexed him that Patrick might make the same sort of trouble for himself again.

"I see you trailed a bunch of cattle into town," Turknet said.

"You got an eagle eye, old hoss," Cal said as he refilled his glass. "You fixin' to steal them?"

Turknet laughed. "Why bother? Coghlan ain't buying rustled beef right now."

"That's mighty comforting." Cal raised his glass and slugged back the whiskey.

"You got a buyer for those cows?" Turknet asked.

"I surely do," Cal answered.

"Good for you." Turknet spun a coin on the bar to pay for the drinks. "Adios."

"So long," Cal said.

Turknet and his companions filed out of the saloon. Cal gave the ruffians a quick once-over. Their boots were dusty, their hats battered and sweat stained, but their tied-down six-shooters looked whistle clean. He doubted any of them had forked a horse as hired hands much.

Ten minutes later, Patrick sauntered into the saloon from the door to the wagon yard, where the hurdy-gurdy girls had their rooms. He spotted Cal at the bar and came over.

"You got nothing better to do than snoop on me?" Patrick asked.

"Whoa, haul in your neck," Cal said. "I just stopped in to wet my

whistle." A young, slender soiled dove stepped into the saloon looking none the worse for wear, but she didn't look sunny and chipper
either as she moved toward a lone customer at a back table.

"You quit me over a whore," Patrick snapped.

"No, I quit you over what you did to a whore," Cal replied, "and
I'll do it again if need be."

Patrick nodded at the girl. "Does she look beat-up?"

"Not that I can tell."

"That's right," Patrick said, "because I'll never give you cause to
try to take the Double K away from me like you did last time."

Cal looked at Patrick in amazement. "Have you got air between
your ears? This idea you got stuck in your *cabeza* that I tried to
swindle you is plumb loco. Didn't you read the papers in my desk?
You stand to own the whole shebang, just like your pappy wanted."

"I read them. It doesn't mean you can't change your mind and
have a lawyer draw new papers."

"You're talking crazy," Cal said, "and we've got no time for it
right now. Dick Turknet and his outfit are planning to steal our
cattle and we'll need help to stop them."

"How do you know?"

"Because he's chuckleheaded."

"How many men does he have?"

"Counting Turknet, five that I know of."

"Who can we get?"

"I'm hoping Ignacio and his brother Antonio will join up. They
can close herd the cows while you, me, and George find a way to
persuade Turknet and his lads to steal livestock elsewhere. They'll
shadow us by daylight and make their move at dusk when they think
we're about to make camp. And it won't be peaceable."

"How do we stop them?" Patrick asked.

"We'll surround them."

"Now who's loco?"

"I'll explain later," Cal replied. "Let's get going. Turknet will make his move before we get too far off the basin. You tell George, while I talk with Ignacio."

* * *

An hour before the first stirring of dawn, George, Ignacio, and his father, Cesario—who refused to be left out of the scheme—started the herd east toward Round Mountain. Behind an abandoned nester's shack within sight of the wagon road, Cal, Patrick, and Antonio waited. As the sun topped Sierra Blanca and splashed the day across the Tularosa, Dick Turknet and his four companions loped by, trailing one pack animal.

"I do believe old Dick lied to me more than once yesterday," Cal said when the riders were beyond earshot.

"How so?" Patrick asked.

"Because one pack animal can't carry enough victuals and such to get five riders very far. I'm guessing those lads are still working for Coghlan and he plans to sell our cattle to pay some debts."

"Coghlan," Antonio said, "is a *puta,* and his riders *ladrones.*" He spit to accentuate his point.

Cal smiled at Antonio, who looked a lot like Ignacio except his nose wasn't crooked from getting broken in a fistfight. "I agree they're whores and thieves, amigo. A low-down bunch, every mother's son of them."

They waited thirty minutes before following Turknet and his gang. About a mile up the road, the horse tracks veered out of the canyon and onto a game trail that climbed a rocky foothill where only the stumps of trees and scant underbrush remained after years of woodcutting by the villagers. The last scramble up the trail brought them to a rise, where they drew rein and could just make out miniature men on horseback beyond, cresting an equally barren hill.

"Best we stay back a bit more," Cal said.

Topping the next hill, they found a stand of mesquite in a hollow and watched as Turknet and his lads paced slowly down toward the canyon to the thin ribbon of wagon road that made a slow curl toward Round Mountain.

When the horsemen passed out of sight, they trailed behind, careful not to show themselves. To be sure they hadn't been spotted, Cal sent Patrick on a long loop to see if Turknet had dropped one of his men behind to cut sign. Patrick came back with an all clear and the trio moved cautiously on.

Cal had told George to bed down the cattle outside of Bent, a small ranching area about ten miles east of Tularosa with a wide-open pasture of good grass and water. He figured it would be a perfect spot for Turknet to make his move. He'd most likely want to attack the camp directly, gun down any opposition, and night drive the cattle to the Three Rivers Ranch.

With the sun about to touch the highest peaks of the San Andres to the west, Cal left Patrick and Antonio behind in a hollow and went on foot up a stiff trail above the canyon until the sound of horses and the smell of tobacco smoke brought him to a stop. He moved quietly through a stand of cedar and juniper trees and sidestepped a tangle of mountain mahogany. He worked his way down the canyon wall to a shelf that overlooked the pasture where the Herefords were grazing under George's watchful eye. Ignacio and Cesario were busy setting up camp by the creek. Below him,

Dick Turknet and his boys were in among some pine trees, likewise watching.

Cal silently backtracked to the hollow and scratched a map in the dirt for Patrick and Antonio.

"We go in slow and easy," he said. "Once we're in the trees behind Turknet and his boys, Patrick, you take the right flank and, you take the left, Antonio. I'll come in from the rear.

"I'll give Turknet a warning. When the gunplay starts, George knows to cut off any riders trying to escape in his direction. Ignacio and his father will mill the cattle to keep them from stampeding."

"You got it all sorted out, do you?" Patrick said.

He looked at Patrick. "That's right. Don't stop shooting until they do. Picket the horses, get your rifles, and follow me. Not a sound."

It took the good part of an hour to work their way to where Turknet and his men waited. As Patrick and Antonio veered off to their positions, the memory of the Hembrillo Canyon battle where Ignacio had been wounded passed through Cal's mind. He was about to go to war again, with Ignacio and another Kerney on his side. Life sure threw strange twists of fate at a body.

Silently he counted off two minutes as he watched the outlaws. They were hunkered down, holding the reins to their ponies, ready to mount and ride.

"Turknet," Cal called out from behind a tree, his rifle aimed at Dick's broad back. "You and your boys throw down your guns and ride away before somebody gets killed."

Turknet wheeled and drew his six-gun. Cal shot him in the side as he pulled the trigger. He twisted and fell to the ground. His men poured lead at Cal, bullets gouging the tree trunk and slashing through the branches.

Patrick and Antonio opened up, and the frightened screech of a wounded pony sliced over the gunfire. A rustler pitched backward as he tried to mount, and his riderless horse galloped into the pasture headed straight for George. Another outlaw crumpled to his knees. Suddenly the shooting stopped, followed by a long silence. Cal could make out one man huddled behind the dead pony and another pressed flat against a large log.

"We're done," one of the outlaws finally said. "Don't kill us."

"Get up, leave your guns on the ground, and step out into the clear," Cal said.

Two men rose with their hands above their heads and walked into the open. Light was fading fast and the spooked cattle had stopped milling. Cal sent George back to help settle the critters down, told Patrick to guard the prisoners, and had Antonio ride back on one of the rustlers' ponies to get their horses. He checked the two dead men and found Dick Turknet propped up against a tree trunk still breathing.

"I'm bucked out, old hoss," Turknet said. "Was it you that killed me?"

"It was."

Turknet coughed. "Good. I'd hate to have had some green hand shoot me dead."

"Were you planning to trail the cattle to Three Rivers?" Cal asked.

Turknet shook his head. "No," he wheezed. "Coghlan has a chuck wagon and some waddies waiting near the White Oaks road to San Antonio. The beef was to be trailed there pronto, sold, and shipped east."

"Smart."

"He wanted you dead."

"Not yet," Cal said.

Turknet coughed and stopped breathing. Cal closed his eyes, stretched him out on the ground, went to Patrick, and told him to have the two captives bury their dead partners. It was dark when the men finished and Patrick brought them into camp.

After feeding them some beans and tortillas, George tied them up for the night. "Who gets to take these boys to jail?" he asked.

Cesario grinned. "Me and my *hijos* will do it."

"*Gracias,* Cesario," Cal said.

"*Por nada,* amigo. It has been fun to help catch Coghlan's *ladrones* in the act. I will enjoy telling the marshal. Maybe this time Coghlan will be arrested."

"Don't count on it," Cal replied.

The gunplay had pretty much taken all the steam out of the men, so there wasn't much more talk around the campfire that night.

34

In the morning, Cesario and his sons rode off with their captives to Tularosa while Cal, Patrick, and George started the cattle toward Mescalero. They raised the village by midday. Tucked into a narrow valley surrounded by a deep pine forest, the headquarters for the Indian agency was spit-and-polish tidy, just like the army officer who ran it. A large administration building dominated the village. Nearby stood an adobe school with separate dormitories for boys and girls, the agent's residence, some smaller staff cottages, and an assortment of barns, outbuildings, and corrals. On a grassy plain in front of the government building, the Stars and Stripes flew on a flagpole. A small herd of sheep tended by an old Apache quickly scattered as the cattle clattered into the open field behind the buildings.

Some Apaches lived close by in shabby log cabins and a few wickiups and tepees scattered over a level meadow near a clear mountain spring that cascaded down a small mesa. The tepees faced east, with woodpiles stacked along the north side, and the log cabins were small, one-room buildings made from rough lumber milled on the reservation.

Cal had Patrick and George rest the critters while he met with the agent. First Lieutenant Victor Emanuel Stottler, a West Point graduate, had come to his post with the strong support of evangelists bent on saving the souls of the savage Apaches. An unfriendly man with thin lips and a double chin, Stottler greeted Cal with no more than a nod and quickly showed him on a map where the cattle were to be taken.

"It's another day's journey through mountain passes to Pine Tree Canyon," Stottler said, tapping the map with a wooden pointer. "There is ample grass and water along the way. One of my Apache police officers will guide you. You'll be paid after the cattle are inspected by my livestock superintendent."

"Fair enough," Cal said. "But why bed these critters down so far away?"

Stottler raised an eyebrow. "That is not your business, Mr. Doran. Just deliver the animals. My man will be at Pine Tree to conduct the inspection."

"Whatever you say, Lieutenant," Cal replied.

"Very good," Stottler said with the hint of a frown as he looked out his window at the browsing cattle. "Please move your cows along at once. The children at the school are sometimes allowed to play in the meadow behind the cabins and they are by disposition lazy and filthy enough in spite of our best attempts to teach them otherwise. I'll not have them tracking fresh cow manure into the dormitories or the classrooms."

"Glad to oblige," Cal replied.

Outside, a young Apache police officer waited next to a wagon loaded with supplies and pulled by two mules. His hair was short under his wide-brimmed hat and he had high cheekbones and a very narrow, long nose that gave him a serious look. He nodded at Cal without speaking, climbed onto the seat, and headed the team down a rutted road toward a gap in the thick mountain forest.

Cal signaled to Patrick and George to get the cattle moving, and by the time they joined up they were deep in a long canyon with tall evergreen trees so thick on the steep mountainsides that sunlight danced and dappled through the shadows. In the quiet forest, the cattle plodded along contentedly behind the wagon, hardly making a sound, never wandering into the scrub oak that lined the road. Cal figured it to be the most tranquil trail drive an old brushpopper could ever imagine.

The Apache police officer stopped his wagon long before sunset at a stream bank thick with grass that widened into a beautiful open field fringed by stately evergreens.

"Tomorrow, Pine Tree Canyon, half day," he said to Cal as he unhitched his mules.

"You speak American," Cal said. There was something familiar about the Apache, but Cal couldn't place him.

"All police must," the Apache replied. "Bear and wolves come here. Be careful."

He walked his mules to the stream to drink, and Cal loped his pony to tell Patrick and George, who were watching over the loitering animals, that they were bedding down for the night.

At camp, with time to fix a good meal, George got the Dutch oven going over hot coals, greased it, sliced beef off a quarter section he'd wrapped in canvas, put it in the pot, threw in some salt, and covered it with hot coals. While the beef cooked, he cut potatoes into a skillet greased with bacon fat and got the coffeepot going. When the beef was far enough along, he fried the potatoes up brown and added a can of corn when they were cooked.

Except for not having hot biscuits, Cal allowed that it was the best trail meal he'd had in a long time. He kept his eye on the Apache policeman, who sat across from Patrick, staring at him over the coffee cup he cradled in his hands. He hadn't said a word since joining the crew for supper.

"Walks Alone," he finally said, throwing a stone at Patrick. It hit him in the chest.

"What?" Patrick asked, startled.

"You threw rocks at me. You sat next to me under the window where my sister lay. I gave you the name Walks Alone because you always hid from your father."

"That was you?"

The Apache nodded.

"You never spoke."

"You are white eyes. Nothing to say."

"What's your name?" Patrick asked.

"James Kaytennae. They call my sister Crooked Running Woman because of her leg. Once, she ran like the wind, beating all the boys, now no more. Where is your father, Walks Alone?"

"Dead," Patrick said flatly. "Don't call me that."

James Kaytennae turned to Cal. "You captured me in the mountains with his father."

"I remember that," Cal said.

"I have been told you are a policeman."

"I have been sometimes," Cal replied.

Kaytennae lifted his hat. "They make us cut our hair like you white eyes. If I grow it, Stottler puts me in guardhouse and takes my allotment of food. No longer policeman."

"That's no kind of law to pay any mind to," Cal said.

"It's Stottler who makes law here. Children run away from school to the camps, he puts parents in guardhouse, sometimes the children. School boss too nice to the children, he sends school boss away. To leave Mescalero, you must have paper from Stottler. Here, everybody is in his guardhouse, except no walls."

"That's not so hard to take," Patrick said, remembering the walls at Yuma Prison.

"Better I should have died before I stole the chicken from your father's ranchero."

A wolf howled in the distance. Patrick dumped his plate in the wash bucket. "Well, you ain't dead," he said. "Leastways, not yet."

"Dead inside is worse," Kaytennae replied, looking him in the eye.

"I wouldn't know about that," Patrick said. He turned away and reached for Cuidado's reins. "I'll take first watch."

Cal stretched out. "That's fine with me. Tonight maybe we should call you Rides Alone."

"That's not funny," Patrick snapped.

Across the campfire, James Kaytennae almost smiled.

* * *

The road to Pine Tree Canyon left the meadow and climbed the side of a mountain before dropping down to a long woodland funnel between two peaks. They emerged into a sun-drenched serpentine canyon that gradually became an expansive high-country valley. An adobe house sat at the foot of a parklike hill. A nearby rushing stream tumbled down from the mountains and fed a big pond next to a large log barn and a horse corral.

"Sure is a pretty slice of country," George said.

"Good water, good grass," Cal agreed, "but I'd miss the views across the Tularosa."

"But not the dust, I reckon," Patrick added.

"Not the dust," Cal echoed.

They set the cattle to graze in the pasture unattended and dismounted at the house, where James Kaytennae was unloading the wagon, helped by two women. The youngest one caught Patrick's eye. She had dark, curly hair, bright blue eyes, an oval face with high cheekbones, and a slender figure. The other woman wasn't much older, Patrick reckoned, and looked to be the girl's sister, although she wasn't near as fetching.

He tipped his hat in the girl's direction and got a startled look in response.

"You men might as well light," the older woman said as she shouldered a bag of beans. "I'm Ruth Dunphy. I expect my husband to be here shortly. There's coffee on the stove."

She turned and hurried toward the open door.

"Thank you, ma'am," Cal called after her, easing out of his saddle.

The pretty girl followed along behind with big tins of coffee wrapped in her arms.

"You coming?" Patrick asked Kaytennae as he slid to the ground.

Kaytennae shook his head. "Work to do, and Tom Dunphy doesn't like Apaches unless they're Christians."

"I'll lend a hand," Patrick said as Cal and George jingled their way inside.

He pitched in, handing sacks, boxes, and tins to the two women, who came and went together, never out of each other's sight, rushing as fast as they could to get the stores into the house. The younger woman was small boned, light-footed, and soft curved. Her hair was piled high in a messy way that charmed Patrick.

He tried conversation when she stumbled carrying a bag of flour. "Are you hurt?"

She shook her head mutely in reply as Dunphy's wife gave him a sharp look.

He tried again when he handed her a carton of canned peaches. "The juice at the bottom of the can is what I like the best," he said awkwardly. "How about you?"

It won him an alarmed look from the girl and a glowering stare from Dunphy's wife.

"What's her name?" he asked Kaytennae after the wagon was emptied and the women had gone inside.

"Emma. Her family was rubbed out someplace far away in Texas. Her sister is Dunphy's wife. She came here five moons ago."

"She sure ain't much of a talker," Patrick said.

Kaytennae shrugged. "When I first bring her here in the wagon, she talked, talked, talked, all the time. Now, not so much."

"She seemed scared," Patrick said.

"Dunphy has a heavy hand," Kaytennae said.

Inside the house, Emma had disappeared. Dunphy's wife gave Patrick a weak smile and poured him a cup of coffee.

"Mr. Dunphy will be here soon," she said nervously.

"Yes, ma'am," Patrick replied. "Where's your sister?"

"She's not feeling well."

"Sorry to hear it," Patrick said, thinking the girl hadn't looked sick at all.

Mrs. Dunphy turned her attention to the boxes, sacks, and tins of food and supplies stacked on the floor and began putting them on the shelves of a big cabinet near the cookstove or in large tin and wooden boxes that sat on the dirt floor. Everything in the room, including the round dining table, the chairs, even the stove, looked scrubbed spotless. There wasn't a speck of dust or dirt around the firewood box, and under a small window a brightly polished lamp sat on a small table next to an open Bible. Patrick had never seen such a clean house.

"Can we help, ma'am?" Cal asked.

Ruth Dunphy turned and bushed hair from her face. "No. It all must be done exactly so. A place for everything, and everything in its place."

"Well, then, we'll wait for your husband on the porch," Cal said.

"Yes, that would be best," Ruth Dunphy replied as she carefully put the last can of peaches with all the others, label side out.

Patrick left his untouched coffee and followed Cal and George to the porch. "Did the girl look sick to you?" he asked.

"Didn't have much of a chance to tell," Cal replied. "Dunphy's missus herded her into the other room as soon as the supplies were unloaded."

"I never saw a woman in such a panic to get her victuals stowed," George said.

"That girl isn't sick; she's scared," Patrick said. "Kaytennae says Dunphy is hard on the women."

"That may be," Cal said, "but it's Dunphy's home and we've no cause to interfere because of it."

Down by the pond, James Kaytennae had unhitched his team of mules and was washing them down.

"I'll water the horses," Patrick said as he grabbed the reins and started them toward the pond.

"You've only seen that girl Emma once before?" he asked Kaytennae at the pond after the ponies were watered.

"You not see her again inside?" Kaytennae asked.

"Nope, she disappeared."

"It is same with me. Many times I come here and I don't see her much. Today is different; Dunphy not here yet. Other times, he hides her."

"Where?"

Kaytennae shrugged.

"Does he hide his wife?"

"Not the wife," Kaytennae replied.

"That's mighty peculiar."

Kaytennae shrugged again, looked over Patrick's shoulder, and raised his chin. "Dunphy coming now."

In the distance a rider hazing a string of horses cantered toward them.

"Be careful around him, Walks Alone," James said. "He has snake in him."

"My name is Patrick, not Walks Alone."

"It is good to have more than one name," Kaytennae replied with a slight smile.

As Dunphy drew near, Patrick stepped over to the horse corral, opened the gate, and looked up at the man as he drove the ponies into the enclosure. He had close-set eyes under thick brows and a heavy jaw that gave him an ornery expression.

"Are you Cal Doran?" he demanded as Patrick swung the gate closed.

"Nope, he's over at the house waiting on you," Patrick answered.

Dunphy wheeled his horse. "Saddle up and bring those ponies along. I want to take a look at each and every one of them cows you brought."

Patrick ambled back to the horses as Dunphy cantered toward the house. "That's one thorny character," he said to James Kaytennae as he climbed on Cuidado.

"He stirs many to anger," Kaytennae replied. "Someday he gets killed, I think."

* * *

At the end of the day, after the cattle had been inspected and tallied and the paper for payment signed, Tom Dunphy invited Cal, Patrick, and George to the house for supper and offered them the barn to bed down in overnight. Excluded from Dunphy's hospitality, James Kaytennae spread his bedroll under the wagon, where he would dine on jerked beef and cold biscuits.

As they cleaned up at the well before supper, Patrick repeated to Cal and George what James Kaytennae had told him about Dunphy and the girl.

"Maybe it's none of our business," George said as he slicked down his hair.

"Something's not right," Patrick retorted hotly.

The notion that Patrick seemed genuinely concerned about the girl pleased Cal, and from what he'd heard, Patrick had cause to fret. "If she's not at supper, we'll ask about her," he said, "but not right away."

Patrick smiled, an honest, true smile. "Good."

There was no sign of Emma as the men settled down at the table to eat. Ruth Dunphy served up a stew and silently picked at her meal while her husband jawboned about how hard it was to get the heathen Apaches to care for the five thousand sheep Lieutenant Stottler had purchased as part of his scheme to turn the Indians into responsible farmers.

"Out in the camps, all they do is slaughter a lamb and cook it when they get hungry," Dunphy complained. "Nobody looks after the animals. It's easy pickings for the wolves and coyotes."

"Can't say I'd like herding sheep either," Cal said.

"They're all just lazy beggars, getting everything for free," Dunphy added.

"Once they were free," Cal replied as he pushed his empty plate away. "That was mighty good stew, ma'am."

"A bit more?" Ruth Dunphy asked.

"I'd be obliged if you would let me take some of your cooking to the Indian, ma'am. Doesn't seem fair to cut him out of such good fixings."

Her hand froze in midair.

"By thunder, no," Dunphy said sharply.

Cal ignored Dunphy and smiled at his wife. "Sure would be mighty Christian of you, ma'am."

"I said no," Dunphy sputtered. "We break bread only with God-fearing folks in this house."

"Where's Emma?" Patrick asked softly.

Cal swung his gaze to Dunphy. "That's been troubling my mind, also. Where is that pretty girl?"

Dunphy glared at his wife.

"Where is she?" Patrick prodded.

"Sickly tonight," Dunphy replied slowly, his gaze locked on his wife. "Isn't that right?"

Ruth Dunphy nodded and dropped her gaze.

"She seemed all right earlier," Patrick said.

"I said she's sick," Dunphy said, his voice rising.

"You are not a plausible liar, sir," Cal said, placing his six-gun on the table, his hand on the grip.

Dunphy's face turned red. "No need for that."

"Maybe not," Cal said. "Take a look, Patrick."

Dunphy's wife started praying, head lowered, hands clasped, eyes squeezed shut. Color drained from Dunphy's face.

In the bedroom Patrick found Emma gagged and bound to the bed. A straw mattress and a blanket were on the floor next to the bed. He wondered if that was where Dunphy's wife slept. He freed Emma's hands, removed the gag, and asked if she wanted to leave.

She whispered, "Yes, yes, yes."

He led her out of the bedroom past where husband and wife sat like statues under the watchful eyes of Cal and George, who'd gathered up Dunphy's six-gun and rifle.

"We're leaving now," Patrick said to Ruth Dunphy. "You're welcome to come with us."

Ruth Dunphy shook her head no.

Cal waited for Patrick and the girl to pass outside. "I sure hope there aren't any more young womenfolk back home planning to come and stay with y'all," he said. "If I hear different, it may prompt me to pay another visit."

* * *

The party arrived at Mescalero and stopped at James Kaytennae's cabin, a one-room affair not much bigger than a tepee, with a cookstove in the middle of the room vented by a pipe through the ceiling. The dirt floor was covered in blankets, animal skins, and boxes that held Kaytennae's important possessions. Several long rifles rested against a wall, and a coat and several hats hung on pegs near the door. There were no chairs, so everyone sat on the floor while Kaytennae got a fire going to boil coffee.

"Please don't say anything about what happened to me," Emma pleaded. It was the first she'd spoken since leaving Pine Tree Canyon.

"The man should be made to answer," Patrick said.

Emma shook her head. "I'm sorry, I can't. Please don't tell."

"Why is that, miss?" Cal asked.

"I'm going to have a baby," she said.

George shook his head. "It ain't right what he done. Nor what your sister allowed."

"Maybe I will shoot him," James Kaytennae said matter-of-factly.

Emma looked at the solemn-faced men. "You've all been so good and brave to help me; please do me this one last favor."

Each man nodded.

"Thank you."

"How are you going to get by?" Patrick asked.

"I don't know."

"Without folks asking a passel of questions?" Cal added.

"I don't know."

"Why don't you come with us to Tularosa?" Cal suggested. "We've got friends there who might help."

"I have nowhere else to go," Emma said.

"Then it's settled," Patrick announced.

"I'll take you in the wagon," James Kaytennae said as he poured coffee into tin cups. "Stottler will go loco and give me the boot like he did the school boss."

Emma shook her head. "I wouldn't want that."

Kaytennae grinned. "It's okay. Time for somebody else to be police."

35

On the eve of her seventeenth birthday, after a long, difficult labor, Emma Murray gave birth to a baby girl. She'd spent sixteen hours in constant pain, sweating and swearing with each contraction. When the baby came, it made no sound for what seemed the longest time, and in her exhausted state, Emma believed it to be dead. Teresa slapped it on the bottom and the baby uttered a feeble cry. She cut the umbilical cord, cleaned up the afterbirth, bathed the infant, and put her in Emma's arms before sending Ignacio on his way across the Tularosa to the Double K with news of the event.

"She is *bella*," Teresa said. "Beautiful."

Emma looked down at her daughter. She was bright pink, with damp, dark hair on her tiny head. She wiggled her little legs, gave a tiny wail, and smacked her lips.

"Yes," Emma replied as she smiled at her daughter, "she is."

"Do you have a name for the little one?" Teresa asked.

"Molly," Emma answered, "after my mother. Only she loved me."

"And now you have Molly to love," Teresa said.

"What will happen next, little Molly?" Emma crooned as she studied her baby girl.

"Your *hija* will sleep, and then she will want your milk."

Emma smiled. "No, I mean in the future."

"Patrick has come to visit you more times than I can count," Teresa said. "He rides here from the ranch just to see you. A very long, hard journey. Has there been no talk of a future between you?"

"I do most of the talking," Emma replied. "He sits and looks at me. Sometimes he smiles."

"And says nothing?"

"Almost. He'll talk about the horses he's training, or how the cattle are doing, but not much more than that. I know he's not stupid."

Teresa laughed as she adjusted Emma's blanket. "Patricio *estúpido*? He has faults, but that is not one of them."

"Cal told me about his early years before his father found him," Emma said.

"*Muy* dreadful. Yet he is not uncaring to you," Teresa said with a smile. "He comes to see you over and over. Surely you must know that he finds you beautiful."

Emma nodded. Since she was twelve years old, men had looked at her with more than passing interest. Until Thomas Dunphy, she'd not minded their attention. "Yes, but I want more from a man than silent company."

"He will be here again before a day passes. Ask him of his intentions."

"I know what his intentions are," Emma said, shaking her head. "He wants to either marry me or have me for his own. I wish I could live my life beholden to no man."

Teresa patted Emma's hand. "To do that, you'd be forced to lay with many vaqueros at Coghlan's saloon, and still you would not be free. Rest now. Soon Molly will be hungry."

"You have been so good to me," Emma said sleepily.

"Hush," Teresa said as she slipped out of the room and closed the door.

For the next several hours she sat in the chair she'd placed by the door, listening for any sounds, ready to jump up to help Emma and the baby if needed. As soon as the *hija* arrived and the danger passed, Teresa's mother had hurried Juan, Sofia, Bernardo, and Miguel away. The house, normally filled with the sound of children's laughter and voices, was unusually quiet.

She thought about Patrick and Emma, wondering if they could make a life together, have some happiness.

* * *

Patrick arrived the following evening. Before he could enter the courtyard, Teresa intercepted him.

"Come," she said, blocking his entry through the gate, "you must help me catch a rooster that has flown into the pasture by the river."

"Can't you get one of your children to help?" Patrick asked.

"They are all at their *abuela*'s house. Come, all I ask is a small favor. You will see Emma soon enough."

"She's all right?" he asked.

"*Sí,*" Teresa said as she stepped out of the courtyard and closed the gate. "And so is the baby. Her name is Molly."

She hurried him down the lane to the pasture. A small bunch of sheep scattered as they approached.

"I don't see a rooster," Patrick said.

"It is not here. Before you see Emma, first we will talk."

"About what?"

"I have come to think of Emma as a sister," Teresa replied, "and

I feel she is now one of our family. So I want no harm to come to her."

"From who?"

"From you, Patricio. That is why we are talking."

Patrick turned away. "Loco talk, if you ask me."

Teresa touched his elbow and he turned back to her. "I know you've heard about your father many times, but never from me. He rescued Ignacio from a beating, gave him work, taught him to be a vaquero, and saved his life. He took care of Ignacio just as he took care of you after searching so long to find you. Since your father's death, Cal has raised you as his own flesh and blood. Both men did more for you than anyone could have asked."

"What's this got to do with me hurting Emma?"

"Because I have watched you trample on every kindness, every fine thing that has been done for you, with *apatía*—how you say, indifference. You must not treat Emma that way."

Patrick looked at Teresa with impatience. "I don't need to be told how to be or what to do."

"*Verdad?*"

"Yes, that's so."

Teresa glared at Patrick. "Still I tell you to treat her with respect. She deserves no less."

Patrick snorted. "Whatever happens between Emma and me is our business." He turned and marched away.

Teresa watched him go. Once again, he'd rebuffed her with his stubborn nature. For years, she'd tried to love him, only to be met by his suspicion. Her heart went out to Emma, who might soon be living with a man who seemed to have no kindness in him at all. She saw no joy in the future for either of them, alone or together.

Teresa walked slowly home, grateful for all she had with her family that couldn't be counted in coin.

* * *

Patrick sat on the floor across from Emma in the small bedroom. She was propped up in bed with pillows behind her head, her hair spread out like a fan, her baby asleep in her arms.

He wanted her so intently, he was easily and often tongue-tied. Only the dim light in the room hid his blush.

He gazed at her hair, the line of her neck, her small, delicate hands, her high cheekbones, her flashing blue eyes, which seemed to bore into him. He wanted to reach out and touch her warm skin, brown and freckled from the sun. When she smiled his heart raced, but today there were no smiles. She looked cold and stern, as though she wanted nothing to do with him. Her eyes fluttered closed and her breathing slowed. He sat quietly and listened and watched.

Over the months, he'd come to realize she had a sharp mind. She was far more intelligent than any woman he'd known, except maybe Mrs. Ingalls at the Yuma Prison, and although he would never admit it to anyone, he figured she was a touch smarter than he was. So he kept his idle talk to what he knew best: horses and cattle, ranching and working.

He loved listening to her talk, although she troubled him with some of her helter-skelter ideas. She dreamt of being alone with a room full of books for a year, being a beekeeper, learning to draw like the illustrators in the eastern magazines, becoming a doctor, traveling across China, meeting the queen of England, hiking the hills of Scotland. It was all pipe-dream stuff.

Once he'd asked her what had happened to her family, and she started to say something about her father, shook her head, turned stone-faced, and stopped talking for a long while. He never mentioned it again, but it made him think she knew misery as well as he did and had secrets to keep as well.

The baby was sleeping now. He looked at it and remembered that Teresa hadn't paid much attention to Ignacio after her children were born because the little ones needed a lot of tending. He figured it would be the same with Emma, and he didn't cotton to the notion. He wanted her all to himself.

She was almost asleep, her eyes closed, her breath a whisper across the small room. He thought about how nice it would be to join her on that bed.

"I'm not sleeping," Emma said softly, opening her eyes. "What did you come here to say to me?"

Patrick sat upright, his back against the adobe wall of the small room. "What do you mean?"

Emma looked at him in silence.

"I don't know what to say," Patrick finally blurted, forcing a smile.

"What do you want?" Emma held his gaze as she stroked Molly's head.

"You," Patrick answered slowly.

"Not my baby?"

"Both of you," Patrick said.

Emma had expected his lie. "I will not marry you yet," she said.

Patrick stood. "Then I might as well git."

"Wait."

"What for?" he blustered.

"Hear me out. I will come to the ranch and live in the casita

Ignacio built for Teresa. I will cook and tend house for you, Cal, and George, but you must pay me wages."

"Why should I do that?" Patrick demanded.

Emma chose her words carefully. "Because it is the only way I will ever consider marrying you."

"You're loco," Patrick said.

Emma smiled and looked down at her baby daughter. "Yes or no?"

Patrick hesitated, then nodded. "I'll come get you in a week."

"We'll be ready," Emma said.

Emma watched him leave. She knew it was desire that drove Patrick to her, maybe even love, but she had no illusions about her own feelings for him. Although she felt no great passion, she might very well give herself to him anyway. But no man would ever again take her against her will the way Thomas Dunphy had done.

36

Time passed quickly for Emma at the Double K. From sunup to nightfall she kept busy housekeeping and cooking for Patrick, Cal, and George and caring for Molly, who at ten months was wobbling around on her tiny feet, frequently falling down, and letting out surprised wails each time her unsteady legs gave way beneath her.

Once a month she accompanied George, Cal, or Patrick to town for supplies and food. Most often Patrick drove the wagon, and she sat quietly next to him with Molly on her lap as he tried valiantly to make conversation.

Since her arrival at the Double K, she realized that she made him nervous. Alone in her company he was like an unsure little boy. His hands trembled, he stumbled over words, he blushed, and he looked at her with such longing that at times it almost made her giggle. When she was silent he became anxious, sometimes irritable. He had no soft words of affection for her, but she expected none from him. She was of a mind to believe that he had the good sense not to try to rape her, but she remained wary nonetheless.

Based on his lack of interest in Molly, she wondered what kind of father he would be. Not once had she seen him reach out to touch or hold her delightful little girl, who bubbled with inquisitiveness, as both Cal and George often did. Rarely did he bother to speak to her. Emma imagined that perhaps he had no warmth in his heart for children. Had he given any genuine attention to her daughter, she might have already given herself to him, for she found him handsome.

On an early morning in late January, with a thick carpet of low, gray skies covering the Tularosa, Emma and Molly rode in the wagon with Cal as they crossed the basin to town. With the pressure of Patrick's constant attention left behind, the trip felt like a holiday to her. Alone with Cal she could relax, sometimes to the point of feeling girlish. He was like an uncle to her, and little Molly dearly loved him. She eagerly tottered to him whenever he came into sight.

They had left before dawn, and a brisk wind had them bundled up against the biting cold. Frost on the ground crackled underneath the wagon wheels.

"We'll get some moisture out of those clouds," Cal declared. "Maybe snow."

"I'd love that," Emma replied with a hopeful sigh.

"It's a sight to see, all right," Cal agreed, "as long as you don't have to snake cattle out of snowdrifts." He glanced at Emma. "I should tie Molly behind you and put you both on the back of a pony." He'd once said about the same thing to John Kerney. "That would turn you into a hand."

Emma laughed and bounced Molly on her knee, who giggled and clapped her hands. "I'd like that. So would Molly, I bet."

"Are you gonna spend any of your wages on yourself in town this time?" Cal asked.

Emma shook her head. "I just need a few things for Molly."

"I don't fault you for putting money aside, but you shouldn't be so stingy on yourself."

"Are you about to give me a talking-to?"

Cal chuckled. "Wouldn't do a bit of good. I will say you've got that lad back at the ranch about half civilized, but I doubt you can hold him off much longer."

"I know it," Emma replied.

In the time that Emma and Molly had been at the ranch, Patrick had been on his good behavior, hoping to win Emma over. It was amazing how a woman could gentle a man, but in Patrick's case Cal wasn't sure it would last forever. The lad had a lot of wild oats tugging at him and had lately become as restless as a wildcat.

"Will you stay or skedaddle?" he asked.

"Whatever do you mean?" she asked, faking innocence.

"Either you're going to share a blanket with Patrick or you'll leave the Double K. I can't see it any other way."

"There is no other way."

"In all the years I've known him, I've never seen him so partial to anyone."

"I wonder if he loves me," Emma said.

"I reckon he does. Will you marry him?"

"I don't know."

"I'd sure hate to see you go. George would too."

Emma smiled. "I didn't say I would leave, just that I might not marry him."

Cal shot her a surprised look. "Well, I'll be. You're a bold one; I'll give you that. But you've got cause to be cautious."

Emma placed her hand on Cal's sleeve. "I knew you would understand. I wish Patrick was more like you."

"Give over that silly talk, missy," Cal said gruffly.

"I will not," Emma replied with a laugh.

They traveled the rest of the way to Tularosa through a growing snowstorm that turned the entire basin white under a bank of flat, dark clouds that hung above like a massive ceiling blocking the sky, hiding the mountains from view. In town, they went directly to Ignacio's casa, where they were greeted with food and an invitation to spend the night.

After eating, Cal and Ignacio went off to the cantina. Emma tucked Molly into bed with Sofia and rejoined Teresa, who had sent Juan, Bernardo, and Miguel to spend the night with their grandfather Cesario, who lived alone and enjoyed their company.

"I think I'll have at least three more children," Emma said merrily.

Teresa looked at her in the lamplight. "Have you decided to marry Patrick?"

"Not yet. I may want different men to give me my babies."

"Emma," Teresa cried, startled and shocked by the thought of it.

Emma smiled mischievously.

"Do you love Patrick at all?" Teresa asked.

"I don't know if I can," Emma replied, a touch of sadness in her voice. "Perhaps we're a perfect match."

Teresa reached for her hand and the two women sat silent in the lamplight for a time.

"Are you happy?" she finally asked Emma.

"I'm safe," Emma answered. "That might be about the best I can do."

37

Overnight the skies had cleared and the day was bitter cold. To the west above the San Andres, dull clouds gathered, pushed eastward by a stiff breeze. Snow covered the mountains and the basin, creating a glistening landscape. Icicles danced on the bare branches of the trees that lined the village acequias, and chimney smoke filled the air with the aroma of pine and piñon logs.

Cal and Emma had spent the morning buying and loading the wagon with supplies. Earlier, they decided to stay over another night before returning to the Double K in hopes the cold snap would end and the weather would clear. But Cal figured more snow was on the way as he stomped his boots clean on the front porch of the general store, where two horses hitched to a buckboard waited. Tied to the back of the wagon was a little pinto pony.

He stepped into the warmth of the general store and spotted the lawyer Albert Fountain with his young son, Henry, warming their hands at the potbellied stove.

Years ago, Fountain had drawn up the papers giving Cal guardianship of Patrick, making the boy his sole heir, and giving him half ownership of the Double K. During Cal's times as a deputy sheriff, official business had brought him into contact with Fountain every now and then, and he'd watched the lawyer become a powerful and influential politician. He had held elected and appointed offices, had served in the militia, rising to the rank of colonel, and had become an enemy of Oliver Lee and his compadres, who some said were rustling on the Tularosa. Since Cal had no proof that Lee was a rustler and got along just fine with the man, he paid no attention to the rumors. Cal was one of the few Texans on the Tularosa who'd never found cause to dislike Albert Fountain in spite of not agreeing with his politics. Fountain fought for what he believed in, and Cal admired that quality. He also figured any man willing to take on the cattle rustlers was worthy of his respect, and Fountain was doing just that as counsel to a newly formed stock-growers association. He was relentlessly pursuing the stock thieves by legal means and had already scored convictions on one gang operating near Socorro along the Rio Grande. Word had it that he was now poised to go after Oliver Lee.

Cal touched his hat brim as he stepped to the stove. "Good morning, Colonel."

Fountain turned. A muscular man with a high forehead and wide-spaced eyes, he was clean shaven except for a neatly trimmed mustache. Fountain smiled. "Good day to you, sir."

"What brings you to Tularosa?" Cal asked.

"Young Henry and I are on our way home to Las Cruces from Lincoln."

"There's more snow sure to come before nightfall."

"I believe you're right," Fountain replied. "We'll stay over tonight in La Luz. Have you seen anything of Oliver Lee and his friends in town?"

"Can't say I have," Cal replied. "Are you looking to find those lads?"

"Not yet," Fountain said, forcing a smile. "Come, Henry, pick out some hard candy and let's be on our way."

"Have a safe trip home," Cal said.

Fountain gave him a quizzical look. "Yes, by all means."

Cal sought out the proprietor's wife, who was busy arranging notions and fabrics on a table near a display of women's fashions.

"Do you recall that young woman in here with me this morning?" he asked.

"Yes, of course I do," the woman replied.

"Would you help me pick out an outfit or two for her?"

"Certainly. What would you like for her?"

"Nothing fancy," Cal replied. "She's pretty enough as is. Something she'd enjoy wearing every day. And can you wrap it up nice?"

"With pleasure."

After half an hour with the woman's expert help, Cal left the store with a parcel tied with a pretty red ribbon under his arm. In it were two dresses and some undergarments the proprietor's wife had picked out.

With the storm approaching, he hurried back to Ignacio's casa, covered the loaded wagon with a tarp, and fed the team some oats just as the first flakes began to fall. Inside, he put the parcel on the table in front of Emma.

"What's this?" she asked, as Ignacio, Teresa, and their children gathered around.

"Open it," Cal said.

Emma handed Molly to Teresa, carefully untied the ribbon, and peeled back the paper. "Oh, my," she said, her fingers caressing the fabric. Her eyes were bright and wet as she stood and held a dress in front of her. "Oh, my."

"Maybe you should court her, my amigo," Ignacio said.

"Watch what you say, old pard," Cal cautioned.

Ignacio belly laughed as Emma swirled across the room with the new dress pressed against her body.

She stopped and looked at Cal. For an instant she was no longer a bold, fiercely independent woman, but just a delighted, charming young lady brimming with pleasure.

"I never . . . ," she stammered before throwing herself into his arms. "You are the sweetest man."

Cal gave her a small hug and pushed her away. "Now, I've told you before, give over that kind of talk."

She gave him a quick kiss on the cheek and danced away.

* * *

Two days after their return to the ranch, on a clear, cool, early morning, Patrick confronted Cal as he climbed down from the windmill.

"Do you want her for yourself, old man?" he asked.

"What are you all puffed up about?" Cal asked as he crossed toward the barn, grease can in hand, Patrick at his heels.

"You know damn well what it is," Patrick spat, "buying her dresses and all. She told me."

"That girl needed some new duds and I made her a present. Nothing more to it than that."

"You've got no hankering for her?" Patrick demanded.

"If I were young and inclined to want to settle down with a woman, I'd pay my respects to her, hat in hand," Cal replied as he stowed the grease can on a shelf in the barn. "But I'm neither young nor the marrying kind."

"So you do fancy her," Patrick said, half snarling.

Cal grabbed a rag and wiped his hands. "What man wouldn't? But I ain't standing in your way or trying to queer your play."

"You expect me to believe that?"

"Why is it you can't see the honest truth when it's told to you straight out? If you want to call me a liar, we can knock each other's ears down right here and now."

Patrick backed up a step. "I ain't looking for a fight."

"Good," Cal said on his way to the saddle shed. "You've been mooning over Emma for nigh onto a year, and it's about time you stopped being flummoxed by her."

"I ain't confused at all."

"Like hell you ain't." Cal grabbed his tack and started for the corral, where his pony waited. "I know you don't like to take advice, but here's some for you anyway: Go tell that girl what you want, listen to what she wants, and see if you two can cinch something up together."

"I've already done that."

"Do it again and be nice about it," Cal said as he entered the corral with his tack. Bandit, his pony, trotted over. "You got all day and night to get it done, with no one around. I don't think we lost any stock in the storm, but it's best to prowl around and check. George is on his way to Big Sheep, and I'm headed to North Canyon. We'll be back tomorrow. Go talk to that gal."

"All right," Patrick said. "Maybe I will."

Cal blew on the bit to warm it, put it in Bandit's mouth, secured his saddlebags and scabbard, mounted, and smiled down at Patrick. "Way I see it, Emma has been real good medicine for you. *Buena suerte.*"

He rode out of the corral and broke Bandit into a trot. Behind him, he heard the gate swing closed. He'd finally said his piece to Patrick. He hoped some of it had sunk in.

* * *

While Molly slept soundly, Emma cleaned the ashes out of the cookstove, brought in more wood, and scrubbed the kitchen floor. When she finished, she washed her face in a basin of hot water, sat at the kitchen table, and brushed her long, thick hair with slow strokes, the feel of it pleasant and soothing.

Cal and George had ridden away earlier in the day, and Patrick was still in the corral working with one of the horses he was training. Usually when he was with the ponies he came in for a midmorning cup of coffee, knowing she always kept a fresh pot ready. Today she'd yet to hear his footsteps. She emptied the basin of water outside and paused to watch him for a minute. He reined the pony from a canter to a quick stop and trotted it around the corral. He bent low over the pony's neck, patting and talking to it before dismounting. She found it mystifying that he was gentle and patient with animals and so sharp and irritable with people.

She was about to wave and call to him that fresh coffee was ready when Molly started crying. She changed the baby's dirty diaper and nursed her for a time before Patrick stomped into the kitchen.

He nodded, crossed to the stove, poured his coffee, and sat across from her at the table.

"Molly's getting big," he said after taking a swallow. "How long a time before she stops nursing?" He had no idea how long it took but thought once it stopped maybe Emma might show more interest in him.

Emma looked at him with surprise. It was unlike him to comment about Molly at all. "Another year or so."

"That's good, I guess," Patrick said, falling silent. He wet his lips, ran a finger around the rim of his cup, and said in a rush, "I know I'm not much for courting, but I'm thinking we should get married."

Emma looked at him without changing her expression.

"Well?" he prodded.

"Will you hear me out and not get riled by what I have to say?" Emma asked.

"Are you turning me down?" Patrick asked, ready to hate what he might hear.

"You're starting up already," Emma replied evenly. "Will you hear me out?"

Patrick shifted uneasily in the chair. "I will."

"Promise?"

"Okay," he said. Across the table, a milk bubble formed on Molly's lips and she burped.

"You can have me," Emma said, patting Molly's back, "but I will not marry you yet."

Patrick's eyebrows went up. "Why not?"

"We can live as man and wife for now."

"I ain't good enough to marry?"

"I won't be owned by any man."

"What's that mean?"

"I won't be bossed around, tied up and locked in a room, or forced to do whatever a man wants. You can have no rights over me."

"I'm not like that," he replied, half believing his words.

"If you ever force yourself on me, raise a hand to me or Molly, come to our bed drunk and dirty, I will leave. If you ever lie to me, steal from me, or treat me like a servant or a whore, I'll leave. Those are my terms."

"You got this all figured out, don't you?" Patrick said.

Emma nodded. "If you don't like it, walk away."

"You ain't never gonna marry me?"

"I didn't say that."

Patrick stared at her. He didn't know what he meant to her and probably never would. She seemed to take him as he was and wasn't frightened of him at all. He liked that. There was a part of her he didn't understand, but he knew it was as tough as rawhide. Maybe even dangerous.

He'd thought about all of this every day for a year, trying to shake her off and be done with her. But all he could think of was being with her, pressed belly to belly, her legs wrapped around him, her dark hair coiled in his fingers, lips on lips, his hands exploring every inch of her warm body.

"I ain't walking away," he finally said.

"Tonight, after Molly goes to sleep, you can visit me. Take a bath before you come."

"Tonight, then," Patrick said.

"Yes," Emma replied with a small smile, wondering if he would kiss her before he climbed on her. If he did not, it would be dreadful.

3 8

I n the morning, Cal and George met up on the trail back to the ranch, and after exchanging the happy news of the good condition of the stock at Big Sheep and North Canyon, they rode together in comfortable silence under a razor-sharp blue February sky.

All was quiet upon their arrival, with no sign of Patrick, Emma, or Molly. Cuidado, Patrick's pony, loitered in the pasture with the other horses, and the wagon was parked in the barn, causing George to worry.

"Something ain't right," he said as he slid out of the saddle. "None of the corral chores have been done, and this is Emma's wash day and there ain't no clothes on the line. Besides that, the wagon is here, Patrick's pony is here, and there's not a sound to be heard or person to be seen."

"Rein it in," Cal replied.

"Well then, where the hoot is everybody?" George countered. "What's going on?"

"Let's get these ponies brushed, watered, and fed," Cal replied, nodding toward the casita, "and take our good time doing it."

The worried look on George's face faded into a grin. "You ain't saying . . ."

"I'm hoping," Cal replied.

"I'll be damned," George chuckled. "If Patrick's done cinched her up, it will sure make it a lot easier around here on us old boys."

"Amen," Cal replied.

They looked after their ponies with great, deliberate care and turned them loose in the pasture just as Deputy Sheriff Tito Barela rode up.

"What brings you out here, Tito?" Cal asked. Built low to the ground, Tito had a chubby face and sunny disposition that belied his toughness.

"Colonel Fountain and his son Henry are missing," Tito replied. "A stage driver who met the colonel on the road said three horsemen were following Fountain. He was carrying grand jury indictments against Oliver Lee and his sidekicks for cattle larceny and defacing brands." Tito slid off his pony.

"I saw Fountain in Tularosa on his way home," Cal said, "and he asked me if Lee and his amigos were in town."

"Did he say anything about being followed?" Tito asked.

Cal shook his head. "Nope. How sure are you about foul play?"

"There were bloodstains and many horse tracks where the wagon left the road, and we found one of the colonel's horses and his buckboard miles to the east, his papers missing, everything scattered about."

"Bad business," Cal said.

"It's a big *tumulto*," Tito said. "Posses are out looking for the bodies, big rewards have been raised, and people are demanding the arrest of Lee and his compadres for murder. There's talk of a lynching when they're brought in."

Tito held out a star. "The sheriff wants you back on the job. I'm to bring you to Las Cruces pronto."

Cal hesitated. He wasn't about to go galloping off to do the sheriff's bidding without first knowing if Patrick and Emma had cinched up.

"You go on ahead," he said as he took the star from Tito's hand. "Tell the sheriff I'll be there in a couple of days."

Tito nodded and threw a leg up on his pony. "Adios."

"So long," Cal replied.

"I thought you weren't gonna be a lawman anymore," George said as Tito rode away.

"Well, curiosity has got the best of me, I reckon," Cal said with a slow grin. "Besides, we can always use the money, and between you and Patrick, I know things will get looked after around here."

He slapped George on the back. "I'm hungry. Let's get a cup of coffee and see if there are any victuals warming on the stove."

* * *

Patrick eased into the kitchen, poured a cup of coffee, and joined Cal and George at the table, where the men were mopping up the last of their bowls of stew with slices of Emma's homemade bread. Both nodded howdy but didn't say a word.

"Did we lose any stock from the storm?" Patrick finally asked.

"Didn't find any carcasses," Cal said, giving Patrick a once-over. His hair was mussed and he looked more relaxed than anytime Cal could recall since he returned home. Also, he was clean shaven and smelled like soap. "Our tallies at Big Sheep and North Canyon were about right."

"Maybe a wolf or bear took one or two of the yearlings," George said. "That's about all we lost."

"And we're gonna have some good grass up there come spring," Cal noted as he went to the stove for the coffeepot. "But we need to start moving the cattle to new pastures real soon."

"Who came to visit?" Patrick asked.

"Tito Barela." Cal refilled his cup and passed the pot to George. "Seems Albert Fountain and his youngest son were bushwhacked on their way home from Lincoln. Posses are out looking for their bodies. Oliver Lee and some of his boys are suspects."

He took the star out of his shirt pocket. "I've been asked to ride for the law again. I'll leave in the morning. Now that you've dropped your rope on Emma, mind if George moves back into your old room? I'm tired of having him bunk with me anyway."

"That's okay by me," Patrick replied, coloring slightly.

"*Bueno.*" Cal stood, drained his coffee, and juggled the badge in his hand. "Best I get my outfit together. Can't go chasing *cabrons* unshucked."

"How long will you be gone?" Patrick asked.

"Don't know," Cal replied, "but it would sure be nice if you could have some of them cow ponies ready to sell when I get back. That's if you can find the time."

"Want to make that a bit plainer?" Patrick asked, holding back a grin.

"No need, from the looks of it," Cal said with a smile.

George pushed back his chair and chuckled at Patrick. "You look a little peaked, old son, like you're coming down with something. Better rest up today. See if Emma has a remedy you can take. I'll look after the chores that need doing."

"I swear someday when Cal's not around I'm gonna fire you," Patrick said, suppressing a smile.

"I know it," George replied.

"And I'll hire him right back," Cal announced.

"I know that too," George said, pulling his work gloves on as he headed for the door.

"In case you don't know it, that old boy there is a friend of yours," Cal said after George was gone.

"I'm beginning to get a glimmer of that idea," Patrick replied.

* * *

Patrick moved out of his room and George didn't waste any time taking it over when he finished doing chores. Cal packed his bedroll and saddlebags thinking he and George might soon be sharing the casita if Patrick and Emma got busy making babies. Cal liked the notion of the house someday filled with children. It would be a tribute to all that John Kerney had wanted for his son.

He spread an oilcloth on his bed and got out his artillery. He would take a shotgun, a rifle, two pistols, a Bowie knife, and enough ammunition to get through a daylong gunfight if necessary. When you wore a star you had to expect to go to war.

He was cleaning his shotgun when Emma appeared in the open door, wearing one of the dresses Cal had given her. Unlike Patrick, she seemed no different than before, which came as no surprise. From what Cal had observed, women quickly returned to their ordinary selves after they'd given themselves to a man, until the next time, when it happened all over again. It was a mystery he hadn't quite figured out.

"Patrick told me," she said. "I'll miss you."

Cal put the shotgun down and gave her a good look-see. There was no sign that she'd been mistreated, and she seemed calm and collected. "I shouldn't be gone all that long," he replied. "Are you doing all right, missy?"

Emma nodded and smiled. "I'm fine."

"You're staying on, then?"

"I'm staying."

"Good."

"Will you do me a favor?"

"What's that?" Cal asked.

"When you're in town, buy me two pairs of boys' pants." She held out a piece of paper and some silver coins. "I wrote down the size to get. They won't fit exactly, but I'll alter them."

"For you, are they?" Cal asked, taking the coins and the paper from her hand.

"How did you know?" Emma replied.

"I saw you down in the pasture with Patrick. He picked out a pony to give you, didn't he?"

Emma nodded and beamed. "A sweet gelding and a saddle that fits me just fine."

"That's real good."

"I'll pack some food for you in the morning before you go."

"Why, thank you, ma'am."

"Don't be so formal."

"Why not?" Cal replied. "After all, you're the woman of the house now, not just hired help anymore. Should I send a preacher out from town to hitch you two?"

Emma looked shocked. "Don't you dare." She gave him a bright smile and disappeared from sight.

Cal went back to cleaning his shotgun, thinking Emma had

seemed more pleased with her new pony than with Patrick, but that was okay. They were just getting started.

It was the book writers and poets who made a big deal about cooing, courting, love, and romance. In a hard country there wasn't much room for all of that. Maybe Patrick and Emma had come about as close to it as they would ever get. If so and they were happy, that would be mighty fine in Cal's book.

39

Cal Doran arrived in Las Cruces in the midst of a political ruckus that had been brewing for more than a year. The last election for sheriff had turned into a court fight when a group of citizens intercepted the Tularosa messenger transporting the ballot box and burned its contents, throwing the results in favor of the Democrats, led by Albert Fall, Colonel Fountain's political rival. Under Fountain's leadership, the Republicans had sued in court and Fall had spent months fighting the challenge with delaying tactics.

With Fountain murdered, the Republicans were continuing to press their case, but losing their leader had hurt their effectiveness. Meanwhile, the Democratic incumbent, Guadalupe Ascarate, held on to the sheriff's office. At Fall's suggestion, Ascarate had deputized Oliver Lee and his amigos, in spite of the rumors and accusations floating around them about the Fountain murders.

Ascarate had served two terms as sheriff back in the eighties, and Cal had found him decent and reasonably competent. But first and foremost Guadalupe was a politician, and folks like that were usually corrupt enough to bend, twist, and maybe even break the law to hold on to power and influence.

As Cal stepped toward the sheriff's office he wondered what scheme Judge Fall and Sheriff Ascarate had hatched for him. He sure didn't think they were counting on him to pronounce Oliver Lee citizen of the year and demand satisfaction from all who disagreed.

The only people inside the office were a jailer and a hobo in lockup. The jailer directed Cal to the Arcade Saloon, where he found Ascarate at a table with Albert Fall. Both men stood and shook Cal's hand.

"Good of you to agree to serve as a deputy," Judge Albert Bacon Fall said. Originally from Kentucky, he had a soft, pleasant drawl. Although he was back in private practice as a lawyer and no longer sat on the bench, Fall savored his honorary title.

"*Sí*," Guadalupe Ascarate said. "Sit."

"What have you boys got in mind for me?" Cal asked.

Judge Fall smiled. "Straight to the point. I like that."

Ascarate smiled and nodded in agreement.

Fall, square jawed under a droopy mustache, had wispy hair thinning on top. Ascarate's narrow face was hidden by a beard and topped off by a carpet of thick hair. Both men were still flashing their teeth, but neither man's eyes were smiling.

"You know about this court case over the sheriff's office," Fall said, smile gone. "Well, with Fountain and his young boy missing and presumed killed, Guadalupe has been unjustly criticized because he hasn't rushed out to arrest Oliver Lee and his men."

"I've heard a passel of evidence points in Lee's direction," Cal offered.

"All spurious. The fact is Fountain's oldest son, Albert Jr., has been making unfounded accusations about a plot in the sheriff's office to hide and destroy evidence that could convict Oliver."

"Nothing could be further from the truth," Ascarate said pompously.

"Exactly." Fall leaned forward. "We've tried to put the rumors to rest. Guadalupe and his opponent, Numa Reymond, met with Governor Thornton. Thornton proposed that if Guadalupe stepped down as sheriff and Reymond refused the office, he'd appoint Pat Garrett to the job. Guadalupe agreed but Reymond would have none of it. The Republicans are on a witch hunt for Oliver and aren't about to let it rest."

"They're no better than a lynch mob," Ascarate put in.

"A Pinkerton agent by the name of Fraser has been trying to tie the Fountain case to Oliver Lee," Fall continued. "But all he's done is spread a lot of gossip to Thornton up in Santa Fe. Until this election is settled, we need to keep things from getting out of hand. That's where you come in. Everyone knows you've never taken sides for or against me or Fountain and that you're a fair and honest lawman. We need you to take over the investigation."

"Unhindered?" Cal asked.

"Of course," Fall said.

"With the help I need?"

"*Sí*," Guadalupe replied.

Cal leaned back and studied the two men. "I'll want to see all the evidence, talk to all the people involved, and visit all the locations."

"I'd expect no less," Fall said.

Cal turned to Ascarate. "Nobody gets arrested unless I say so, and you keep Lee and his boys from flaunting their authority as deputies."

"You're asking a lot," Fall said.

"Those are my terms," Cal replied.

Ascarate looked at Fall, who nodded slightly, and then turned back to Cal. "You must move quickly," he said.

"Give me a month. Let the newspapers know that I was deputized to look into the Fountain disappearances and that I am not interested in arresting anybody for any other crimes."

"Very savvy," Judge Fall said as he stood. "I'm due in court, gentlemen. I'll leave you to make all the necessary arrangements. Good day."

Fall left, and Ascarate pushed back his chair. "Come, let's get you sworn in."

* * *

After meeting with the men who'd scoured the Tularosa for Fountain and his son, Cal left Las Cruces the following morning headed for Lincoln. He'd read all the reports turned in by the posses that had searched for Colonel Fountain, including the discovery of the ambush site, the tracking of the bushwhackers east toward the Sacramento Mountains, and finding the buckboard and one of the harness horses abandoned in the desert.

He'd carefully studied the evidence Fountain had used to present his indictments against Oliver Lee and his partners, William McNew and Jim Gilliland, and found it compelling. He thumbed through stock-thieving warrants filed by Texas Rangers against Lee and his companions and found them equally persuasive.

Fountain had been attacked by three riders at the eastern foot of Chalk Hill. Saturnino Barela, the stage driver, had seen three unidentified men following Fountain at a distance when he stopped to talk to the colonel. And the Apache scout who had followed the killers' tracks from Chalk Hill lost them a mere three miles from Oliver Lee's Dog Canyon ranch, where a herd of cattle had been driven across the tracks, obliterating all sign, a questionable coincidence.

At the eastern foot of Chalk Hill, Cal stopped to look over the spot where the colonel and Henry Fountain had been attacked. As he expected, all traces of the incident had disappeared, blown away by wind and covered by sand. The leader of the posse that came upon the scene had reported finding a pool of blood and the tracks of the three killers, along with two powder-burned coins and a bloody handkerchief.

Cal thought on all of that for a spell. Dried blood had been found on the seat of the buckboard, so Fountain most likely was shot while driving. Putting it together, Cal reckoned Fountain died on the spot and the killers had quickly moved the wagon off the road and out of sight. He imagined a terrified young Henry clutching the coins left over from the money his father had given him to buy some candy. He pictured a momentarily remorseful killer wiping blood off the boy's face with the handkerchief after he'd been shot dead.

Even if the killers had worn masks to hide their identities or were strangers in the territory, Henry had seen too much to live. Any eight-year-old worth his salt could describe the ponies, recognize a brand, remember what the killers wore, or recall a distinctive saddle or a fancy long gun or six-shooter.

In Tularosa, on the day Cal had run into Fountain and his son in the general store, he'd glanced at their buckboard. On the seat was a lap robe with dogs' heads on it, surely belonging to Henry, and a handmade quilt. Neither the lap robe nor the quilt had been recovered. Cal figured the killers had wrapped Henry's body in the robe and the colonel's in the quilt. Then they lashed the boy's body to the pony, put Fountain's body in the buckboard, and rode away, with one of the murderers driving the wagon. Maybe one of the killers had simply used the handkerchief to wipe blood off his hands. The attack had been a cold-blooded deed, premeditated, not a crime of passion.

Cal moved on, wondering why only one harness horse had been found near the abandoned buckboard. Had the killers also lashed Fountain's body to one of the horses? If so, did the trio separate sometime after the tracks were erased, with two killers taking the victims one way, while the third man drove the wagon in the opposite direction to throw off anyone who might follow?

That could explain why only one horse had been corralled near the buckboard and why the other animals hadn't been found yet. Maybe they had been disposed of along with their gruesome cargo.

For the time being, Cal figured focusing only on Oliver Lee and his boys would simply stir up more unrest. Best to first see if witnesses could identify any other likely suspects during the colonel's fateful journey.

He pushed on until he raised up La Luz, where he spoke with Dave Sutherland, who'd hosted Fountain and Henry the night before they disappeared. Sutherland said he'd talked politics with his old friend, but there had been no mention of any worries on Fountain's part about being followed by riders.

Cal stood with Sutherland on his front porch and asked if there were any suspicious characters or strangers around in the village during Fountain's overnight visit.

Sutherland shook his head. "There was nobody like that," he said. "You know, I believe Albert and Henry would be alive today

if Miss Fannie Stevenson hadn't changed her mind about riding
to Las Cruces with Albert because of the bad weather."

"Or maybe she'd be dead too," Cal said. "Is Miss Stevenson in
town?"

"Yep, she's at her place up the road a small piece on the right,"
Sutherland replied. "Doing poorly. She has weak lungs. Look for
the picket fence."

Cal thanked Sutherland, made his way to Fannie Stevenson's
cottage, and knocked on the door. A tiny, frail woman in her middle years who looked liked a stiff breeze could easily bowl her over
opened the door. After he introduced himself and stated his business, Miss Stevenson invited him in.

"Tragic, simply tragic," she said when Cal mentioned the Fountains' disappearance again. She sat primly on a fancy cushioned
sofa with a high stuffed back. An oval cast-iron mirror hung on the
wall behind her.

"On the day the colonel and Henry left for Las Cruces, you
decided not to travel with them," Cal said.

"Yes, that morning the weather was terrible." She put a hand to
her chest. "I walked down to Mr. Sutherland's to tell Colonel Fountain I'd changed my mind about going, and my lungs burned the
whole way. They would have certainly failed me in the cold during
such a long trip."

"Did you see any strangers on your walk?"

"Yes, one man I didn't recognize," Fanny replied. "He was red
faced and had a full beard. He was on horseback, leading a pack
animal."

"Heading in what direction?"

Fannie coughed politely into a lace handkerchief. "West, out of
town."

"Did he wear an eye patch?"

"I'm not sure."

"Did you see anyone else you didn't know?" Cal asked.

"No. You must catch the men responsible for these terrible crimes, Deputy."

"I'll do my best," Cal replied. "I'm obliged for your time, Miss Fannie."

"Come visit any time," Miss Fannie said wistfully.

Outside, he mounted Bandit and thought about the red-faced bearded man Miss Fannie had seen that morning. He'd been traveling west—the same direction the colonel and his son would take on their journey home. One-Eye Bill Carr, an Oliver Lee saddle partner, fit her description almost perfectly.

He stopped at Meyer's store and asked if the colonel had come in before leaving La Luz.

"He sure did," Meyer replied. "Came in early with his son, who had a sweet tooth. His pa gave him a quarter to buy some candy. He made a ten-cent purchase and tucked his change in the corner of his handkerchief."

A nickel and a dime, change for a quarter, had been found at the foot of Chalk Hill, along with a bloody handkerchief. Now he knew that the handkerchief belonged to Henry, he could probably forget his speculations about how blood came to be on it.

"Did the colonel say anything about being shadowed by riders?" he asked.

Meyer shook his head. "All he said was he was anxious to get home."

"Did you see Bill Carr in town around the same time? Or somebody who looks like him?"

"I sure didn't."

"Thank you kindly," Cal said.

He bought a tin of canned peaches and rode to the livery, where he fed his pony some oats and turned it out in the corral. He talked to the owner and asked if he saw any strangers the night Fountain and his son had stayed with Sutherland.

"Two riders trailing a packhorse stopped for water and feed, but they moved on before nightfall," the man answered.

"Did you know them?"

"Strangers, like you said."

"Not Bill Carr?" Cal asked.

"I know One-Eye Bill, and it weren't him," the man replied, "although folks might have mistaken him to be Bill with the same beard and all. About the same height too. Both men had beards."

"What about their ponies?"

"A red chestnut and a brown. Pack animal was a flea-bitten gray."

Cal thanked the man, paid for stabling his pony and a place to rest his head, broke out the biscuits and jerky he'd purchased in Las Cruces, and finished his cold meal with the canned peaches for dessert. He put Bandit in a stall and settled down for the night on a bed of straw with a soft wind whistling through the cracks in the stable walls. He fell asleep quickly, but not until the thought of young Henry Fountain gunned down so heartlessly cleared from his mind.

* * *

In Tularosa the following morning, Cal talked to Adam Dieter, the proprietor of the general store where he'd met the Fountains on the day they had passed through town.

"I invited them to stay for a meal," Dieter said, "but Colonel

Fountain wanted to push on to La Luz. Besides the hard candy for
Henry, he bought some horse feed, forty pounds of oats."

"Did he talk about being followed on the road from Lincoln?"
Cal asked.

"Nope," Dieter replied. "But you should talk to Saturnino Barela,
the stage driver."

"I already have. Did you see Bill Carr on the day Colonel Fountain and his boy were here?"

Dieter shook his head. "I haven't seen Bill or any of Mr. Lee's
associates for a while."

Before Cal could take his leave, Dieter's missus stepped over to
ask how Emma liked the dresses he'd bought her.

"Just fine," Cal replied, suddenly remembering his promise to
get Emma the pants she wanted. He pulled out the piece of paper
with the sizes on it and gave it to Mrs. Dieter. "She'd like some pants
now, ma'am."

"We have what she needs right over here," she said.

Within ten minutes, he was at Ignacio's house carrying a package for Emma. He spied Ignacio plowing a nearby field by the river,
gave a shout, and rode over through the rich, dark, moist soil.

"Isn't it early to be planting?" Cal asked.

"Plowing and planting are two different things," Ignacio said
with a laugh. "Better you stick to ranching, my amigo, and leave
farming to me. You're wearing a badge again. Why is that?"

"The Fountain murders."

Ignacio's smile faded. "Have the bodies been found?"

Cal shook his head. "I doubt they ever will be." He held out the
package. "If I leave this at the casa, can you get it out to Emma at
the ranch?"

"More clothes?" Ignacio asked, raising an eyebrow.

"Yep, but this time she paid for them, so don't give me that look."

Ignacio raised a hand in mock surrender. "Okay. Teresa has been asking me to take her to the ranch to visit Emma. We should do it now before winter is gone. This week or next maybe."

"I'm obliged."

"How is Patrick doing with his courting?"

"He's moved in with Emma."

"Madre de Dios," Ignacio said, crossing himself and grinning. "A miracle."

"Well, it sure has seemed to improve his disposition," Cal said, "so I guess that's something of a miracle."

Ignacio chuckled. "Come, Teresa will want to hear all the news. I will leave this stubborn mule stuck here in the mud and we will go eat."

"You don't have to ask me twice," Cal replied.

HARD COUNTRY

4 0

Filled up with good food and pleasant talk, Cal rode at a leisurely pace to Blazer's Mill, located on the south fork of the
Tularosa River. Surrounded by the Mescalero Apache Reservation,
it was the home of Dr. Joseph Blazer, a former dentist and a friend
of Albert Fountain. The tiny settlement, tucked in a narrow valley,
consisted of Blazer's two-story house, a smaller residence, a sawmill
and gristmill along the ten-foot-wide river, a general store, and
some barns and corrals. Once there had been a post office, but it
had been moved to the Indian agent's headquarters in the Mescalero village down the road a piece.

It was here John Kerney had bought the milled lumber to build
the barn he planned to raise, only to die carting it home.

Cal reined in at Blazer's adobe house next to a saddled pony
hitched to the post. The house had a cupola on top of the second
story that looked over the sawmill and gristmill two hundred feet
downstream. Blazer stepped out to greet him before he could dismount. An old-timer who'd come to the territory soon after the
War Between the States, Blazer was in his late sixties. He had a full
white beard, white hair, and a long face with narrow eyes.

Doc Blazer had been a witness to one of the most famous gun-fights of the Lincoln County War: a shootout in which Billy the Kid and the Regulators traded lead with Buckshot Roberts at the grist-mill. The fight had left a Regulator dead and Roberts mortally wounded.

"Cal Doran," Doc Blazer said genially. "Light and set a spell. There's fresh coffee on the stove."

"Now, that's a remedy I could use on this bone-chilling day," Cal said as he eased out of the saddle.

Doc Blazer ushered him into the kitchen, where James Kayten-nae sat at the table with his hat pushed back, feet crossed, and a biscuit in his hand, completely at ease. A tribal police officer badge was pinned to his shirt. He nodded a wordless greeting.

"I thought you'd given up on the police," Cal said as he shucked his coat.

"I tried," James answered, eyeing the tin star on Cal's shirt, "but Lieutenant Stottler says I track too good and speak too good white-eyes lingo to go back to being a camp Indian. Seems you the same."

Cal nodded. "Yep, I got drafted into keeping the peace again. I've been hankering to hear about the Apache who gave Henry Fountain that pony. What can you tell me?"

"He went to live at White Tail. Somebody said the colonel had long time done a favor for the old man; that's why he gave the pony."

Cal waited for Kaytennae to say more, but he ate another biscuit instead.

"I wonder if the old man saw any strangers following Fountain," Cal said.

Doc Blazer brought the coffeepot to the table, poured a cup for

Michael McGarrity

Cal, one for himself, and sat. "If he didn't, I did," he said. "Albert and Henry spent the night here on their way home. Much later after they left, I saw two riders pass by. Although I could not see their faces clearly, as they were some distance away, I was worried for the colonel because he told me he recognized some suspicious characters on the road from Lincoln."

"Was it two riders, or one rider and a pack animal?" Cal asked.

"Just two riders," Doc Blazer replied. "I didn't see a pack animal."

"Were they bearded or clean shaven?"

"Bearded, as best I could tell."

"Did Fountain mention any names?" Cal asked.

"No, but he feared for his safety. Someone had handed him a piece of paper at the Lincoln courthouse before he met with the grand jury on the cattle cases. It said, 'If you drop this we will be your friends. If you go on with it you will never reach home alive.' He showed it to me."

"Who gave him the note?" Cal asked.

"He didn't say."

"I found his lost horses two days past," James Kaytennae said quietly. "One buckboard pony and the pinto, long ride apart. Big stain on the wagon horse. Maybe blood. No more tracks. I sent ponies to the sheriff with the stage driver."

"Where did you find them?" Cal asked.

"West and south. Sheriff will send men to look. I think the bodies are gone forever."

"Probably so," Cal said.

Doc Blazer sighed. "The colonel said he could take care of any trouble if it arose. He seemed to think no man would dare to harm him with young Henry at his side."

"White eyes would," James Kaytennae said flatly.

Neither Cal nor Doc Blazer protested the comment. The three men finished their coffee in silence.

* * *

After bidding Doc Blazer good-bye, Cal and James Kaytennae rode together to Mescalero. On the way, Cal told Kaytennae that Patrick was living with Emma and her daughter, Molly, at the Double K.

Kaytennae grunted his approval. "It is good that she has taken Walks Alone to her bed."

"It surely does seem to be a tonic for the lad," Cal replied.

The wind picked up and lashed the snow that had fallen earlier in the week into their faces. They turned up their collars, lowered their hats and high-loped the horses to the agency headquarters.

"It's too late for you to ride on," James announced as they arrived at his one-room cabin. "Birds say much colder tonight. You stay here. Bring saddle inside. Otherwise my uncle will take it. He likes stealing things from white eyes."

"What about my pony?" Cal asked.

Kaytennae shook his head. "Too big for his treasure bag."

They fed and watered their horses, put them out to pasture, and carried their gear inside. James lit a fire and put the coffeepot on the stove.

"Is Lieutenant Stottler still locking up parents who won't send their children to school?" Cal asked as he sat on a sheepskin rug.

Kaytennae nodded sadly and grinned at the same time. "More bad than that now. Lieutenant locks up the grandmothers and stops rations to the parents. It big mistake to make war on Apache grandmothers. Somebody put witchcraft on him. He won't live to be old man, for sure."

"How long does he have?" Cal asked.

"Not soon enough, grandmothers say," James replied. "They upset he make all the men wear white eyes clothes and fence a piece of land for farming. Many warriors just get drunk instead. You hear Tom Dunphy's wife dead?"

"No, what happened?"

"Hung herself in the barn. Dunphy dead too."

"What happened to him?"

"Somebody shot him. Stottler sent me to bring Dunphy to Mescalero for meeting and I found him on the front porch with hole in his head. Some cattle missing too, maybe fifty. I left Dunphy there and followed the cattle to the Upper Penasco, but trail died. White eyes steal them."

"I didn't hear about any cattle thieves up this way," Cal said.

Kaytennae shrugged. "Maybe rustlers come from Seven Rivers."

"That would have been a long trek off the plains to steal fifty cows," Cal said. "Besides, why didn't they take all those critters? We trailed a hundred and fifty up here."

Kaytennae shrugged again.

"Doesn't make sense. So who killed Dunphy?"

Kaytennae shook his head. "Only tracks I found around the house were my own. I told Lieutenant Stottler and he sent out some white eyes to bury him Christian next to his woman."

Over a meal of mutton, Cal and James Kaytennae talked about the Fountain murders. Kaytennae questioned how white-eyes law could trust men to tell the truth when the white-eyes fathers lied and stole from the Apache all the time. Cal told him most of the time the law wasn't about truth but who was the better liar. During the evening, he tried to get James to talk more about the murder of Tom Dunphy but got nowhere with it.

In the morning, Cal said thanks and adios. James asked him to give his greetings to Walks Alone.

"I'll do it," Cal replied, "although he doesn't much appreciate the moniker."

"Moniker?" Kaytennae inquired with a puzzled look.

"The name you gave him."

Kaytennae nodded. "Tell him it's good to have an Apache name. All the tribe knows who he is."

"And that's good?"

Kaytennae shrugged. "Maybe my uncle won't steal from him."

Cal laughed. "I'll tell him that."

He rode off pretty much convinced that James Kaytennae had shot Tom Dunphy and that a number of Apache families were supplementing their meager government rations with cuts of prime Hereford beef. The idea of it made him smile, but his smile faded when he thought about telling Emma what had happened to Dunphy and her sister.

He wondered if it would throw her off her feed to be told. Probably not. He hadn't heard her mention either one of them by name since the day she left Pine Tree Canyon. He figured the presence of little Molly had to be a constant reminder of her ordeal at the hands of Dunphy and her sister, but not once had Emma shown that baby girl anything but love. He marveled at her grit.

41

Lincoln, once known as La Placita del Rio Bonito, sat in a narrow, lush valley along the Rio Bonito. Rich farm- and pastureland bordered the watercourse, and steep hills rose up on both sides of the town. Houses, hotels, saloons, and businesses lined the wagon road through the busy county seat. The only prominent structure remaining from the original Spanish settlement was a large circular tower called a torreón, where early villagers had gathered for safety during the many Apache raids.

Across from the two-story adobe courthouse stood the Wortley Hotel, a low-slung building with a sloping roof and veranda sheltered by a line of trees. Cal put Bandit in the livery, took a room for the night, and went looking for Curly Long, an old-timer who never missed a jury trial or a hanging if he could help it and never turned down a free drink.

Curly was a harmless, stove-up old wrangler without a lick of hair on his head, and Cal found him in the saloon next door to the hotel watching a game of billiards. He asked Curly what he knew about Fountain's time in town with the grand jury.

"Things were already popping with excitement by the time the colonel got here," Curly said. "Folks came from miles around to see if Lee and his partner Bill McNew would be indicted for cattle thieving, and when Colonel Fountain had that calf skin spread out on the courtroom floor showing the altered brand, everyone figured their gooses were cooked."

"Did you see anyone pass Fountain a note on the last day?" Cal asked.

Curly scratched his beard and peered at Cal with his bleary red eyes. "All this talking makes a man parched."

"Get us a bottle," Cal said, handing Curly some coins, "and we'll sit a spell."

Curly showed his crooked, stained teeth, hurried to the bar at the back of the room, and returned with a bottle and two glasses.

"About that note given to Fountain," Cal prodded.

"Didn't know nothing about it until after the colonel and his boy disappeared. Then there was talk." Curly paused to knock back a glass. "I hear tell the note was pressed on him by someone in the crowd waiting to get into the courtroom. Some folks are saying the note came from one of Oliver Lee's cowboys, but I was there and those boys were giving the colonel a wide berth. Not one was within ten feet of him. In fact, several had skinned out of town the night before."

"What about Bill Carr?" Cal asked.

"One-Eye Bill Carr? He weren't around at all."

"You certain?" Cal asked.

"I rode with Bill, so I should knowed him."

"How about somebody who looked like old Bill?" Cal asked.

Curly stroked his beard. "There was a fella. Him and a pard had a room at the Wortley. But he had two good eyes."

After a glass with Curly, Cal returned to the Wortley and asked the innkeeper about the men.

"Yes," the innkeeper replied after checking his register, "a Mr. Wilson and a Mr. Jones. They took a room a day before the grand jury convened and stayed through the whole proceedings. They left soon after the indictments were announced."

"How soon?" Cal inquired.

"Before Colonel Fountain, who was sent off amidst much congratulations."

Cal questioned the innkeeper further and learned the men had kept to themselves and caused no trouble during their stay. He came away with descriptions of the two along with the innkeeper's strong opinion that neither Wilson nor Jones looked a lick like One-Eye Bill Carr.

Cal spent the rest of the day visiting with folks who'd been at the courthouse during the grand jury proceedings. No one recalled seeing a note passed to Fountain, or seeing Bill Carr in town at the time.

The next day he talked to the Lincoln County sheriff and his deputies, all the merchants and innkeepers, town folks who knew just about every living soul in the county, and several area ranchers who sided against Oliver Lee and his boys. Some allowed they'd seen two strangers in town that might have been Wilson and Jones, but those who knew him swore Bill Carr hadn't been around at all.

Two days of asking questions seemed only to cloud Cal's investigation. Rumors about the Fountain murders abounded: One mysterious man allegedly shadowed the colonel after he left Lincoln; four unknown men had followed him to Blazer's Mill; three of Lee's riders had been seen on the Tularosa Road to Las Cruces.

Some said for certain that two years past, Lee and his partner Bill McNew had offered five hundred dollars to have Fountain killed. Others speculated that Judge Fall had masterminded the whole affair.

There was talk that outside killers had been imported to do the job, while others argued there would have been no need to murder little Henry if that had been the case. The Lee partisans Cal spoke to put the whole affair at the feet of some former members of a band of rustlers known as the Socorro Gang, which Fountain had recently busted up and sent to prison.

After a night of poor sleep pondering on what to do next, Cal saddled up in the morning with the idea of making a wide circle around the basin, stopping at every settlement, town, and ranch. He needed to find the mysterious Mr. Wilson and Mr. Jones, try to get a lead on any of the ghostly riders who'd supposedly been seen trailing Fountain, and discover if there was any truth to the notion that members of the Socorro Gang had done the killing.

On the outskirts of town, he met up with George Curry, a politician, former sheriff, and local businessman, returning from White Oaks.

Cal reined in next to Curry's buckboard. He had added some heft to his bones and his face had filled out since Cal had last seen him. "George, you may be the only Lincoln citizen I haven't talked to about the Fountain murders."

"Let us correct that grievous error," Curry replied amicably.

"Folks tell me you dined with the colonel the night before he left."

"Very cordially," Curry replied, "and with no mention of court business, I might add. If he had a premonition of danger, nothing in his manner showed it."

"Were you introduced to two men named Wilson and Jones during their stay at the Wortley Hotel?"

"I was," Curry answered. "They'd come over from Socorro, as I recall."

Cal had heard the same from several other town folk. "Did they state their business in Lincoln?"

"Not to me," Curry said, "but I figured them to be courthouse spectators, not dangerous at all. I'll wager you'll find them poor suspects for murder. If I were you, I'd go looking for José Chávez y Chávez."

Chávez y Chávez, part Indian and Mexican, had ridden with Billy the Kid during the Lincoln County War and at various times had been both an outlaw and a lawman. He had a mean streak a mile long and was reported to have killed some people in Las Vegas.

"Why so?" Cal asked, pleased to hear of possible new information.

"I saw him a day or two before Colonel Fountain left Lincoln. He bought me a drink at the saloon across from the courthouse and said he would keep his promise to me not to cause trouble in town, but that he would get Fountain if he had to hang for it. Those were his exact words."

"What was his grievance?" Cal asked.

"Fountain had gone after José at the grand jury for cattle stealing, but they refused to issue an indictment."

"Do you know where he lit out to?" Cal inquired.

"I can't help you there," Curry said. "José is a drifter. He could be just about anywhere. I heard tell that he was seen at Luna's Well near the White Sands the night before Fountain and his boy were gunned down."

"Who saw him?" Cal asked.

"Can't say that I know," Curry said.

Cal thanked Curry for his time and started down the road to Fort Stanton. From there, he'd swing a wide loop to Seaborn Gray's ranch on Salado Flats, the town of White Oaks at the foot of the Jicarilla Mountains, and Socorro along the Rio Grande, trail down the Jornada del Muerto to Engle and Las Cruces, and finally cut back across the Tularosa to Oliver Lee's Dog Canyon ranch. Hopefully, the journey would shake something out of the brush useful to the investigation.

At Fort Stanton, Cal found the army post mostly shuttered, the silent quadrangle under a blanket of melting snow, and the buildings empty except for two small units of soldiers. He met with Lieutenant Wright, the commanding officer, who told him José Chávez y Chávez rode through on his way to Tularosa before Colonel Fountain had passed by, and that the fort would officially close in August. A caretaker detachment of soldiers would remain behind to protect the property from vandalism. Neither Lieutenant Wright nor his quartermaster recalled seeing Mr. Wilson and Mr. Jones traveling through on their way to Socorro.

Since Cal figured to be in the saddle a good two weeks or more, he decided to buy a pack animal at Seaborn Gray's ranch and get provisions for the trip at the store. The letter of credit Sheriff Ascarate had given him would cover the expense.

He made it to the ranch in good time and bargained with Seaborn for a surefooted gelding, which he got at a fair price. At the store, he bought a fourteen-dollar packsaddle along with all the victuals and supplies he needed, charged again to the sheriff, and set out on the road to White Oaks, a good thirty miles distant. The road crossed the Nogal Divide to the flats and wound around the

Carrizo Mountain before turning north to White Oaks. Except for a few large spreads along the route, it was that big, wondrous country of high mountains and vast rangeland he'd first seen with John Kerney during his quest to find Patrick so many years ago.

After several days of constant jawboning with the good citizens of Lincoln, Cal looked forward to having as much time to himself as the remainder of the trip allowed. He would camp under the fast-approaching starry night sky and happily not mutter another word, except to his pony, until he reached White Oaks.

* * *

In White Oaks, Cal took a room at a two-story brick hotel that offered the best accommodations in town. Most of the old gold and silver mines had shut down, but White Oaks still remained a center of commerce and banking as well as the major stage and mail stop from San Antonio on the Rio Grande to Lincoln. Sawmills and coal mines in the nearby mountains operated at full capacity, and the Old Abe, the richest and most productive mine, continued to produce vast quantities of high-grade ore. The prosperous town sported an athletic club, a fine schoolhouse, a variety of stores, and several churches.

He made the rounds asking about Wilson, Jones, and Chávez y Chávez, drew a busted flush, and left the next day, trailing east toward San Antonio along a rough road that crossed the dangerous lava flow on the north side of the Tularosa Basin.

He stopped overnight at the Ozanne Springs stage stop in the Oscura Mountains and learned that Wilson and Jones had stayed there the day Colonel Fountain and his son Henry were murdered at Chalk Hill. The station manager described the two men to Cal's

satisfaction, which left only José Chávez y Chávez as a suspect, unless the rumors about the Socorro Gang held any truth.

Morning came and he rode on, past the site of Carthage, a
company-owned coal-mining town that had been moved lock,
stock, and barrel to coal fields south of Santa Fe. All the spur-line
tracks, coal chutes, and machinery had been ripped up or dis-
mantled, and the dwelling houses and stores taken down, so that
only a small cemetery, the barren strip dumps, and a few melting
adobe structures remained.

At San Antonio, he paid for a room at a boardinghouse, and
after a bath, a good meal, and a night in a soft bed, he decided
to head to Socorro early the next day and meet personally with
Mr. Wilson and Mr. Jones to satisfy any doubts he might have as
to their innocence. He found them at the Santa Fe Railroad offices, where they were employed to survey a proposed spur line
planned to run from the cow town of Magdalena, west of Socorro,
across the San Agustin Plains to a mining town in the Mogollon
Mountains.

After a brief conversation, he wished them luck in their endeav-
ors and went to see Holm Bursum, the county sheriff. Bursum
advised him that Slick Miller and most of the Socorro Gang Colonel Fountain had prosecuted were still in the territorial penitentiary, except for Doc Evans and Lee Williams, who had served their
time and were out. He hadn't seen either of them since their re-
lease, but both were known to work at some of the smaller spreads
along the Rio Grande valley when not engaged in stock stealing.
The sheriff held an outstanding warrant for their arrest on a charge
of altering brands.

Bursum also gave Cal a look-see at a thick report by a Pinkerton
agent that detailed an assassination plot hatched two years earlier

to kill Fountain. Supposedly, the Socorro Gang had been in ca-hoots with Bill Carr to exterminate the colonel and dispose of his body in the San Andres.

"If you see Evans and Williams," Bursum said, "send them my way so I can lock them up."

"I might want to lock them up myself," Cal replied.

He left Socorro looking for four men: José Chávez y Chávez, Doc Evans, Lee Williams, and One-Eye Bill Carr, who had become interesting once again. He knew all four, having met each hombre a number of times over the years. He was convinced they would not have risked the Fountain murders on their own say-so.

For several days he worked his way slowly from ranch to ranch, making inquiries, talking to the hired hands, and getting nowhere. His only accomplishments consisted of filling his belly with some fine home-cooked meals served up by the ranchers' wives and resting his head on comfortable beds in warm bunkhouses.

He rode into Engle on a bright, sunny day, the sky crowded with towering clouds more reminiscent of summer than of winter, debating whether to telegraph his resignation to Sheriff Ascarate and head for home or continue the search. At the train station he decided to ask around town about his four suspects and then send a report of his findings, such as they were, to Ascarate. He stopped at all the saloons, the small brothel, where a lone, weary-looking whore greeted him with a thin smile, and the hotel.

He spied Doc Evans and Lee Williams in the hotel dining room about to dig into large mounds of food heaped on their plates. Although both men were thieves and not shootists, he approached them cautiously nonetheless.

"What are you boys doing down this way?" Cal asked pleasantly, his gun hand close to his six-shooter.

Doc Evans dropped his fork on his plate and gave Cal a disgusted look. "Well, if you ain't the ruination of my day."

Short and scrawny, Evans had a pockmarked face and long, greasy hair that hung down over his ears.

"I asked you a polite question," Cal said evenly.

Evans stabbed a piece of meat with his fork. "We was having a peaceful meal until you showed up."

Lee Williams had his head lowered over this plate, shoveling food into his mouth, a good deal of it sticking to his mustache. Of the two, Williams was the slower thinker, and that wasn't saying much for Evans.

"I don't like that answer," Cal said. "Try again."

Evans curled his lip. "We've been riding the chuck line."

From his stops at the ranches, Cal knew there wasn't a lick of truth to Doc's lie.

"The sheriff up in Socorro told me you were part of a scheme several years back to kill Albert Fountain," he countered.

"Weren't us," Evans replied. "Don't know anything about it."

"If it weren't you, who was it?" Cal demanded.

"I said I didn't know."

Evans looked at Williams, who burped, wiped his sleeve across his mouth, and nodded in agreement.

"Stand up, both of you," Cal ordered.

"What for?" Evans asked.

"I'm arresting you for altering brands and stealing stock."

"You don't got a lick of proof about that," Williams said, his mouth full of food.

"Shut up, Lee," Evans barked.

Cal pulled his leg iron. "Let's go, boys. Do it nice and easy so I don't have to kill you both."

"I ain't finished eating," Williams whined.

"Get up," Cal said, gesturing with his six-gun, "and keep your hands on the table."

* * *

With the help of the train conductor and two willing citizens, Cal got Doc Evans and Lee Williams to Las Cruces without incident. Cal had notified Ascarate by telegraph of his impending arrival with prisoners, and the sheriff and Deputy Tito Barela were there to greet him when the train pulled into the station. He turned his prisoners over to Tito and went with Ascarate to the Arcade Saloon, where Judge Fall waited.

Fall flashed a friendly smile as Cal joined him at the table. "Sheriff Ascarate was kind enough to share the telegraph you sent him about your investigation. You've done a good piece of work."

Cal reached for the whiskey bottle and a clean glass, poured a shot, and drank it. "All I've done is give you some bona fide desperados you can point to as possible suspects if Oliver Lee ever goes to trial for Fountain's murder."

Fall's expression turned thoughtful. "You don't think Doc Evans and Lee Williams are likely candidates?"

Cal shook his head. "I talked to those old boys on the train ride down here. They swear they didn't kill Fountain and I believe them. Besides, they ain't the kind someone would hire to do murder, and they ain't bright enough to come up with a plan to do it on their own."

"Do they have alibis?" Fall asked.

"Nope, they've been drifting."

Fall smiled. "What about Chávez y Chávez?"

"I've been pondering what George Curry told me about José ever since I left Lincoln. It's no secret George and Oliver have been on cordial terms for a long time. Could be, George was looking out for a friend."

Fall showed his teeth. "Are you suggesting Sheriff Curry deliberately misled you?"

Cal smiled back at Fall. "I didn't say that, Judge, but loyalty can't be scoffed at."

"Indeed not," Fall replied. "I take it you haven't crossed paths with Chávez y Chávez."

"I haven't seen hide or hair of him," Cal admitted. "Curry said he'd heard José was at Luna's Well around the time of the murders, but that's just talk, as far as I know."

"And Bill Carr?" Fall asked.

"Bill will do whatever Oliver asks of him, including murder, I reckon. But I'll bet you a dozen good men and true who side with Lee will step forward and give Bill an alibi if he needs one."

Fall nodded. "Once again, I admire your directness." He turned to Guadalupe Ascarate. "Will you be needing Cal to stay on as a deputy?"

Ascarate shook his head.

Cal stood and put his star and the bill of sale for the gelding and supplies he'd bought from Seaborn Gray on the table in front of Ascarate. "You own a packhorse now, Sheriff. It's a good, stout animal and comes with a saddle. I'll hitch it outside the jail."

"You can keep it," Ascarate said, pocketing the badge.

"That wouldn't be right," Cal replied. "Adios."

Fall didn't rise. "You've done the territory a great service."

Cal smiled at Fall's disingenuous flattery. "Sowing doubt about who the killers might be isn't gonna keep a whole passel of folks from believing Oliver Lee was behind the murders."

"Every little bit helps," Fall replied. "Especially with no bodies to prove the foul deed."

"You're right about that," Cal said.

Anxious to get home, he left the men to their palavering, bought a ticket to Engle, parked the pack animal at the jail, and returned to the depot to wait for the northbound freight, due in an hour. With his hat pulled low he sat hunched on a bench, hoping to be ignored and left alone. Approaching footsteps on the wooden platform made him look up to see Oliver Lee coming his way.

He hadn't seen Lee in a while, but the man hadn't changed much. He had a purposeful stride and moved easily and with a certain grace. He was taller than average, slender and fit, with large black eyes. He stopped in front of Cal, pushed back his wide hat, revealing a broad forehead and coal black hair, and smiled pleasantly. A tin star was pinned to his coat.

Cal got to his feet and looked Oliver level in the eye.

"Did you find Fountain's killers?" Lee asked with a smile.

"I heard that when you were asked to help search for Fountain you said you didn't care about the damned son of a bitch," Cal answered. "Why start now?"

Oliver Lee laughed. "I still don't care a lick about him, but I don't like being called a murderer."

"I can't help you shed that handle," Cal replied.

"Are you standing against me?"

"I didn't the last time you asked me that question, and I'm not taking sides this time either."

Lee's smile widened. "That's good. It's time for things to quiet down."

Cal nodded in agreement. "They will for a spell, I reckon. But I suspect you will be hunted if old Guadalupe gets booted out of office and Pat Garrett takes over."

"Maybe when that time comes, old Pat will take you on as a deputy."

"I want no part of gunning for you."

"So you think I'm innocent."

"I didn't say that," Cal replied.

"I've never figured why you didn't join with us to stand against the big outfits."

"I don't give my loyalty to quarrelsome men."

Lee's jaw tightened. He touched the brim of his hat. "Adios."

"So long," Cal replied. Oliver Lee turned and walked away. In the distance came the sound of the train whistle. Cal went to fetch Bandit so he could load him on the stock car waiting at the siding.

* * *

Crossing the San Andres cleared Cal's mind of thoughts of Albert Fountain and Oliver Lee. He was glad to see the first sign of grass in the high pastures and find several bunches of healthy-looking Double K cattle lounging at some watering holes. Fresh bear scat along the trails signaled the end of winter no matter what the calendar read, and the occasional springs coursing down the mountainsides were filled with gurgling runoff. If the days stayed mild for a while and the summer monsoons came on time, it might well be a good year.

The weeks he'd been away felt like months, and he hurried his pony through the last canyon that hid the ranch from view, only to draw rein at the sight of a small group of people assembled on the hillside near John Kerney's grave. He spurred ahead at a gallop, searching faces as he got closer. Ignacio, Teresa, and their children were there, George and Patrick also. And on her knees, bent over a small coffin near an open grave, was Emma.

42

Emma found Molly dead in her crib the morning after Ignacio, Teresa, and the children arrived for a visit. It happened suddenly for no apparent reason. As the next few days passed, the loss turned Emma empty eyed, wooden, and silent.

She rebuffed all of Patrick's attempts to console her. When he tried to talk to her, she turned away. When he touched her, she recoiled as though snakebit. She made it clear she wanted nothing to do with him, so he moved back into the ranch house, hoping time would ease her grief, but it got no better. She kept the house clean, washed the clothes, cooked the meals, ate alone, and retreated to her casita at night, where she stayed until morning. Each day, she emerged hollow eyed and listless. Each day, Patrick half expected to return to the ranch house to find she had run away, collapsed from exhaustion, or died by her own hand.

Her black mood was so disagreeable, the three men took to avoiding her and the ranch house as much as possible. After a solid two weeks of gathering cattle and branding calves for the spring works, they set about shoeing all the horses, greasing the windmills, training the cow ponies, rebuilding the dirt stock tanks, patching saddles, fixing the leaky barn roof, and repairing corral fences. Within a month, every major job had been done and the ranch was in tiptop shape, while Emma remained mired in bitter despair.

Late one afternoon as they finished the last of the barn chores and turned the ponies out in the pasture, Cal hooked a boot on the corral gate and looked at the house.

"It ain't natural," he said as he rolled a smoke, "her holed up like that all the time."

"And she ain't eating or sleeping right," George added as he rolled one of his own. "There's no meat on her bones at all, and she looks dead tired."

"What are we gonna do?" Patrick asked. "Last time I tried talking to her, she told me I'd never see her again if I said another word about how she's been acting."

"We're the gloomiest outfit in the whole damn valley," Cal said, getting a light from George, "and I'm tired of tippy-toeing around while she wastes away to nothing."

"You try talking to her." Patrick picked up a stick and cleaned some manure from his boots.

"I have," Cal said. "So has George. We need to figure something that'll make her shake this off."

"Like what?" George asked.

"We could put her in the wagon and take her to town," Patrick answered. "Get her away from here for a spell."

"Busting her out of the house for a spell ain't a half-bad idea," Cal said. "We've been letting her run roughshod over us with her sulky ways."

"How about we go after that old brindle longhorn up-country and take her with us?" George suggested.

"I thought you wanted to leave that critter be," Patrick said.

"Well, I do," George replied. "But we need to corral him away from the cows. He's just running them ragged. We could bring him back here and pen him. Besides, if we take her to town, she'll just hide out with Teresa. That gal needs some clean mountain air and sunshine to get a fresh outlook."

Cal smiled. "George, I swear you're a bright old boy. A good jolt to get her out of her vapors is just what's called for, and some time in the saddle away from here just might do the trick. I say it's worth a try."

Patrick nodded in agreement.

At mealtime, when Emma put the food on the table, Cal pushed out a chair and told her to sit.

With a wary glance at the men, she sat down slowly, her body as tight as a mainspring. From the looks on their faces, they were up to something, and she wanted none of it.

"You're coming with us to the high country tomorrow. Pack a bedroll, some clothes, put together enough victuals for four days, and be ready to ride at first light. We'll need an early breakfast."

Emma shook her head forcefully and glared at Cal. "You can't make me go."

"We'll tie you across the saddle if we have to," Cal answered, staring her down. "You're going."

Emma glanced from Cal to Patrick to George. "Why are you doing this?"

"Because sometimes a young'un will die before their time," Cal answered. "It's just the way of the world. There's no reason for it and it's nobody fault. We're all tired of waiting on you to start showing some gumption about life again."

"You are mean, heartless men," she said spitefully.

"Think what you will." Cal spooned food on his empty plate and pushed it in front of Emma. "And starting right now, you eat with us."

Patrick held out his fork, and she yanked it from his hand.

* * *

Emma had often ridden the lower canyons near the Double K headquarters, and during the first morning of her forced march on horseback, the familiar landscape was dreary and uninteresting to her. Not even the tall, graceful sotol and agave plants that peppered the rocky soil or the glistening silvery white sands on the basin below held her attention. As they passed along the trail they startled flocks of Gambel's quail, which scattered into the sky, and frightened black-tailed jackrabbits, which scampered for safety. Once, the sight of the animals would have pleased her. Today, she cared not a lick.

Cal led the expedition, with Patrick next, then Emma, and George in the rear trailing the pack animals. To avoid being lashed to the saddle, Emma had promised not to bolt or misbehave but had made no other concessions. Since they had threatened her with physical force to come along, she had no intention of talking to them or doing a smidgen of work during her abduction.

She fully expected them to try to pester her into talking, but so far they were ignoring her. That suited her just fine. She passed the morning hours silently, listening to the sounds of clattering hooves and creaking leather, her thoughts straying over and over again to the moment she found Molly's lifeless body in the crib.

With the noon sun high above and the day warming, they entered a large pasture that stretched for several miles to the base of a mountain that looked like a gigantic fortress carved out of rock. Stone turrets, battlements, towers, and parapets rose and stretched in colossal proportions across the summit as the sun washed the mountain golden.

Emma caught her breath. She had never seen anything like it. For weeks since Molly's death, she'd cried each night into her pillow. Sometimes tears of sadness, sometimes tears of anger, but always tears for the emptiness inside that cut into her heart like a two-edged sword. How she missed that sweet child.

She gazed at the mountain with the sun warm on her face. Knowing Molly would never see such a sight, she felt like crying again. Instead, she lowered her gaze, sniffled, and held back the tears.

They drew near a spring concealed at the base of the mountain by a small stand of wispy desert willow and feathery bushes. On the sheer cliffs above, a small herd of mountain sheep looked down on them suspiciously before scurrying away, bounding over boulders.

When they stopped for a meal, Emma found herself surprised once again by her captors. No orders were given for her to cook or do anything at all. Instead, George started a campfire, Patrick made coffee, and Cal put strips of beef and canned corn in a skillet.

"Dinner now, supper this evening," he explained, without waiting for her to ask. "There's rough country ahead and we'll need to make tracks until nightfall."

"How far?" Emma asked, astonished that the question had tumbled out of her mouth so easily.

"A tidy step," Cal replied.

Emma winced. She'd been in the saddle a good six hours and

didn't look forward to spending the rest of the day on horseback. Her body already ached, especially her back.

By the time they ate and moved on, she felt somewhat better. Cal led them around the fortress mountain across another large pasture that ran against a mountain range cut by dozens of narrow slot canyons, which drained the east slopes. Some of them burrowed deep into the tumbled rocks at the base of the peaks; others ran like long fingers down impossibly steep inclines. Cal pointed them toward a canyon, and soon they were climbing single file up a rocky trail, sunlight blocked by the towering walls. The ponies moved slowly through twists and turns, and as they gained each ridge, another appeared above in an endless progression.

Throughout the day, Patrick had been in front of her, and with his broad back and square shoulders, she had to admit he cut a handsome figure in the saddle.

They came out of the dim light into gathering dusk and picked their way cautiously along a narrow ledge that looked over a hundred-foot crevice. By the time they got off the ledge into a high meadow of tall pine trees, night had fallen.

Sore, exhausted, and cold, Emma dismounted slowly. Her nerves were stretched thin from the final harrowing ride up the mountain. It was all she could do to pull the saddle off her pony and picket it with the others. George had a small fire going, with coffee heating up, and Patrick had set out some hardtack and jerked beef for supper. Cal was with the pack animals, removing their heavy loads. A half-moon hung in the sky, and through the trees a million stars filled the heavens like specks of diamond dust.

She warmed herself by the fire before spreading out her bedroll on a cushion of pine needles some distance from the men. She stretched out just for a minute to ease her weary bones and listened to George and Patrick's chatter, the crackling fire, and the soft whinnying of the ponies.

She was almost asleep when she heard footsteps. She sat bolt upright.

"Easy, Emma," Cal said gently, hunkering down to see her face. "There's something I think it's time for you to hear. Thomas Dunphy is dead, shot in the head some months back. Nobody knows who did it, but I think it was James Kaytennae."

He paused for a second to let her take it in. "One more thing: Your sister is dead. She hung herself in the barn before Dunphy was murdered."

Emma took a deep breath.

"It's over and done, Emma, whenever you want it to be," Cal said. "You savvy?"

Emma looked at Cal and nodded.

"Good." Cal rose up. "You want supper?"

Emma shook her head.

"Good night."

After Cal moved away, Emma stuck her fist in her mouth and sobbed into her blanket, letting all the pent-up rage she had about her sister and Tom Dunphy come out. She was glad Ruth had died by her own hand, happy Tom Dunphy had been shot down like the dog he was. For the first time since her escape from Dunphy's cabin, she fell into a dreamless sleep.

43

On the afternoon of the second day, they spotted the longhorn in the clearing of a deep, rock-strewn, heavily treed canyon. They reined in upwind a good half mile from the brindle, and the old bull raised his head and shook it in their direction.

"Now, that's a sight," George said.

"He knows we're here," Patrick said.

"The spread of them horns is at least a good six feet," George said admiringly, "and he looks sleek and well fed."

Cal studied the trail down the canyon to where the longhorn stood. "There's only one way in from here," he said, "and he'll probably bolt before we're halfway down."

Emma switched her attention away from the powerful beast to the three riders lined up in a row studying the animal. She wondered how in the blazes they planned to catch it.

Beyond the longhorn and the canyon, the boundless tablelands of the Jornada del Muerto, flat and desolate in the midday sun, sparkled clear in sharp relief. Miles away a dust devil rose from the desert floor and whirled into oblivion on the western horizon. Here the San Andres were a thick forest of piñon and juniper trees, the mountains sloping gently down to sandy, water-less, flats.

All morning they had ridden through rugged wilderness on faint game trails and climbed boulder-strewn ridges, sometimes cresting to breathtaking vistas embracing a hundred miles of broken mountain ranges stacked against the horizon. Even though she'd had her first good sleep since Molly's passing, Emma was saddle sore and bone weary again. Yet she felt less fatigued in her mind than she had in days.

"I don't cotton to wasting time trying to circle around that old brindle," George said. "It would be a long, tiresome ride for nothing."

"I reckon you're right," Cal said.

"Let's just ride down the trail and see what he does," Patrick said. "If he spooks we can track him."

Cal raised an eyebrow. "That old mossy-horn can run twenty miles between now and sunset."

"Or he'll hunker down somewhere in the brush and we'll never spot him," George added.

"Don't make me do this by myself," Patrick replied with a laugh as he started down the trail. "Come on, old-timers, we've got him outgunned. If he charges, one of us will snare him."

As the riders walked their ponies single file down the canyon, the brindle stood his ground, head raised, tail slowly swishing. A hundred yards away, they stopped on a wide, level shelf and the bull shook his horns at them.

George gave Emma the reins to the pack animals. "You stay here, missy," he whispered. "All right?"

Emma nodded, stared at the bull, and glanced at Cal. "Can you really catch him?" she asked.

Cal, lariat in hand, shrugged. "We'll see. That old brindle is wily and fleet." He glanced at Patrick and George. "Ready?"

Both men nodded.

In unison, the three men spurred their ponies to a gallop. Cal and George fanned out in a flanking maneuver as Patrick rode straight at the old bull. At fifty yards the longhorn dropped his head, pawed the ground, bellowed, and with the coarse hair on his back standing straight up, charged straight for Patrick.

Cal and George closed in from both sides, hollering like banshees, ropes low. The longhorn stopped and whirled at the fast-approaching riders. Spooked, George's pony reared back on hind legs as George grabbed leather. Cal closed but his rope missed, the lasso sliding off the brindle's shoulder. The old bull spun back toward Patrick, who made a perfect throw, the loop settling over the head and one horn.

He looped the rope around his saddle horn and turned Cuidado away from the charging bull. Before the brindle could swing around, Cuidado dug in his hooves and squatted. The rope tightened and the saddle cinch broke, pulling the saddle and Patrick over Cuidado's head. He landed still straddling his saddle and tumbled head over heels into the dirt. As he struggled to get on his feet, the brindle spun, thundered past him, and hooked a horn into Cuidado's breast.

The pony went down, screaming and thrashing, blood pouring from the wound. The bull pulled free and headed for the trees, with Cal and George in pursuit.

Cuidado rolled on his side, kicking his legs, lifting his head, his eyes wide and wild, screaming an unworldly sound. Patrick stumbled over to him. He knelt, rubbed Cuidado's neck, patted his forehead, and whispered in his ear.

Cuidado's breathing slowed, and he nickered softly. Patrick shot him with his six-gun, the sound echoing through the canyon.

Off in the distance he heard Cal and George hooting and hollering as they chased the old bull. He turned and looked at Emma as she came down the trail with the pack animals, her face a mask of worry.

"It's all right," he called, trying to believe it himself. "It's all right."

* * *

The rocky canyon soil made it impossible to bury Cuidado deep. But with Emma's help, Patrick scratched out a shallow depression and used one of the packhorses to snake Cuidado into it. Together they covered him with a layer of dirt, large rocks, and some small boulders Patrick managed to roll on top of the makeshift grave.

"Wolves will be here feeding come night," Patrick said, "but I couldn't just leave him lying there."

"I know," Emma said.

"He was the best pony a man could ever want."

"I know," Emma said, studying Patrick's sad eyes. She'd never seen him so solemn before.

At the mouth of the canyon, Cal and George appeared, loped over to them, reined in, and said nothing as they looked at the mound covering Cuidado.

Patrick hoisted his saddle. "I'll ride one of the packhorses home."

"We've got that brindle bull snubbed to a tree down yonder a ways." Cal slid to the ground and held out the reins. "You can take my pony and go shoot him."

Patrick reached for his long gun, hesitated, and then slowly shook his head. "No, let him go."

"You certain?" Cal asked.

"Yep, I'm certain."

"I'll cut him loose," George said. He turned his pony and trotted away.

Cal picked up Patrick's bedroll and his sheathed rifle. "Let's get you mounted."

Emma watched Patrick and Cal walk to the packhorses, thinking that they and George were the best men she'd ever met—and that included her father, God rest his drunken, tortured soul. She had all but given up on life, and they had pulled her back into the world. And with the loss of Cuidado, Patrick had paid a terrible price to do it. Wasn't that true affection?

Emma believed it was.

44

As the early days of summer passed quickly, Emma slowly regained her good nature and vibrant spirit. With her health restored she seemed even more comely than before, so much so that she took Patrick's breath away.

Before Molly's death, Patrick always felt that she took no genuine pleasure in his company. Now she was more comfortable and lighthearted with him, although she'd yet to invite him to move back into the casita. He figured she just needed more time to heal up from all her past misery, so he waited patiently, spending his free time training his new honey-colored pony he'd named Jefe.

Occasionally he took Emma horseback riding in the cool of the evening after supper. They headed up one of the nearby canyons or out onto the basin and watched the fading light soften the harsh, sun-scorched, sandblasted land. They didn't talk much or ride far, but it didn't matter to Patrick. It was the best part of his day.

Emma had taken to studying Patrick on their evening rides. He hadn't once tried to kiss her, even though she felt ready for that and more.

During their trips to town they got the latest news about the Fountain murder investigation. After the court decided that Sheriff Ascarate's opponent, Numa Reymond, had won the election, the political shenanigans began. Reymond took office, appointed Pat Garrett chief deputy, and promptly left town for an extended tour of Italy, paid for, as rumor had it, by those who wanted to give Garrett a free hand hunting down Oliver Lee and his partners.

To the disgust of his supporters, Garrett had done nothing so far. The investigation dragged on, with Lee proclaiming to all who would listen that Garrett planned to shoot him in the back and collect the huge reward as soon as he could get a judge to sign an arrest warrant against him.

Late in the summer, Numa Reymond resigned and Pat Garrett became sheriff. From a reliable source, Cal heard that Albert Fall had argued against Garrett's appointment. Since he'd always believed Fall had lied to him about wanting Garrett to be sheriff, it didn't surprise him none.

The Double K finished fall works with a tidy profit from the sale of their cattle. They also sold a dozen top cow ponies to the Diamond A outfit, one of the biggest spreads in the territory. In Engle, Patrick and Cal turned the ponies over to the Diamond A wrangler, spent the night in the hotel, and did some shopping the following day, with Patrick coming away with a fancy saddle for Emma.

"Are you gonna propose?" Cal asked as they lugged their purchases back to the hotel.

"Not yet."

"Why not?"

"Because I don't want her to turn me down again."

"That ain't gonna happen," Cal said as they climbed the stairs to their room. "Buy her a ring, give her the saddle, and ask her to marry you. Then we'll all go to town, get you two hitched, and have a party."

Patrick dropped the saddle on the bed. "You got it all figured, do you?"

Cal tied the new bandanna he'd bought around his neck and studied himself in the mirror. "I reckon I do. We're her family now, and she's gonna stay right where she is. She's been keeping you at bay to see what you'll do, and you've done right to not pester her for a time until she got her legs back under her."

Cal adjusted the bandanna and turned to face Patrick. "Tell the little lady you propose to marry her and you have my blessings."

"You aren't her father," Patrick said.

Cal chortled. "I'm about the closest thing to a pa either one of you has."

The truth of Cal's words struck home. "Will you stand up for me?" Patrick asked.

"I will gladly," Cal replied, looking Patrick straight in the eyes, "if you promise to stick by her, never raise a hand against her, and love her the best that you can."

Patrick laughed. "You have my word, but damn if you don't sound like a preacher."

Cal grinned and slapped Patrick on the back. "First time I've ever been called that, old son. Let's head on home."

* * *

Cal's calculation that Emma would accept Patrick's marriage proposal proved accurate, and within days the Double K outfit decamped to Tularosa to get the couple hitched. In town, Emma stayed with Ignacio and Teresa while the men took rooms at the hotel. After a whirlwind three days of shopping, finding a preacher, and making arrangements, the evening ceremony was held in the Chávez hacienda courtyard. Patrick wore his new sack suit, and Emma was gussied up in a pretty dark blue dress with a touch of white crepe at the collar and flowers in her hair. George gave Emma away, Teresa was matron of honor, and Cal served as Patrick's best man. The invited guests consisted of all of Ignacio and Teresa's children and relatives, who filled the courtyard to capacity.

After the vows were exchanged, Cal gave Emma a whirl to the music before turning her over to Patrick, and the *fiesta de boda* officially began. There was dancing, a lavish feast, and much drinking as the evening wore on. After a final round of toasts to the bride and groom, Ignacio drove them to the hotel in his wagon, which had been festooned with flowers by his children.

In the morning, Cal and George headed home to the Double K, leaving the newlyweds behind. They rode silently past the green fields and tall shade trees of the village into the sandy desert of the immense basin that stretched before them.

"That was a fine party," George said, bleary-eyed and hungover.

"As drunk as you were, I'm amazed you remember it," Cal replied with a smile.

"Don't you vex me none about it," George grumped. "Man's got a right to enjoy himself now and again."

"I've got no sermon for you," Cal said. "In fact I was glad to see it. You ain't had a good drunk for nigh on a year."

George trotted his pony alongside Cal and gave him a serious once-over. "How come you look like the cat that licked up all the cream? You've been acting like that since yesterday."

"There was a time I had doubts I'd ever get that boy raised up right. Now that the job is done I'm feeling tolerable good about it."

"Does that mean you're gonna sit on the veranda with your feet up and leave all the work to me and that newlywed fella we left at the hotel in town?"

Cal laughed. "I may not kick up my heels like a colt anymore, but not yet, old-timer, not yet."

* * *

Upon Patrick and Emma's return to the ranch, they found that Cal and George had turned the casita into a bunkhouse, moved Emma out, and moved themselves in. Emma set about giving the main house a woman's touch, and by the time winter arrived there were curtains in the windows, pictures on the walls, shelves in the kitchen, and in the sitting room some new furniture Patrick had bought in Las Cruces.

Everything was dandy until February, when Emma lost the baby she was carrying. Although she kept up with her cooking and daily chores, it threw her into a black mood for a month, making her near unapproachable. Except for mealtimes, Cal and George hid out in the casita bunkhouse to avoid the glumness, leaving Patrick to sit alone and silent in the front room, with Emma closeted behind her bedroom door. He took to sleeping in his old room, which Emma had planned to turn into a nursery.

Cal had just about given up on expecting any improvement to the situation when one morning Emma emerged from the bedroom rosy cheeked, smiling, and wearing a pretty dress.

"You look tolerable well," he said.

"I have decided not to brood anymore."

"Is that a promise to yourself?" he asked.

"I don't know," Emma replied.

With spring works about to start, her recovery couldn't have come at a better time. For the next two weeks the whole outfit went out gathering and branding on the flats and in the high country, with Emma handling the chuck wagon chores.

Gene Rhodes came over from the horse camp that he'd proved up next to his father's homestead to lend a hand, and the Bar Cross and Diamond A ranches sent stray men to trim the herd and throw their stock over to the home range.

Twice during the roundup, Cal, George, and Patrick saw the brindle longhorn at a distance. They reined in and watched the old bull until it shook its head, gave a bellow, and loped away. George swore the longhorn was just saying howdy.

When the gathering was complete, Cal tallied the herd. A goodly number of healthy calves had been born. It augured a nice profit down the road if on-the-hoof prices stayed steady.

They turned the steers, yearlings, and barren cows loose in the high pastures, brought the mothers and their babies down closer to the ranch where the grass had come back in the sandy soil, and celebrated with a cookout and some good whiskey to thank the boys who'd come to lend a hand.

Over steaks cut from a maverick steer nobody had claimed during the roundup, Patrick sat with Gene Rhodes at the long table where the cowboys were sawing into meat and eyeing Emma appreciatively as she served platters of vegetables, potatoes, and beans.

One of the best bronc riders on the basin, Gene was a mite undersized and weighed no more than a hundred and fifty pounds, but he was all muscle and sinew. He had bright blue eyes, a cowlick he kept hidden under his hat, and a slight cleft palate that gave him a peculiar way of speaking, although it didn't spoil his looks. He'd studied at a California college for two years, working odd jobs to do it, and after coming home had taught school for a spell before starting up his spread.

The two men talked horses and books for a time, until Gene brought up the Fountain murders. Lincoln County had dropped the indictments against Oliver Lee and Bill McNew, and Gene, a good and true friend of Lee, wanted to know if Pat Garrett had come around asking Cal to sign on as a deputy.

"He paid a visit," Patrick replied. "He wanted Cal to help round up some witnesses who may have heard Oliver and McNew plotting to kill Fountain in '95. He's mule headed about getting another indictment."

"It's a damn ugly and dangerous feud," Gene replied, lighting a cigarette. "I plan to shun the politicians who have caused it for the rest of my days. Either that, or I mean to fisticuff a few of them."

Patrick laughed. Gene was known as the scrappiest boxer around, taking on all comers, no matter how big they were.

"I'm heading home," Gene said as he stood.

"Stop by anytime," Patrick said.

"I may have to do that," Gene said. "The Double K is about the only place on the Tularosa where a body can avoid getting into a gunfight over this sorry business."

* * *

Gene's reckoning of the tension between the Lee and Garrett factions proved to be near perfect. On his next visit to Las Cruces, Patrick found that some old boys were on the prod for misguided citizens sitting on the wrong side of the political aisle, opposing newspapers had gone to war in print, and just about everybody in the town was holding their breath waiting for the lead to start flying. At the mercantile store, he picked out some trees Emma had asked him to buy for the courtyard and left for home with a load of supplies and the saplings wrapped in damp paper, glad to be leaving the uneasiness in town behind.

With the passing of summer into fall, Patrick became more and more convinced that Emma's bad moods were a thing of the past. But when she miscarried in the early days of another pregnancy, anger and grief took hold of her once again and she would have nothing to do with him at all.

Unwilling to put up with her damnable silence and brooding, he bundled her in blankets and took her against her will to see a doctor in Las Cruces, who examined her in private. When he finished, he told Patrick there was nothing physically wrong with Emma, and during her next pregnancy she was to repose in bed and avoid all mental and physical effort during the first two to three months.

"Should she show signs of fever, chill, nausea, or indisposition, she must rest," the doctor said. "If the symptoms worsen to pains in the lower back or abdomen and a discharge, you must call for me to come right away."

"Our ranch is out a ways in the San Andres east of Engle," Patrick said.

The doctor peered at the couple over his eyeglasses. "I see. This is her second miscarriage, which means she will very likely have difficulty again. If that is the case, you would be wise to rent a place here in town as soon as it is apparent she is pregnant so that she can have proper care."

"I don't want to get pregnant again," Emma said bluntly. "Ever."

The doctor smiled sympathetically. "You're excessively distressed right now, but that will pass."

Emma shook her head. "I can't bear the thought of losing another baby."

"Then we'll just have to make sure that you don't," he replied. "The most dangerous time to lose a baby is from the tenth to the twentieth week."

He turned to Patrick. "Bring her to see me as soon as she misses a menstrual cycle, so that I can arrest any possibility of expulsion and quiet the womb."

"I will," Patrick said. "I'm obliged."

He settled up with the doctor and walked with Emma down the street to the hotel where they were staying for the night.

"I'll never have another baby," Emma snapped angrily as she moved rapidly away from Patrick.

He caught up and grabbed her arm. "Of course we're gonna have children. It'll be all right. I'll rent us a house here in town like the doctor said. It will be all right."

"Let go of me." She jerked free, stormed into the hotel, and didn't say another word for hours.

That night, Patrick drank whiskey at a bar until he was sure Emma was asleep before he returned to their room. He stretched out on the creaky bed and listened to her breathing, wondering how long she'd be cantankerous this time before it wore off. He was certain that she wanted children, and he'd taken to the idea for her sake, although he doubted he would make much of a father.

45

In the spring of 1898, about the same time Pat Garrett was fixing to do battle with Oliver Lee, the government decided to go to war with Spain over the sinking of the battleship *Maine* in the Havana Harbor. A call was made to raise three volunteer cavalry regiments authorized by Congress, and Patrick decided to sign up.

He was more eager to get away from Emma and her unsettled ways than he was to fight the Spaniards. Most of the time she seemed fine, but then out of nowhere she'd snap at him without cause, or start a fight over something he'd said that didn't amount to spit. When that happened, she took to leaving the house in a huff, being gone for hours on her pony, with Patrick out chasing her down to get her home before nightfall.

She hadn't kicked him out of her bed, but she hadn't gotten pregnant again either. Patrick took to thinking she was wishing herself not to have a baby and succeeding at it, although he didn't exactly know how.

Cal told him war wouldn't be the glory he expected it to be, but Patrick would hear none of it. On a sunny morning in late April he arrived in Las Cruces and presented himself to William Llewellyn, the speaker of the territorial House of Representatives, who had been asked by the governor to recruit volunteers. He signed up, passed a physical examination, got mustered in, and was assigned to Troop G, commanded by Llewellyn, who'd been made a captain.

Within a few days the troop's quota had been filled, and the men marched down to the depot for the trip to San Antonio, where the First United States Volunteer Cavalry would be assembled and trained. As the train left the station, the citizens of Las Cruces gave them a big send-off.

Although Patrick kept mostly to himself, there was a lot of laughter, jawboning, drinking, and card playing on the train ride to San Antonio. Very few of Patrick's fellow troopers were complete strangers to him. Most he'd either met or seen in passing here or there, and just about all were cowboys, hardened to the saddle. By the time the train pulled into San Antonio, the eighty men of Troop G all knew one another by their given names or favorite handles.

They unloaded at the fairgrounds southwest of town, where earlier arriving troops had set up camp. They got tents raised and equipment stowed, which took the rest of the day, ate supper, and turned in for the night. Come morning, Captain Llewellyn sent Patrick and five other riders over to Fort Sam Houston to bring back horses for the troopers. The detail brought back a remuda of tough, half-wild Texas and Mexican ponies that needed to be shod, and the captain set the boys to the task.

Once the training started, Patrick fell easily into the military routine. It wasn't much different than the life he'd always known of getting up early and working hard throughout the day. The regiment drilled on horseback and on foot, and by the end of a week most of the ponies had been gentled enough to ride. Somehow the senior officers, Colonel Wood and Colonel Roosevelt, had managed to equip and supply the regiment with first-rate Krag-Jørgenson carbines, which the men took to with ease. About the only things Patrick didn't like were the sticky weather, which made him sweat, and the low horizon of thick forest that had him constantly looking for mountains that weren't there.

By the end of the second week, the troop had lost five men to accidents, illness, and one death, when a fella got thrown by an outlaw bronc that stomped on him before he could get up.

Replacements were sent to bring the troop up to full strength, and one of the new boys was Jake Jacobi, who came over from one of the Arizona outfits.

"Pat Kerney," Jake said, looking Patrick over with a grin as the men lined up for chow, which most days consisted of hard bread and corned beef. "Now, ain't you a sight."

Patrick grinned back at the one man who'd been a true friend during his time at the Wilcox ranch. "Howdy, Jake," he said. "Did you shuck California?"

Jake shook his head. "Hell no, I stuck there permanent like. But when the Spaniards blew up the *Maine* this old sailor couldn't stand the thought of missing out on the fight. I hightailed it back to Arizona just in time to sign on."

"Well, I ain't sorry to see you," Patrick said. "Captain has me working with the ponies and I've got a passel more that needs gentling. You're just the old boy to help me do it."

"Just like old times," Jake said.

"That might be so," Patrick replied.

Excused from drilling with the regiment, Patrick and Jake spent long hours breaking horses. Because time was short, they were forced to use the quirt and handle the animals a bit rougher than usual. Together they made dozens of cavalry horses out of pitching, snorting, wild-eyed ponies without ever spoiling one.

At night Patrick fell asleep in his tent too tired, sore, and bruised to think about the Double K or Emma. After enough ponies had been saddle broke, Patrick and Jake began drilling again with the regiment, which they allowed was a whole lot easier than starting horses.

On a morning in late May, Captain Llewellyn assembled the troopers and told them they would be leaving soon for Tampa, Florida, where they would embark for Cuba.

"If you have letters to write, do it now," he said, before dismissing the men.

Patrick went back to his tent, sat down with paper and pen, and wrote to Emma.

Dear Emma,

Our captain says we'll be on our way to Florida soon and we best write home. Here in Texas we've been busy getting ready for the fight, training ponies, doing maneuvers, and drilling on horseback. Our commanding officer of the whole shebang is Col. Wood, who told us New Mexico boys we were a right smart outfit. They got us outfitted in new uniforms with leggings and equipped with new rifles and six-shooters that will sure take care of those Spaniards.

My captain is William Llewellyn, and he's a good officer.

*Cal knows him for sure and I'm betting George does too.
Lawyer Fall is here and so is George Curry. Both are captains
in other troops of our squadron. The folks here in Texas have
taken to calling us Rough Riders, so I guess that's our new
handle. Most of the men are from out of the West, but there
are college boys and easterners here also, including Col.
Wood's second in command, Col. Roosevelt, who some say
once bossed the police in New York City and had a ranch in
the Dakota Territory for a time. He sure likes the way I work
with the ponies and told me so. Said I did a bully job, and I
had to ask someone what it meant.*

*The officers make us drill on horseback every day,
sometimes in close formation, other times wheeling and
galloping our ponies in practice charges, or fanning out at a
high lope in a flanking maneuver. All the boys like the
horseback drills best.*

*Can't say much for the weather here. Hot and sticky at
night, so it's hard to sleep. And lots of mosquitoes, which us
New Mexico boys just ain't used to. We sure are a mixed
bunch, cowboys, miners, storekeepers, lawyers, even a
preacher who serves as a private, just like most of the rest of
us. Didn't think those eastern college boys would fit in, but
they do and they're a good sort. Surprised one of them by
having read a book or two.*

*Captain says there will be a post office in Tampa, so you
can write to me there if you want. Hope the ranch is okay and
the stock is healthy. Say howdy to Cal and George for me.*

Affectionately, your husband,
Patrick Kerney

He sealed the letter in an envelope and went to mail it, walking through a cloud of dust kicked up on the edge of the fairgrounds by a bunch of troopers racing their ponies. On the way back to his tent, he felt a touch of longing for Emma, the Double K, and even Cal and George.

HARD COUNTRY 413

He sealed the letter in an envelope and went to mail it, walking
through a cloud of dust kicked up on the edge of the fairgrounds
by a bunch of troopers racing their ponies. On the way back to his
tent, he felt a touch of longing for Emma, the Double K, and even
Cal and George.

46

On May 28, Patrick Kerney marched with more than a thousand men and more than twelve hundred animals out of their hot, dusty camp to the San Antonio train station for the trip to Tampa. It took the rest of the day and all night to get everything loaded. At dawn, the passenger trains arrived and the regiment finally got under way. The men spent four uncomfortable days in the cramped quarters of the train, the only relief coming with an occasional stop, where the men were given a few hours of leave. Aside from card games, idle chatter, and some illicit whiskey drinking, the only other distraction along the way came from folks who turned out to greet and cheer the regiment, bringing flowers, fruit, and pails of milk. There were pretty southern girls who waved flags and begged for mementos of buttons and cartridges. Many of the boys obliged.

In Tampa, getting unloaded was no less of a disorganized mess, and when everything finally did get sorted out, the men were marched across pine-covered sand flats to a campground. The land struck Patrick as odd. There were no branches on the lower trunks of the pine trees for a good twenty feet or more, and the sand was as hot as the blistering dunes of the Tularosa.

There wasn't much to Tampa: a big hotel, some homes and boardinghouses, and a number of saloons, diners, and business establishments along dusty streets. A single railroad track led to a port some eight or nine miles away. The clammy weather was worse than San Antonio, with the temperature over a hundred degrees. But in spite of that, the town was packed with folks eager to cheer on the troops and see the flotilla anchored in the harbor.

The officers kept the men busy practicing skirmish drills in the woods, and the regiment as a whole did several mounted drills, which were the most fun of all. On the regiment's last evening in Tampa, Patrick went down to the harbor and looked out at the water. As pretty as it was, with the bay filled with all kinds of civilian and navy ships, the sea beyond the port seemed unnaturally endless to him. He wasn't sure how he would like being on a boat. Jake had told him about how some people got seasick even when the water was fairly calm, but Patrick was more worried about not seeing land. He didn't like the notion of that at all.

He'd taken to smoking more since joining the volunteers. Away from the piers, where he could have some peace and quiet, he sat on the beach and rolled a smoke. After he finished, he wrote another letter to Emma.

Dear Wife,

I'm in Tampa now, ready to sail for Cuba tomorrow. I went to the post office hoping for a letter but there was none. I reckon you haven't been to town lately so maybe my letter hasn't gotten to you yet. I finally got paid, and the government gave me thirteen dollars in wages. Tell George I'm earning less than him now. It'll bring a smile, I bet.

Yesterday, our captain told us the horses are gonna stay behind, which means all that work I did with ponies for our troop in San Antonio is for naught. I guess you could call us the horseless Rough Riders.

Not all the boys are gonna get to go, and those to be left behind are plenty sorrowful. Tell Cal that George Curry and Albert Fall won't be going to war leastways in Cuba. But I'm sure they'll make up for it once they get back home, if Pat Garrett hasn't already killed Oliver Lee.

I met up with an old pard who rode for the brand with me in Arizona. Jake is his name, and he was a sailor before he took to being a hand. He's told me all about going to sea, but since it's a short trip I'm hoping to do all right.

It's possible that our next post office will be Havana, and I'll write again, if not from there, then from wherever the regiment lands. I am all right and going to war with the best men a fellow could ask to be with in dangerous times. Col. Roosevelt told us he knew of no better men more willing to do their duty.

Tell Cal that Captain Llewellyn sends his regards. He remembers him most kindly. Ask George to make sure he takes Jefe for a ride once in a while so he doesn't get fat or ornery while I'm gone.

Your affectionate husband,
Patrick Kerney

He rolled another cigarette and watched the sun dip low on the horizon, turning the shimmering water golden. It was sure pretty enough, but he didn't like the empty surface of the vast ocean at all.

* * *

Rumors of lurking Spanish warships off the Florida coast kept the invasion fleet of warships and transports, loaded with thousands of soldiers and tons of supplies, in port for seven days before sailing. Because of a lack of ships, only the officers' ponies had been loaded, which meant all the boys would be on foot. Nobody liked the idea of it at all.

On smelly, hot, overcrowded ships the men sweltered, cursed, and made do without adequate food or water. When the fleet finally weighed anchor, the Rough Riders were about ready to rebel against the generals who bossed the army and the admirals who ran the navy.

They steamed for six days, and the big, empty ocean didn't bother Patrick that much, not with thirty-five ships stretched out over the water. At night, the ship's lights made it look like a town floating on the sea.

When the fleet raised Santiago, the ships stopped. Ahead, navy picket ships, tiny in the distance against the high mountains of the coast that rose from the water's edge, blocked the harbor. Set back from the bay with its narrow passage to the sea overlooked by a large castle on a high bluff, Santiago didn't strike Patrick as a promising place to start a war. His doubts were eased after Captain Llewellyn told the troops the Spanish ships were bottled up inside the bay and the regiment would disembark at a place called Daiquirí, a small mining village down the coast.

Most of the boys were glad to see land and were eager to shuck the ship. The flotilla steamed a short ways and after warships shelled the village and other settlements close by, the troops went ashore in rowboats that were tossed around in the heavy seas. The officers' horses brought on the deck jumped off the ship. Most swam to shore, but some drowned out to sea.

Patrick managed to keep his food down on the boat to shore but felt unsteady for a time after reaching dry land. Jake said it was because of sea legs.

There were no Spanish to fight in Daiquirí, which was a darn good thing, because getting the camp organized turned into a mess just like in Tampa. This time they set up in a grove of palm trees, with the colored Buffalo Soldiers of the Tenth Cavalry camped next to them.

In the morning, a trooper from another outfit brought over a mail pouch that had been put on the wrong ship in Tampa. In it was a letter to Patrick from Cal.

Patrick,

Emma shared your letter and I read it to George, who is laid up with a bad case of gout these several weeks that has settled in his knee, causing considerable pain. He chuckled at your message to him and it raised his spirits mightily. If he doesn't improve shortly, I'll haul him to town and have the doctor look him over.

With George hobbled up, Emma has pitched right in to help with the ranch and I tell you she has the makings of a hand. That little gal works as hard as any cowboy and shirks from no chore. I swear, taking on a man's work suits her as she is now as cheerful and lively as she was in the past. I suspect you'll be greeted by a wife who's a top hand when you come home. And I can tell you for a fact she is pining for your return.

Here we've got our own war brewing. Oliver Lee and
several of his pards have been hiding from Pat Garrett, who
put together a posse of Republicans bound to hunt Lee down.
Last week, I came upon Lee and Jim Gilliland with Gene
Rhodes on Double K land. They said they were just moseying
through, but I figure they were scouting hideouts for once the
shooting starts.

I reckon they're using Gene's ranch as their headquarters
right now.

I'll take this letter along with one Emma has written to
you to town tomorrow with the hope that you are safe, healthy,
and unharmed.

Your partner,
Cal

Patrick put the letter in his pocket, found the trooper who'd
brought the mail pouch, and asked if there was another letter for
him that might have been misplaced.

The old boy shook his head. "All that came was in that there
pouch," the trooper replied.

Patrick returned to his troop, cogitating on the unhappy idea
that with George laid up, Cal and Emma were getting along just
fine at the Double K without him. He didn't like it at all but had
no time to brood, as the troops were soon assembled and the regiment moved out.

* * *

They marched all day and into the night. Patrick was certain his
sore feet would give out, but he made it without complaint, al-

though he sure did miss his pony. When they arrived in Siboney, a coastal town abandoned by the Spanish, Captain Llewellyn explained that the troops were now part of the Fifth Corps, with orders to encircle the town of Santiago, twelve miles distant, where the Spanish waited in great numbers.

"There will be fighting up ahead before we get there, boys," Llewellyn added, "so eat and rest."

They made fires, cooked pork and coffee, and filled their bellies before a tropical storm soaked them for several hours. Jake and Patrick cut huge palm leaves and used them for shelter. When it ended, they dried out as best they could and rested for a time on soggy ground before moving out at first light up a narrow mountain trail surrounded by heavy timber. As they neared the front, the advance guards came under fire.

Captain Llewellyn soon had the boys in the midst of the fighting, pushing their way through thick jungle against a hidden enemy firing down from several mountain positions. They moved forward under a withering attack from camouflaged soldiers using smokeless powder, with no clear targets to shoot at.

Clutching their rifles, Patrick and Jake Jacobi plodded through a clearing of chest-high grass with men on their left and right. It was slow going, with everybody ducking for cover as the Spanish poured down fire. Behind them the units had gotten all mixed together during the advance, and troopers and regular soldiers were right on their backs. Men fell and never got up.

On the far side of the grassy clearing, Patrick and Jake dropped on their bellies, wiggled under wire fences strung in the dense jungle, and worked their way cautiously to a ridge at the foot of a sheer mountain. Bullets clipped the brush around them. On either side, troopers joined the line.

"Where are those sons o' bitches so I can shoot them?" Jake griped as he pressed himself to the ground.

"Damn if I know," Patrick replied, his chin buried in spongy dirt. Craning his neck, all he could see were trees climbing the steep incline. "Maybe Captain Llewellyn can tell us."

Jake looked around. "He ain't nearby, so I guess we're on our own."

Close to the right, they heard heavy firing from some troopers. Crouching low, they ran under a hail of bullets to join the fray. Through an opening in the jungle they could see a group of men advancing slowly on some red-tiled ranch buildings. They joined up where the troopers had taken cover in thick underbrush to find Colonel Roosevelt in command.

Roosevelt smiled at them, his teeth flashing. "Ah, my two New Mexico bronc riders. If you can fight as well as you break horses, we'll have these rascals whipped in a jiffy."

"I'm from the Arizona troop, Colonel," Jake Jacobi said.

Roosevelt clamped a hand on Jake's shoulder. "No matter, my boy; we're all Americans."

A cheer went up from some troops down the line, and Roosevelt sprang to his feet. "I believe Colonel Wood has made his charge. Let's join in the fight."

The troopers rose as one and rushed the buildings. Heavy firing passed over their heads and then abruptly stopped. Out of breath, they reached the buildings, to find two dead Spanish soldiers. The rest had retreated.

"Well done, men," Roosevelt boomed delightedly.

The boys heartily congratulated each other before moving ahead.

After the shooting stopped for the day, Patrick learned they had fought the first land battle of the war at a place called Las Guasi-mas. The Rough Riders had eight men killed and thirty-four wounded. In all, sixteen American soldiers had died and fifty-two were wounded.

The next morning, Patrick and Jake helped bury the dead troopers on a hillside near a big tree with vultures circling over-head. A chaplain read a service, and the men bared their heads, sang "Rock of Ages," and walked silently back to camp.

* * *

The Fifth Corps moved camp several miles to a marsh next to a pleasant stream and awaited orders that didn't come for five days, making all the boys restless. When the corps finally started march-ing toward Santiago, the regiment was bunched in the back of a long column of Regular Army soldiers. During the long, hot slog, they waded through streams, plodded through thick jungle, and pushed on until nightfall, when they stopped and slept on open ground with no cover, near an abandoned ranch on a hill.

Up before dawn, the men ate a quick breakfast and assembled as the sun rose in a clear sky. A battery of field guns arrived, pulled by huge horses. Once the guns were placed and trained on the enemy above, the men were much pleased. They gave a shout when the cannons opened up on the Spanish, filling the sky with great clouds of white smoke.

A minute or more passed before the Spanish artillery replied and shells started exploding overhead, sending shrapnel into the assembled troops. A piece of shrapnel sliced the skin off a knuckle on Patrick's left hand, but it hurt no more than a skinned shin. Four men were wounded and one lost a leg.

Colonel Roosevelt hurried the regiment over the crest of the hill into some thickets and re-formed the columns. When the big guns fell silent, he moved the troops behind Colonel Wood's brigade down a trail to a ford in the San Juan River. They crossed under heavy rifle fire and passed through a field of smooth, high grass, men pitching forward or sinking out of sight as they got hit.

They entered a sunken lane, fenced by wire on either side, that led straight up between two hills where the Spanish were entrenched, the Mauser bullets from their rifles whirling and popping in the air. They found cover were they could, but a few of the boys got shot anyway.

To the right and left of the regiment, soldiers were advancing slowly up the hill with a logjam of men behind them.

Patrick and Jake were flat on their stomachs ten feet away from the colonel when his orderly collapsed, shot dead.

Roosevelt called Jake over to him.

Bent low, Jake moved quickly to Roosevelt's side.

"Trooper, find Colonel Wood and ask if we've been given permission to advance. Tell him we are being much cut up."

"Yes, sir." Jake stood and pitched forward across Roosevelt's knees with a bullet through his throat.

Patrick reached Jake in a single leap and pulled him off the colonel. Blood was pumping from his cut artery. Patrick tried to stem the flow with his hand.

"It's no use," Roosevelt said quietly, his face grim, his leggings covered in Jake's blood.

Patrick waited until Jake stopped breathing and closed his eyes. "I'll carry the message for you, Colonel."

"Good lad," Roosevelt said over the sound of renewed fighting.

Down the line another trooper slumped, shot through the mouth. "Be careful, my boy."

"Yes, sir," Patrick replied. He crawled to the end of the trench, bent low, and started running. A bullet caught him in the side, spun him around, and knocked him off his feet. He looked over at the colonel, who waved at him to return to the trench. He shook his head, got up, and started running again, slowed by the pain. The ball had hit bone, probably a rib, and it hurt like the blazes.

On the other side of the river he came upon a general on horseback and gave him Colonel Roosevelt's message.

"He is to advance," the officer said. "I'll go to him immediately. Have your wound attended to."

Patrick pulled out his shirttail and inspected the wound. It was bleeding, but not badly. He could feel the exit hole in his back, so he knew the bullet had passed through. He wadded his neckerchief against his side, secured it with his belt, and got back to the line in time to join the last contingent of men advancing up the hill.

He moved slowly, dizzily forward, telling himself not to quit the fight or go yellow. Up ahead he could see Colonel Roosevelt moving back and forth across the line, encouraging the men. He kept ducking bullets even though he knew they had already passed by. Suddenly, he felt faint and crumpled to the ground. The next thing he saw was an officer kneeling next to him.

"You've been nipped in the side," the officer said as he inspected Patrick's wound.

"I know it," Patrick said. "Anywhere else?"

"Not that I can tell." The officer finished dressing the wound. "You'll live. Let's get you down the hill."

"I can go on," Patrick said.

"Not today. You got a bit of a fever." He called a soldier over as he helped Patrick to his feet. "Take this man to the field hospital."

Woozy and wobbly, Patrick made his way slowly down the hill on the soldier's helpful arm. By the time a surgeon had him stretched out on the ground at the field hospital, he was burning up.

Not today. You got a bit of a fever. He called an orderly over to help Patrick to his feet. "Take this man to the field hospital."

Woozy and wobbly, Patrick made his way slowly down the hill on the soldier's helpful arm. By the time a surgeon had him stretched out on the ground at the field hospital, he was burning up.

47

I n early May 1899, ten months after his return from Cuba, Private Patrick Kerney was released from the post hospital at Fort Monroe, Virginia. He'd survived a Spanish bullet, malaria, dysentery, pneumonia, and the hospital at Camp Wikoff on Montauk Point, Long Island, where all the sick and wounded men were first treated upon their arrival home.

Thousands of men had been hospitalized at the camp. The lucky ones, who were not sick or who had recovered from their wounds, remained quarantined with their units until they mustered out. Most of Patrick's troop left for home in September. The very ill were sent to civilian and military hospitals for further treatment. Fortunately for Patrick, the doctors and nurses at Fort Monroe had kept him alive through some rough times with fever that often made him senseless. When he wasn't delirious, unconscious, and racked with pain, he suffered from chills, headaches, vomiting, diarrhea, and a raw, dry cough. There were days he was too weak to move from his bed, and when he did get up, exhaustion quickly overtook him. At times his deliriums took him back to the ranch, except it wasn't Emma waiting for him at home, but Ida. When he did dream of Emma, she was with Cal, not him.

As he slowly recovered, the doctors told him he had miraculously survived the most dangerous, potentially life-threatening form of malaria. He believed them. Back in the hospital wards at Camp Wikoff he had seen men as sick or sicker, dying like flies. Thousands had died of the disease, far more than those shot down by Spanish guns. It was a grim business.

Wearing a brand-spanking-new Rough Riders uniform with almost a year's pay in his pocket, Patrick left the massive, six-sided stone fortress, which had been built decades before the Civil War. Situated on a point of land at the tip of the ocean, completely surrounded by a moat, Fort Monroe had brought back memories of Yuma Prison. He was glad to be rid of it.

He bought a train ticket all the way to Engle and sent a telegraph to Ignacio in Tularosa, asking him to let Emma and Cal know he would be arriving in four days. He'd written home a week before saying he would soon be released and asking that they bring his pony to the station so he could ride home. Now with his energy low again, he wasn't sure that had been such a good idea.

In Baltimore, there was a two-hour wait for his train. He passed the time rereading the letters from home he'd received over the months. Cal and Emma had written faithfully, mostly with news of the ranch and doings on the basin.

George had recovered from gout only to crack his head on a fall from his horse in rough country. He'd healed up nicely under Emma's care and was back in the saddle. Last summer's rains had brought more grass back in the high pastures, and a couple of winter storms had put a good mantle of snow on the peaks.

Patrick had missed both the fall and spring works, but Cal wrote about them in detail, praising Emma's growing skills as a hand. With her help, the outfit had made enough profit from stock sales in the fall to put a little money in the bank and build a line cabin in the high country. Cal reckoned he'd reached a point where he didn't need to sleep on the cold, hard ground anymore when he was out tending cattle. The cabin had been supplied with a stove, two cots, firewood, and provisions. Cal figured it would add some years to his life if he could avoid gunfights and accidents.

With George's help, Emma had built a chicken coop near the barn and had stocked it with six hens and a rooster. So far, the hens were producing a steady quantity of eggs, much to Cal and George's delight at breakfast. Within a month of getting the chickens, Emma had shot a coyote and a bobcat trying to raid the henhouse. She wrote that some Troop G boys back in Las Cruces had told her about how Patrick had gotten wounded carrying a message for Colonel Roosevelt, and she was eager to hear all about it when he got home.

He wondered how long he'd be worthless once he returned to the ranch. He'd lost thirty pounds, was as pale as a banker, and ran out of steam real fast. The doctors had told him getting back to his old self could take a while and he could expect to have relapses that might be mild or severe. But he'd fixed on the notion that no matter how long it took him to get well, he damn sure wasn't gonna let Emma, Cal, or George coddle him like some invalid. He'd had enough of that in the hospital.

He mostly worried how he and Emma would get on. Her letters hadn't been filled with tender feelings, but then neither were his. He remembered the times when she'd stormed out of the house in a fury and wondered if he could put up with the dark moods that came over her. Maybe she was done with all of that and they could start fresh, start a family.

He paged through newspaper clippings Emma had sent along in some of her letters. The war with Spain hadn't kept the skirmish over the Fountain murders from heating up on the basin. There had been a gunfight at Wildy Well between Pat Garrett and his deputies against Oliver Lee and his partners. A deputy sheriff had been killed and Lee and Jim Gilliland had gone on the dodge. Cal had seen them riding with Gene Rhodes in the San Andres backcountry. This time the three men sported long beards that made them almost unrecognizable.

In Cal's last letter, he wrote that Lee and Gilliland had given themselves up and were about to go on trial for the Fountain murders in Hillsboro, the Sierra County seat north of Las Cruces. Newspapers from around the country had sent reporters to cover the event, and Patrick had been following the goings-on and the hullabaloo as best he could. He had no druthers as to how it might turn out but wouldn't mind being in the courtroom to hear all the lies that were sure to be told by both sides.

Other than the pending trial, the big excitement on the basin was the coming of the railroad. While Patrick was in Cuba, the tracks had reached the new town site of Alamogordo on the eastern side of the Tularosa and building lots were being laid out and sold. The territorial legislature had carved a new county out of parts of Doña Ana and Lincoln counties and named it for the sitting governor, Miguel Otero. The seat of county government was to be the new town, which just about guaranteed its future prosperity. Patrick wondered if newcomers had already started pouring in. He didn't doubt it. Would he even recognize the place once he got home?

He boarded the train and settled down in an empty seat, hoping folks would let him be, but his uniform attracted too much atten-

tion. Men came up to him and shook his hand, women were thrilled
to meet a Rough Rider, and a young, wide-eyed button traveling
with his mother asked if he'd been shot in Cuba. Patrick allowed
that it was so, sent him back to his seat pronto, pulled his campaign
hat down low, and pretended to sleep. It wasn't long before he
drifted off.

* * *

During the next few days, Patrick stayed to himself as much as
possible, watching the countryside pass by through the railcar windows. The doctors had told him to avoid hard spirits, and he stuck
to their advice when offered a drink now and then by fellow pas-
sengers who wanted to hear all about the Rough Riders.

The Midwest was a big, fertile country and he was glad to see it,
but he missed the mountains that screened the endless sun-blasted
Tularosa, the huge skies that capped the heaving sand dunes and
jumbled lava flows, and the purple sunsets that danced over the
San Andres.

There were moments when his mind returned to the war. He
flinched at the thought of Jake Jacobi dying in his arms, blood
pulsing from his throat. Or he remembered the Spanish artillery
shell that took off the trooper's leg at the battle for Kettle Hill, the
limb tumbling end over end in the air. He had almost no memory
of getting shot but recalled clearly the days he spent lying on the
spongy, moist ground burning up with fever, his wound infected,
his mind a confused jumble, watching the sand crabs crawling
toward the bodies of the men who had died.

He put thoughts of war aside when the Rocky Mountains rose
in the distance, and during the remainder of the trip his spirits

revived. From Socorro south into the Jornada del Muerto he drank in the sight of the raw desert and rugged mountains he knew and loved so well.

As the train chugged into Engle, he spotted Emma, Cal, and George standing on the platform, waving gaily. George looked older; Emma, browned by the sun and still about as pretty as a girl could be, looked as though she'd grown an inch or two; and Cal sported a bushy white mustache that gave him a distinguished air.

Seeing them brought feelings of delight and apprehension Patrick hadn't expected. As the train ground to a stop, he grabbed his bag and headed for the exit. They had all changed some, he reckoned, and with the new century just months away he wondered what the future would bring and just how he might fit into it on the Double K.

⋙ THREE ⋘

Emma Kerney

48

Patrick stayed close to the ranch after his return home, happy to be back on the Tularosa. He grew stronger every day, and when the fevers and chills came, he recovered faster each time, thanks to Emma's care. She had welcomed him back to her bed without hesitation, and although the sex was satisfying, Patrick seemed indifferent toward her, something she'd never experienced with him before. Many nights he fell asleep in a porch rocking chair and came to bed in the wee hours.

When Patrick left to go to war, Emma had felt a twinge of jealousy. Had she been a man, she would have done the same. Not for the fighting, but to see faraway places, walk big-city streets, and watch ocean waves lap sandy shores. It had always been her dream to see the world.

Their first night in bed together after he got home, she touched the bullet-hole scar in his side. "Does it hurt?"

"Leave that be," he said, pushing her hand away.

"Tell me what happened."

"I didn't get into this bed buck naked to tell you a story," he said as his hand slid to her thigh.

"Will you tell me sometime?"

"Maybe so, but I doubt it."

At breakfast the next morning she asked him about the ocean. "I've always wanted to see it."

"Didn't like it," Patrick said. "It ain't a friendly place. Empty and dangerous."

He went outside and she followed. "I don't mean to rile you, but you've seen places I can only dream about."

"I didn't go on a pleasure trip."

"I know that," Emma said, touching his arm.

Patrick pulled away. "Let it be."

That night he came into the bedroom just as she was putting away the letters he'd written to her.

"You should burn those," he said.

"They're mine to keep," she said. "I've been reading them again. What happened to that Arizona friend of yours?"

"Jake got shot in the neck and died," he answered grimly, staring at her.

"I'm sorry."

"There's nothing about the war that you need to know, so stop pestering me about it."

He turned, stomped away, and was gone all night.

In the morning, she sought Cal out and told him what had happened.

Cal nodded sympathetically. He had served in the Eighth Texas Cavalry, known as Terry's Texas Raiders, during the War of Secession, and fought at Shiloh, Chickamauga, and Chattanooga. Near the end of the fighting, he'd slipped through Union lines with a hundred and fifty fellow Confederate cavalrymen to avoid capture.

Thirty-four years later, he had no desire to talk about the horrors he'd experienced, although they still haunted him at times.

Emma looked at Cal. "Was I pestering?"

"Nope," he replied, "but war ain't an easy subject to talk about. It's the worst kind of killing. There ain't nothing to compare. It changes a body forever."

"Have you been in a war?" Emma asked.

Cal nodded. "And it still troubles my mind to think about it." He patted Emma's arm. "Just like it must vex you to recollect what happened at Pine Tree Canyon."

Emma shivered and her expression clouded. "Yes, of course."

"Don't fret," Cal said. "You ain't been contrary about it."

"I'll leave him be, promise," Emma said.

Cal smiled. "Don't you do that. You're his best medicine. Maybe he'll tell you on his own someday."

"I hope so."

During his next trip to town, Cal found issues of *Scribner's Magazine* that contained Colonel Roosevelt's serialized accounts of his war exploits in Cuba and brought them home to Emma, who studied them eagerly. Patrick also read them and allowed that the colonel had told the story true enough.

"Except he makes it sound like it was heroic, which it weren't," he added.

"Then what was it like?" Emma asked.

"A bunch of blundering fools creeping up hills to their deaths," he replied. "Cal was right; there ain't no glory in war."

Emma bit her lip. "No one was brave?"

"Lots of boys were," Patrick replied. "But it was still nothing but a god-awful mess."

Live cattle prices had jumped during the war, and the trend had held into 1899. Before Patrick's return, Cal had struck a deal with a cattle buyer that guaranteed another prosperous year for the outfit. With enough grass in the high pastures to winter over more than just the steers, cows, and calves, Cal had held back some of the yearlings to sell as two-year-olds. It meant greater profit, and if prices held steady he planned to do it again.

There was always the risk another drought could upend his plans. But with the ranch almost in the black and the bank loan about to be paid off, Cal figured it to be a good time to take the gamble. After he explained his thinking on the matter, Patrick readily went along.

The two men had worked as stray riders on the John Cross, 7TX, and Bar Cross roundups, so when the time came to get the Double K fall works under way, cowboys from all three spreads showed up, along with Gene Rhodes.

"I thought you went off to get married," Cal said as Gene slid off his saddle.

Colonel Fountain's and his son's bodies had never been found, and after the acquittal of his friends Oliver Lee and Jim Gilliland in the murder trial, Gene Rhodes had gone back east to marry a lady he'd been romancing by mail.

"I did and I am," Gene replied as he nodded at Patrick. "Went all the way to New York State. Sure is different than this hot, dusty basin, but I can't say I like it any better. Family will join me shortly, but until then I need work and a place to lie low."

"What did you go and do?" Patrick asked.

Gene pulled an earlobe. "Seems the old boy I hired to look after my place while I was gone went and said the cow I'd slaughtered for him to eat was stolen. Of course, that was after he ate the beef.

To clear matters up, I had to bend my pistol over his head and escort him to Texas."

"Are there warrants for your arrest?" Cal asked.

"After what I done to him, there could be," Gene replied. "So I'd just as soon not be too easy to find for a spell."

"You're not gathering any cattle this fall?"

Gene shook his head. "I sold them sometime back, and my pa is wintering over his stock. I'm looking to hire on as a hand somewhere for a time."

"We'll take you on for fall works," Patrick said, "and if you've a need, you can hunker down in our line cabin after we finish up."

Gene smiled. "That's mighty neighborly, and I'm obliged. Besides the hands from the John Cross, the 7TX, and the Bar Cross, who else is joining up?"

"That's it," Cal said.

"Should be enough," Gene said, glancing at Patrick. "I sure hope your missus is gonna be the trail cook. She fixes a mighty fine table, as I recall."

"Old George will be driving the chuck wagon and fixing the victuals," Cal said. "He can't fork a horse the way he used to, and Patrick's wife, Emma, makes a hand."

"Sorry to hear that about George," Gene said, giving Patrick a glance. "Your wife makes a hand, does she? Why, that's worth seeing, I reckon."

"Maybe so," Patrick said with a shrug.

* * *

Before the fall works, Cal and Patrick had moved most of the Double K cattle to a south pasture, a high-country valley with adequate water and good browse that stretched for ten miles through shallow canyons and around solitary peaks. There were some old, played-out mines tunneled into mountainsides, but it was all government land that had never been homesteaded or proved up, so the grasses hadn't been overgrazed before the ruinous three-year drought.

The crew left the ranch before sunup and reached the valley campsite at noon, pushing stray stock they picked up ahead of them along the way. It was a mixed bunch of thirty-six half-wild steers, ornery mother cows, and bawling calves, all looking to skedaddle into nearby side canyons.

George had set up camp in a grassy field with browse nearby for the remuda, wood to fuel the cook fire, and a stream under a ridgeline that ran clear and cold. A fire was going when the waddies arrived, and George was busy cutting freshly butchered steaks from a side of beef he'd kept cool and covered in a washtub.

He'd fed the crew a breakfast of eggs and bacon at four in the morning, and they'd eaten until they were stacked to the fill. But that was eight hours ago and he'd hear gripes real quick if supper was late. He wasted no time frying the steaks, heating up canned corn seared in beef drippings, boiling rice, and warming up biscuits and gravy.

Patrick herded the remuda into a rope corral, and the riders picked out and saddled their fresh cutting horses for the afternoon's work. When they finished, George called the crew to chow, and to a man they stood aside and let Emma go first. She didn't hesitate to step to the head of the line.

At the stream where he was watering the stray cattle, Gene Rhodes watched the courtly display with amusement. He knew a number of hardworking womenfolk who toiled from daybreak to nighttime, but never one who made a hand. Stock raising was men's work, and most women were glad to have nothing to do with it. Cal Doran was not a man given to exaggeration, so he was keen to see exactly how well Emma Kerney could fork a horse. Watching her make tracks from the ranch to camp didn't prove anything one way or the other, but he had hopes she'd show spunk and grit when they started cutting and branding after supper.

With two years of college in California under his belt plus some audited courses he'd taken at the new agriculture and mechanical college in Las Cruces, Gene had an eye on becoming a writer. A story about a comely, slender, hard-riding cowgirl who put the boys to shame on a roundup just might sell to a magazine, even if it was a bit shy of the truth in the telling of it. The more he thought about it, the better he liked the idea.

With a big beefsteak draped on his plate along with all the other fixings, he sat on a log across from Emma Kerney and gave her a close gander to sear her features in his mind's eye.

"You stare at me like I ought to be home scrubbing the floor," Emma said.

Gene blushed. "I don't mean to be rude, ma'am, but I never worked a roundup with a woman before."

"Is that what your wife does?" Emma asked, ignoring Gene's comment. "Scrub and darn and clean and such?"

Gene blushed again, this time in irritation. "I reckon so. She sure doesn't cowboy like I hear you do."

"Don't get her riled," George cautioned as he sat down next to Gene and cut a slice off his steak.

"You don't think I can do it?" Emma said, glaring at Rhodes.

"I didn't say that," Gene replied, looking to Patrick for help.

Patrick shook his head and cut another bite of steak.

"She's riled," George muttered.

"I'm not riled," Emma snapped.

"I sure hope you can cowboy, ma'am," Gene replied softly. "I truly do."

Emma's glare didn't soften. "And why is that?"

"Because it would be a heck of a story," Gene answered, "and one I'd be happy to tell around a campfire to a bunch of old boys."

Emma studied Gene hard to judge if he was funning her.

"I mean it," Gene said sincerely.

Emma stopped glaring and smiled. "I believe you."

"I am truly relieved that you do," Gene replied.

After dinner, the crew filled the wreck pan with dirty dishes and rode into the pasture to make the first cut. No one needed to be told what to do. They would gather all the stock, separate out the steers, brand the strays, and point the herd along in the direction of the next day's roundup.

Emma had saddled up a cutting pony named Biscuit that looked thrifty enough for any good hand to fork. She didn't hesitate going after a reluctant, bellowing steer that wanted to stay in the center of the shifting, nervous herd. She showed Biscuit the animal she wanted and the pony went right for it. The steer dodged, and Emma's pony dodged with it. The steer twisted toward the center of the herd, and Biscuit cut it off, settling back on its heels, forcing the steer toward the perimeter. In the midst of the herd, Biscuit and the steer turned and dodged in lightning-fast, whirligig unison, until Emma cleared her quarry.

Gene dropped his lariat over the steer and tipped his hat to Emma as he led the panting animal away.

Emma smiled as she wheeled Biscuit back to cut out another critter.

Gene parked the steer with the others that had already been cut out, plunged his pony into the riled herd, whirled a steer to the fringe, and quickly cleared it, thinking he might not need to color up a story about a top-hand cowgirl after all.

By the time all the steers were separated and they began working the cows and calves, he was damn sure convinced that Emma made a hand.

He watched her go after an irritated mother cow bent on protecting her baby. It was a ticklish business, but Emma didn't hesitate to turn Biscuit loose. The cow wheeled and charged. Biscuit dodged, closed on the animal, and hounded it until it broke away from its calf. Not once did Emma grab leather, and she dropped her lariat on the frightened calf in her first try and pulled it to the branding fire.

Gene followed along, dismounted, threw the quaking calf to the ground, twisted it until it was on its side, and held its head while a Bar Cross cowboy stomped his boot on a rear leg, pushed it forward, and pulled the other leg far to the rear to keep it from kicking.

Cal seared the Double K brand into its hide, clipped an ear, and castrated it.

"You weren't blowing smoke about that gal," Gene said as he released the bawling calf and threw the next one down. "Patrick has got himself one humdinger of a wife."

Cal chuckled, repeated the same procedure on the calf, and said, "That's a fact, although he's still getting used to her."

"I can see why," Gene said. "She's no ordinary filly."

The outfit worked until sundown. Most of the gathered cattle belonged to the Double K, so there was no need for the stray men to begin separating the animals by brand. After supper, the first two night guards, Patrick and Emma, rode out to bed down the restless herd.

That slip of a gal purely amazed Gene. She had worked as hard as any hand during the day and seemed to take to the job like she was born to it. He started thinking on another story he could pen about a ranch-savvy gal who bamboozles a young cowboy into believing she is helpless in order to win his affection. He wanted to start in on it right away but was too darn weary. Instead he jotted the idea in a pocket notebook, along with the one about a girl who goes on a roundup and puts the boys to shame, rolled up in his blanket, put his head on his saddle, and went to sleep.

49

The camp stayed put the next two days as the riders popped stray cattle out of the nearby canyons and nudged them off surrounding mountainsides. The effort added eighty head of drifted steers, cows, calves, and a few yearlings to the growing herd, belonging mostly to the other outfits. There were even a few of Gene's cows in the bunch, which pleased him greatly. He'd trail them to town with the Double K cut and sell them there.

The drifted critters were a mite unruly, which kept the night guards alert during the cool, starlit dark hours. But by the time they were on the move to the new campground, they ambled along with the Double K herd without complaint. All together the tally reached over two hundred head.

At the new camp, the crew settled the cows, saddled fresh ponies for the afternoon roundup, and lined up with their plates waiting for George to spoon out the hot stew that was simmering over the fire in Dutch ovens. Along with it came stewed prunes, hot biscuits, and Arbuckles' coffee.

"George, I swear you're a better cook than you were a cowboy," one of the Bar Cross boys joked as he walked away with a full plate.

A 7TX hand slapped his knee and hooted in agreement.

"Watch what you say or you'll find grease in your boots come morning," George growled.

The campground was in a shallow depression hard against a ridgeline that made a good holding area. From here, once the gathering was complete and branding done, the stray men from the other outfits would cut out their critters and trail them west over the rough mountain pass to the big spreads on the Jornada. The Double K would trail its beef herd east to the new town of Alamogordo, where the cattle buyer had arranged for stock cars to take the animals south to El Paso and east from there. Although it would be a longer trail drive by half a day, it would be less stressful on the animals and easier on the outfit.

"I'll trail my cattle with yours, if you don't mind," Gene said to Patrick. He had eleven critters consisting of six cows, four calves, and a young steer.

"I thought you needed to lay low," Patrick replied. He put his plate aside and rolled a cigarette.

"I got a hankering to see Alamogordo again." Gene finished his Arbuckles' coffee. "Last time I was there, it was the end of the tracks with a signboard on a bare patch of ground six miles from water. I hear it's grown considerable."

George sat himself down next to Gene, wiped his hands on his pants, and looked around at the crew. They were covered in dust from head to foot, kicked up by hundreds of hooves. He shook his head. "I don't see the need for another town. We already got La Luz and Tularosa. Makes the whole damn valley seem crowded."

"Now, hold on a minute, George," Cal said. "A new town means more whiskey and women, and you're partial to both, as I recall."

"Don't you go make Emma think bad of me," George snapped.

"Why, I'd never," Emma said in mock protest.

"See there," George said, shaking a finger at Cal. "You've already gone and done it."

"I hear whiskey and saloons have been outlawed," Gene said.

"Then the town ain't needed at all," George said.

"Don't you want to see it?" Emma asked.

"Once, maybe," George grumbled.

The boys started teasing George about some of his more memorable drunks when he'd been a Bar Cross hand, and after they finished, Emma told them about George getting drunk at her wedding.

Gene watched, thinking she seemed a hell of a lot more at ease with Cal, old George, and a bunch of dusty cowboys she hardly knew than she did with her own husband. On top of that, Patrick didn't seem troubled by it at all. That was something worth pondering but likely wouldn't suit the story he had in mind.

He turned to Patrick. "This sure is broken country, with timber and rough canyons where cows can hide."

Patrick nodded. "I know it. Four hands will hold the steers and cows separate while the rest of us pop strays. We should get it done by nightfall tomorrow. One more day to work the herd and we'll be trailing our way to Alamogordo the morning after."

"I'd be obliged if you don't put me to minding those critters we've already gathered," Gene said.

"I had no such idea," Patrick replied as he stubbed out his cigarette and stood. "Time to start chasing strays," he announced to the hands.

As the end of the roundup neared, the work got downright monotonous, but the boys didn't tire of busting startled cattle from the thickets, breaks, and canyons out into the open. With a skill they knew few people had and without a grumble or complaint, the men rode out laughing and joking under a clear New Mexico sky.

* * *

The morning after the last of the cows were gathered, Cal and Patrick grazed the animals before starting them for Alamogordo. They'd turned most of the small remuda loose, knowing some would return to the ranch headquarters while others would need to be brought in before winter came.

The boys from the other outfits were long gone, pushing their strays up the foothills of the San Andres Mountains. Telltale dust hanging over the hills put them a good five miles away.

Storm clouds had moved in overnight, and the sun broke through in patches, blotted out by fast-moving, steel gray clouds with brilliant white thunderheads that gathered near the eastern Sacramentos.

Cal gave the sky a wary eye. The storm could stall and rain buckets forty miles away or blow west and unleash a gully washer on them before day's end. Under good weather conditions, four hands could easily handle driving a beef herd of three hundred cows forty miles over the flats. But a stampede would scatter the herd, cause cattle to be killed or lost, and reduce their profit for the year.

"If the storm doesn't wander this way before we get out on the flats, we should be okay," Patrick said.

Cal nodded. "Tell George to saddle his horse, hitch it behind the wagon, and be ready to pitch in if the cattle get a notion to run. I'll get Gene and Emma to pick up the pace."

Patrick nodded, turned his pony, and cantered toward the wagon.

As fast as they could without spooking them, they moved the nervous herd through a long canyon that fanned out to the flats. Across the basin the storm tarried a while. Lightning blots speared the Sacramento peaks, cracked over the desert, and jumped from cloud to cloud. Blustery winds above swirled and pulsed. A curtain of rain blocked the Sacramentos from view. Slowly the storm moved out over the basin, coming right at them. It stopped halfway, drenched the sugar white sand dunes as the thunder roared and rumbled, and then faded away to the north, masking Sierra Blanca.

"Lordy, lordy," George said as Cal drew near. "That there storm didn't stop me from ever praying for rain again, but it sure did come close."

"Don't make a noon camp," Cal said. "We'll push on till dusk."

"Okay by me," George replied as he slapped the reins against the team's haunches. "I'm getting low on victuals anyway."

They made camp at sundown, with the sweep of the needle-sharp Organ Mountains to the west tinted red against a thin ribbon of yellow sky. The herd bedded down without complaint in the cool of the night. A full moon washed over the white sands that stretched for miles across the basin, creating a magical landscape of rolling, milky dunes cut by shadowy, wandering crevasses. It was a sight that had them talking in whispers.

In the morning they gained the Tularosa road and drove the herd at a good pace, pausing at some of the shallow sinks filled with rainwater from the storm to let the critters drink. It was as peaceable a drive with a mixed herd as Cal could remember.

They skirted the sand dunes before stopping for supper. Dusk

found them a half mile off the road on a bedding ground with
little browse that rose to the canyons at the base of the sheer Sacramentos.

The sound of a train whistle coursing through the thin air told
them civilization was close at hand. They would raise up Alamogordo in the morning.

* * *

At midmorning under another threatening sky, they reached the
outskirts of Alamogordo. On the west side of the railroad tracks,
the sandy soil of the basin sprinkled with bunchgrass and mesquite
held sway, but on the east side a town had magically sprung up. As
they drew closer, George pulled the wagon team to a stop and the
four riders reined in, astonished by the sight before them, the beef
herd momentarily forgotten.

In addition to a two-story train station, a large domed water
tower, machine shops, and rail sidings, there were houses, commercial buildings, mercantile shops, general stores, and a huge
hotel clustered near the station. On streets laid out in grids, a
dozen or more buildings were under construction. A wide road
ran east toward Alamo Canyon in the Sacramento foothills, and
along the boulevard several fancy houses had been thrown up.
Close to the station a string of pretty little cottages with tile roofs
lined lanes that paralleled the tracks. North of the train station an
open ribbon of land was being transformed into a park. There were
buggies and wagons on the streets, people on cement sidewalks,
and crews of laborers trenching for water pipes. Evenly spaced
electric light poles marched up the main street along with freshly
planted cottonwood saplings.

"I'll be," Gene Rhodes said. "There are at least a hundred buildings out there. It's a marvel of modern ingenuity."

"Whatever that means, it don't make it right," George groused.

Cal laughed. "There's nothing we can do about it."

George started the wagon team. "We can avoid it," he replied.

At the stockyards, they cut out Gene's critters, put them in a small corral, and penned the Double K herd next to waiting stock cars.

"I'll quit you here," Gene said to Cal, "and go scare up a butcher or two to buy my cows."

Cal gave Gene his wages. "You'll get more selling to a cattle buyer."

"I know it," Gene replied, "but right now I don't need anybody else accusing me of rustling. Some in that bunch of mine are mavericks that wandered onto my spread and picked up my brand by accident."

"No stockman on the Tularosa would find fault with that," Cal said.

"Maybe so," Gene answered, "but look around; this place got started from nothing lickety-split. It's a new town, a new county, and a new county seat all rolled into one. The old ways are on their way out, and I don't hanker to get caught in the squeeze. Especially now that I'm a married man."

"Good luck to you and your gal," Cal said. "Bring her by to visit once you fetch her and get settled."

"I surely will."

Gene tipped his hat to Emma and rode away, cogitating about the sentence he needed to write to start a story about the gal who made a hand.

50

While Cal, Patrick, and Emma stocked up on clothes and sundries at the big mercantile store capped by a domed tower a few steps from the hotel, George ambled down the sidewalk and discovered that Alamogordo wasn't quite as dry as Gene Rhodes had made it out to be. There was one legal watering hole in town, owned and operated by the railroad company, and it was no hurdy-gurdy house. A long, polished bar with a brass foot rail ran the length of one wall. Behind it were large curved mirrors surrounded by carved, ornamental wooden pillars. A big nickel-plated cash register sat on a shelf in front of the mirrors along with bottles of whiskey and glasses. Along the opposite wall was a row of high-back upholstered booths crowned with wood molding. The tables and chairs in the center of the room showed no sign of wear or abuse at all. The place was brightly lit by chandeliers and big windows that looked out on the street.

Although there were plenty of patrons, there wasn't another cowboy in sight. In a bar full of pilgrims, with no girlies around for companionship, George lost all desire to stay and get drunk. He reckoned there had not been one fight in the place since the day it opened. He bought a double shot of rye whiskey, downed it, and walked out, leaving behind a trail of dusty boot prints on the wooden floor.

He found Cal, Patrick, and Emma in front of the store next to the wagon with parcels under their arms.

"We're gonna stay over the night at the hotel," Patrick said.

George looked skyward. The threat of a storm had passed, and except for a few mare's tails over the San Andres, it was sunny and clear. "If it's all the same, I'll draw my wages now and start back to the ranch," he said.

Cal counted out George's pay. "Are you stopping in Tularosa?" he asked.

George nodded as he took the bills. Cal had paid him twice what a hand made, which was the going rate for a cook on roundup. He felt real flush. "Ain't that far, a dozen miles or so, and the saloons there are more congenial." He cast a quick glance at Emma, who gave him an innocent smile.

"Take the wagon," Patrick said, handing George a piece of paper, "get the supplies we need at the store, and put it on our account. It's all written down."

George nodded and put the paper in his shirt pocket.

"And don't forget to take a bath before you go looking for congenial company," Emma said sweetly.

Only George's leathery skin, browned by nearly sixty years in the saddle, hid his blush. He turned to Patrick. "That little lady of yours gives me no peace of mind."

Patrick grinned. "Don't go feeling picked on. She gets after all of us now and then."

"Humph," George replied as he started the team on the road to Tularosa.

With Alamogordo behind him, his pony hitched to the wagon, and the wide-open country and towering mountains sharp in the sparkling light, George settled the team into a slow trot. In all his years, never had he been so worn down. As a young man, he'd helped trail five thousand head along the Western Trail from San Antonio to Dodge City. He'd driven cattle from Abilene to Cheyenne, crossing flooded rivers and fighting off Comanche raiding parties along the way. In 1866, he'd been on the first drive that blazed the Goodnight-Loving Trail to Fort Sumner, where the army had kept thousands of Navajos and Apaches rounded up and under guard for a time.

George had argued hard with Cal not to take him off the back of a horse during fall works, but secretly he'd been glad to shuck his pony for the chuck wagon. That wasn't to say cooking for a crew was easy, for it weren't. You got up first and went to bed late. He thought it would surely be a mite easier than forking a horse but found it just as wearisome.

In Tularosa, he parked the wagon at the livery, unhitched the team, and paid for their keep before riding his pony over to Coghlan's saloon. Once it had been as brand-spanking new as the watering hole in Alamogordo. Not as fancy, but a respectable place to get a stiff drink and a good poke and play a friendly hand of cards. As Pat Coghlan's fortunes kept sinking, the place had gotten seedier. Still, George preferred it simply out of habit.

Inside, he found the same crowd of out-of-work cowboys, town drunks, gamblers, and a few drifters. He ordered whiskey at the bar and gave a nod at Leonia, his favorite soiled dove.

She sashayed over and linked her arm around his. "Are you going to buy me a drink first?"

George smiled down at her. She was older than the other girls—

maybe forty—and built the way he liked his women: short, round, and full figured, with wide hips and a big bottom he could grab onto.

"I'm gonna get a bottle, buy us a dinner, rent a room at the hotel, and spend the night with you, cash on the barrelhead," he said with a grin. "But not until I have a bath and get a shave."

Leonia pinched George's cheek. "Have you gone and robbed a bank?"

"I ain't done nothing desperate," George said.

Leonia rubbed her breast against George's arm, ran her hand down to his crotch, and gave him a gentle squeeze. "Either way, I'm all yours tonight, handsome."

* * *

George felt as fit as a fiddle, the aches and pains of yesterday forgotten. It was way past dawn when he pulled himself out of bed. Although he'd had a fine supper last night with Leonia, his stomach was grumbling for breakfast. After she'd tiptoed out of the room, he'd snoozed for a time before getting dressed and counting his remaining wages. His night with her had set him back some, but he still had enough money for breakfast, a new pair of pants, some tobacco and cigarette papers, a small sack of hard candy, and a blue silk neckerchief he'd taken a shine to last time he was in Adam Dieter's store.

After breakfast, he fed the animals, hitched the team, tied his saddle pony to the back of the wagon, and stopped at Dieter's store to get the provisions on Patrick's list. Dieter got busy right away filling the order while his missus gathered together George's purchases. He signed for the ranch order, put on his new neckerchief, and admired himself in the countertop mirror.

"You look right smart, George," Adam Dieter said.

George smiled in agreement. Last night with Leonia had taken ten years off him. "I sure ain't dead yet."

Dieter helped load the wagon, and in a jiffy George was on his way. The new train tracks ran along the western fringe of the village, skirting Tularosa entirely. He reckoned there had to be some reason why the railroad company decided to build a whole new town a short piece away in Alamogordo, but he couldn't figure out why. A few years back, Pat Coghlan and the other merchants in town had been selling land to nesters on the promise that the railroad would turn Tularosa into a Garden of Eden in the desert. After seeing Alamogordo, George was surefire glad Coghlan's plan had turned to dust.

He stopped in front of Ignacio's hacienda and gave a holler. Teresa stepped outside and he tipped his hat. "Howdy, Señora."

"*Buenos días,* George. Are you alone in town?"

"Cal and them should be along sometime today," he answered. "They stayed the night in Alamogordo."

"Come inside. I have fresh coffee."

"Thank you kindly, but there's a storm brewing and I need to make tracks."

He tipped his hat again and started the team down the road to the basin. Over the years, he'd worked with Cal to improve the road, and now it was a lot less dangerous. Still, there were some passages over wide, sandy arroyos prone to flash floods, and cuts across rocky slopes given to slides and washouts. Either could thwart man and beast.

The sky was dark with thunderheads, and a stiff wind whipped out of the southwest, bending the mesquite and greasewood, whistling through the yucca groves, blowing stinging sand. George pulled his hat down around his ears and used his new neckerchief as a mask to protect his face from the sand.

Five miles outside Tularosa, the storm let loose a thick sheet of rain. Rolling thunder and lightning broke above George's head, spooking the team. He stopped the wagon, tied the critters to a mesquite, and crawled under the wagon to wait it out. The wind turned cold and the rain kept coming until George couldn't see three feet in front of him. When it finally stopped, he was sitting in a shallow stream of water running down the middle of the road.

On the flats George wasn't worried much about getting stuck. The parched ground could take a good, heavy soaking without getting saturated. He crawled out from under the wagon and walked down the road apiece. It was soggy and there were puddles in spots, but it wasn't muddy much at all. He led the team by the reins a ways, and the wagon wheels sank no more than a half inch. He climbed up on the seat and started the team slowly down the road. The black sky had turned gray, and thirty miles to the west a thick veil of clouds masked the San Andres. It was raining hard at the ranch and up north around the Carrizozo Flat. To the southwest there was no sign of clearing. George was certain more rain was coming. How much and when he could only guess.

He kept the team moving at a slow, steady pace. The wind died to a gentle breeze and a light mist rolled off the San Andres. He reached the first big arroyo late in the day and gave it a close look. It was shallow and wide, a good tenth of a mile across. There was no fresh debris or sign of recent erosion to signal a recent flash flood. He walked across it, stopping several times to dig into the sand with his hands. Only the top three inches were wet.

Once the runoff from the mountains reached the arroyo, he'd be stranded for a day before he could cross. Best to jingle his spurs, make camp on the other side, and worry about the next arroyo crossing in the morning. He started the team across and got his front wheels stuck less than fifty feet from the far side. One wheel was sunk down to the axle, making the wagon lean hard to the side.

He needed to get moving in a hurry. He brought his saddle pony forward and tried to break the wagon free using more horsepower. The wagon lurched forward a bit, stopped, and sank back into the sand. He tried again with no luck, got a shovel, trenched around the front wheels, piled mesquite branches and rocks in the trenches, and urged the horses forward. The wheels turned and caught firmer ground just as the skies opened up.

Safely across, George hurried the team away from the arroyo to a small hill near a stand of mesquite off the road. He put on his slicker, picketed the animals to keep them from straying, and fed them some oats before grabbing a tarp and ducking under the wagon for shelter. He spread the tarp on the ground and went back out into the storm to get his saddle, bedroll, and some food.

Lightning cracked overhead as he settled in under the wagon. He was stopped for the night, maybe longer. He shed his slicker, wrapped it around his bedroll to keep it dry, and ate hard tack, jerky, and a can of pears for his supper.

Finished, George drank the juice from the can and leaned against the rear axle. The arroyo was running full tilt, a dull roar growing louder above the sound of the thunder. Out on the desert he could see lightning strikes sparking and arcing into the ground.

His aches and twinges were back worse than ever, and he had a stabbing pain in his left arm all the way up to his shoulder he'd never felt before. He rubbed his arm hard to ease the discomfort, but it didn't help at all.

The storm raged on, wind whipping the rain in every direction, including flat-out straight into his face. It was a humdinger of a blow, sure to be talked about for a long time to come. He figured to have a good time funnin' Cal for staying warm and dry while he got the wagonload of supplies safely to the ranch through storm and flood.

The pain hit him hard again, so hard it made him gasp. It took a long time to pass, and he stayed tensed up until it did. Cold and wet, he was too tired to move. He stayed still, listening to the rain, the wind, the thunder, the torrent of water in the arroyo, until he fell asleep.

* * *

The storm rattled the windows and caused a dozen leaks in the dirt roof of Ignacio's hacienda before it stopped a few hours before dawn. As Cal helped Ignacio and his oldest son, Juan, clean up and patch the leaks, he wondered how much damage had been caused at the ranch. The ranch house and casita had probably fared well on the higher ground, but the barn, outbuildings, and corrals were smack in the middle of a pasture cut by an arroyo that drained runoff from the mountains. He decided to figure on the worst amount of damage.

Yesterday, he'd left Alamogordo on his own hoping to catch up with George, but the bad weather kept him at Ignacio's instead. Cal worried about the old boy. He was prone to sickness, had lost a step or two to gout, and seemed worn down more than usual. Cal kicked himself for letting George head home alone.

He left Tularosa under a pale blue peaceful sky and dancing light from the morning sun that made the rain-drenched village

glitter. Adobe walls had melted, the narrow lanes were deeply rutted, the main road had turned into a mud bog, and water ran in
gushing rivulets off the flat roofs. Men, women, and children were
cleaning up dark pools of water lapping at their doors, hanging
soaked garments and bedding out to dry, shoring up walls, and
patching leaky roofs.

Every little arroyo, ditch, and gully had overflowed. The river
had spilled its banks, and frothing white water rushed into the
basin, spreading over the flats. Crop fields were flooded, and where
the water had receded, a dead lamb, partially covered in mud,
rested against a fence post.

Some of the old cottonwoods were shorn of leaves, with branches
and limbs split off. A big tree had fallen into the river, snaring
debris pushed downstream by the rapid current. A lone chicken
perched on a branch, clucking pitifully.

Cal slowed Bandit to a walk as they started across the floodplain
on the flats. At times, Bandit's legs sank above the fetlocks. Each
time he pulled himself free, shook his head, snorted, and moved
on. The road had washed out in places, but not badly enough to
slow Cal down considerably, and by early afternoon he reached the
first arroyo.

It had grown a good ten feet in width and deepened a foot in
places. There were standing pools of water along the banks, and
slow-moving eddies disappeared into the sandy bed. Tree trunks
and boulders had washed down from the high country miles away.
The storm had been as powerful out on the basin as it had been
in town, which only made Cal worry more about George.

He dismounted, gave the arroyo a close look, and decided he
couldn't risk getting stuck in quicksand. He followed the arroyo
south for a time, found a safe crossing, and doubled back to the

road. Within minutes he saw the wagon and the animals in the distance. He spurred Bandit ahead and called out.

At the wagon, his feet hit the ground before Bandit came to a complete stop. It was tightly covered and securely lashed. He looked under it. George lay on a tarp, his eyes wide open, his face a frozen mask of surprise.

Cal crawled to him and gently closed his old friend's eyes. "Dammit all, George," he said. "Dammit."

At the wagon, his feet hit the ground before Bandit came to a
complete stop. It was tightly covered and securely lashed. He looked

51

The storm had splintered the Double K saddle shed, chicken
coop, and corrals into sticks scattered across the pasture and
the flats. Floodwaters had cut a new channel through the pasture
directly under the barn, collapsing it into a pile of debris. Nearby,
the windmill tilted precariously over the rock rubble of what had
been the stock tank. Saddles and bridles were waterlogged and ru-
ined. Hand tools, wagon wheels, barrels, rolls of wire, and ladders lay
partially buried in mud. Two cow ponies had been swept away, and
all of Emma's chickens drowned. Only the ranch house and casita,
on higher ground, stood intact, but barely, with roofs in need of
patching and several adobe walls in need of shoring. Bedding, linens,
and clothing had to be aired and dried in order to be salvaged.

In the high country, rock slides had blocked trails to the pastures, and most of the dirt water tanks had either burst or filled
with silt. Some of the big old willows in the seeps were uprooted,
and several slot canyons were completely blocked by landslides. Six
inches of mud had flowed into the line cabin, knocking down the
stove and taking the door off its hinges. On the basin, the wagon
road to Tularosa was washed out in half a dozen places.

After they put the ranch house in livable order and threw up some temporary corrals, Cal, Patrick, and Emma went looking for their livestock. For two weeks they trekked through the San Andres and the northern half of the basin, gathering animals. They trailed home seventy-six steers, cows, and calves, half a dozen yearlings, nine ponies, and eighteen strays. Counting the carcasses they found along the way, Cal figured half of their herd and six ponies had either been lost in the storm or drifted a good distance off the Tularosa.

That night at the dinner table, they talked about what needed to get fixed.

"The windmill, stock tank, and corrals right away," Cal said. "We need to get all that done pronto."

"You get no argument from me," Patrick said as he started a list. "But first we should fence the pasture to keep our critters nearby while we rebuild. We'll have to cut and haul a good amount of timber to do it."

"At least the timber is free, so it won't cost except for our labor," Cal replied, pleased with Patrick's reasoning. "Same for the windmill and the stock tank."

"I say we take out a bank loan to get it all done in one swoop," Patrick announced, putting the list aside. "We can rebuild the barn, fix the line cabin, throw up a new chicken coop, and restock the herd. Do the whole caboodle and make this place better than it was before. It might take the good part of a year, but we could hire a hand to help out."

He looked at Cal and Emma expectantly, awaiting their approval.

"I'm not partial to borrowing against the ranch," Cal replied quietly, wondering how Patrick's good thinking could drift astray so easily. "We built our brand slowly, and I reckon it's best to put the outfit back together the same way."

"The bank will loan us the money sure enough," Patrick said, trying to gather support, "and now's the time to do it, with cattle prices strong. We can pay it back in a year or two."

Cal and Emma said nothing.

"Why are y'all locking horns with me on this?" he asked.

"I've seen many a stockman owe everybody he could owe when the hard times came," Cal said, "and I damn sure don't want to have us end up like that."

"This outfit has always paid its creditors, merchants and bankers alike," Patrick replied.

"Because we've never owed much and have made do with less when times were tight," Cal said evenly. "I say we stay on that same trail now."

Emma nodded. "Cal's right, Patrick."

Patrick glared at her. "Why do you always side with Cal over me?" he snapped.

"That's not true," Emma said, stiffening in her chair.

"Maybe so, but just remember, you're my wife, not a partner in this outfit, so what you say about how we run things don't mean spit."

Emma clamped her jaw shut, pushed her chair back, and stomped outside.

Patrick shook his head as he watched her go. "That woman," he grumbled.

"You had no cause to barrel into her like that," Cal said. "Best go make amends."

Patrick shook his head. "Not this old boy, and I don't need you giving me advice."

"Yes, you do, and I'll say my piece whenever it suits me."

"Someday I'm gonna run this outfit as I see fit, old man, without you meddling in my marriage."

"Can't see that I'm meddling when you spat with her in front of me."

"How come you back her up the way you do?"

"That gal has earned the right to have a say," Cal replied, "and you know it."

"Maybe so, maybe not," Patrick snapped. He stood and walked out of the kitchen.

Cal heard the bedroom door close, leaned back in his chair, and lit a cigar, thinking Emma would return shortly. When she didn't, he went looking and found her on the hill standing over Molly's grave.

"I miss her," she said softly as he came near.

"I know it."

"Just like you miss George. I miss him too."

In the moonlight Cal stared at George's grave, covered in fresh dirt from the hole he'd dug with Patrick's help. Next to it was John Kerney's grave, now a grassy mound. "I miss all three of the folks buried here."

They stood in the silence of the night for a moment.

"I'm pregnant," Emma said softly.

"Does Patrick know?"

"Not yet, and I don't want him to if it means we have to borrow money for me to live in town until the baby comes."

"You'd risk your life and losing the child to save this outfit from taking on some debt?"

"I would."

Cal shook his head. "Earlier, I thought it was just Patrick who had stopped thinking straight. How far along are you?"

"Two months."

"You go tell your husband right now," Cal said gruffly. "It should've been him to know first. Wake him up if you have to. When he asks if I know, lie to him. Otherwise it will start a ruckus."

"Then what?"

"Patrick will want to find out if I knew before him. When he comes, I'll ease his mind. Then we'll palaver and make plans."

"I'll not be left out of it," Emma snipped.

"This time you will do as I say," Cal replied. "Now, git."

The angry look on Cal's face hurried Emma along.

A half hour passed before Patrick banged on Cal's door. He opened it to a worried-looking man.

"Do you know?" Patrick demanded.

"Know what?" Cal asked, hoping Emma had done as she'd been told.

Patrick studied him close before replying. "Emma's pregnant."

"Well, I'll be," Cal said, smiling big. "It's high time, old son. Let's have a drink on it to celebrate."

He got a bottle out of the dresser and handed it to Patrick, who took a long swig.

"I ain't gonna let her lose this one," he said, passing the bottle over.

"Of course you ain't." Cal paused to drink. "I'll go along with whatever you and Emma decide needs doing."

"We're leaving for town come morning to see the doctor, and she'll stay there until the baby's born, just like he said she needed to the last time we talked to him. I told her straight out she had no choice in the matter."

"Good for you," Cal said.

"We'll find a place to rent and fix it up some."

"I'll ride along," Cal said, "and we'll borrow the money to get her set up in town."

"You ain't opposed to the idea?"

"Hell no."

Patrick looked relieved. "I'm obliged."

"No call for that," Cal replied. "It about time the Double K raised more than just cows and ponies."

52

In Las Cruces, Cal met up with Patrick and Emma at the hotel after their appointment with the doctor.

"What did the sawbones say?" Cal asked.

"I'm fine," Emma replied, "but because I lost the last two after the third month, I'm not to do heavy physical work and must rest frequently."

"No riding your pony either," Patrick reminded her. "She's to see the doctor every two weeks until the baby comes."

"We can get you a buggy for town, if need be," Cal said.

"I'm not an invalid," Emma said sharply. "I can walk."

As they left the hotel for the bank, an automobile pulled to a stop outside. The driver cut the engine, jumped out, pulled off his goggles, and went up the steps looking about as pleased as a man could be.

Cal, Patrick, and Emma gave the machine a close look. It was a lot like a buggy, with a front seat and a backseat, a stiff high top, big back wheels, little front ones with hard tires, and a carbide lamp. Cal allowed the only thing it lacked was a horse, and although it had made one hell of a racket and fouled the air, the contraption intrigued him. If a mechanical engine could cart people around, maybe it could be used to pump water out of the ground. That appealed to Cal as a much more practical use.

Patrick wanted to buy one. Emma wanted to be taken for a ride in it.

"I bet it will get stuck in a ditch five miles out of town or just up and quit running for no reason," Cal predicted.

"Maybe so," Patrick said, peering at the wheel sticking up from the floor, which somehow steered the thing. "But the time will come when people will trade their horses for these machines."

"I don't think I want to be part of a world where folks give up riding ponies."

Patrick laughed. "You're getting downright cantankerous, old man."

"And I plan to stay that way too," Cal replied as he headed Patrick and Emma down the street toward the bank.

Inside they met with banker George Bowman and his son Henry, who looked over the ranch deed and title papers Patrick had brought along, inquired about the outfit's outstanding debts—the Double K owed sixty-five dollars to Adam Dieter's mercantile in Tularosa and thirty dollars to a feed store—and asked what the loan was for.

"My wife is having a baby and the doctor says she needs to stay in town under his care until then," Patrick answered. "There have been some problems in the past, if you get my drift."

"Ah," George Bowman said. A heavyset man with a round face covered with whiskers, he gave Emma a concerned look. "I'm sure we can accommodate you and the missus. Do you have an amount in mind?"

Patrick nodded and glanced at Emma. "We've been thinking with rent, food, furnishings, cooking and heating wood, doctor bills, and all, until the baby comes, five hundred dollars."

"You should think of buying instead of renting," Henry Bowman said. A thin fellow with a receding hairline, Henry sported a droopy mustache that covered his upper lip. "Real estate is booming. We've got over three thousand citizens living here now and more folks are arriving every month. Prices on houses have gone up ten percent in just the last year."

Patrick glanced at Cal. "What would it take to buy a place?" he asked.

"You can get a good house on a small lot near the new Women's Improvement Park for about what you want to borrow, perhaps a little more," George Bowman replied. "It would be a wise investment."

"If you'd like something more modest," Henry added, "there are a few smaller adobes along Griggs Avenue for sale. It's a lovely, tree-shaded lane."

"Buying makes sense," Cal said. "It's better to own property rather than put *dinero* into some landlord's pocket. I say we should do it. I'll add my John Hancock to the loan papers, but put the title to the house in Patrick and Emma's name."

"You'd like them to own it jointly?" George Bowman asked.

"Yep."

"Are you agreed?" George Bowman asked Patrick and Emma.

"That's fine by us," Patrick said.

"Yes, yes," Emma said, almost speechless. The thought of owning a house in town was so grand it nearly bowled her over. She had never considered the possibility before.

"Then it's settled," Cal said, getting to his feet. "I'll leave it to you to work out the details. Just make sure the loan amount is enough to cover buying a place and all that they'll need for Emma's stay in town."

"Certainly," George Bowman said, turning his attention to Patrick and Emma. "You can start looking right away. If you find something you like, Henry here can negotiate on your behalf with the owner."

"Where are you headed?" Patrick asked Cal, who had his hand on the doorknob.

"You ain't the only ones with business in town," Cal replied with a smile and a wave. "See you at supper."

* * *

On the street, Cal hurried quickly to Albert Fall's law offices, where he waited half an hour to see the judge.

"It's been a while, Cal," Fall said with a smile as they shook hands in his office, a wood-paneled room with shelves filled with thick law books. "What brings you to see me?"

"I want to draw up a new will leaving my half of the Double K outfit to Patrick Kerney's wife, Emma."

Fall motioned Cal to sit. "Do you currently have a will?"

Cal nodded and handed Fall his copy of the will Albert Fountain had drawn up years ago.

Fall read it quickly. "Do you want to completely remove Patrick as your inheritor?"

"Nope," Cal said. "Just the ranch part, including livestock. He'll still get my personal possessions."

"I see," Fall said. "How familiar are you with the legal rights of married women?"

"Since I never married, not one bit," Cal replied.

"New Mexico law is based on old Spanish law," Fall said, "which gives Patrick's missus certain protections. Whatever they earn or own during the marriage belongs to both parties, regardless of who earned it or whose name is on the title. And should she survive him, she'll have full legal access to Patrick's estate. Also, during their union she's entitled to a privy examination before a judge to make sure she isn't being pressured by her husband to sell property belonging to her in whole or part."

"That's all well and good, Judge, but we both know laws change, and not always for the better. I want Patrick and Emma to share owning the Double K no matter what, with an equal say in it."

Fall raised an eyebrow. "Is there trouble between them?"

Cal shook his head. "No more than what any couple bickers about, I reckon. Truth is I favor them both as if they were my own children, and I want that made clear to them."

"You can put those very words in your will," Fall said.

Cal nodded. "Good enough."

"Do you have any additional instructions or advice you wish to give either of them?" Fall asked.

"I'm not looking to turn this into a sermon, Judge," Cal said.

Fall smiled. "Earlier, you said you wanted them to have equal say in the ranch. That could be spelled out as a condition of your bequest, making it more binding on both parties."

"I like that notion," Cal said. "Put it in."

Fall nodded. "Very good. I'll have the document drawn up by

my clerk immediately. Come by in the morning and we'll go over it together."

Cal got to his feet. "I'll see you then."

"I understand Sheriff Baker in Otero County is looking for an experienced deputy," Fall said as he walked Cal to the door. "I could put in a word for you, if you're so inclined."

"I'm obliged but not interested," Cal replied. "I'm too long in the tooth to be riding for the law and have enough work for three men at the ranch. See you *mañana*."

Cal stepped outside Fall's office feeling good about what he'd done. Las Cruces was golden brown in the afternoon sun. To the east the fluted peaks of the Organ Mountains, showing every wrinkle and cleft in the brilliant light, dominated the horizon. Near the town, the rich farmland along the river valley muted the surrounding desert with a ribbon of green. A team of mules pulled a wagon with hay bales stacked eight rows high down the dusty street past a mercantile store where a group of Mescaleros were loading up supplies.

Cal approached the group hoping to find James Kaytennae among them, but he wasn't there. He asked an old Apache man sitting in a wagon if James had come to town.

"Who are you?" the Apache asked, squinting at Cal from under his hat.

"Cal Doran."

The old man nodded. "I know that name. James not here."

"*Gracias.*"

"Now you ask me another question," the Apache said.

"What question is that?" Cal asked.

"Why I give Henry Fountain a pony. James tells me you want to know."

Cal laughed and slapped his leg. "It's not important any-more."

The old man grunted. "Good, because I not say why to you anyway."

Cal smiled. "That's fine by me. Tell James howdy for me."

The old man grunted again.

Cal nodded good-bye, strolled across the street to the Tip-Top Saloon, ordered a whiskey, and glanced around the crowded room. There was nothing fancy about the place, and no familiar faces, but it looked like a rowdy crowd had gathered, ready to get drunk and run wild.

Cal finished his drink, turned to leave, and found Doc Evans blocking his way. Evans's long greasy hair had been cut short and his skin was pasty, sure signs he'd been cooling his heels in prison for a spell.

"I spent two years locked up in the Santa Fe Penitentiary because of you," Evans said loudly, slurring his words a bit.

"Doc, I didn't recognize you," Cal replied amiably, easing his hand to his six-shooter.

"Did you hear what I said?" Evans snapped, about as drunk as a man could get and remain standing. He leaned to one side and almost lost his balance.

"All I did was arrest you for altering brands."

"If you'd let me be in Engle, I would have moseyed on down into Mexico and put that little confusion behind me."

"That makes it a damn shame for you, all right."

"If I wasn't drunk I'd call you out," Evans said.

"Now, there's no sense getting shot if you're gonna be too drunk to remember it."

"You ain't funny and you ain't the law no more," Evans said, wagging his finger. "Watch yourself or maybe you'll go missing like Albert Fountain and his little boy did."

He wobbled away to a table and plopped down on a chair next to his old saddle partner Lee Williams.

Cal didn't ease his hand away from his leg iron until he was out the door. He waited a few minutes to make sure Evans didn't come stumbling out of the Tip-Top bent on murder, before terrapinning his way to the hotel.

53

Over supper at the Don Bernardo Hotel, Emma and Patrick told Cal about the house they liked the best.

"It's on Griggs Avenue, close to the park, and made of adobe," Patrick said, "but the owner has added a low, hipped roof, like the one on the ranch house. Should keep it nice and dry inside."

Cal nodded his approval as he cut a thigh off the roasted chicken and put it on his plate.

"It needs a coat of mud plaster on the outside," Patrick continued as he sliced white meat off the fowl. "And the floors are dirt sealed in ox blood."

"How many rooms?" Cal asked.

"Four," Patrick replied as he passed the plate of chicken to Emma. "It's a box cut into squares. Kitchen and front room at the street side, two bedrooms at the back. The front room has a fireplace."

"It's got water in the kitchen and a good cookstove," Emma said, her eyes sparkling, "and windows in every room, with a nice big tree in the front yard."

"Out back there's a privy, a covered shed large enough to hold firewood and a buggy," Patrick added. "The adobe wall in back needs work, but the house is solid. Out front is a picket fence."

"Are you gonna buy it?" Cal asked.

"If we don't find something better for what we can afford," Emma said.

"Will it do for you?" Cal asked her.

She nodded. "It's more than I ever figured on. Will you come look at it with us tomorrow?"

"I will, if you'll wait on me until I finish some business."

"What's all this business you've got to take care of?" Patrick asked as he poured gravy on his chicken.

"I'm too hungry to talk anymore right now," Cal answered, reaching for the bowl of vegetables. "Pass the biscuits."

* * *

The house Patrick and Emma described over supper turned out to be the one they decided to buy. By the following morning the only thing lacking for the deal to go through was Cal's signature on the Double K mortgage papers. Before heading to the bank, where George and Henry Bowman waited on him, Cal packed his gear and walked with Patrick to the livery, where he saddled Bandit for the ride home to the ranch.

"I'll be along as soon as Emma's settled in," Patrick said as Cal led Bandit out of the stall.

"No hurry, old son," Cal replied. "Take care of your woman first. The work will still be there when you get home."

"You should look to hire us a hand," Patrick said.

Cal cinched the saddle and put the bit in Bandit's mouth. "Since I expect you'll be making regular visits to town until the baby comes, I've been thinking in that same direction myself."

"I'll still pull my weight," Patrick said.

"I know you will," Cal said as he walked Bandit outside and paid the stable owner. "Where's that wife of yours?"

"She said she wasn't hungry and wanted no breakfast," Patrick replied with a shrug and grin. "Truth is she's in the hotel room making a list of what we need for the house."

Cal laughed as he threw a leg over Bandit. "I bet she comes up with things you ain't even thought of."

"Maybe so," Patrick said. "Do you need me to come along to the bank?"

Cal shook his head as he turned Bandit in the direction of the bank. "Ain't necessary. See you at the ranch."

Inside the bank, George and Henry Bowman watched Cal carefully read the loan and real estate papers before signing his name.

"We'll put the remaining proceeds into Patrick's new account after the real estate sale is satisfied," Henry Bowman said as he gathered up the documents.

Cal leaned back and raised an eyebrow. "Can Emma get the money she needs when Patrick is back at the ranch?"

"She'll be on a monthly allowance that we can disperse to her as needed up to a certain amount," George Bowman replied. "Patrick will establish credit accounts at the various merchants and pay the household bills when he comes to town."

Cal wondered if Emma had squawked in protest and decided she would never make her objections known publicly.

"I'd be obliged if you would do me a favor," he said.

"If it's within our power, certainly," George Bowman replied.

"I want to write a letter to Emma and have you personally take it to her after Patrick leaves town for the ranch. Will you do that?"

"It would be our pleasure," George Bowman said as he stood and glanced at Henry. "We have papers to file at the courthouse. Please use the office to write your letter."

He placed pen, paper, and an envelope on the desk. "Just leave it here when you're finished and I promise it will be delivered as you asked."

"Again, I'm obliged."

After George and Henry left, Cal scooted his chair close to the big walnut desk and started writing. He folded greenbacks into the letter, put her name on the envelope, sealed it, left it on the desk, and rode out of town.

He'd yet to tell Patrick or Emma about his new will and testament and didn't plan to until he was permanently stove up, broke down, or plain feeble. He figured that was sometime off because except for some aches, pains, and a slower step or two, he still felt lively.

* * *

The night before Patrick left for the ranch, Emma could hardly contain her excitement. The prospect of living alone by herself in town and in her own house was beyond the scope of anything she'd ever imagined. The only drawback was being put on an allowance like a child and having to go ask George or Henry Bowman for money. She held her tongue about it for now but planned to demand full access to the account when Patrick next came to town.

His visits during the coming months wouldn't be a bother at all. In fact, having him in the house and in her bed briefly every now and then was perfect. She looked forward to the freedom of living her own life for a while with some occasional satisfying sex, and without the unending chore of caring for a man.

Last night in bed Patrick had talked happily about another child after this one, and maybe a third. Such talk would have confused her if she hadn't already concluded that he wanted children so she wouldn't leave him. She doubted when the baby came he'd show any more interest in it than he had in Molly, and she wasn't sure if she could tolerate that. She knew in her heart he loved her as best he could but would never stop expecting to be betrayed and abandoned. What the future held, Emma wasn't sure, but she looked forward with great anticipation to her time in town on her own.

To contain her eagerness to see Patrick off to the ranch come morning, she quietly stitched new curtains for the windows by lamplight at the kitchen table. It was a wobbly table Patrick had repaired by bracing the legs with wood. The rest of the furniture they'd bought was of about the same quality, except for the brand-new bed. The secondhand kitchen chairs weren't rickety, the old bedroom dresser lacked only a few drawer pulls, which Patrick had already replaced, and the used sofa in the front room sagged a little but was comfortable. There was still more furniture to buy, but it could wait.

After Patrick was on his way, Emma planned to spend the first week finishing the curtains, making the house look better with some elbow grease and paint, and shopping for some more of the supplies, sundries, and linens she needed. She relished the idea of wandering down Main Street, exploring all the stores, and watching the people in their carriages, buggies, and wagons driving up and down the long thoroughfare through town. On her list was a visit to Faulkner's General Store, where she'd spotted a shelf full of books and magazines for sale. The mere thought of a day spent reading with no other care brought a smile to her face.

Her eyes grew tired and her fingers began to ache. She put the sewing aside and went to bed. Patrick was on his stomach, breathing softly. Through the open window she could hear the sounds of the town, so different from the silence of the ranch at night. She listened to the receding clatter of wagon wheels on Griggs Avenue, the distant laughter of people drifting over from Main Street, the whistle of an approaching train, the braying of a neighbor's mule. She'd never felt happier.

* * *

Patrick pushed aside his empty plate, patted his belly, and smiled at Emma. "A man could get fat and lazy eating your cooking and living in town," he said.

"I'll not have a fat, lazy man in my bed," Emma said gaily as she poured him more coffee. "Best you get back to the ranch."

"Can't wait to see me off, can you?"

"I've got woman's work to do here and you'd just get in the way."

"Fix it up all you like, so I can make a fair profit from it when the time comes to sell."

Emma's smile faded. "It will take both of us to agree to that."

Patrick nodded. "I suppose so." He drank his coffee and looked out the window. The sky had begun to lighten. It had been three days since Cal had left for the ranch, and he wanted to be on the road by sunrise. Out on the street, the team was hitched to the wagon and ready to go. "I'm gonna jingle my spurs out of here."

"When will you be back?" Emma asked.

"I figure three weeks." He finished his coffee and stood. "We should have the corrals up and the windmill working by then. If Cal has hired a hand, it'll go even faster."

"Three weeks," Emma said, barely containing a smile. She gave him a kiss and a swift hug.

"You be careful with all that woman's work," Patrick cautioned. "Rest every day like the doctor said."

"Making curtains is restful enough," Emma answered.

She went outside with Patrick and stayed there until his wagon disappeared from sight. Back in the kitchen she whirled around in a happy little dance, quickly washed the breakfast dishes, and began working on the kitchen curtains so she could hang them before the morning passed.

She was carefully hemming the final border to the last curtain when a knock came at the door. Wondering who it could possibly be, she opened it to find Henry Bowman on the front step.

"Mr. Bowman."

"Ma'am." Henry tipped his hat, smiled, and handed Emma an envelope.

"What's this?" she asked.

"A letter from Cal Doran," Henry replied.

Emma's eyes widened in surprise. "Why would Cal write me?"

"I don't know."

She put the envelope in her apron pocket. "Would you like to come in for a cup of coffee?"

Henry shook his head. "I regret I must get back to the office. Good day."

"Good day, and thank you," Emma called out as Bowman hurried away.

At the kitchen table, she opened the envelope, took out a letter and some folding money, and read what Cal had written.

Emma,

> *Long before you came to the Double K, Patrick sold his half of the outfit to me and set out on his own. I don't know if he ever told you about the time he was gone, but I figure he didn't because he don't talk about it much. Anyway, to shorten this tale up a mite, he came home after a long spell and bought back into the spread with this dinero I've held on to all this time. I've decided to give it to you. I'd appreciate it if you'd put it to the care of yourself and your unborn baby, but use it as you see fit. I'll come visit when I can, and don't you worry about the Double K. We'll get it whipped back into shape all right.*

Cal

She counted the money. Four hundred dollars; a year's wages for a good hand. It was a fortune to her. She read the letter again and burst into tears.

5 4

By the start of his third day back at the ranch, Cal was kicking himself for not hiring help in Las Cruces. He wasn't worn down by the work, just beleaguered by all that needed to get done. On top of that, with no water at the ranch headquarters and nobody left behind to watch the critters, the animals had drifted. Since there was no pen built to hold them yet, he hadn't bothered trailing after them.

Cutting and hauling timber for the corrals, pasture fence, and damaged windmill tower would take at least two hands, so he was stuck waiting on Patrick's return before those jobs could get started. While he waited, he turned his attention to the stock tank, digging out two feet of dried mud and buried rocks. He figured to lay a rock-and-mortar foundation and build a shallow dirt tank above it as a stopgap measure until something more substantial could be put up.

He was on his knees sorting rocks by size when he heard a horse snort at his back. He turned quickly to see James Kaytennae no more than five feet away, looking down at him from the back of a thrifty pinto.

"Big storm come here too," James said, looking around at the wreckage.

"What are you doing sneaking up on me like that?" Cal asked, getting to his feet.

"He Who Steals Horses said you asked me to come here," James answered.

"Who?"

"The old man you spoke to in Las Cruces."

"I just asked after you and told him to say howdy."

James shrugged. "That's not what he says."

"He Who Steals Horses," Cal said. "That's a name that tells you a lot about a fella."

James shrugged again.

"So who is he?"

James shrugged a third time.

Cal tried a different tack. "What brings you here?"

"You have plenty of work. I need work."

"You're not a tribal policeman anymore?"

James shook his head. "They want to make me a farmer, but I don't like that. No Apache does. Someday, Mescaleros will kick the white eyes off our land, and I want to learn what you do with cattle so we can take over when they're gone."

"Is that a fact?" Cal asked with a smile.

"Sure. Maybe not soon, but someday whites eyes will go."

"I meant do you really want to learn to cowboy?"

James nodded. "You give me a job?"

"Okay. Room, board, browse for your pony, and thirty dollars a month."

"I start now?" James asked as he swung out of the saddle.

"Right now," Cal replied.

* * *

By the first hard freeze in early December, the pasture fence had been thrown up and the corrals rebuilt, and the restored windmill pumped water into the new stock tank. Cal decided with the ponies close by under James Kaytennae's watchful eye and the cattle fenced in at the North Canyon with water and grass, it was a good time to visit Emma.

Patrick had been riding into town twice a month and reporting back that all was going well and there were no problems with Emma's pregnancy. He had left that morning for Las Cruces, and Cal planned to follow come sunup. He missed Emma's company and wanted to see her at least once before the baby came.

After supper, he packed a few things in his saddlebags, put together his bedroll, and went to the kitchen, where James sat at the table working on a flute he had started making several months ago. He had cut a bloom stalk off an agave plant, hollowed out three holes, notched an end, covered it in leather, and etched a geometric pattern on it. Now he was attaching blue and white beads hung on leather strips to the bottom of the flute.

"I've been meaning to ask if you can play that thing," Cal said as he joined James at the table.

James shook his head and blew on it, and only a squeak came out. "It is to be a gift."

Cal sat and gave the flute in James's hand a close look. "Well, that's a right fine-looking gift. What's the occasion?"

James looked confused.

"Is it for a birthday?" Cal asked.

James smiled. "No, it's a courting flute. A marriage present."

"Does it work?"

James tied off the last strand of beads and handed it to Cal. "Finished now. Try it."

Cal blew through the notched end and only the sound of air came out.

James smiled. "You play bad as me."

"Appears so. I hope who gets it can play it. Who's getting married?"

James patted his chest with a finger.

"You?" Cal said with a grin. "Well, I'll be. When?"

"When the sun travels to warm us again."

"That's real fine," Cal said. "Will you stay on till spring?"

James nodded as he wrapped the flute in a cloth. "I have promised her father horses. I will buy some ponies from you before I leave."

Cal smiled. "That's a damn fine gift for anyone. I'll give you a good price. Pick out the ones you want."

"I have done that," James replied.

Cal laughed. "That figures. I'm turning in. See you *mañana*."

James nodded good night. After Cal left, James crossed the courtyard to the casita, tucked the flute away in the bedroom dresser, and prepared for bed, spreading his blankets and hides on the floor.

Before he returned to Mescalero, he would buy four good saddle ponies to give to his bride's father. At home, he had two others He Who Steals Horses was keeping for him. That made six. He'd promised eight. He might have to raid a ranch or go to Texas with He Who Steals Horses for the other two, but he would keep his word.

Cal left before sunup next morning under a full moon in a clear sky. At first light, bundled in a blanket against the cold, James rode into the pasture and tracked the ponies several miles from the ranch house, where they had clustered near the fence line. The horses whinnied, snorted, and trotted away as he approached, their breath rising like smoke in the freezing air. He did a count. Six were missing, including a brown and a calico he'd picked out to buy.

He backtracked in a widening circle until he found sign that two riders had cut the six horses from the herd and driven them to the eastern edge of the pasture bordering the basin flats. Fence wires dangled to the ground.

He stopped, dismounted, and studied the riders' horse tracks, fixing them in his mind. They were fresh and ran southeast across the basin toward the white sands, the stolen horses following strung together.

Tse-yahnka, an old trail once used by his people, skirted the low edge of the vast dunes. As a young boy he'd traveled it with his family to gather salt in sack-shaped hides, late in the summer when the lake beds were dry. He doubted the rustlers knew of it.

The horse tracks also showed they were moving at a slow trot toward the Jarilla Mountains, a distant, small range on the basin that was divided by a low pass that led directly to El Paso and Mexico.

The horses would need water long before reaching the Jarillas. On the McNew ranch just southeast of the dunes, there was a well used by travelers on the road from Tularosa to Las Cruces. The rustlers would stop there.

If he followed *tse-yahnka,* he might be able to cut them off before they reached the ranch. James spurred his pony.

* * *

Since leaving the Double K with the ponies, Doc Evans had been counting on Cal Doran to come after him. Yet with more than four hours on the trail, there was no sign of him. Every so often he fell back to take another look-see, while Lee Williams kept moving the ponies.

A cold breeze out of the northwest made the day chilly in spite of a cloudless sky, and Doc stayed buttoned up against the wind.

Cal Doran's Double K Ranch was known far and wide for prime saddle stock. The ponies would bring top prices in Mexico, enough to pay for a month or more of whiskey and women in Juárez. Doc decided to be content with that prospect for now. He'd kill Cal Doran another day.

As he scanned the horizon, Doc pondered the notion of getting some of the old gang together after he got back from Mexico, returning to the Double K, and stealing every pony on the spread. That would surely get Doran tracking him. Then he'd kill him.

He glanced skyward and figured by the angle of the sun they'd raise Bill McNew's spread by dusk. Bill was a friend, so nobody would ask any questions about the string of ponies.

Doc gave another look northward, studying the low dunes and the shallow arroyos lined with mesquite, where a rider could easily hide. Beyond, running to the San Andres, the baked, empty alkali flats stretched out for miles. He saw no telltale dust signs of a horse and rider.

Ahead, Lee and the ponies had disappeared over a small rise. Doc caught up with him just as a lone rider appeared out of the southeast, traveling at a slow walk.

It was an Apache by his looks, wrapped in a blanket, wearing a Mexican sombrero and riding a sturdy pinto pony that would bring a good price in Juárez. Doc winked at Lee, who grinned back.

The Apache reined in ten feet away.

"You speak American?" Doc asked.

The Apache shook his head. "No savvy."

Smiling friendly like, Doc closed in. "Shoot him when I grab the pony's reins," he said to Lee.

James held his six-gun underneath his blanket. When the white eyes drew near, he flipped the blanket back, shot him in the head, and put two bullets in the other gringo's chest. Both men slumped over and fell out of their saddles as their horses bolted.

James waited to make sure they were dead before going after the stolen ponies. He put the stock in a temporary rope corral and returned to the bodies. He thought fleetingly about taking the white eyes' ponies and decided against it. Saddled, riderless horses would bring out a posse and the hoofprints could get him hung as a murdering, renegade Apache. He made a careful job of erasing all the horse tracks and headed the Double K ponies back toward the ranch across the low dunes, where all traces of his passage were quickly swallowed, and on to the flats, where the wind hid his sign.

55

Emma hurried with her baby to the doctor's office. To her embarrassment, he cried so loudly that people on the street turned to look as she rushed by with him in her arms.

Until a week ago, he'd been an almost perfect baby, content and happy when awake, sleeping soundly at night, and cranky only when his diapers needed changing or he was hungry. But on the day he turned three months old, he began crying for hours at a time, especially after nursing. He flailed his arms and legs, wouldn't sleep, and fussed often for no reason. His little tummy got bloated and hard, and he swallowed air when he cried, which gave him gas and made him even more uncomfortable.

Emma was beside herself with worry. For two days she'd tried everything she could think of to calm him, rocking him for hours on end, rubbing his tummy, bathing him in warm water, burping him to relieve the gas. Nothing worked.

Her doctor had left town and Emma had yet to meet the physician who'd bought the practice. She'd heard from a neighbor that he was an older man from St. Louis who had been an army surgeon. His wife served as his nurse. Emma hoped she wouldn't have to wait long to see him.

His office consisted of two front rooms of a house with a lovely covered porch and a nice front yard. The sign next to the door read: DR. HORACE DRUMMOND.

There was no one in the small waiting room. She sighed in relief and sat nervously with her baby in her arms, silently trying to will him to stop crying, but he kept howling as though he was in awful pain. She felt like the worst possible mother.

Across the room, a framed medical diploma and a membership certificate from a medical society were hung on a wall above a small table holding a colorful oriental vase decorated with dragons. She kept her gaze fixed on the vase, trying to maintain her composure, convinced the doctor would find fault and scold her for being unfit.

In a few minutes a man with a neatly trimmed beard and gray hair came into the room. He took off his eyeglasses, peered closely at her wailing baby, and smiled.

"I'm Dr. Drummond," he said as he took the baby from her arms. "Colicky, I would say. Very unsettling for a new mother. Boy or girl?"

"A boy," Emma replied, forcing a smile.

"What's his name?" Drummond asked above the crying.

"Clifford John Kerney. His daddy has taken to calling him CJ, and I've started falling into the habit myself."

"Then I take it you're Mrs. Kerney."

"Yes, Emma."

"Come into my office."

"Is he very sick?" Emma asked as she followed along.

Drummond held the howling CJ at arm's length. "He looks healthy enough. And his lungs certainly sound strong."

He poked and felt CJ's stomach in three places, listened to his heart and lungs, inspected his buttocks and penis, felt his limbs, and peered into his mouth. CJ kept crying.

"Does he cry for a long time?" he asked.

"Yes, for hours."

"How often?"

"At least three times a day, mostly after he nurses," Emma answered.

Drummond nodded again. "He has colic. Make some light fennel tea for yourself and drink it twice a day. It will take a day or two before it has an effect on your milk, but it will help his digestion. Also, put a mustard plaster on his stomach when he's uncomfortable and keep him sitting upright as much as possible. Make sure the poultice doesn't blister his tender skin. Many mothers have told me that rubbing the baby's feet helps relieve the discomfort. He looks to be about three months old, so this should be over soon."

"I hope so," Emma said with a sigh.

Drummond smiled reassuringly. "It will be. Let me fetch my wife to hold CJ while I examine you."

"I'm fine," Emma said.

"I'm sure you are," Dr. Drummond replied soothingly as he stepped to the door, "but I require it of all my new patients. It will take but a few minutes."

He returned with his wife, a portly woman with a round, sour face and a faint mustache on her upper lip, who introduced herself curtly as Mrs. Drummond. She picked CJ up and sat silently in a chair by the door as her husband listened to Emma's lungs and heart through his stethoscope and examined her throat, ears, and eyes. He felt the pulse in her neck and listened to her heart a second time before putting his stethoscope away.

"Did you have a severe fever as a child?" he asked over CJ's crying.

Emma nodded. "A real bad one, when I was ten. I broke out in a rash and had a high fever, and my bones ached something fierce. Why?"

"Do you ever get dizzy?"

"No."

"Do you have fainting spells?"

"Like the fancy ladies in novels?" Emma replied, trying to sound lighthearted. "No."

Drummond smiled. "Have you had chest pains?"

Emma shook her head. The doctor's questions were becoming worrisome.

"Do you get short of breath?" Drummond asked.

"I don't think I ever have been."

"Does your nose bleed frequently?"

"No," Emma replied with growing alarm. "Why are you asking me these things?"

"You have a heart murmur."

Emma stiffened. "What does that mean?"

"It means your heart is working harder than it should. I can hear it through my stethoscope."

"What can be done about it?"

"You must be careful not to overwork yourself, and if you should feel dizzy, faint, have trouble breathing, or have chest pains, rest immediately and come see me right away."

Emma nodded and took CJ from Mrs. Drummond. His crying had eased to a whimper. The thought of not living long enough to raise him shook her to the core. "Is my heart going to give out on me?" she asked.

"I wouldn't worry about that," Drummond replied gently. "You're young and in excellent health otherwise. Just don't overwork. Give yourself time to rest. A slow pace would be best."

"I can do normal things?"

Dr. Drummond nodded. "Don't overdo. I know that won't be easy caring for a baby and such, but you must try. I want you to come back in two months. Sooner, of course, if CJ doesn't get better."

"I will," Emma said. "Thank you, Doctor."

She paid her bill and left, with CJ making a ruckus as she hurried down the street. Her time in Las Cruces was coming to an end. Within the week Patrick would arrive to take her back to the ranch. She had to start putting things away and closing up the house. During his last visit to town he'd proposed renting the place for the extra income, but Emma talked him out of it. Although she looked forward to returning to the ranch, her months in town mostly on her own had been pure bliss. She'd come to appreciate time to herself away from the demands of men and had come to believe that she could live completely on her own if necessary. Much more than a house in town, the casita on Griggs Avenue was now her sanctuary, a place she could go and just be herself.

Back home, she sat in the rocking chair with CJ on her lap and put her hand over her heart. She could feel it beating. She felt the pulse at her neck. As far as she could tell, everything was fine. She had seen only three doctors in her entire life, and the other two had never said anything about a heart murmur. Maybe Dr. Drummond was mistaken.

Still, she worried. She should have asked him more questions. What exactly was a heart murmur? How did it make her heart work harder? Did she get it from the fever she had as a child years ago?

CJ continued crying. Emma propped him on her hip and made a mustard plaster: four tablespoons flour, two tablespoons dry mustard, and a pinch of some baking soda to prevent burning. She mixed it into a paste with lukewarm water, spread it along the top of a flour-sack towel, folded it, and put it on CJ's tummy. As soon as he calmed down she would carry him to the store, buy fennel, and make some tea.

She thought more about what the doctor had told her and decided he must be wrong. She worked as hard as any man at the ranch, and on the range few matched her stamina. She decided not to say a word about the heart murmur to Patrick or Cal. There was no cause to worry them over nothing.

56

After her return to the ranch, Emma's fear that Patrick wouldn't take to his son at first seemed to come true. Although her spirits sank initially, she soon decided there was no reason to scold him about it. He could help a mother cow through a difficult birth but was completely awkward, unsure, and helpless around CJ. To overcome Patrick's uneasiness, Emma used every excuse she could to thrust CJ into his arms. He would hold CJ for a minute or two, looking completely befuddled, before returning him. To a certain extent her strategy worked. By the time CJ was six months old, Patrick was less uncomfortable and occasionally even playful with him, scooping him up and holding him high above his head as he squealed with delight.

When CJ started toddling around on his long, unsteady legs, Emma constantly chased him down as he tried to follow Patrick and Cal everywhere. She found him climbing down the porch steps or scooting out the courtyard gate, or halfway to the corrals and barn. As she herded him home, he fussed all the way back.

After dinner, he was constantly underfoot as the men braided rope, made brindle reins, sharpened knives, and cleaned their gear. When they played cards, he sat on their laps to watch or fiddled at their feet with the wooden toy animals Cal had carved for him.

The world and all its critters fascinated CJ. He loved the ponies and the cows, chased the hens in the chicken coop, had to be rescued from a baby rattlesnake he tried to capture in the courtyard, and ran after the spotted lizards that whipped across the porch. He stalked the solitary roadrunner that lived in a stand of nearby mesquite and clattered in the low branches of the big cottonwoods John Kerney had planted years ago, and caught frogs that lived in the reeds and cattails near the spring that fed the well.

At the age of two, CJ was on the back of a pony with Patrick, and by three he was in the saddle alone, being led around the horse corral or the fenced pasture. At four, CJ had his own little pony named Buddy, and once he finished practicing his numbers and letters on the slate chalkboard Emma bought for him, he busted out the door, ready to ride. Cal swore he had the makings of a stockman from his boots on up.

When Patrick and Cal were out day herding, busy working the ponies, moving stock to fresh pasture, or checking the fence lines, Emma took CJ riding on the flats. Away from the menfolk and housework for a time, and alone with her son, it was the best part of her day.

Inquisitive by nature, CJ was always asking questions. He wanted to know what kind of animals lived in the holes that dotted the desert floor, why ponies needed to wear horseshoes, and what made the wind blow. Emma was determined to have CJ get a proper education beyond what she could teach him. She had every intention to move to town with him when he was old enough for school.

In the evening, after CJ was tucked into bed, Emma sometimes read aloud as Patrick and Cal worked at their chores. Patrick had lost all interest in books—hadn't picked up one in years—and while Cal wouldn't admit it, his eyesight had failed some and he frequently squinted when reading.

Newspaper and magazine stories about the Boxer Rebellion in China and the Boer War in South Africa had captured Emma's interest, so she'd ordered two books by men who had lived through those exciting events. She'd just finished a story about a British medical missionary in China who had barely escaped being killed on the streets of Peking, and had begun reading *London to Lady-smith via Pretoria*, a book of field dispatches about the Boer War written by a British correspondent named Winston Churchill. Both books had her dreaming of seeing more of the world, which she knew would probably never happen. But it no longer made her sad. She was happy with her life far more than ever before.

Some evenings Cal, Patrick, and Emma talked over ranch matters. Changes in the cattle business had happened like lightning after a stock market panic in 1901, caused when railroad tycoons trying to outsmart each other started a recession. Live cattle prices plummeted, newfangled refrigerated railcars began shipping dressed beef to big-city markets across the country, and regional slaughterhouses had sprung up in St. Louis, Omaha, and most recently Fort Worth.

The time had passed when just about any cow a stockman delivered under contract got shipped. And packers weren't just selling whole beef carcasses to butchers and grocers anymore. Now they were marketing high-quality quarters and halves direct to big-city restaurants and wholesalers. Cattle buyers were looking for cows that would meet the changing tastes of customers, who wanted better cuts of meat. They culled out unwanted animals prior to shipping, leaving the stockman to either unload the critters at a loss or throw them back on the range for another season.

For three years, the Double K sold all the Herefords they trailed to market but made no profit at all. And with lots of outfits struggling to get by, they made only a little money selling cow ponies to other spreads. To pay the bills, restock, and keep operating, they carried a five-thousand-dollar bank loan at ten percent interest paid semiannually. Fortunately, they'd been able to rent the house in town for enough to cover the interest on the bank loan.

Emma missed having her sanctuary in town where she could escape the menfolk, enjoy the occasional company of other women, and have the niceties of civilization close at hand. The western side of the Tularosa remained mostly unsettled, and the few ranches thereabouts were a long ride away, which made visiting difficult. Except for a rare overnight trip to see Ignacio and Teresa in Tularosa and the infrequent trips to Alamogordo and Las Cruces to buy supplies, her life was CJ and the ranch.

In another year, CJ would be ready for school. Emma had squirreled away the four hundred dollars Cal had given her when she was pregnant and planned to use it to move the renters out of her house and pay the interest on the bank loan. If that wasn't enough to cover the interest, she'd find work in one of the stores on Main Street. She was determined CJ would be schooled.

She had said nothing about her supposedly weak heart. Soon after her second visit to see Dr. Drummond, he suddenly closed his practice and left the territory to return to St. Louis. The rumor was his wife hadn't liked New Mexico one bit.

Feeling fit and healthy, Emma had no desire to find another doctor, and all the niggling concerns Dr. Drummond had planted in her mind about fainting or getting nosebleeds or having trouble breathing faded away.

During spring and fall works she went out on the trail with CJ at her side, driving the chuck wagon and cooking for the boys. The rest of the year, she worked hard from sunup past sundown and slept like a baby except when CJ woke her up with a cold, an ear infection, or a toothache.

Patrick had learned to use a gentle hand with her in bed, and she couldn't imagine their lovemaking getting any better, but it did. She would have liked him to be more affectionate with CJ, but it wasn't his temperament. He did, however, take pleasure in CJ's company and didn't mind him trailing around as he worked.

On a spring day when Patrick and Cal left early for a trip to the cabin in the high country to grease the windmills and clean out the dirt tanks, Emma yearned for some company. The men had taken CJ with them, Patrick and CJ on horseback—CJ with his cowboy hat pulled down over his ears and a big grin on his face— and Cal driving a wagon full of supplies for the cabin, with a pony named Cactus trailing behind. She'd never seen her son look so happy.

It was the first time CJ had ever been away from her for a day and a night, and it made her a little anxious and lonely.

All spring, angry winds had kicked up dirt and turned the sky smoky gray for days on end. Today the winds were calm enough to be outside without the dust and sand whipping in her face. She worked in the courtyard making soap from wood ash and bacon fat, churning butter, and mending shirts until the warm sun was noontime high. She finished stitching a tear at the elbow of one of Patrick's shirts and looked up to see a rider approaching from the mountain trail that led south to Gene Rhodes's cabin and horse camp, which had been washed away sometime back in a bad flood. She fetched the rifle kept by the kitchen door, leaned it against the courtyard wall, and waited for the rider to draw closer, wondering who it might be.

* * *

The sight of the Double K ranch house raised Gene Rhodes's spirits. Two days ago he'd left the gold camp at Orogrande in the Jarillas Mountains in a hurry, after an argument over a crap game led to a fight with a colored man. Gene busted a half dozen beer bottles over the man's head in order to lay him out cold and got banged up a bit in return. The man's brother, who didn't take too kindly to the outcome of the disagreement, came looking for Gene the next morning. He'd skedaddled before the brother found him or the law got on him.

Four years ago, his wife, May, had taken their young son, Alan, back east to her family's home in New York State. Since then, Gene had faced hard times and some bad luck. He'd mortgaged his spread to Oliver Lee for two hundred and fifty dollars to pay May's fare home, and lost the cabin and improvements in a flood after settling accounts with Oliver. His attempt to get the ranch going again and make a profit had fallen short during the recession, so the money he'd sunk into building a new tank had been for naught. He broke some horses that sold for not much money and finally had to take a job working for Oliver laying pipe in an irrigation ditch to carry water out of the Sacramento Mountains to the Orogrande gold camp. It was hard, grueling labor, but he worked with a number of old boys he'd ridden with in earlier times, so at least the companionship was enjoyable.

The only good to come out of his predicament since May left was that some of his stories and poems had been published. It wasn't enough to pay for victuals, smoking tobacco, or feed for his pony for a month, but it kept him writing, twelve, fourteen hours a day when he had some time to himself or wasn't working as a hand. It blunted the unhappiness he felt being so long separated from his family and the mortification he suffered for his shameful failure to provide for them.

Up ahead he saw a woman standing in the ranch house courtyard watching him approach. He reckoned it was Pat Kerney's wife, Emma. He'd finally written that story about her making a hand on a roundup and sent it off to the editor at *Out West* magazine, thinking it the best yarn he'd set down yet. The editor rejected it as too unbelievable, saying his readers wouldn't abide a female character who took on the attire and manners of rough-hewn cowmen. Gene had written back that he had a particular inability to write anything that didn't ring true and hoped his pathetic failing wouldn't keep the magazine from considering other stories he planned to submit.

He reined in at the corral and gave a howdy to Emma.

"Step down from that pony, Gene," Emma said, "and I'll feed you supper."

"I'm obliged," Gene replied. "But there's no need for you to go to any trouble on my account. Are Pat and Cal around?"

"No, they're not. I'm about to fix myself a meal and would appreciate your company. So light and come have some supper with me."

"Since I know firsthand what a good cook you are, I can't say no to you twice," Gene said with a grin as he slid out of the saddle.

When he drew close, Emma saw that his left eye was swollen shut, he had a gash on his cheek, and his lips were bruised and puffy.

"I think I'd better patch you up before we eat," she said. "Who did you tangle with?"

Gene shrugged. "Just some old boy who didn't know better when to quit fighting."

Emma sat him down at the kitchen table, cleaned his wounds, put some iodine on the gash, and covered it with a plaster.

"You'll heal up in a day or two," she said.

"I appreciate your kindness," Gene said. "Where's that youngster of yours?"

"He's with his daddy and Cal up at the cabin."

"I was hoping to stay there myself for a few days until I hear whether I'm in trouble with the law over the row I got into."

"You can stay there as long as you like," Emma replied as she stirred the simmering pot of stew. "Patrick and Cal will be glad for your company. Now, for supper, I've got stew, fresh-baked bread, and coffee. Will that suit you?"

"It will be the best meal I've had in weeks," Gene said with a grin.

Emma served up a plate of stew and they ate and talked for a time about doings on the basin and along the Rio Grande. There was talk the Reclamation Service of the federal government might start building a dam on the river due west of Engle, where it swerved against a long, high bluff and veered toward the fertile farmlands of the Mesilla Valley. If the dam got built, it would create the largest manmade lake in the world and would tame a river that could be as dry as a wagon road one year and flood out every village along its banks the next. A new spur line from Engle would carry supplies and materials to the site by train, and a thousand men would work years to build it.

Gene talked about the ride he'd taken on the railroad that ran from Alamogordo to Cloudcroft. He described how the tracks climbed twenty-six miles, twisting and turning high into the Sacramento Mountains across deep, wide canyons spanned by long, curving timber trestles, and the spectacular views of the basin and western mountains on the switchbacks.

"It's a genuine engineering marvel," he added.

"I'd love to see it," Emma sighed, thinking that while she was dreaming about China and South Africa there were things right in her own backyard she was missing out on.

"You'll never forget it, guaranteed." Gene sopped up the last of the stew gravy on his plate with a piece of bread. "I've been meaning to tell you, I wrote a story about how you made a hand on that roundup I hired on for, and sent it off to a magazine."

Emma's eyes widened in surprise. "It's about me? I didn't know you were a writer."

Gene blushed slightly. "I'm trying hard to become one. I've had some luck with a few yarns getting published, but I've a far piece to go still. Not many folks know about my scribblings."

"What happened to the story?"

Gene shrugged. "It didn't come to anything. The editor turned it down. I'm gonna rework it some and try again."

Emma's eyes sparkled. "You'll be famous someday; I just know it. I'd love to read it."

"If I get it published, I'll send you a copy."

"Promise?"

"I swear to it." Gene finished his coffee and stood. "I best be on my way. Thank you kindly for the tasty meal."

"You're welcome. Come by anytime."

They said good-bye on the porch and Emma watched Gene ride off. She wanted to ask about his wife and young son back east but thought better about it. Rumor had it that May Rhodes had disliked the immensity of the Tularosa Basin, yearned for the orderly boundaries and tranquil fields of her home state, couldn't abide the constant loneliness and unrelenting winds, and desperately missed her parents.

She wondered why Gene hadn't left the territory to be with his family or found a way to bring them back to New Mexico. Did he miss them? Some men seemed careless about holding their families together, but Gene didn't strike her that way. Maybe it was just that hard times had befallen him.

Turning her attention to her next chore, Emma cleared off the table and moved it to the corner of the room. With the men gone for several days, she'd give the wood floor in the kitchen a good cleaning and polishing. She filled a wash pan with soapy water, got down on her hands and knees, and started scrubbing, trying not to worry about CJ. She knew he was safe with Cal and Patrick.

57

Cal's favorite pony, Bandit, had come up lame a few weeks back and still favored his left rear leg, so he'd cut out Cactus, a bald-faced black, to take up to the cabin. Cactus had sharp teeth and a free and easy gait and liked to pitch a few times after being saddled in the morning. He was the last of the pure mustangs in the Double K remuda Cal and Patrick had gathered in Chihuahua some years back. He'd earned his name by pitching Patrick into a stand of chollas the first time he was ridden on the open range.

More a range pony than a cow horse, Cactus did fine in among the more gentle ponies. But once he got free, his wild blood took over and he ran like the wind for the high country and was almost impossible to corral. He got sold to an outfit on the Jornada, but Cal had to take him back after he broke free on his way to his new home and took to the mountains. A month later, Patrick found him in the north pasture nipping at two old breeding mares in heat that had been separated from the herd.

On level ground or on a rocky hillside, Cactus could change strides as smooth as silk. That made for an easy day in the saddle, so Cal didn't mind if the pony did some casueying first thing. After one or two mild bucks to assert himself, Cactus settled down and did as asked without complaint.

After reaching the cabin, unpacking their gear, and eating a quick cold dinner of jerky and biscuits, Cal, Patrick, and CJ went separate ways. Patrick and CJ rode north to grease the windmill, and Cal drifted west to check on a dirt tank in a high summer pasture. Near a stand of pine trees, the tank captured rainwater and snowmelt. Given the unusually dry winter they'd just had, it cheered Cal considerably to see the tank a little more than three-fourths full, thanks to some early spring storms that had parked over the mountains.

But dirt tanks leaked no matter what, watered seeped into the ground no matter what, and water evaporated in the hot sun no matter what, so to save as much water as possible for livestock, the leaks needed to be plugged. He reckoned there was enough water to serve fifty to seventy-five head for a month if they didn't dally moving them up to the pasture. The grass was blue grama, the best on the ranch, and cows thrived on it.

He walked the perimeter. The tank was spoon shaped, with a gentle grade that descended to the water, which was held back by a five-foot earthen berm. Cal and John Kerney had built the tank years ago by hand and the berm was now covered with grasses and shrubs, which kept it firmly in place. At the base, water was leaking out in rivulets. Cattle had been moved off the pasture during fall works, but there was plenty of fresh sign of other critters drinking at the tank, including turkey, bear, cougar, and deer.

Cal patched the leaks with rocks and dirt, slowing the water to a trickle. Then he piled mounds of dirt against the berm to stem the last of the flow, and tamped everything down. Although a cool breeze whispered through the pines, he'd worked up a sweat. He gave his efforts a quick inspection and rested against the trunk of a pine tree with a view of the Tularosa Basin, looking peaceful and empty as far as the eye could see. The gray, the brown, the stark black-and-white colors of the land, ebbed and flowed as clouds momentarily masked the sun, creating a pale yellow, billowy ivory sky. Except for Sierra Blanca peak thrusting toward the heavens, the Sacramentos melted into a single mysterious wall.

He was bone weary. It was 1906 and he'd turned sixty-six years old. He'd slowed down more than just a step, and although he tried to hide it, Emma had taken to watching him with a careful eye when he came home sore and tired at the end of the day.

He looked skyward. If he left now, he'd be back at the cabin fixing supper long before Patrick and CJ returned. He took a last swig of water from his canteen, climbed on Cactus, and started down the trail into the shadowy canyon. Cactus saw the black bear coming out of a shrub thicket before Cal did. He reared up on his hind legs, nostrils flared, snorting in fear.

The bear rose in reply, snarling and showing teeth. By the size and weight of it, it was male. Cal grabbed for his rifle as the bear bounded straight at him. Cactus dropped down to all fours and bared his teeth. The bear struck Cactus hard across the face with a paw. Cal fired point-blank, emptying his rifle into the beast as he fell astride Cactus, into a shallow defile off the trail. He dropped his rifle, grabbed for the horn, tumbled out of the saddle, and slammed his back hard against a boulder. Something snapped, and pain hit like a lightning bolt.

Cactus rolled and stood, shaking in his tracks. Blood flowed from a deep claw cut on his face. Above him on the trail, the bear lay motionless.

Cal hurt so much he didn't want to move, but there was no time to waste. He had to get to Cactus before the pony bolted; otherwise, he'd be wrecked and afoot. He wiggled his hands and legs, gratified that all but his right arm worked. Whatever he'd busted was high up on the right side of his back, and each time he moved his arm it felt like a hot poker burning a hole in his chest. Pulling his arm close to his side, he stood very slowly and paused to let his head clear. He walked to Cactus, talking gentle and low to him, and grabbed the reins. He used his bandanna to clean the gash on the pony's face as best he could. Then he hooked his boot in the stirrup and mounted. The pain made him dizzy.

Cactus shivered and pawed the ground.

"Let's go, boy," Cal said, turning the pony away from the dead bear. "Slow and easy."

Cactus settled into a faltering walk and picked his way carefully down the hillside on the switchback. Cal fought hard to stay alert, but his head kept dropping to his chest. On level ground, he got Cactus headed toward the cabin in an uneasy trot that sent needles of pain up and down his arm and through his body. He was breathing hard for no cause except shock, he reckoned. It took what seemed forever to raise the cabin. The wagon was parked out front, the team was in the corral, and a strange pony was hitched to a fence post. Smoke poured from the cabin chimney, and a fella was chopping kindling at the woodpile. Patrick and CJ's ponies were nowhere in sight.

Everything looked peaceful enough, but Cal took no chances. He wrapped the reins around the horn, fumbled across his waist for his six-shooter with his left hand, lifted it from the holster, and laid it in his lap. The man saw him coming, stopped chopping, and waved a greeting. Cal wasn't seeing all that good and didn't recognize the fellow until he reined in by the woodpile.

"Why, Gene, I'm glad to see you," he said as his leg iron slipped off his lap and fell to the ground. "I've been wrecked some and could use a hand."

Gene helped Cal down from his pony and walked him to the cabin. He was unsteady on his feet, and his ashen face was covered in sweat. He clutched his right arm to his side and with each step winced in pain.

"Is it your arm that's stove up?" Gene asked as he eased Cal down on the bed.

"That and my back," Cal said. "I think something broke off and got stuck inside. It sure feels that way. You'll have to cut my vest and shirt off for a look-see. I ain't about to try to move the arm."

"Stay still," Gene said. He got a knife and cut off Cal's vest and bloody shirt. Part of a bone stuck out of his upper arm, and his shoulder blade looked liked it had been crushed by a cannon ball. The skin was angry red and bloody.

"You're busted up all right and need a doctor, pronto," Gene said. "I'm gonna clean you up some, carry you home in the wagon, and fetch one from town."

"I'm obliged," Cal said, nodding at the shelves where the supplies were kept. "Bring me that bottle of whiskey."

Gene used some of the whiskey on Cal's arm before giving him the bottle, wrapped the arm tight against his side with some cut-up cloth, and put a light mud plaster over the broken bone.

Cal had lapped up half the bottle by the time Gene finished.

"I'll get the team hitched," Gene said.

"I'll be right here waiting on you," Cal replied with a faint smile as he lifted the whiskey bottle. "If I was a critter, you would have already shot me."

"I don't believe bullets can kill you, old son," Gene replied.

At the corral he made quick work of roping the team and hitching them to the wagon. He unsaddled Cal's pony, put him in the corral, and went back to check on Cal. He was unconscious but breathing. Gene gathered up the bedrolls that were stowed against the wall, spread them out in the wagon, and woke Cal up.

"Time to get along," Gene said, helping Cal to his feet. He wrapped a blanket around him.

Cal nodded but didn't speak.

He got Cal in the wagon, laid him on his side, covered him with another blanket, propped his head against some clean straw, tied his pony to the wagon, and started the team down the rutted trail toward the Double K headquarters.

It would be dark long before he reached the ranch house, and there would be no moonlight on the trail. He hee-hawed the team along at a faster pace, hoping they knew the way home and Cal would still be alive when they got there.

58

The long day in the saddle had been hard on CJ, and he was plumb wore out by the time Patrick had greased the windmill, worked on the dirt tank, and repaired the barbwire fence at the mouth of the canyon. He hoisted CJ up with him, and leading his son's little pony started back to the cabin at a slow pace. CJ fell asleep within minutes. Patrick figured Cal would have supper waiting and be fretting about where they were by the time they arrived.

He reached the cabin with the sun dipping behind the San Andres. The cabin door was open, the wagon and team of horses were gone, and Cactus was alone in the corral. Patrick urged his horse forward in a gallop, jolting CJ awake.

"What's wrong?" CJ asked.

"Be quiet now, boy," Patrick snapped, wrapping an arm around CJ as he reached for his six-gun.

* * *

Hard pounding on the door brought Emma out of a sound sleep. She heard her name being called and footsteps inside the house.

She quickly lit a lamp and rushed out of the bedroom to find Gene
Rhodes holding Cal upright and dragging him to the couch.

"Not there," Emma snapped, turning toward the open bedroom
door. "Bring him in here."

Gene followed Emma into the bedroom. "We can't lay him on his
back," he said. "He's hurt bad there and his right arm is fractured."

Emma helped Gene stretch Cal out on his side and peeled away
the blanket. His right shoulder blade was shattered and the skin
around it badly bruised. A bone protruded through the mud plaster on his upper arm. His face had lost all color and he was barely
conscious.

"Stoke up the fire in the cookstove and get some water boiling,"
Emma said.

Gene hesitated at the door. "He thinks something broke inside."

"Hurry with that water," Emma said as she rushed past him for
laudanum tonic and turpentine liniment from the kitchen cabinet.

She grabbed a spoon, returned to Cal, made him swallow some
tonic, and smiled when he opened his eyes.

"What fool thing did you do?" she asked.

"Tangled with a bear," Cal replied in a thin voice. "Got the best
of him too. Leastways for the time being."

"I'm sending Gene for a doctor."

Cal shook his head. "Don't waste that cowboy's time. I'll be dead
long before the doctor gets here and you'll still have to pay him
five cents a mile, coming and going for nothing."

"Don't talk that way," Emma scolded, holding back a sob.

"I got a hole inside me sucking air out of my lungs," Cal said
with a grimace. "No sawbones is gonna fix it."

"Don't be silly," Emma said, stroking his face. "You'll be fine.
Where are Patrick and CJ?"

Cal coughed, and blood foamed at his mouth. "Don't know for certain, but I suspect on their way here."

He glanced up as Gene stepped into the bedroom and stood at the foot of the bed. "I'd be obliged if you'd let Ignacio Chávez and his family know of my passing. I'd like them to help lay me to rest, if they've a mind to."

"I'll fetch them," Gene said.

Emma wiped the blood from the corner of Cal's mouth. "Don't talk nonsense."

Cal patted her hand. "Put me up on the hill next to John Kerney, Molly, and George. I've always liked that view."

"You stop that talk," Emma snapped.

Cal squeezed Emma's hand. "Don't you fret, now. There's an old pistol box under my bed. Bring it here to me."

Emma shook her head. "I'm staying right by your side."

Cal smiled. "I ain't quite ready to quit this world yet. Go get it, girl. It's important."

Emma let go of his hand and hurried out of the room.

"I'll be heading out," Gene said.

"Don't jingle your spurs on my account," Cal replied. "Besides, you look plumb wore out."

Gene stepped closer to Cal. "I can sleep in the saddle. Are you sure you don't want a doctor?"

Cal shook his head. "It would do me no good. I always figured I'd get shot down by some desperado, not killed by a bear. How's my pony?"

"I doctored him some and put him in the corral at the cabin. He'll be fine."

"Good." Cal winced and caught his breath.

"I'll be on my way," Gene said.

"Adios and thanks for getting me home," Cal replied. "Much obliged. Don't get old and busted up. It's no damn fun."

Gene smiled at Cal's sand. "Now, that's a homily a man can take to heart. So long."

Gene left. Cal took a breath and held it against the pain that shot through his chest. He forced a smile when Emma returned, put the pistol box down on the chair, and set about washing his face with hot water. She sat him upright, leaned him forward, cleaned around his crushed shoulder blade, and bound his fractured arm tight against his side.

"I told Gene to bring the doctor," Emma said as she lowered him tenderly down to his side.

"Foolish waste of his time and your money," Cal replied. "That box contains my will. Don't you read it until you fetch some whiskey for me."

She got a bottle from the bottom drawer of the desk, kneeled at the side of the bed, lifted his head, tilted the full glass to his lips, and watched him drink.

"Give me two more just like that," he said, "and keep the bottle handy."

When he'd finished drinking, she put the bottle on the floor and read the will. She would inherit half the ranch. Stunned, she looked at Cal in disbelief.

"I was planning to tell you and Patrick both," Cal said, "but just didn't get around to it."

With tears in her eyes, Emma read the document again. "You didn't need to do this."

"The Double K is my home, and you, Patrick, and CJ are the only family I've got. You've earned an equal say in this outfit, so fair is fair. Besides, there's no man on this planet that can boss you around anyway."

Emma smiled. "Only you."

"When you've a mind to let me. I'm gonna rest now. I'm feeling wore out."

"Sleep." Emma leaned over and kissed him. "I'll be right here."

She covered him with a blanket, turned down the lamp, pulled her chair close to the bed, and watched him doze off. She couldn't imagine the ranch without Cal, or what life without him might be. He was the kindest, best person she had ever known.

59

Cal lost consciousness before Patrick and CJ got home, and died two days later without waking. Leaving Patrick and CJ to fend on their own, Emma never left Cal's side, sleeping in the chair next to the bed, holding his hand, wiping his feverish face, talking and reading to him in the hopes he would awake.

Cal stopped breathing several hours after Gene Rhodes arrived with the doctor, who announced that nothing could be done, expressed his sympathies, collected his fee, and left.

In Tularosa, Gene had spread the word about Cal's bad wreck, and it got passed on by telegraph to people in Alamogordo, Las Cruces, and Engle. A number of folks rode out to the Double K to pay respects and say good-bye. Ignacio, Teresa, and their children were on hand, as were some of the boys and stockmen from other spreads on the Tularosa and Jornada. James Kaytennae came in alone from Mescalero, traveling day and night to get there in time, and former deputy sheriff Tito Barela from Las Cruces showed up. Adam Dieter, the shopkeeper in Tularosa, made the long trek, as did Oliver Lee and some other Texans Cal had known in the old days.

Leland and Maude Carter and Earl and Addie Hightower, two couples who ranched on small spreads in the San Andres, showed up early with their children to help out. Leland and Earl slaughtered a maverick cow, and Maude and Addie helped Emma roast it on a spit over an open pit and prepare the rest of the fixings.

They buried Cal next to John Kerney under a carved wooden cross Ignacio fashioned from mesquite wood. All the folks gathered around except James Kaytennae, who remained astride his pony on the adjacent hilltop to avoid getting ghost sickness from the dead. Gene Rhodes took off his hat and read the epitaph he'd written:

In this hard country where coin is scarce and loyal friends pure gold,

Here lies a man known to all as true and good and bold.

He lived by his word, upheld the law, and tamed this desert land,

Not many more will pass this way with his true grit and sand.

He gave the epitaph to Emma. Gene had signed it. She folded it carefully, wiped away some tears, and hurried to the ranch house with CJ in hand. All she could allow herself to think about was feeding the folks who'd come to say good-bye to Cal. If she stayed focused on that and that alone, maybe she wouldn't break down in front of everybody.

While the men carved the beef, Emma got busy with Addie and Maude preparing platters of chicken, biscuits, boiled vegetables, and pies and setting out plates on the long plank table in the courtyard. After everyone ate, the menfolk smoked, sipped whiskey, and told stories about Cal, while the women cleaned up and the children played. When the last person had left and the last dish was washed and put away, Emma collapsed in her bed and slept.

CJ woke her up by shaking her. It was well into the morning, with full daylight streaming though the window.

"Pa wants you to get up," he said, as he climbed on the bed and sat next to her.

Emma rumpled his hair. "All right."

"Don't do that," CJ said, pulling away.

"Don't you like it?" Emma asked.

"No. Get up. Pa says so."

Emma sat up and looked at her son. "You're pretty bossy."

CJ grinned. "I know."

His face and hands were dirty and his hair was matted and unwashed. "You need a bath and a change of clothes," Emma said.

CJ made a sour face.

"Tell your pa I'll be right there."

CJ jumped off the bed and ran out of the room.

Emma dressed, ran a brush through her hair, and found Patrick in the front room at the desk sorting through papers. "Do I need to fix you some food?" she asked.

Patrick shook his head sharply and said nothing.

She sat down across from him and waited. He'd barely spoken to her since the night Cal had been brought home by Gene Rhodes busted up and dying. She hadn't minded Patrick's silence or his careful avoidance of her over the last few days, although she knew it was due to the contents of Cal's will. The anger on his face after he read it told her so.

Patrick continued staring at her silently. She thought about walking out of the room to protest his childish ways, but that would only fuel his anger. She could outlast him when it came to holding her tongue, but that too only served to rile him.

"What is it?" she finally asked.

"You know damn well what it is," Patrick snapped. "How often did you have to lift your skirts to get into Cal's will? Did it start when I was in Cuba? Before that maybe? Maybe it was going on right up until the day he died."

Emma stood up and glared at Patrick. "That's not true. Don't you ever say that to me again."

"I'll say what I please. This was supposed to be my ranch. Mine. And Cal broke his word."

"It's still your ranch," Emma replied.

"Half yours doesn't make it all mine."

"Is that what you want?" Emma asked.

"That's what I was promised."

"Cal loved us both and he wanted us to share. He said so in his will."

Patrick smiled lewdly at her.

"Don't you dare say a word," Emma spat, "or I will hate you forever."

"I know what he wrote. That doesn't make it right. I want my ranch." Patrick slammed his hand on the desk.

Emma shook her head. "No."

"You're no wife to me," Patrick said as he came out of his chair in a rage.

She wouldn't give in to him. The forsaken, lost little boy who lived inside of Patrick made him who he was, but that didn't give him the right to bully her. She turned, went to the bedroom, and started packing. She had known for some time it might come to this and felt no twinge of regret about leaving. She wasn't sure if it was permanent or not. But she did know that if Patrick tried to stop her from taking CJ he would never see either of them ever again.

60

Fall works always ended the same way for CJ. After everything was packed and loaded in the wagon, Pa would stand silently on the porch and watch him and his ma leave for town without saying a word or even giving a wave. Never a "good-bye," "so long," or "adios" passed between them. But this time it was even more strained. Last night his parents had argued something fierce.

CJ usually rode his pony, Buddy, alongside the wagon while Ma chattered about how glad she was to be returning to town and how happy she would be to see CJ back in school. She was always sunniest when they were leaving the Double K, even though she seemed to like it well enough while they were there. Not today. She drove the wagon away from the house stone-faced and silent, her eyes hard and red, her chin set, which happened only when she was really angry.

Last night, he'd snuck out on the porch after bedtime and listened to them arguing in the kitchen, raising their voices at each other and sounding fit to be tied. Pa wanted CJ to stay at the Double K and go to a one-room schoolhouse Earl Hightower had built for his three girls on his ranch. Earl's wife Addie was to be the teacher, and Leland and Maude Carter, the Hightowers' neighbors, were planning to send their two boys to it.

Ma was having none of it. While she liked Addie, she wanted CJ to go to a modern school with college-educated teachers, good textbooks for reading, writing, and arithmetic, desks for every student, and maps and globes in every classroom. Besides, she argued, it would be too far to ride back and forth every day.

To CJ the idea of a school close to the ranch sounded just about perfect. They had passed through the Hightower spread during fall works and he'd seen the school, a new log building in a pretty area of grassy flats and red hills. He could get there on Buddy in little more than an hour.

Pa had argued that if CJ was ever going to ranch he needed to learn to do it firsthand, and schooling in town wouldn't get him ready to run the spread when the time came for him to take over. That made good sense to CJ, who loved every minute he spent at the Double K. Besides, he was ten years old now and not some little kid that needed to be looked after every minute by his ma, even though he liked town and loved his school. His teacher was already talking to him about going on to college when he got older, saying he had the makings of a scholar.

He'd overheard arguments before between his parents, and Pa never won any of them, so after a time when it was clear Pa didn't stand a chance, he quit eavesdropping and snuck back to bed. It wasn't that Pa was bad at arguing; he just wasn't as good at it as Ma. He'd watched her talk the school principal into letting him skip a grade, and seen her convince his teacher to let him use an eighth-grade reader when he was still in the fourth grade. When she set her mind to it, she was almost certain to have her way.

He fell asleep only to get woken up an hour later by an awful row between his parents. They were yelling at each other in the courtyard at the top of their lungs. Ma was calling Pa a son of a bitch, telling him to let go of her, and screaming no over and over again. Pa was yelling back, calling her a bitch, and sounding drunk and angry.

Suddenly, CJ heard the door to the casita, where Pa bunked while they were at the ranch, slam shut. After that, all he heard were muffled shouts. He sat bolt upright in bed thinking he should go listen at the door, but everything soon got quiet. It was late when he finally got back to sleep. Ma got him up before first light. She was about as angry looking as he'd ever seen her and had a big red welt across her cheek. She gave him a quick kiss, told him to dress and get ready for breakfast, and flew out of his bedroom.

In the kitchen, Pa was nowhere to be found. Ma said barely a word as she fixed breakfast just for the two of them. When he asked why Pa wasn't eating with them, she told him to hush. He could hear Pa's footsteps on the porch, but he didn't come inside.

After breakfast, CJ wanted to go looking for him to say good-bye, but Ma hurried him along, not even bothering to clear off the table or wash the dishes. They loaded the wagon, hitched the horse to it, and saddled Buddy before the sun broke over the Sacramentos.

"I need to say good-bye to Pa," CJ said.

"We're leaving now," Ma said. "Get on Buddy and come with me or I'll take a switch to you."

CJ looked at her in disbelief. Never once had she raised a hand to him, but the look on her face told him she meant it. He mounted Buddy and rode next to the wagon in silence, hoping she would say that everything would be all right and not to worry, like she always did after she fought with Pa. This time she wouldn't even look at him.

He kept glancing at her and then back at the ranch house, thinking Pa would be on the porch watching them leave like always, but he wasn't there.

CJ reckoned something mighty bad had happened between his parents last night. They'd never cussed each other so hard or shouted and yelled like that before, and he'd never seen Ma stay so angry. It scared him.

* * *

Patrick watched from the side of the barn as Emma and CJ faded into specks at the far end of the pasture. Whatever good there was in his marriage had been wiped out last night; whatever affection Emma had for him had been erased. All because he'd gotten a little drunk after their argument about CJ's schooling, pulled her out of her bed, yanked her along to the casita, and forced her to have sex.

She'd kept him out of her bed all summer long with one excuse or another. She felt dizzy, had indigestion, or was too tired. As far as Patrick could tell, there wasn't a damn thing wrong with her except she'd gotten skinny, slept longer, and had soured on sex.

After he got liquored up a little, he'd decided he had rights he hankered to exercise. She was huffy when he went to her room and grabbed at her, so he slapped her for acting uppity. She slapped him back, broke away, and ran into the courtyard. He caught up and slapped her again, and she yelled like a banshee, clawing his face and calling him a son of a bitch. He yanked her into the casita, threw her on the bed, lifted her nightgown, forced her legs apart, and took her. She froze up under him until he finished. He rolled off, his face throbbing from her scratches.

"Don't you ever touch me again," she whispered harshly.

Patrick laughed as he rose to his feet. "Why would I want to? You ain't the gal I remember from before. I can get more pleasure from a five-dollar whore than from you."

Emma got up and pulled her nightgown down. "I told you what would happen if you ever raped me."

"I'm your husband, so it ain't rape," he said as he pushed her toward the door. "Now, git."

"We won't be coming back."

"You ain't welcome," Patrick replied, "but by God I'll have CJ back here where he belongs. Tell me true, is Cal CJ's pappy?"

"You son of a bitch," Emma spat. She slammed the door behind her.

Patrick stopped running the memory of last night through his mind as he walked to the horse corral. If it was over, so be it, he thought. On his next trip to town he'd see what could be done to buy her out and get a judge to give him CJ. He was darn certain she'd want a divorce. There had to be some way to get the boy to live with him, although judges were mostly on the side of women when it came to raising children.

If she really was feeling poorly, he might have a chance to get CJ if he could prove she couldn't take proper care of him. Thinking back over the summer, he saw that Emma hadn't been herself. She'd worked hard and all, but her mood had been different, more serious and less lively. Maybe she'd just up and die. That would solve everything.

Whatever happened, he was already feeling good to be rid of her. The lie made Patrick's stomach turn over. It was pure bull. He knew what he'd done was wrong, and lying to himself about wanting her gone wouldn't make the hurt of losing her go away. He'd never get over her. He was a spineless fool for letting a woman worm inside him that way.

He got busy with the ponies. It was best to concentrate on work and forget about her. He'd sold six ranch horses to a stockman north of Carrizozo, a new village that had sprung up a few years back along the railroad on the far-north side of the Tularosa. He'd have the ponies finished in a month, deliver them, then head to Las Cruces to make a bank payment and find himself a lawyer to talk to.

He wondered what it would take to get Emma to turn CJ over to him, at least partways. He damn sure wasn't willing to lose both a wife and a son completely. Then he'd be back to having nobody, and he couldn't cotton to that.

He shouldn't have forced himself on her like he did. His gut seized up with the memory of it, and he quickly brushed it away, determined not to think of it again.

61

The day Emma's period was late she knew she was pregnant. She waited another month before seeking out a doctor, who confirmed she was with child and spent a long time listening to her heart through his stethoscope.

"You have a heart murmur," Dr. Fielder finally said.

Emma's spirits sank. Ever since the start of summer, she'd been lightheaded, sometimes even dizzy, and often out of breath. After returning to Las Cruces from the ranch, she'd done a good job of hiding her ailment from CJ and her employer, Sam Miller, who owned a dry-goods store on Main Street.

She nodded.

Dr. Fielder raised an eyebrow. "You're not surprised?"

In a way, he reminded Emma of Cal with his soft Texas drawl and quiet air of confidence.

"I know about it," she said with a slight smile, "but I haven't let it slow me down."

"Do you want to have this baby, Mrs. Kerney?"

The question startled Emma. "Why would you even ask me that?" she demanded.

"I'm worried about your health," Fielder replied gently. "With your heart condition you could easily lose it." He paused and gave her a serious look. "Or the child might be motherless."

Emma's eyes widened. Both possibilities were unimaginable to her. Losing Molly had been hard enough. That would not happen again. She would have this child and live to raise it. "What should I do?"

"Do you have kinfolks who can help during your pregnancy?"

Emma shook her head. "I live alone with my son and have to work. I have a job at Miller's Dry Goods."

Dr. Fielder looked grave. "You must avoid excitement and strenuous work. Being on your feet all day won't do for you or your baby. You'll need plenty of rest so as not to strain your heart. The delivery could do tremendous damage to your heart. Do you understand what I'm saying?"

"That I could die giving birth," Emma replied.

"Or before," Fielder added. "I take it you have no husband?"

"I do," Emma replied, "but not for long."

"I see. I must tell you directly, Mrs. Kerney, that in order to give every advantage to you and the baby, you must cease work, have only a very light housekeeping burden, and rest in bed every day. In addition, you'll need to have nursing care as your time approaches. Otherwise, I fear for the worst. Is there some way this might be possible?"

"Yes."

Fielder smiled. "Good. I'll want to see you in a month and then twice a month after that until the baby comes."

Fielder reached for a pen and wrote something down.

"Miss Strauss is a nurse who took her diploma at a New York hospital. She is quite capable and also an excellent midwife, although I will attend you at delivery." He handed the paper to Emma. "Get in touch with her as soon as possible."

"Thank you," Emma said.

She walked slowly home in the late afternoon coolness of the day, with gray skies covering the valley and rain clouds gathering above the Organ Mountains. She kept her head lowered to hide her tears. To protect her unborn child and give it a chance for life, she needed money to get though the pregnancy and pay all the bills. That meant she would have to come to terms with Patrick. He'd offered through his lawyer to sign over the house and give her a cash settlement equal to a third of the value of the ranch if she agreed to let CJ live with him and go to Addie Hightower's one-room schoolhouse.

Emma hated the idea of CJ giving up the chance to get a good enough education to go to college. More than that, she feared Patrick's influence over him. Although she would never say it to him, CJ was a sweet boy, honest and caring. He had none of his father's suspicious attitudes toward people or his sharp temper. But most of all, her heart broke at the thought of losing him. It felt almost as bad as Molly's death.

It seemed fate had conspired to force her to give up her son for an unborn baby that might not even survive. She had no choice but to do all she could to bring her baby into the world and raise it. But she would never completely surrender CJ to Patrick in order to do it.

At home, CJ was at the kitchen table studying a Spalding Athletic Library book on the manly art of boxing that he'd bought last Saturday for ten cents. Emma had seen him in his room shadow boxing and practicing the various poses illustrated in the book. He smiled and closed the cover as Emma kissed him on the cheek.

"If I let you live with your father at the ranch for one school term and here in town with me for the other, would you like that? Summers you could stay at the ranch as always, if you like, or be here with me. It will be your choice."

CJ's eyes widened with pleasure for a second before he gave his mother a sharp look. "Does that mean you and Pa are for certain getting divorced?"

Emma took a deep breath. "I told you that we were. It isn't going to change."

CJ's expression turned stormy.

"I know you don't like it," Emma said gently.

"I hate it!" CJ snapped. "Don't do it."

She reached for his hand, but he pulled it away. "Someday you're going to be your pa's partner in the Double K," Emma said as she sat down beside him. "I know you love the ranch and would rather be there than any other place. Your pa can teach you all he knows, just like before. In the fall, you can live in town with me. That way, your pa and I get to share you. It's the best way to do things."

CJ turned his head. "It's not best for me without you with us."

Emma stood and reached for the apron on the hook by the kitchen door. She wasn't sure if she could keep from wrapping her arms around CJ and never letting him go.

"You think about the idea while I get started on supper," she said as she tied the apron strings. "It just might be perfect for you. Your pa will help you become the best rancher on the basin, and with all your schooling you'll be smarter and more savvy than the whole lot of them."

CJ stood. "I'm going to my room," he said, sounding surly.

"Bring in some wood for the cookstove before you do," Emma said, trying to keep her voice from trembling.

* * *

Patrick's attorney, Alan Lipscomb, met him a block away from the offices of Wallace Claiborne Hale, Emma's lawyer.

"They're waiting for us," Lipscomb said, consulting his pocket watch. He ran a handkerchief across his forehead. It was a hot day for the middle of November, and a stiff breeze kicked across the valley. On Main Street, dust swirled up and down the boulevard. Only a few people were out. A wagon rattled past and several automobiles chugged by, billowing smoke. A huge tumbleweed followed one of the motorcars down the street. In spite of the bountiful crops harvested earlier in the fall along the Rio Grande, Las Cruces looked dried out and thirsty.

"They can wait," Patrick replied, looking at the baby-faced lawyer in his three-piece suit. "Are you sure they agreed to my terms?"

Lipscomb nodded. "You pay her one-third the value of the ranch, livestock, and improvements, and she gets the house free and clear plus any remaining cash from the dissolution of the partnership and the marriage."

Patrick hated the idea of borrowing the money to settle the divorce, but there was no other way to do it. "What about CJ?" he demanded. "I want my boy."

"That's what we're here to find out. Mr. Hale says they're willing to make an offer."

"What kind of offer?"

Lipscomb shrugged. "Best you can plan on is seeing your son in town and having him out at the ranch when he's not in school. There isn't a judge in the district who will give you custody of the boy over his mother's objections. And as far as we know, there are no moral or health issues that would hold up against her. She has all the cards."

Lipscomb waited for his client to react. A tall man who towered over him, Patrick Kerney had a face that gave nothing away. In his two prior meetings with the man, Lipscomb had come to think of Kerney as taciturn and vindictive. Why else would he want to deny his wife custody of their son? Mrs. Kerney was well liked and respected by all who knew her in town. Many folks, particularly the men who frequented Miller's Dry Goods, found her remarkably interesting and vivacious. Lipscomb was one of those men.

Patrick said nothing. "Are you ready?" Lipscomb asked.

Patrick nodded and stepped off briskly down the sidewalk toward Hale's office. Lipscomb hurried to catch up and drew even with Kerney at the front door, just as he flung it open and stepped inside. A male secretary scrambled to his feet to greet them.

"Where is my wife?" Kerney demanded curtly.

The secretary nodded at the closed door to the inner office. "Go right in."

Kerney stormed in. Lipscomb, in his wake, wondered if all hell was going to break loose. Instead, Kerney glanced quickly at his wife, sitting in a chair across from Hale's desk, and locked his eyes on Hale, who rose, hand extended.

He shook Hale's hand across the desk, sat stiffly in an empty chair away from his wife, and said, "Let's hear what you have to say."

Lipscomb took a seat between Kerney and his missus. As always, he was struck by Emma's natural attractiveness. She had lively eyes, pleasing full lips, high cheekbones, and lustrous dark hair done up in a bun.

"Yes, of course," Wallace Hale said, settling down behind his desk. "To the business at hand." He passed a document across the desk to Lipscomb.

"What's this?" Lipscomb said, reaching for his reading spectacles.

"Once signed, it testifies, declares, and acknowledges that Mr. Kerney is the father of Mrs. Kerney's unborn child," Hale replied. "By his signature, Mr. Kerney furthermore agrees to make the unborn child an equal heir to his estate."

Stunned, red faced, and angry looking, Patrick turned to Emma and sputtered, "What damn unborn child?"

Wallace Hart held up his hand to stop him. "Enough, Mr. Kerney. If you are about to challenge my client's claim that you are the father of this child, I advise against it. If you do so, all pending agreements regarding the divorce settlement will dissolve here and now, and we will see you and your counsel in court, where you will not fare well."

Patrick Kerney clenched his jaw and shot another glance at Emma, who sat calmly, ignoring him.

"Just what does my client get out of this?" Lipscomb asked.

"Along with the already agreed-upon division of property and cash assets, Mrs. Kerney will graciously agree to allow CJ to stay with your client on the ranch each year from the start of the New Year through fall works, providing that CJ returns to his mother's house during the summer should he so desire and your client agrees to return CJ home to his mother in time to attend school in the fall. Furthermore, Mr. Kerney must ensure that CJ attends school at the Hightower Ranch while it is in session during the time the boy resides at the Double K."

Hale handed Lipscomb another document and watched as he

read it. "Do you need a moment in private with your client?" he asked.

"Just how far along are you?" Patrick demanded of Emma before Lipscomb could reply to Hale.

"You should know," Emma said evenly, refusing to look at him, "unless you'd like to forget what you did."

Patrick gripped the arms of his chair and glared at her.

Hale passed another paper to Lipscomb. "Dr. Fielder is attending to Mrs. Kerney. She is approaching the end of her third month. He attests to it in his letter."

"Did you figure out how to do all this all on your own?" Patrick snapped at Emma. "Is this how you pay me back for getting you away from Tom Dunphy and your loco sister? Taking you in when you had nothing and giving you a home and a family?"

Emma straightened her back and stared at the wall of books behind Hale's desk.

"Do you want a moment with your client?" Hale repeated.

Lipscomb nodded.

"Use my office," Hale said as he escorted Emma to the door. "If you agree to Mrs. Kerney's conditions, call for my secretary. He'll have the necessary documents for Mr. Kerney to sign."

Patrick waited until the door closed. "Maybe I should get me a lawyer who will stand up for me."

"Another lawyer might be more than willing to advise you to take the matter before a judge," Lipscomb replied. "But I feel it will serve no good purpose, although folks hereabouts will certainly find plenty reason to gossip about what gets disclosed in court."

"That kind of talk won't bother me none out on the Double K," Patrick replied.

"But it will surely bother your son here in town," Lipscomb responded.

"Dammit," Patrick snorted.

"If you have any knowledge that Mrs. Kerney has been unfaithful with another man, we can proceed with a counterproposal or take the entire custody question before a judge. Otherwise, I suggest you accept the terms."

Patrick fell silent.

"Do you wish to contest Mrs. Kerney's assertion that you are the father of her unborn child?"

Patrick sighed. "I want to be done with this and with her."

"Very well." Lipscomb opened the door and called for Hale's secretary.

Papers in hand, Patrick and Lipscomb read though the documents carefully. After Patrick signed, Lipscomb witnessed his signature, and the two men left Hale's office. The secretary was alone in the front office. Emma and Hale were nowhere in sight.

In spite of his bluster, Patrick wanted to see her again. He wanted to talk her out of the mule-headed stubbornness that had caused her to leave him. He wanted her to give him another chance, like any decent wife should.

That wasn't going to happen, and he knew it. Right there, on the spot, with Lipscomb saying something that didn't register, Patrick decided he would have nothing at all to do with the baby Emma carried. Not now, not ever.

62

As winter approached, news of impending statehood filled the newspapers. In the diners, saloons, hotels, and stores along Main Street, it was about the only subject of conversation. Rumor had it that New Mexico would become a state soon after Congress convened in the New Year. The city fathers were already planning a day of celebration.

Emma used some of the money she received from the divorce settlement to have electricity installed in her house. Workmen ran a wire from the poles in the alley, cut a hole through the adobe wall, put in switches, outlets, and ceiling lights, and attached the wires to everything. As soon as they were done, Emma bought table lamps and lightbulbs for each room. Every day at dusk, she and CJ turned all the lights on just because it was such a marvel. After supper, they sat together in the front room. Emma usually sewed while CJ did his studies, and when he finished they read aloud to each other until his bedtime.

For a nickel, she had bought a dog-eared, used copy of *A Lady's Life in the Rocky Mountains,* by an Englishwoman named Isabella Bird. The book totally enthralled her, and CJ enjoyed it as well.

It was a series of letters written in 1873 by Isabella to her sister back in England as she traveled alone in the Rocky Mountains, meeting up with a one-eyed desperado, surviving blizzards, climbing fourteen-thousand-foot mountains, weathering cold and hunger in a mountain cabin during an ice storm, staying in flea-infested houses, and traveling on foot through the forest after being thrown by her horse when a bear attacked. Not only were the tales exciting, but the author's descriptions of all she'd seen were splendid.

The night she finished reading aloud the last chapter to CJ, Emma came to a decision. Isabella Bird had inspired her. She would not leave this world without first seeing something of it, no matter if it was only a small slice.

She closed the book and looked at CJ. "You and I are going to take a trip before you leave for the ranch."

CJ's eyes lit up. "Where to?"

"California. I want to see the Pacific Ocean and dip my toes in the water. We'll stop at the Grand Canyon on the way back."

CJ grinned. "I'd like that a whole bunch. Maybe we could visit Inscription Rock, where all the Spanish conquistadors and early explorers signed their names," he added excitedly. "It's over north-west from here."

"I don't see why not," Emma said, almost giggling. "On our way home we can stay over a few days in Albuquerque, go to Santa Fe, and visit some of the Indian pueblos along the Rio Grande. I've never been to any of those places."

"When are we going?" CJ asked.

"Soon. I'll go to the train depot in the morning and get sched-ules and brochures. We'll plan our adventure tomorrow after you're home from school."

"Do you really mean it?" CJ asked, barely able to contain himself.

"Yes, I do."

"Whoopee!" CJ shouted with a grin.

"We'll have such fun," Emma said. She pulled him out of his chair and danced him gaily around the room.

* * *

In the predawn darkness of a cold, early January morning, CJ stepped out of his mother's house, walked through the gate of the picket fence, put his heavy parcels and bags in the back of the wagon, tied Buddy to the tailgate, and climbed up on the seat next to his father. He could see Ma's outline in the front-room window. She'd been crying a little when she kissed him good-bye, and CJ wasn't feeling too good to be leaving her for so long a time himself.

On their trip to California, he'd seen more, done more, and had more fun than his two best friends, Austin Feather and Billy McFie, could imagine. He must have told them about his adventures more than a dozen times, describing the ocean, which went on forever, filling up the horizon more than the desert ever could, and recounting his first look into the Grand Canyon, spotting the thin ribbon of the river in the deep gorge thousands of feet below, and how scary it was to peer down into it. He told them about Inscription Rock, where for hundreds of years a pool of clear water had drawn travelers, who chiseled their names and initials in stone on the towering, sheer cliff. He talked about the people he saw on the trains, the land he saw from the railcar windows, the fancy two-story buildings that lined the Santa Fe Plaza, and the Indians at the pueblos.

Envious of all CJ had seen, Billy and Austin declared Mrs. Kerney to be the swellest mother in town to take him on such an adventure. CJ felt the same.

"I see she's got electricity now," Pa said as he started the team down the street.

"Sure makes it easier on the eyes come nightfall," CJ allowed with a nod of his head.

"I suppose so. Waste of money, as I see it." Patrick reached for a blanket on the floorboard. "Here, in case you get cold."

"I'm fine, Pa," CJ replied, stuffing the blanket between them on the seat.

"What have you got in those parcels?" Patrick asked.

"Schoolbooks," CJ replied. "Ma doesn't want me falling behind in my studies. I'm to give the books to Mrs. Hightower, so she can make assignments for me from them."

"Sam Miller told me your ma stopped working for him and took you on a trip to California."

"Yep," CJ said enthusiastically, "and it was some humdinger too. We saw the ocean, the Grand Canyon . . ."

"Damn wasteful foolishness," Patrick scolded. "I'll hear nothing about it."

CJ dropped his head. "But you saw the ocean, even rode on a ship to Cuba and back."

"That was different; that was war. The government paid for it."

"How come you don't talk about the war?"

"Because the only friend I had got shot down in front of my eyes and I wanted no more to do with losing people I took a liking to. Came close to dying myself. I don't like those memories." The vision of Jake Jacobi dead and bloody at Colonel Roosevelt's feet passed through Patrick's mind.

"Are we gonna come back to town when Ma has the baby?" CJ asked.

"I'll hear no talk of that," Patrick snapped. "Not now or ever again. And you won't be coming back here until you start school in the fall. I've moved all my business dealings to Alamogordo, so that's where we'll go when we need victuals, supplies, and such. I'd like it fine if this is the last I ever see of Las Cruces."

"Why can't you and Ma get along?"

"Ask your ma. It wasn't me who did any of this. You'll be starting school in a week, but your chores come first, understand? I don't want you lollygagging at the ranch."

"Yes, Pa."

"No school unless the chores get done."

"Yes, Pa."

Patrick gave him a tight smile. "You and me are gonna run the best outfit on the Tularosa. Ain't that right?"

"Yes, sir," CJ replied.

A weak sun broke over the top of the snow-tipped Organ Mountains, and a chill wind coursed down San Augustin Pass. Suddenly, CJ felt cold. He turned his collar up, wrapped the blanket around his legs, and felt a quick stab of regret about leaving Las Cruces, his school pals, and his ma.

* * *

CJ soon discovered the ranch wasn't the same without Ma there. Pa had turned the house into a messy workshop of sorts, with tools, ropes, buckets, saddles, and other gear spread out all over the front room and the kitchen table. He'd taken up drinking, although not when CJ was around, and the whiskey bottles were in plain sight.

Pa had given CJ Cal's old room, and he'd fixed it up with a table made out of scrap wood, which he used for studying in the evening after supper. Most nights he was dog tired from his chores. First off, he had to clean out the barn stalls and rake the horse apples out of the corrals every morning. Then he had to feed the critters and turn them out for water on the pasture. Pa usually had breakfast ready by then, and after cleaning the dishes and washing up, CJ hurried off on the trail to the Hightowers' for school. Some mornings he about froze before he got there.

With daily ranch chores to be done by the three Hightower girls and the two young Carter boys needing to travel a long way home, school didn't last more than four hours a day. Mrs. Hightower was a real nice lady, and CJ liked her a lot, but she sure wasn't much of a teacher when it came to answering his questions, especially about science and mathematics. Still, the schoolbooks he'd brought along kept him learning, and he was able to figure a lot of stuff out by himself.

The oldest Hightower girl, Amy, was a year younger than CJ and a real pest. A redhead with a temper, she always chased him during recess when they played tag.

However, she was smart, and CJ liked her for that.

Because he was the oldest student at school, CJ had to tend the woodstove, chop wood and kindling, haul water, and watch the younger children when Mrs. Hightower got called away by her husband for one reason or another. Sometimes she was gone for a half hour or more.

For lunch he mostly brought canned fruit, crackers, and beef jerky. Once in a while, Mrs. Hightower fixed him a sandwich or gave him a hard-boiled egg.

Back home after school, CJ chopped kindling, cleaned out the cookstove, set a new fire in the fireplace, and helped out with the ponies. He also had to keep the kitchen clean. When Pa wasn't back in time from day herding, he fixed supper, getting scolded when he burned the meat or didn't have the food ready and waiting.

In early March, Mrs. Hightower let school out for spring works, and CJ stayed busy helping with the gathering, his studies pleasantly forgotten. Pa let him work the calves during branding, and he felt real grown-up, hazing the critters to catch hands, who roped the animals and brought them to the bulldoggers to earmark, castrate, and brand with a hot iron. More than once CJ had to shoo away an upset mother cow riled by her calf's blatting. One of the boys from another outfit gave him a nod of thanks and a wink for keeping a charging cow from wrecking into him. CJ felt real good about that.

Spring works turned out to be the best time he had since returning to the Double K. Pa wasn't so gloomy and bossy, which made the days more pleasant, and the lighthearted company of the waddies from the other outfits lifted CJ's spirits.

By the time it ended, every stockman on the northwestern quarter of the basin had thrown over their cattle or was trailing them home. After returning to the Double K, Pa paid off Joe, the temporary hand he'd hired for the works. The next morning CJ and Pa set out for Alamogordo.

The town had grown some since CJ had seen it last. There were new buildings with fancy brickwork and marble along Pennsylvania and New York avenues, and a three-story state asylum for the blind filled up several large lots near the north edge of town. The cottonwood trees in the long park that bordered the railroad tracks were now tall enough to shade the big green lawns, and at the south end of the park a man-made lake was home to a small flock of beautiful white swans.

CJ had never seen such pretty birds, and he slowed his pony to take a closer look, only to be hurried along by Pa in the wagon, who wanted a drink, a bath, a meal, and a room. They stopped at the Hotel Southwestern, which looked out over the lake. Pa got them a room for the night and walked across the street for a drink at the only saloon in town, while CJ put the wagon and ponies up at the stables near the hotel. Waiting for Pa to return, he walked over to the lake and watched the swans cruise silently back and forth across the water. An hour passed before Pa found CJ at the lake.

"I've been looking for you," he said gruffly. "Half reckoned you'd run away."

"Sorry," CJ said. "Didn't mean to worry you."

"I would have tracked you down," Pa said, handing him a soda pop. "I got this at the grocery store to wet your whistle."

The cold, sweet liquid tasted delicious. CJ gulped it down.

"Don't get drunk on that stuff," Pa cautioned.

CJ grinned. It wasn't like Pa to make a joke. He felt a surge of warmth run through him. Maybe Pa liked him after all.

At the barber's, CJ took a turn in the bathwater after Pa finished in the tub and watched as the barber gave him a shave. Pa had grown a mustache, which made him look older.

"Are you gonna have him shave the mustache off?" he asked, as the barber ran his straightedge razor up Pa's neck.

"Nope," Pa replied. "Don't you like it?"

CJ shrugged.

"Wouldn't matter a lick to me if you did or didn't," Pa said. "I'm keeping it."

The barber chuckled like it was some kind of joke, but CJ didn't think it very funny.

At supper in the hotel restaurant, Pa ordered a whole chicken, a slew of vegetables, and a big cherry pie for desert. It was the best meal CJ had eaten since leaving Las Cruces and his mother's good cooking. He'd learned not to say a word about her to Pa, but there were times he wanted to, especially when he missed her badly.

After they cleaned their plates, Pa gave CJ the key to their room and told him he would be back later.

"You're on your own, but don't wait up for me," he said, handing CJ a dime. "The druggist one block over sells soda pop. Go get you one."

"Thanks."

"In the morning we'll get supplies and head home."

"Okay."

He got his soda pop from the druggist and went back to the lake. One swan, motionless near the far shore, had his head tucked under his wing. The others floated effortlessly in the center of the lake. Three children ran ahead of their parents along the park walkway, screeching and chasing each other down the path. A couple strolled by whispering to each other. On the main street, wagons rolled by, draft horses whinnied, and motorcars chugged along.

CJ sat by the lakeshore in the gathering dusk feeling totally alone. The lights from inside the hotel spread out across the water, making the ripples glisten. He got up, went to the room, undressed, and got into bed. Hours later Pa came in smelling like whiskey and perfume.

* * *

In the morning, Patrick walked CJ to Wolfinger's Dry Goods and told him to pick out two shirts, two pairs of pants, a pair of boots, a new hat, a vest, and some underclothes. He told the clerk to put CJ's purchases on the ranch account and left CJ there to go to the bank. At the First National, he talked to Sam Gilbert about renewing his loan for another year. Gilbert agreed, Patrick signed the paperwork, and Sam gave him an envelope addressed to CJ in Emma's handwriting.

"This came for CJ included in some documents Henry Bowman sent over from your old bank in Las Cruces," Sam explained. "I've been holding it for him."

"Thank you kindly," Patrick said. On the street, he tore open the envelope and read the letter.

Dear CJ,

You have a baby brother. He was born early and had a hard time of it for a spell, but he is now gaining weight and growing fast. If he's anything like you, I'll be plumb worn out chasing him down once he starts walking.

His name is Matthew. It's an old name from my side of the family that was given to my baby brother, who died when he was very, very young. I'm sure you'll start calling him Matt right away. I've told him all about you and he is very eager to meet you.

I'd hoped you might come to town to see me before school starts in the fall, but Mr. Bowman at the bank told me your pa has moved all his business dealings to Alamogordo, so I guess you won't be coming here until then. But remember, if you want to come home for the summer, just tell your pa and he'll bring you.

I'll close for now, hoping you are happy and healthy at the
ranch and you have a kind thought now and then for your
loving mother. I'm about beside myself missing you.

With all my love,
Mother

Patrick tore up the letter and threw it in a trash can at Pop
Weigele's store, where he dropped off the grocery list to be filled.
"I'll need it ready pronto," he told the clerk as he hurried out
the door to corral CJ.

The boy would probably find out about the baby soon enough,
but not from him.

6 3

CJ was nearly fourteen the year war broke out in Europe. The news stories and dispatches from the front fascinated him and his two best pals, Austin Feather and Billy McFie. During his time in town with Ma and his baby brother, Matt, he spent hours with his friends discussing the armies, the battles, and especially the pilots who flew reconnaissance airplanes over enemy lines. None of them had ever seen a real airplane, only pictures in the newspapers, but they all agreed being a pilot in the war was about the best job a soldier could have.

When they weren't dreaming about flying airplanes, they imagined themselves as marines with the Atlantic Fleet landing in Veracruz to fight the Mexicans. All three hoped the United States joined with the English and French to fight the Hun and the war lasted long enough for them to enlist and see action overseas.

In the meantime, CJ liked his school in Las Cruces. The teachers made him buckle down to his mathematics studies and the natural sciences, a subject he really enjoyed. Living with Ma and Matt was a lot easier than what Pa had him doing at the ranch, and he had free time on the weekends to explore the countryside outside of town with his two pals.

CJ didn't mind hard work at the ranch, but Pa hardly took an interest in him except to correct, scold, or talk some about the critters that needed doctoring or the fix-up work to be done. He never gave a thought to letting CJ take a breather now and then.

With Ma, on the other hand, once his chores and schoolwork were done, she was willing to see him go off with his friends or let him relax in the evening with a magazine or a book.

He had warmed to Matt right from the get-go, and Ma wasted no time teaching CJ how to care for the squirt, right down to diaper changing. When a dizzy spell came over Ma, CJ kept an eye on Matt. When Ma went to bed early feeling faint, he sat with Matt at the kitchen table and let him draw pictures on butcher paper while he did his studies. Sometimes when Ma napped in the afternoon, he took Matt to watch the trains come into the depot. Matt loved trains.

At three, Matt also loved taking things apart. CJ figured him to become a railroad engineer or some sort of mechanical genius.

That summer at the ranch, CJ rode his pony to Engle and took the train to Las Cruces once a month to visit Ma and Matt for a couple of days. It didn't sit well with Pa, who tried to talk him out of going and never had much to say once he returned. Although Pa never raised a hand to him, CJ always felt he wanted to, especially when he went against his wishes and talked about Matt and Ma.

Aside from Pa's stubborn rejection of Ma and Matt, as long as CJ stayed busy at the ranch and did as he was asked, things went along without a hitch. He'd gotten used to the idea that Pa would never be good company, but the ranch sure was. CJ truly loved the pretty slice of mountains, canyons, and flats bordering the Tularosa that made up the Double K. Every year he learned more and more about what it took to be a good stockman and horse trainer, and he loved that part of it, too, especially the ponies.

About twice every summer Pa and CJ rode to Alamogordo for supplies, and in the evenings Pa left him at the hotel to go visit a whorehouse on the south side of town, where the Mexican families lived in little adobe casitas. CJ knew it was a whorehouse because once he followed Pa to find out where he went. The painted ladies sitting on the porch made it a real easy giveaway. Las Cruces had some of the same kinds of places.

The war in Europe was good for the cattle market, so Pa had plenty of money to spend on soiled doves and whiskey. The English were buying large amounts of beef for their boys in the trenches, and with the prosperity at home, folks were consuming more meat. Pa had expanded the herd to meet demand and every year had a contract in his pocket that brought a nice profit come selling time.

On top of that, the outfit had the reputation for the best cow and ranch ponies in the southwest and the army was buying all the saddle-broke stock that Pa and CJ could provide. Pa felt so flush he'd hired a wrecked old cowboy named Curtis to do the cooking and tend to the chores around the ranch, so he and CJ could concentrate on gentling the ponies and day herding the cows.

Given to talking to himself and mumbling, Curtis wasn't much better company than Pa, except he was a mite more friendly and easygoing. He had a long beard that he combed every day, wore a cowboy hat that he never took off except to sleep, and walked with a bad limp due to one leg being shorter than the other. He was a fair cook, ran a tidy kitchen, and didn't mind any chore Pa gave him.

By the time CJ turned fifteen he was nearly as tall as Pa and had filled out considerably. Each night as Curtis spooned a second helping on CJ's plate, he accused him of eating enough grub to feed a bunkhouse full of hungry cowpunchers.

CJ loved working with the ponies. He had a steady, gentle hand and an even temperament that calmed even the most skittish horse. Solid in the saddle, he rode all but the roughest-pitching ones with ease. When he did get bucked off by a snot-snorting, mean bronc, he never took it out on the critter. Once, after CJ outlasted a truly cussed pony that twisted something fierce in midair and spun completely around before thudding down on all fours, Pa allowed that CJ had glue on his pants. The compliment floored him. Pa hardly ever praised anybody.

By the end of fall works, CJ stood a hair under six feet, weighed a good one-sixty, and had a cowboy's sundrenched tan face and the hands of a working man. A stranger had to look close under CJ's cowboy hat to see he wasn't quite full grown.

Early in the morning, Patrick found CJ in his room packing to get ready for his return to Las Cruces. Each night during the last month, after CJ had gone to bed, Patrick had fixed up Cal's old saddle until it looked almost brand-new. The deep, rich leather gleamed. He heaved it on CJ's bed.

"That's for you," he said. "It was Cal's. He'd want you to have it. I fixed it up some."

CJ caught his breath. "It sure is a beaut."

Patrick counted out some greenbacks and placed them on the dresser.

"You're paying me wages?" CJ asked in amazement.

Pa nodded. "I can afford to this year. Top-hand wages at that, for the whole summer. Don't spend it all on women."

"I'm obliged," CJ said, smiling at Pa's attempt to joke.

"You earned it," Patrick replied. "You best be on your way."

"I'm about to go," CJ replied.

"I'm keeping Curtis on," Patrick said.

"That's good," CJ said.

Patrick nodded. "Don't lose that saddle in a poker game." He turned and left the room before CJ could respond.

CJ couldn't figure what had come over Pa. Any show of generosity was unlike him. And what did he mean about betting the saddle? Was it just another bad joke? He sat on the bed and gave the saddle a real close look. Every little rip and tear had been carefully repaired and all the metal polished. Pa had even carved CJ's initials on the cantle.

He counted out the money. It was more than he'd ever held in his hand in his entire life. He stuffed the bills in his pocket thinking maybe Pa appreciated him a little after all.

64

A week after CJ returned home from the ranch, Emma got a telegraph message that Ignacio Chávez was sick with cancer and about to die. She telegraphed Teresa that she was coming, took CJ out of school, quickly packed for their trip, and with Matthew on her lap and CJ driving the buggy, set out on the journey. Along the way, she told CJ some of the stories she'd heard from Cal, including how John Kerney had shot down an outlaw riding with Billy the Kid who was about to kill Ignacio in cold blood, and the battle the three friends had fought with Buffalo Soldiers in Hembrillo Canyon against Victorio and his band of Apaches.

The road to Tularosa had been improved considerably, but it was still more than a day's travel from Las Cruces to the village. They stayed overnight in Alamogordo at the Hotel Southwestern, and after supper CJ took Ma and Matt to see the swans on the lake.

"Aren't they beautiful?" CJ said. "They mate for life, you know."

"That's the way it should be," Emma replied softly.

A distant engine whistle sounded three times.

"I'm going to see the train," Matt announced happily as he scooted toward the depot.

CJ ran after him, lifted him up, and carried him on his shoulders to the depot. Emma followed along, smiling with pride at her two wonderful sons.

The next morning dawned hot and windy, and with dust stinging their eyes, they set a rapid pace to Tularosa. They arrived at the hacienda, where the Chávez family and relatives, some who had traveled from as far away as El Paso, and many of their village friends were gathered. The adults talked in hushed tones while the young children played noisily in the courtyard.

Teresa welcomed Emma with a hug and whispered, "Patrick is here."

Emma stiffened. She'd not seen him since the day he agreed to her terms for the divorce. "Where?"

"He's staying at the hotel. He saw Ignacio last night."

"Can I see Ignacio?" Emma asked.

"*Sí*, he would like that very much. Take CJ with you. That would please him also. I'll care for the little one. He looks much like Patrick."

In the dim light of the bedroom, Ignacio looked old, thin, and frail. On the blanket chest stood a hand-carved wooden statue of the Virgin of Guadalupe surrounded by candles and wild roses. Propped up by some pillows, he grasped Emma's hand, managed a smile, and looked at CJ.

"Who is this hombre?" he said. "Not CJ, all grown-up? He looks much like his *abuelo*, John Kerney."

"Ma's been telling me stories about you, Cal, and my grandpa," CJ said.

"Good stories, I hope," Ignacio said. "More than once your *abuelo* saved my life." He made the sign of the cross, gasped in pain, and waited for it to pass before continuing. "When the pain comes I have few words. Where is your little *hijo*, Emma?"

"With Teresa," Emma answered.

"Ah." Ignacio forced a smile. "I must meet him."

"I'll bring him to you later," Emma said.

Ignacio smiled. "Good. Now, sit with me for a while. I would like that very much."

CJ sat on a chair against the wall and Emma perched on the edge of the bed. Haltingly, Ignacio told the story of how John Kerney found him bleeding, beaten, and robbed in La Luz, patched him up, and gave him a job.

"Years later, I met the man who robbed me and I beat him up," he said, making a fist. "Cal and your *abuelo* did many kindnesses for me and my family. I still miss them both."

Ignacio drifted off. Outside his bedroom Emma said, "I would have liked to have known your grandfather."

"Me too," CJ replied.

In the courtyard, some of Teresa's grandchildren were leading Matt around on the back of a small donkey. He was grinning from ear to ear, kicking his heels against the donkey's sides, asking to go faster, faster.

"What can I do to help?" Emma asked Teresa.

"*Nada*," Teresa replied. "I have too much help already. I am sorry I have no room for you to stay with us."

"You don't need us underfoot." Emma stroked her friend's hand. She looked weary and sad, and yet she seemed completely composed. "I must do something to help while I'm here."

"You are here," Teresa said. "That is enough."

Later in the afternoon, accompanied by Teresa, Emma took Matt to meet Ignacio.

"Come here, little one," Ignacio said, his voice shaky and weak.

"You look much like your mother and your father. Very handsome. The girls will like you *mucho*."

Matt stepped tentatively to the side of the bed.

"Are you sick?" he asked.

"*Sí*," Ignacio answered.

"When my mom feels sick she takes a nap," Matt said.

"A *siesta* is a good thing. Do you know the word *siesta*?"

Matt nodded. "It means nap. I don't like naps."

"That's because you are young and have much to do," Ignacio said.

Matt looked up at his mom. "Tell my ma that."

"I just did," Ignacio said with a chuckle. "Thank you for coming to see me."

"You're welcome."

"Now I must sleep for a while."

"Okay," Matt said.

Teary eyed, Emma kissed Ignacio good-bye, hugged Teresa, and walked with her boys to the hotel. As they approached the entrance, Patrick emerged. He pulled up short and quickly tried to get around them.

Emma blocked his way. "Don't you dare pass us by." She yanked Matt squarely in front of Patrick. "This is your son Matthew. Look at him. Speak to him."

Patrick glared at her. He smelled of whiskey and looked a little wobbly.

"Talk to him, Pa," CJ pleaded.

"Don't you tell me what to do, boy," Patrick snapped, refusing to look at the child.

Emma kneeled at Matt's side. "This is your father, Matthew. Say hello to him."

"Hi," Matt said timidly, taking a step back into his mother's arms.

Patrick glanced at Emma. Her jaw was set and her eyes bored into him. Finally, he looked at the boy, his face a hard mask.

"Howdy," he grumbled as he sidestepped around Emma and the child, walked hurriedly down the street, and ducked into the nearby saloon.

Trembling with anger, Emma rose and marshaled a cheerful smile. "Come on," she said. "Let's rent a nice room and get ready for supper."

CJ took Matt by the hand and followed Ma into the hotel. Never once had she said a bad word against Pa to him. She could be as tough as nails when he didn't measure up, but she was always fair and he knew she loved him. With Pa it was different. He also pushed him hard, as he had a right to, but CJ rarely felt Pa cared a hoot or a holler about him or anybody else. And what he'd just done to Matt irked CJ a lot. It sure didn't make CJ feel proud to be his son.

* * *

The following evening Ignacio's body was laid out in an open casket in the hacienda courtyard, surrounded by lighted tapers that flickered in the early dusk. With the priest away from the village, the mass for the dead would have to wait. Old women in long black shawls prayed the rosary, while funeral hymns were sung by *alabados*.

With the tolling of the church bell, the funeral procession began with some women in front, two of them carrying a richly embroidered banner of Our Lady of Guadalupe. Behind them, two musicians played violins, followed by the wagon bearing Ignacio's body, his coffin covered in muslin with a small cross affixed to the lid. At the rear of the wagon were Teresa, her children and grandchildren, and other members of the family. Behind them came many of the Mexican villagers. Emma, CJ, and Matthew were among a very small group of *americano* merchants and townspeople at the end of the procession. Emma kept glancing back to see if Patrick had joined the procession, but he was nowhere to be seen.

Bonfires lit the way, each tended by a young boy. At the *campo santo*, the holy ground, part of the wooden grave fence with elaborate staves that surrounded the burial site of Ignacio's parents had been removed and a fresh grave dug. At the head of the grave was a hand-carved cross with a sunburst of the Sacred Heart in the center. Little stars adorned the cross.

Solemn men carried the casket from the wagon and, using ropes, gently lowered it into the grave. Women laid roses all around. Surrounded by her children, Teresa knelt, placed the silver cross she wore the day they were married on the casket lid, and quietly began to cry.

Helped to her feet by her two oldest sons, she turned to find a sea of candles lighting the night for the way home. As she neared Emma, CJ, and Matthew, Teresa held out her hand.

"Come," she said softly.

With CJ and Matthew at her side, Emma clasped Teresa's hand and walked with her and the family back to the hacienda. Soon the bell ceased tolling and the musicians began playing their violins once more.

Hand in hand with Teresa, Emma felt a sense of loss, not only for the passing of Ignacio but for the closing of an era on the basin that soon would be forgotten.

65

In the spring of 1916, Patrick bought a string of horses that included a spirited bay with a natural single-footed gait that CJ took a shine to. Barely saddle broke, the pony settled into an even four-beat gait that was smooth as silk and fast. CJ had never ridden a faster horse. He named the bay Traveller and set about training him to be his next cow pony.

Pa didn't like Traveller much because every morning when CJ went to ride him, the horse put on a private rodeo show, pitching and wheeling something fierce. Some days it took CJ a good five minutes to settle Traveller down.

"He'll just rile up the others and spoil them," Pa said. "We don't need that."

"He hasn't yet," CJ replied as he slid out of the saddle and rubbed Traveller's snout.

"I know an outlaw when I see one," Pa replied. "He tries to stay shut of the corral and shies whenever he sees a saddle rope. There's nothing good about him except his gait."

"He's gonna be a great cow pony, maybe one of the best ever," CJ countered. "I want him for my own."

Patrick laughed. "That's tomfoolery."

"I mean it, Pa."

Patrick slapped his gloves against his leg. "I never figured you to have poor horse sense, but if you want him, he's yours. But work him on your own time, hear? If he starts spoiling the herd, he's gone from the Double K. Savvy?"

"I savvy," CJ replied as he swung back into the saddle. "Leave him to me and you'll see what a good one he is."

"I doubt it," Patrick grumbled.

Over the next several months sometimes even CJ questioned his faith in Traveller. The pony played up to any mare in heat and got aggressive when CJ attempted to rein him in, sometimes kicking or rearing in protest. Once he went after another mare for no cause, knocking it down and sinking his teeth into its flank, ripping a large gash.

Pa called him plumb mean, but CJ wasn't ready to give up on him. He took to riding him long and hard as often as he could in the hopes Traveller would settle down, and the strategy seemed to work. There was nothing more fun than to fly across a pasture on Traveller's back when he was in a full, single-footed gallop.

He still pitched every time he was first mounted, but CJ sensed it becoming more of a ritual and less of a contest. CJ figured Traveller to be a one-man pony, and that suited him just fine.

On the long summer evenings, he worked Traveller with some yearling cows, and the pony proved to be tops. Quick of foot, smart, and unrelenting, Traveller could dodge and dart a cow out of a herd with ease, although at times CJ came halfway out of the saddle when the pony made an unexpected move.

Pa still didn't like the horse, and the feeling seemed mutual. Traveller charged him anytime he came near, his neck arched high, teeth bared. One evening he came at Pa with his forelegs flailing and sent him scrambling over the corral fence.

"He's a killer," Pa said, glaring at the pony. "Mark my words. Unless you break him down, he'll get to you."

"He'll be fine," CJ said, patting Traveller's neck to calm him.

"You need to listen to what I'm telling you," Pa snapped.

"I do, most of the time," CJ countered, "but this time I think you're wrong."

"We'll see about that," Pa replied. "Throw a rope on him and tie him to the stubbing post."

"What in blazes for?" CJ asked. "He's not wild and unbroken."

"Just do it," Pa ordered, "and put a bridle on him while I get my saddle."

Pa had taken to sipping whiskey every evening after supper, and today was no exception. "Maybe you should wait until morning to ride him," CJ suggested.

Pa stopped in midstride and glared at CJ. "I can do any damn thing I want on my ranch when I want. Do as you're told and snub him to the damn post."

CJ snubbed Traveller and waited for Pa's return. He came out of the saddle shed with his gear, looking contrary and angry. He saddled Traveller roughly and threw a leg up.

"Turn him loose," Pa ordered.

CJ hesitated. "Maybe you shouldn't . . ."

"Do it!"

CJ released Traveller, and the pony arched his back, bounded three feet in the air, came down on his forelegs, and kicked. Before Pa could regain his seat, the pony spun and threw him smack into the stubbing post.

CJ grabbed the reins as Traveller reared up to stomp on Pa and pulled him away. He tied him to the corral fence and ran to check on Pa, who sat in the dirt holding his head.

"Are you okay?" he asked.

Slowly Pa got to his feet. "Just a knock on my noggin. Unsaddle that outlaw and put him in the pasture while I tend to myself."

CJ calmed Traveller, unsaddled him, and put him out to pasture. The pony paused outside the gate, lifted his head, tossed his mane, and looked at CJ. He whinnied once, a long, loud call, and trotted away with his tail straight out. It was a stallion's victory celebration sure enough, and it made CJ smile.

He was in the saddle shed putting Pa's tack away when he heard the report of a rifle. He dropped everything and darted outside. Pa stood at the corral cradling his long gun. In the pasture Traveller lay on his side, dead.

"No, dammit!" CJ shouted.

He flung himself against Pa and knocked him into the corral fence. Pa kept his balance and punched CJ in the mouth.

CJ slammed Pa into the fence again. "I quit you," he yelled.

Pa balled his fist, hesitated, and pushed past him. "That suits me fine. Get that dead critter out of my pasture before you go," he said flatly.

CJ spit blood. "Do it yourself."

He left for town within the hour, with Pa standing on the porch watching him ride out. Nary a good-bye passed between them.

66

The year 1917 began with war fever spreading across the land. German U-boats were attacking unarmed merchant ships carrying food and supplies to Britain. While still calling for peace, President Wilson had cut off diplomatic ties with Germany and ordered merchant ships armed when Congress failed to give him the authority to do so. Newspaper editors were calling on the government to enter the war and the Brits were asking for an American expeditionary force to come to their aid in the French trenches, where thousands upon thousands had already died in battles that seemed to resolve nothing. Recruiting posters were up all over town, and many men were enlisting in the National Guard and the Regular Army.

Billy McFie, who'd just turned eighteen, had signed up with the Regular Army and was leaving in a week for basic training. Austin Feather would be seventeen in less than a month and had his pa's consent to join the National Guard. Jealous of his friends, CJ had pleaded with his ma to let him join up when he turned seventeen, but she was having none of it.

"There's to be a national draft," she argued, "and you'll be taken quickly enough if the war is still going on. Hopefully it will all be over by then. Stop pestering me about it."

CJ had started classes at the New Mexico College of Agricultural and Mechanical Arts campus a few miles outside of town. With one semester under his belt, he'd decided not to go to the ranch for spring works, but instead stay in town and finish his freshman year. But what he really wanted to do was go to war like his friends Austin and Billy and many of the older college men who'd already left for the service.

On Billy's last night before reporting, the three friends sat under the bare branches of a big cottonwood along the Rio Grande and talked about the war.

"I'm hoping it don't end until I get there," Billy said.

"No chance of that," Austin replied as he lit a cigarette and passed it around. "My pa says it will take years to defeat the Hun. Look how long it's been going on so far."

"If I could get by with lying about my age, I'd enlist," CJ said. "But my ma has already told the recruiters to send me packing if I show up."

Billy shook his head. "That's a damn shame."

"I sure would like it if the three of us could serve together," Austin said.

"The Army Air Service," CJ said wistfully.

"The cavalry," Austin countered.

"In the trenches the cavalry will be on foot," Billy said knowingly, having been told the same by his recruiter.

"Then the field artillery," Austin said. "You can ride in the field artillery."

"You're both making me glum," CJ said.

"Does anybody know you in El Paso?" Billy asked.

"I don't think so," CJ replied.

Billy handed him the cigarette. "Enlist down there. As big as you are, nobody will doubt your word about being eighteen."

CJ laughed.

"What's so funny?" Austin asked.

"I'll do it," CJ said.

"When?" Austin asked.

"Soon," CJ replied, already scheming how to do it without Ma knowing what he was up to.

"How will we know you really did it?" Billy asked.

"I'll write you both."

"It's a deal," Austin said.

The three boys shook hands to seal it and smoked another cigarette.

* * *

Congress declared war on Germany the week before CJ's classes recessed for spring break. He told Ma he was going to the ranch but instead used some of the top-hand wages he'd saved for a train ticket to El Paso, where he enlisted in the Texas National Guard using his mother's maiden name. The recruiter was pleased to have another cowboy sign up and told him to forget about the Army Air Service.

"For now you'll be assigned to the First Texas Cavalry," he said. "You'll train in San Antonio until the army brass and the government figure out what's gonna happen next. Maybe you'll get some field experience along the border, keeping an eye on the Mexicans."

"Where on the border?"

"The Big Bend Country along the Rio Grande."

Happy to have gotten himself enlisted and with the prospect of seeing a new slice of the country, CJ smiled. "When do I leave?"

"In two days, along with eight other recruits."

Before he left, CJ wrote to Billy and Austin telling them he'd been sworn in and assigned to the First Texas Cavalry and was going to San Antonio. He sent a note to the college withdrawing from school and wrote to Pa, saying what he'd done without asking for his understanding or blessing. He stared at an empty sheet of paper for a long time before starting a letter to Ma.

> *Dear Mother,*
>
> *I know how much you'll dislike what I have to tell you, but I've joined up. Please don't try to track me down, because you won't be able to find me as I didn't use my real name when I enlisted. I wrote to Pa and told him so you don't have to. I doubt what I've done will bother him any, but I know you'll be mad at me for lying to you and going against your wishes.*
>
> *I'm doing the right thing and hope you'll understand and forgive me. I'll write you from time to time so you don't have to worry about me. Give Matt my love and tell him I'll be home when the war is over and we'll all have a fine time then.*
>
> *Your loving son,*
>
> *CJ*

In San Antonio, CJ and his fellow new recruits were thrown in with a whole passel of West Texas cowboys who'd also enlisted. The outfit was short on uniforms, so most of the troops wore their civilian duds for a while, until the quartermaster shipments arrived.

Much to everyone's dismay, the rumor that the new recruits were going south to the Big Bend Country for border patrol duty got quickly squashed by the officers and sergeants.

CJ spent his days with the other recruits on stable or barracks duty, cleaning out stalls and latrines, washing dishes and cleaning rifles, standing inspection and studying the rules of military etiquette, marching and riding in formation, and attending lectures in tactics.

Summer brought the arrival of four veteran troops of the First Texas Cavalry up from the Big Bend under the command of Major John Golding, and over the next month field and weapons training intensified. On July 26, the entire First Texas Cavalry detrained in Fort Worth with orders to guard Camp Bowie, a National Guard cantonment under construction. It was one of thirty-two National Guard and army cantonments to be built across the country.

The camp was sited on land overlooking the city about two miles west of downtown. There was a road nearby that gave easy access to the city, which contained a major rail yard, two large meatpacking plants, granaries, a horse and mule market that supplied livestock to the camp, and more than a hundred thousand citizens eager to cash in on the millions of dollars to be spent on military construction and the monthly payroll doled out to the troops.

The troopers arrived to find nothing more than a timekeeper's shack and three thousand laborers working in the hot Texas sun unloading truckloads of lumber, gravel, tools, and raw materials. They pitched their tents and went to work guarding the camp, as roads were built, water-line trenches were dug, a rail spur was laid, telephone lines were strung, and mess halls, warehouses, latrines, and bathhouses were framed and roofed.

More troops arrived soon after, including National Guard en-

gineers from Texas and Oklahoma and six companies of Texas
Infantry. In a month, nine hundred buildings had been put up.
The men had never seen anything like it. On August 23, Major
General Edwin St. John Greble, a Regular Army officer who had
served in the Spanish American War and in El Paso during the
Mexican border crisis, arrived to assume command and announce
the formation of the new Thirty-sixth Division.

As summer turned to fall, more guardsmen and draftees poured
into the camp. Eight-man tents held ten to twelve soldiers; men
lined up outside mess halls waiting their turn for meals that were
served to two hundred and fifty troopers at a time. Some of the
late arriving units were forced to practice tactics with wooden rifles, and most men trained with outdated rifles that were useless
on the battlefield.

When a freezing storm blew in on a late September morning,
thousands were without winter clothing and blankets. Another cold
storm hit the camp in early October, leaving more than half the
units without fuel wood to keep warm. Men went on sick call in
droves, suffering from measles, pneumonia, and meningitis, and
the hospital, the largest structure in camp, overflowed with patients.

CJ took to the training with enthusiasm and tried to keep his
spirits up, although he wondered at times if the army could ever
do anything right. Many of the junior officers didn't know spit
about soldiering, but a few of the sergeants were seasoned troopers,
including CJ's sergeant, a tall, easygoing Texan named John Lockhart. A veteran of the Rough Riders and the Regular Army, Lockhart knew his stuff and treated his men fairly. He had a way of
getting the most out of his men without being bossy. CJ asked
Lockhart if he remembered knowing Patrick Kerney from the New
Mexico troop.

Lockhart said he did. "Was he kin of yours?"

"He's an uncle on my mother's side," CJ lied.

Lockhart looked surprised. "He's alive?"

"Yep."

"I'll be," Lockhart said with a shake of his head. "We were in the same hospital ward at Camp Wikoff. As sick as he was, I figured him to be a goner."

When a corporal in CJ's platoon died of pneumonia, Lockhart recommended him for the promotion, and soon CJ sported stripes on his uniform blouse.

He'd been writing letters to Ma and squirreling them away to send before he left for France. He didn't want her to know where he was stationed for fear she'd demand that he be sent home.

He told her about San Antonio and Fort Worth, the two biggest cities he'd ever seen, and how there were motorcars everywhere and more people on the streets than a body could count. He drew a sketch of the tanks that had been unloaded off the camp's railroad spur and wrote that he'd never seen such marvels of destruction, with their huge tracks that ground deep ruts in the earth and the big rotating guns on both sides. He told her the cavalry boys he served with weren't happy about being turned into foot soldiers and that several had deserted to go back to their farms and ranches.

A week after he got promoted, CJ sat on his cot in the evening and wrote another letter.

Dear Mother,

Today, a British army officer who served in the trenches in France gave a lecture to noncommissioned officers on field

*fortifications. I got to attend it because I am now promoted to
corporal and will be going to various schools here at camp
that teach noncoms and officers how to use the bayonet,
proper ways to protect against poison gas, musketry training,
and a lot of other soldiering skills. I don't get to go to all the
schools, but each company and regiment sends enough
noncoms and officers to them so that the training can get
passed on to every man in the entire division.*

*My sergeant, John Lockhart, says I'm sure to keep getting
promoted, as many of the fellas here don't take well to military
discipline and get their rank taken away for things like
insubordination or being absent without leave. He just got
made a master sergeant himself.*

*Our camp is growing. Our colonel told us there are over
25,000 soldiers here now. We all live in tents that are laid out
like villages in neat squares connected one to the other. It's
quite a sight.*

*The other day just about everybody stopped dead in their
tracks to watch three Army Air Service biplanes fly overhead.
It was something to behold, and we talked about it until
lights-out.*

*They've been back a couple of times since then and it's a
marvel to see what those pilots can do in the air, flying upside
down and twisting the airplane in the sky.*

*I'll close now as I am very weary. We've been digging
makeshift trenches to practice what it's like to go to war in
Europe. A big trench is being built outside of camp a ways
that will be as much like the real McCoy as they can make it.
But until it's finished, we dig for a spell and then practice
how to use hand and rifle grenades, do target shooting—I'm*

expert at that—and build trench fortifications. Drilling and
hard marches round out the day.

This is letter number five. I'll bundle them up and send
them to you before I leave for France. I hope you're proud
about my promotion, and don't worry about me as I am fine.
Tell that little button Matt I miss him.

Your loving son,
CJ

Feeling a touch homesick, he sealed the letter in an envelope and put it with the others. He hadn't written that he was just out of the hospital after a bad case of the measles and that one of his tent mates, Private Buddy Nice from Big Spring, had died from it. That would just worry her to tears when she got the letter.

Several of the men had already turned in and were snoring in their sleep. Two others were cleaning their rifles. Another trooper, Sammy Longbow, a Cherokee Indian, was sharpening the Bowie knife that he valued more than any weapon the army could issue to him.

CJ checked the tent stove, banked the fire, and stepped into the cold November night to round up the rest of his squad before lights-out sounded. He'd taken a shine to army life and was starting to think it just might suit him to make a career of it.

6 7

From winter to the late spring of 1918, CJ worried that he would be left out of the action. Since December, the First Division had been in the trenches with the French, and four more outfits, including two National Guard divisions, had joined the fighting. No one seemed to know when the Thirty-sixth would get overseas orders, and all the officers were tight-lipped about it, but in early June a flurry of paperwork and new orders signaled the division would soon be under way to the Port of New York for embarkation to Europe.

Supplies and equipment were inventoried and supplemented; all soldiers underwent physical exams; mechanized tanks, trucks, and field pieces were inspected and repaired as needed; and daily roll calls were held to limit desertions. A note from one man in CJ's regiment was found on his cot saying he'd be back after he helped his widowed mother on the farm.

Although the impending departure was supposed to be kept secret, the boys were allowed to write home about it, and soon family members were pouring into Fort Worth to see their sons, brothers, and husbands off to war. Passes were granted to men whose loved ones were in town. CJ stayed in camp with the other soldiers who had no kin visiting, and they kept their spirits up in the evenings by writing letters and playing cards until lights-out.

Tapped for promotion to sergeant, CJ received orders to leave early for New York. On July 3 he wrote a quick note to Ma.

Dear Mother,

Tomorrow I leave for France ahead of the division with a small detachment of men and officers who have been promoted and ordered to attend school in France. I am now a sergeant and will be receiving instruction to become a proficient noncommissioned officer.

I'm including some pay I've saved up over the last year, about six months' worth. If you need it that's okay by me, or you can save it for me. But take some and get Matt a present from me. Tell that little rascal I miss him.

You'll get this in a parcel I'll wrap up that has all the letters I've written to you over the last year. I hope when you read them you'll forgive me for worrying you these many months, but I didn't want you trying to take me out of the army for being underage.

I've just written Pa to tell him where I'm going. I figure he has a right to know.

I'll write you again from France and tell you about all the sights I see.

Your loving son,
CJ (Sgt.)

On the early evening of July 4, CJ boarded a train in Fort Worth with a detachment of soldiers including John Lockhart, recently commissioned a second lieutenant, who also had orders to attend school in France. They sat together in a coach car staring out at the rolling hills of the North Texas plains.

"Tell me true, CJ," Lockhart said, "how old are you?"

"Just now nineteen," CJ lied.

"I figured you to be about that," Lockhart said with a smile. "You're the youngest sergeant in the division. Did you know that?"

"No, sir."

"You're gonna be scared when you go to war. Every man is, no matter how many times they do it."

"I reckon that's right," CJ said.

"Sergeants can't show it, though," Lockhart counseled. "It throws the boys under him into a panic and gets a lot of men needlessly killed."

"I sure don't want to falter."

"You won't. Use your noggin. Think things through. Don't rush unless you've got to scamper because of the situation, and don't give stupid orders."

"What if I get stupid orders?" CJ asked.

"For certain you will," Lockhart answered, leaving it at that.

In the gathering darkness the train entered the thick forests of East Texas. The two men smoked in comfortable silence as the trees turned to countless shadows dancing against the windows.

* * *

During the next four days they crossed rivers, including the wide Mississippi, cut through deep forests, passed by rich farmlands with tidy farmhouses, rolled through small towns, and traversed big cities where smokestacks billowed grime and soot into the air. From the train they saw St. Louis, Chicago, and Cleveland. Often they were greeted by flag-waving, cheering crowds lining the tracks in the towns and cities.

On infrequent breaks when they were allowed to stop and stretch their legs, CJ tried hard not to look like a country bumpkin, but sometimes his jaw dropped in amazement at the sight of an enormous stream-driven tractor in a farmer's field or the dozens and dozens of city tenements with folks living stacked up one on top of the other.

Arriving at Camp Merritt in Hoboken, New Jersey, the detachment received orders canceling their early departure and went to work readying for the division's arrival. Across the bay, New York City rose like some futuristic world beyond CJ's imagination. He promised himself to come back and visit it someday.

As the main body of the division began to arrive, men and equipment poured off the trains coming from the south, west, and north, depending on how the different regiments were routed. The outfits were assembled, squared away, and ferried almost immediately across the bay to a camp to prepare for embarkation.

On his last night before boarding for departure, CJ wrote to Ma.

> *Dear Mother,*
>
> *We leave tomorrow for France. I have now traveled from coast to coast and seen more of this great country than most folks I know. The forests and the farmlands are nothing like the land back home. The sky isn't as big and the land crowds you.*
>
> *People lined the rails to cheer us as our train passed by*

and that made us feel good. We're encamped in a weedy,
sandy area favored by pesky mosquitoes, and I'll be glad to get
done with them. Soon I'll be on the ocean and then in France,
but to reach our ship we go by train and ferry back across the
bay. We should be at sea for about twelve days.

We've got a new commanding general, and the old-time
regular sergeants who know him say he's a good one. Strict
but fair.

I'll write to you from Europe and will send mementos to
you and Matt.

Your loving son,

CJ

He sealed the letter in an envelope and put it aside. He was
eager to cross the ocean on a ship and at the same time worried
about it getting sunk by a U-boat. He couldn't swim a lick and the
idea of drowning frightened him.

John Lockhart had said all men go to war scared. CJ figured it
was just happening to him a bit early. He pushed aside his worry
and picked up the noncommissioned officers infantry field guide
John Lockhart had given him to study. At least he'd go to war
prepared.

6 8

I n the port of Brest, CJ left the troopship seasick and miserable. There were times during the voyage when he felt like drowning might not be such a bad way to die after all. Ferried to the dock in barges called lighters, the men were assembled and marched through the town in the rain to a muddy, smelly camp. The fact he was in France registered, but at the moment CJ didn't give a damn. He'd been leaking at both ends for days and was just glad to be on solid ground. After he put up his shelter tent, he fell asleep without bothering to eat chow or take off his boots. John Lockhart woke him the next morning.

"Get moving," he said, handing CJ a lit cigarette. "It seems we're gonna be here for a little while, so the colonel wants us to get our gear in order and squared away. Then it's hot showers, a hot meal, and the rest of the day to ourselves."

CJ tested his land legs and figured he was better. He actually felt hungry. "When do we go to war?" he asked.

Lockhart shrugged. "According to the generals, we ain't fit to fight yet. We're gonna get trained some more before they send us to the front."

"Here?" CJ asked, looking around.

A two-story stone building that made up one side of a large stone-wall enclosure loomed over the sea of tents. A breeze picked up, blowing a foul smell over the camp as it started to rain. CJ clamped on his helmet.

"No," Lockhart answered. "We'll be moved inland to a training center."

The water-soaked pup tents sagged, muddy water filled the puddles, and rivulets ran in the gravel walkways. "I hope it's better than this place," CJ said.

"We'll find out soon enough," Lockhart replied.

That afternoon, feeling better than he had in days, CJ wrote home.

> *Dear Mother,*
>
> We arrived in France yesterday so I haven't seen much of the place. We got marched through town to our camp so the best I can say for now is it's an old country and the folks look poor and ragged. Where we're bivouacked is near a two-story stone barracks where Napoleon housed troops and prisoners a hundred years ago. Leastways that's what I've been told. Of course, that's where the generals and the colonels get to sleep.
>
> It rains here a lot and it is damp and muddy. But we'll leave soon for training and I'll get to see more of the countryside. I'll write again when I can.
>
> *Your loving son,*
> *CJ*

The rain had stopped and the sky cleared when he dropped the letter off to be mailed, so he took a hike away from the camp to stretch his legs. He ambled along a dirt lane past some old farm-houses and cultivated fields partially hidden by hedgerows that were as pretty as a picture. The houses and barns were all stone, with steep roofs that looked like they somehow grew out of the land. Big trees with massive trunks shaded tended lawns. He veered off the lane up a path through a meadow of knee-high coarse grass to the crest of a small hill. Below, an orchard surrounded a white-washed stone cottage, and several goats were in a small paddock near an ancient-looking barn.

He perched on a stone wall, smoked a cigarette, and took it all in, thinking he'd have to remember what he saw because when he got home, Ma would pester him about every detail.

He turned back when it clouded up and started to drizzle. Already there were rumors in camp that the division was to be held in reserve after training. At roll call, the colonel had addressed the regiment to tell them a big push was on to drive the Germans back. The Allies had fought off the spring offensives by the Huns, and a recent French counterattack had smashed their lines on the Western Front. The colonel warned that if the German army collapsed and retreated, the war could be over before the division joined the line.

CJ didn't like that notion at all. If he could help it, he darn sure wasn't going to be left out of the action.

* * *

After two days of rest, the division moved to a training center behind the front lines, near a château, where huts and dozens of buildings had been thrown up in level fields. Twenty-eight thousand men were encamped, and for the next six weeks the troops trained day and night.

They learned how to fire as a line while continuing to advance, how to flank machine-gun nests and use rifle grenades to destroy them. Heavy wire cutters were issued and the men practiced cutting through wire in mud-soaked fields. They were taught to crawl and infiltrate enemy lines, how to cross open fire-swept ground in small units, and how to concentrate fire on an objective.

Told they would lose their stripes if they didn't measure up, CJ and the other noncoms received additional instruction in squad and platoon tactics. They practiced how to control the movement of men on patrol, maneuver platoons across open fields, use cover and concealment, and deploy automatic weapons when attacking the enemy. CJ became expert with the new Browning automatic rifle and was soon teaching others how to use it.

CJ kept his rank, but a number of men got busted down to private. Even some junior officers were sent packing. Assigned to a replacement company to be moved to the front, CJ wrote a note to his mother the night before he left and gave it to John Lockhart, who had been promoted to first lieutenant and ordered to remain with the division pending reassignment to the front.

"Just in case something happens," he said, "please mail this for me, sir."

Lockhart nodded. "I will, CJ. You'll do just fine."

"I sure hope so," CJ said with a tight smile.

"Are you a drinking man, sergeant?" Lockhart asked with an easy smile.

"I got drunk once in Fort Worth," CJ said, "and didn't like it much."

Lockhart laughed and slapped CJ on the back. "I've got a bottle of sipping whiskey that goes down smooth as silk. Let's you and me have a drink together before lights-out."

"I'd like that," CJ said.

Lockhart fetched the bottle from his tent. They walked to the small white church with a soaring spire at the far end of the château, drank some sipping whiskey that indeed went down as smooth as silk, and talked about anything but the war and home.

* * *

CJ marched with the replacement company along a sunken road so deep he could see nothing of the land on either side. Bursting German shells made him want to flinch, but he stiffened his back and plodded through the mud with his head up, covered in dirt from the explosions. Along the way, he passed stretcher-bearers carrying wounded back to medical dressing stations. He glanced at the faces of the wounded men, wondering if his old boyhood pals, Billy and Austin, were up ahead, already in the fight, or if they'd been shot or killed in some earlier battle. He worried about how he'd act when he got the order to go over the top. Would he freeze or run like a scared rabbit for the nearest shell hole in no-man's-land?

They came out of the sunken road to an area that looked at first glance like a plowed field, except the furrows were shell holes separated by mounds of earth. The Germans had retired from the field, and stretcher-bearers were out beyond the wire picking up bodies swarming with blowflies that rose like black clouds from the dead.

CJ thought he had endured all of the awful putrid smells of army life, but once they entered the trenches, the stench was almost unbearable. It smelled of rotting flesh, urine, human waste, the stink of filthy men, and the acid odor of poison mustard gas, which first the Germans and then the Allies had begun to use as a weapon.

He was dropped out of the march along with three other sergeants and a corporal at a regimental command bunker, where a weary lieutenant colonel with a thick New York accent examined them briefly.

"Don't flaunt your stripes, men," he said before sending them down the line to their various companies. "My boys have seen plenty of action and can teach you a thing or two if you'll listen. And for God's sake, don't decide to take a peek over the assault trenches at the German line. You'll be dead from a sniper's bullet in a second, and I damn well can't afford to lose any more replacements. They get killed fast enough as it is."

CJ joined the First Platoon of Company A and reported to Lieutenant Grayson Tyler, who gave him the once-over and asked if he knew how to handle a Browning.

"Yes, sir," CJ replied. "I'm qualified as an instructor."

"Good," Tyler said. "Report to Corporal Morrison. You'll be his BAR man until I decide if you're fit to take over a squad. Do you understand, Sergeant?"

"Yes, sir."

CJ reported to Morrison, an older man with the lobe of his left ear shot off and crudely stitched up.

"I'm your BAR man," CJ said.

"That's lovely," Morrison replied in an Irish brogue, giving CJ a careful look. "Haven't been in the thick of it yet, have you?"

"Not yet."

"It will seize you up soon enough," Morrison said. "Tonight, after the Krauts stop shelling, you'll man an observation post with two privates, Blakely and Ingram. They know the way. It's a disabled

French tank half a kilometer from here. If the Krauts start an attack, send a runner back and provide covering fire before returning to our lines. Have you got that, laddie?"

"Understood, Corporal," CJ replied. "And it's sergeant, not laddie."

Morrison smiled benignly and looked at his watch. "You've got several hours before you go over the top. Come meet Blakely and Ingram. I'm sure they can't wait to address you by your exalted rank."

CJ met Privates Harold Blakely and Osmond Ingram, who looked at his fresh uniform with sergeant's chevrons and grinned as if Corporal Morrison had told them a funny joke. Both soldiers wore mud-encrusted uniforms, had a week's worth of whiskers, and smelled rank.

"The Hun will come at us tonight," Ingram predicted, thrusting a BAR into CJ's hands. "Carry as much ammo as you can, for it's my turn to be runner and I don't wish to be killed."

CJ checked the Browning. It needed to be broken down and cleaned. "What other weapons will we have?"

"There's a light machine gun that's set up in the tank," Blakely replied, "and we'll have our rifles. We'll hold the Krauts off until Ozzie reaches our lines, then retreat."

CJ nodded. "What happened to the other BAR man?"

"Dead," Morrison said. "Have you any more questions?"

CJ shook his head and got to work on the Browning.

That night before moonrise, a German patrol came crawling out of their trench. CJ spotted the movement and sent Ozzie back just as a Kraut machine gun opened up on the tank. Blakely fired back at the German gun position while CJ sprayed the approaching troops, who suddenly rose and started to rush his position. Bullets clanged against the steel. Men in CJ's sights fell.

"It's a whole goddamn platoon of Krauts," Blakely shouted as he turned the machine gun on the advancing men. "It's time to go, time to go."

"Can we be sure Ozzie made it?" CJ shouted.

"Doesn't matter now," Blakely said. "Let's get the hell out of here while we still can."

They left the tank under small-arms fire, zigzagging from shell hole to shell hole. Behind them, German artillery blew the French tank to smithereens, and a roar went up from the Krauts. CJ and Blakely rolled into the trench as shells began to explode around them, answered by American cannon.

Corporal Morrison pulled CJ to his feet as Lieutenant Tyler blew his whistle to signal the counterattack. "Reload and get back over the top," he said. "We've got Germans to kill."

CJ's hands were shaking. He looked around for Private Blakely. "Where's Blakely? Where's Ozzie?"

"Not now." Morrison pushed him up the ladder. "Get going!"

Under a thousand flares, they forced the Germans back. All around CJ men fell, some blown up, some shot down. As he pressed forward next to Corporal Morrison, the horrible hammering, crashing sounds of war surrounded him. The air screamed with shells, hissed with bullets; the moans and cries of dying and wounded men were an unrelenting chorus. Moving from shell hole to mound to shell hole, CJ fired the Browning blindly at the retreating Germans. When the sky went dark and sudden silence came, it was almost as terrifying.

Morrison had to tell CJ to get up and move back. Lugging the BAR, he slogged through mud and dropped down into the trench. Amazed that he was still alive, he tried to catch his breath.

Lieutenant Tyler, his arm in a sling, sought him out. "You'll take over the Second Squad, First Platoon, in the morning, Sergeant. Get some rest."

"Yes, sir," CJ said. "Thank you, sir."

* * *

The regiment overran the German position and held it. Blakely and Ozzie Ingram both survived, only to be blown up by a grenade the next night on outpost duty. Morrison got a field promotion to sergeant and drowned three weeks later crossing a river on a reconnaissance patrol with Lieutenant Tyler, who was severely wounded in the action and sent to the rear. Tyler's replacement was John Lockhart. CJ was delighted to have him as his platoon leader. Over the next month, they pushed ahead with few casualties.

On a morning when the Germans were quiet and the black rats, as big as cats, had disappeared in their holes, John Lockhart stopped by CJ's post.

"Everything okay?" he asked.

"All quiet, Lieutenant," CJ reported. "Nothing's moving."

Lockhart nodded. "We're starting a big push this evening and are ordered to run the Huns out of the forest and sever the railroad line resupplying their troops. We'll be spearheading the assault and will have regiments flanking us on both sides."

"I'm short two men," CJ said.

"Replacements are coming up later today," Lockhart said. "I'll hold a briefing for all noncoms in an hour."

"Yes, sir."

Lockhart squeezed CJ's shoulder. "Take care, Sergeant."

"You too, Lieutenant."

Lockhart moved down the trench, pausing to talk to each soldier, CJ took out his map and studied it. He reckoned it to be three miles to the rail line through a dense forest. They would have to secure a bridge that crossed one river, if it hadn't been destroyed by the Huns before they got there. Field artillery would pound away for hours before the order to advance came. But that didn't mean the Germans would be dislodged. Earlier reconnaissance patrols had located major Hun entrenchments. It could get dangerous in the woods.

He put his map away and went to write a letter to Ma. He hadn't put a word on paper to her since arriving at the front.

* * *

The thunderous roar of artillery barrages rang out for hours. The ground shook and the air screamed with shells. Across the open field, the front of the forest had been obliterated, turned into nothing more than sticks scattered about on the ground, some still upright, burning like candles in the dusk.

When the artillery stopped, the whistles sounded and the regiment came out of the trenches in waves. Waiting for the Germans to open up with a thousand guns, CJ kept his squad right behind John Lockhart. But the only sound came from the hundreds of men running headlong through the mud.

At the forest line, the regiment regrouped in shell holes and behind downed trees while patrols were sent out. CJ assembled his men with rifles at the ready in case of an attack and waited for orders. Small-arms and machine-gun fire erupted in the woods, runners returned, and soon the regiment was up and moving again.

Deep in the forest they encountered a wall of wire, forcing a standstill. As patrols were sent to find a way around it, snipers began picking off the men cutting through the wire. All at once German cannon and mortar let loose, and in the deafening explosions men were blown apart, arms and legs flying through the air.

CJ lost his BAR man before he could gather the rest of his squad. He grabbed the Browning and moved the squad away from the bombardment, looking for a passage through the wire. He found it guarded by three hidden machine-gun nests, the ground in front of them littered with the bodies of the patrol that had been sent to find it.

He hunkered the squad down and sent a private back to report and bring reinforcements. John Lockhart showed up leading the company. The CO had been killed during the bombardment.

Lockhart listened to CJ's report, studied the terrain, and laid out a plan to have men with automatic rifles and light machine guns open up simultaneously on the nests, followed by a company assault.

"We'll overrun them," he said. "Let's do it fast."

CJ crawled into position with a machine gunner and waited for Lockhart's signal. When it came, he opened up on the nest and started creeping forward, the gunner firing at his side. Bullets snapped at his head. Lockhart signaled for the company to move forward and CJ stood to rush the nest.

He felt something slam into his belly, once, twice, and again. It knocked him to his knees. He dropped the Browning and fell on his side across the body of the dead machine gunner. He saw men run past him, heard the gunfire, the grunts, the screams, and then silence.

He closed his eyes and grabbed his belly. It felt like a squishy sausage poking out from under his tunic. A hand touched his shoulder. He turned his head and opened his eyes. John Lockhart looked down at him.

"Sorry," CJ said.

"You did fine, son," Lockhart said softly.

"I just want to go home," CJ said.

"I know."

"To see my ma and my brother. And the ranch."

"I know."

"I don't want to die here."

"Rest now," Lockhart said.

"Yeah," CJ said as his eyes fluttered and closed for the very last time.

69

In early December a letter from France came soon after Matthew arrived home from school. It was from an American army officer in Paris. Emma stared at the envelope in dread.

"Is it from CJ?" he asked excitedly. At six, he was smart and inquisitive, just like his older brother.

Last week, Betty McFie had received a similar letter from France telling her that her boy Billy had lost an arm fighting in the Meuse-Argonne Offensive. Emma sank into a chair at the kitchen table to keep her knees from buckling.

"Is it from CJ?" Matt asked again.

Emma shook her head.

"Who is it from?" Matt asked, studying the envelope in his mother's hands.

"Put on your coat and go play outside," Emma said, fighting to remain calm.

"It's cold. I don't want to."

"Do as I ask," Emma said. "I'll call for you to come in when it's time."

Matt shook his head in protest.

Emma reached for her purse and gave him a quarter. "Buy yourself some candy."

Matt grinned. "Okay." He wasn't allowed candy very often. He put on his coat in a hurry.

Emma waited until the back door slammed before opening the letter. Inside was a second sealed envelope addressed to her in CJ's hand. Her heart sank. She put it aside and read the lieutenant's letter first.

Dear Mrs. Kerney,

I am deeply sorry to tell you of CJ's death on the field of battle. I was with him when he fell. Before he left this world your name was on his lips. I served with him from Texas to France and have never known a young man of greater merit or more courage. He possessed a maturity well beyond his years and was a fine leader of men. In action, CJ was valiant and steadfast, as a person, he was highly respected and well liked. I personally grieve for the loss of his friendship, which I know will never match the pain you must now endure. If it is any consolation, CJ was the best of us.

I have enclosed a letter he asked me to send to you in the event of his death. With my utmost sympathy, I am

Yours truly,
John Lockhart, 1st Lt.
36th Division

Emma pressed CJ's unopened letter against her cheek and sobbed as though life was being sucked out of her. To have lost her sweet little Molly so young and now her brilliant, kindhearted CJ

seemed cruel, unfair. With shaking hands, she opened his letter
and read it.

> *Dear Mother,*
>
> *If you get this letter it's because I won't be coming home.
> But I'm hoping when the war ends, I'll tear it up and write to
> say I'm fine and on my way back to New Mexico. I've been a
> good soldier and done everything I can to prepare myself for
> battle. I've studied and trained hard and think I stand a
> good chance to survive. If I don't, I want you to know that
> I've served honorably. I am glad I did what I did even though
> I know you must still be aggravated that I ran away to enlist.*
>
> *I've thought long and hard about asking you a favor, and
> here it is. Up until I left for the army, I saw how miserable you
> and Pa were after you split up. I don't know what happened
> to cause it and I know Pa can get downright mean and surly
> at times, but you are both mule-headed stubborn in your own
> way, neither willing to give an inch. Maybe you can't set the
> past aside, but if the two of you can make a truce it would
> sure be good for Matt. Since I won't be there for him as an
> older brother, he'll need a father, if Pa is willing. Show him
> my letter and tell him it's my last wish.*
>
> *Your loving son,*
>
> *CJ*

Emma lowered her head, closed her eyes, and cried until she
was gasping for breath. She didn't realize Matthew had returned
until he tugged at her sleeve.

"What's wrong?" he asked, his expression grave with worry.
"Why are you sad?"

She wrapped her arms around Matthew and hesitated for a second before deciding to tell him the truth. "CJ is dead."

"No," Matt said, his voice rising, tears welling in his eyes. "He promised to come home. I don't want him to be dead."

"I don't either, but he is." Emma stroked Matt's face and tried to hold him, but he backed away.

"I don't believe you." His voice broke and he began crying.

Emma pulled him close. "Would I tell you something so terrible if it wasn't true?"

Matt sniffled, wiped his nose on his shirtsleeve, and shook his head. "Does it really say he died in the letter?"

"Yes," Emma whispered.

"Will you read it to me?"

Emma nodded. "Yes. There are two letters, one from CJ and one from his lieutenant. He writes that CJ was very brave."

"Read that one first."

Matthew surprised her by climbing on her lap, something he hadn't done in a year. It was a small balm to her badly wounded heart. She cuddled him close, took a deep breath, and read the letters. When she finished CJ's letter, Matt looked up at her.

"If CJ wrote us a letter, he can't be dead," he said.

"He wrote it before he died," Emma replied.

"No," Matthew said forcefully, rejecting the notion. "He's my big brother, and he's coming home. And I don't want a pa."

Matt had met his father only twice. The first time he barely remembered, but the second time scared him. He'd been with his mother on Main Street when a big, angry man came up and yelled at her. Afterward, Ma told him the man was his father and not to mind him because he was drunk. Matt didn't like him. Other kids' fathers were nice and didn't yell at people on the street.

"We have to tell your father about CJ," Emma said.

"I don't want to see him," Matthew protested as he slid off Emma's lap. "CJ will come home, so I don't have to. Read CJ's letter to me again."

"After we eat." Emma put the letters away in her sewing basket on the top shelf of the kitchen cabinet. Her hands were shaking. She needed to calm herself and keep her wits. "Wash up and set the table while I start supper."

For a moment, Matthew didn't budge.

Emma forced a smile. "Please help."

"Okay," Matthew said grouchily as he slouched to the sink to wash his hands.

Unable to concentrate on cooking, Emma fixed a tasteless vegetable soup and served it with buttered bread. She ate only a few spoonfuls. Matthew sopped his bread in the soup, ate half of it, and pushed the bowl away. She cleared the dishes, rinsed and stacked them in the sink, and began reading CJ's letter to Matthew again.

"He said he's coming back," Matthew interrupted, trying to will it true. "He says so."

"He wanted to," Emma replied.

Matthew stuck his chin out. "I know he will."

"Hush," Emma said. "Let me finish reading it to you." She finished and looked up to find Matthew with his eyes tightly shut, vigorously shaking his head. "Why are you doing that?" she asked.

"I won't go see that man," Matt answered, about to throw a tantrum. "I won't, I won't."

She pulled him to her. He was as stiff as a board. "We don't have to talk about it now."

Slowly he relaxed and almost fell asleep, exhausted, in her arms.

She tucked him into bed with her mind a whirling dust devil scattering her thoughts to the wind. She got out her sewing to keep her hands busy, but it didn't clear her mind. She read CJ's letter again. It had surprised her that he thought the divorce had made her miserable. She'd been unhappy at times, but never wretched, and had built a good life for her sons.

Suddenly she realized the divorce had taken a bigger toll on CJ than she had ever imagined. How could she have missed it? Had CJ hidden his true feelings from her for all those years?

With her doubts about Patrick, she wasn't sure CJ's last wish would result in anything good at all. Patrick had raped her and pushed CJ away by killing a horse he loved. Throughout his life, he'd broken from every person who ever cared about him. Would he do the same to Matthew? She felt obligated to try to fulfill CJ's wish, especially now that she understood some of the hurting he'd endured, but she also had to protect Matt.

She worked on a dress she was making until her fingers stiffened. She put it away, brushed her hair, washed her face, and changed into her nightgown, hoping the routine would calm her. In bed, she barely slept, tossing and turning while memories of CJ crowded her mind with hints of his unhappiness.

She rose early and started breakfast before waking Matthew. "Dress quickly," she said.

"When's my brother coming?" Matthew asked, half-awake.

"I wish for all my heart that was true," Emma replied. "But he's not ever coming home. Now, dress. We're going to do as CJ asked and visit your father at his ranch."

Matt pouted. "I don't want to."

"You will do as you're told," Emma said gently. "We're taking the early morning train to Engle."

Matt stopped pouting. He loved trains. His expression turned worried. "We're not going to live at the ranch, are we?"

"No," Emma answered. "We'll come home after our visit."

"Promise?"

Emma pulled him close. "I promise."

70

The early morning train left Las Cruces with coach cars filled with ranchers, wives, and their children traveling to Albuquerque for a long weekend at the state stockmen's convention. Matthew sat quietly next to Emma in a window seat, gazing at the passing landscape. His silence gave her time to think.

Since leaving Patrick, Emma's only source of reliable information about him came from Addie Hightower, the ranch neighbor who had taught CJ for a time. During Addie's last trip to town, she reported that Patrick had started fixing up the ranch after years of neglecting it and had even asked after Emma. He wanted to know if she was doing all right and if she'd heard from CJ.

It surprised Emma to hear Patrick showed any interest in her at all, and while she didn't take it to mean his hard feelings about her and CJ had softened, it might mean he'd be open to CJ's last wish.

Long ago, when she blamed herself for Molly's death, Cal, Patrick, and George had helped her through it. But this time George and Cal were gone and she was on her own. After CJ ran away, Patrick had accosted her and Matthew on the street, drunkenly accusing her of not doing enough to stop CJ from joining the army. That memory was seared into her mind along with the anger she felt at Patrick for his unjust reproachment. But in her heart she also felt she had failed that wonderful boy.

She gripped her purse tightly to hold back her tears. In it were all of CJ's letters. Patrick should read them to know what a good and honorable man he'd become. And he should meet Matthew and at the very least acknowledge him as his son. If nothing more was accomplished, perhaps that would be enough to honor CJ's wishes.

The engine whistle blew as the train slowed on the approach to the station. Engle was no longer a bustling town fueled by construction of the dam ten miles west on the Rio Grande; its heyday had come and gone. Only the railroad and the big cattle spreads on the Jornada kept it going.

Matthew pointed out the window at the distant San Andres. "Is his ranch in those mountains?"

"On the far side," Emma replied.

"When will we get there?"

"It's a long ride. We'll rent a buggy."

Matthew's expression turned serious. "He won't like me."

"How do you know?"

"I just do," Matthew replied sourly.

* * *

"**B**uggy coming!" Curtis called out from the porch. "It's a far piece yet."

Patrick stepped out of the barn, looked across the pasture at the distant buggy, and glanced up at Curtis. "Who is it?"

"Can't say," Curtis replied, "but it sure ain't any of the neighbors."

"Get the field glasses and take a look."

Curtis got the glasses, studied the approaching buggy, and handed the glasses to Patrick when he reached the porch. "A woman and a button," he reported.

"I'll be damned," Patrick said after a good look.

"Who is it?"

He lowered the glasses. "My ex-wife and her boy."

"Didn't know you had another son. Should I set out two more plates for supper?"

It would be dark in an hour, with a quarter moon rising late. "You'd better," Patrick replied grumpily, wondering what brought Emma and the boy to the Double K. "And fix up the casita. They'll need to spend the night."

Curtis limped back inside, and Patrick studied Emma and the boy through the glasses again. Emma looked a touch older but still about as pretty as a woman could be. She still stirred him like no other woman ever did.

He'd last seen her on the street in Las Cruces after having a few drinks to celebrate filing on six hundred and forty acres he'd bought from a homesteader who'd gone broke. Because the section was in Doña Ana County, he'd had to do the paperwork at the county seat. It had been his first trip to Las Cruces in years, and damn if Emma didn't turn up with that boy right in front of him again. He gave her a chewing on about something but couldn't remember what.

The boy was a pint-size version of CJ. He had the same hair, same square shoulders, and same lean, angular face particular to Kerney men. He'd never admitted any of that to Emma. Facing her cold heart always made him dig in his heels.

A preacher once told him that some men had to reach a certain age before they could accept their failings and follow Jesus to salvation. Patrick reckoned since he already knew what he'd done wrong to his marriage, he didn't need churchgoing forgiveness.

He met the buggy at the corrals, grabbed the reins, and searched Emma's face. She gave nothing away. "What brings you here?" he demanded.

"You remember Matthew," Emma said firmly, her arm around the boy.

Patrick glanced at the boy. "I do. Why are you here?"

"I want to go home," Matthew whispered, tugging Emma's sleeve, eyes wide with apprehension. "I don't like it here."

"I ain't gonna bite you, boy," Patrick snapped, reacting to the sting of Matthew's words.

"Let go of the reins." Emma raised the buggy whip.

"Are you gonna give me a hiding?" Patrick asked, eyeing the whip.

"No, we're going home. Let go of the reins."

Patrick dropped the reins. "Do what suits you."

"CJ is dead," Emma said. "He was killed in France."

Patrick turned ashen gray. "Jesus, no. Not that boy. Not CJ." He stopped the horse before Emma flicked the whip. "Don't leave," he implored.

Emma stared at him hard. "Why not?"

"Please, tell me what you know. I only got two letters from him all the time he's been gone."

"I brought his letters to me for you to read."

"Come inside," Patrick said slowly. "You and the boy stay the night."

Emma didn't move. "His name is Matthew," she said emphatically. "And he's your son."

Patrick nodded. "I know he is. I've known it all along. You and Matthew come inside. Supper's on the stove."

"I'm real hungry, Ma," Matthew said.

"Very well," Emma said as she stepped down from the buggy. Perhaps the trip hadn't been for naught after all.

* * *

Emma sat with Matthew on the living room couch watching Patrick read CJ's letters. After each one, he took a sip of whiskey. When he drained the glass, he splashed a bit more whiskey into it and gave Emma a wary look.

"I don't get drunk anymore," he said as he picked up the last unread letter. "Stopped doing that a while back."

Emma stayed silent.

Twice he read CJ's last wish. Be a pa to Matthew was what CJ wanted. He stared at Matthew. The resemblance to CJ and himself was clear. He thought back to when he was a boy, and not a soul had been there for him. Yet he managed to get by. For so many years he had thought about himself this way. But it was a lie. John Kerney saved him from a life of sheer hell, Cal raised him up out of pure goodness, and Ignacio and Teresa remained his friends even when he repeatedly shunned them.

He put the letter on top of a neat pile and handed it to Emma. "I plumb drove CJ away when I shot that pony he was determined too gentle."

"He told me," Emma said, expecting Patrick to quickly put a share of the fault on her.

"Seems I'm good at that."

"Yes, you are," Emma replied, surprised that he didn't start blaming her.

"If I'd known he wanted to join up, I would have told him what war was really like."

"That didn't work when Cal tried it on you." Emma wondered what it was about men that made them think they'd love war.

"I know it. That's some last wish CJ put on us," Patrick said.

"It is, but if you want to know Matt as your son, you have to stop drinking."

"You'd let me be a father to him?" Patrick wondered if maybe later on she would reconcile with him.

"CJ wanted us to try," Emma replied.

"He was a better man than me, and I give you all the credit for that. You raised him right. I'm obliged that you came out and brought the letters to show me."

"Is that all you have to say?"

"No." Patrick looked at Matthew. "Did your mother read you CJ's letters?"

Matthew nodded.

Patrick smiled. "I'm not always mean and surly like he said."

Matthew stared silently back.

Patrick sighed and sadly shook his head. "I guess he doesn't want a thing to do with me."

Emma's expression turned cold. "Is that going to be your excuse?"

"I wasn't making an excuse."

"Yes, you were," she snapped. "You like to make out that everyone steps away from you, everyone lets you down. I'm sick of it. I've always wanted you to be a father to Matthew. A *good* father."

Patrick bit his lip. "I was only halfway there for CJ, I reckon, so

I need to be all the way there for Matthew. If you'll give me a hand with it, I'd like to try."

Emma had never once heard Patrick ask for help before. She picked up the packet of letters. "Come to town next Sunday sober and we'll talk about it."

"I'll be there."

"Victuals on the table," Curtis called out from the kitchen.

Emma stood and took Matthew's hand. "Let's go wash up for supper."

"I'll join you shortly," Patrick said.

After they left, Patrick poured himself another drink and went out on the veranda. The night was cold and the quarter moon had yet to rise. The vast Tularosa spread out before him, dark and quiet except for the slightest whisper of a breeze.

He remembered CJ gleefully chasing the roadrunner through the cottonwoods, grinning from ear to ear astride his first pony, sitting peacefully in Emma's lap while she read him stories. The thought of those happy times made his heart sink. He damn sure was going to miss him.

The breeze picked up and he felt a wet sting at the corners of his eyes. No point looking back. He had a chance to do right with Matt, and truth be told, without the boy he had no family at all.

He twirled the glass of whiskey in his hands and wondered if Emma would really stick and help him with Matt, or shuck him off the first time he made a mistake. He poured out the whiskey, threw the glass away, heard it shatter, and decided it was time to be the father CJ always wanted him to be, no matter what else happened between him and Emma.

AUTHOR'S NOTE

A great deal of research went into *Hard Country* to make it as his-
torically accurate as possible. For matters pertaining to the world
of the cowboy, *Log of a Twentieth Century Cowboy*, by Daniel G.
Moore, *The Cowboy*, by Philip Ashton Rollins, *A Hundred Years of
Horse Tracks: The Story of the Gray Ranch*, by George Hillard, *The Log
of a Cowboy*, by Andy Adams, and *Cattle Horses & Men*, by John H.
(Jack) Culley, were invaluable.

For information about important historical characters and
events, *A Bar Cross Man: The Life and Personal Writings of Eugene
Manlove Rhodes*, by W. H. Hutchinson, *The Two Alberts: Fountain and
Fall*, by Gordon R. Owen, *The Hired Man on Horseback: My Story of
Eugene Manlove Rhodes*, by May D. Rhodes, *The Life and Death of
Colonel Albert Jennings Fountain*, by A. M. Gibson, *George Curry: 1861–
1947, an Autobiography*, by George Curry, *Tularosa: Last of the Frontier West*, by C. L. Sonnichsen, and *Fort Stanton*, by F. Stanley, were
especially helpful.

On matters pertaining to the Rough Riders, I turned to *The Rise
of Theodore Roosevelt*, by Edmund Morris, *An Oklahoma Rough Rider:
Billy McGinty's Own Story*, edited by Jim Fulbright and Albert

Stehno, and *The Rough Riders,* by Theodore Roosevelt with additional text by Richard Bak.

Lonnie J. White's excellent book, *Panthers to Arrowheads: The 36th (Texas-Oklahoma) Division in World War I,* was an important and valuable source of information about the role of the National Guard in the Great War.

Accurate cowboy lingo came to me by way of *The Dictionary of the American West,* by Win Blevins, and *The Cowboy,* by Rollins. I found Larry D. Ball's *Desert Lawman* helpful in gaining an understanding of law enforcement on the frontier. Randy Steffen's *The Horse Soldier, 1776–1943,* volume 2, and Robert M. Utley's *The Indian Frontier of the American West, 1846–1890* provided valuable insights into the workings of the cavalry in the Southwest. *Indeh: An Apache Odyssey,* by Eve Ball with Nora Henn and Lynda A. Sanchez, Sonnichsen's *The Mescalero Apaches,* Eve Ball's *In the Days of Victorio,* and *Living Life's Circle: Mescalero Apache Cosmovision,* by Claire R. Farrer, provided great insight into the culture and history of a proud people who continue to preserve their traditions and beliefs while making their way in contemporary society. Stephen H. Lekson's *Nana's Raid: Apache Warfare in Southern New Mexico, 1881* added to my understanding of those troubled times for the Apaches in the New Mexico Territory.

The late, masterful writer and renowned storyteller J. Frank Dobie enriched my understanding of Texan pioneers, especially through his books *The Longhorns, Some Part of Myself,* and *Cow People.* Nineteenth- and twentieth-century places came to life for me through *Centennial: Alamogordo New Mexico: 1898–1998,* by David Townsend and Clif McDonald, *Las Cruces, New Mexico, 1849–1999: Multicultural Crossroads,* by Gordon Owen, *Las Cruces, New Mexico 1881,* by Patrick H. Beckett, *An Illustrated History of New Mexico,* by

Thomas E. Chávez, *White Oaks,* by Morris B. Parker, *The Territorial History of Socorro, New Mexico,* by Bruce Ashcroft, and Sonnichsen's *Tularosa: Last of the Frontier West.* Also of great help were White Sands Missile Range Archaeological Reports authored by Peter L. Eidenbach, Linda Hart, Beth Morgan, and Robert L. Hart, and several self-published family histories that put real faces on the people who settled the hard and beautiful country of New Mexico. Mrs. Tom Charles's *Tales of the Tularosa* and *More Tales of the Tularosa* were especially informative.

For fans and scholars of the works of Eugene Manlove Rhodes, I created the epitaph he wrote in *Hard Country* from a careful reading of some of his poems. I hope it does him justice. A select bibliography has been posted on my Web site, www.michaelmcgarrity .com, for readers interested in the primary research materials I used in the development of the story.

Last and most important, Brian Tart, publisher and president of Dutton, is especially thanked for his strong encouragement and support during the past three years. He stuck with me when I stepped into unknown territory as a writer, allowed me the extra time I needed to get the job done, and with his keen editorial eye helped make *Hard Country* a better book. They don't come any better. He "makes a hand."

Santa Fe, New Mexico

Photo by Sean McGarrity

Michael McGarrity is the author of the Anthony Award–nominated *Tularosa, Mexican Hat, Serpent Gate, Hermit's Peak, The Judas Gun, Under the Color of Law,* and *The Big Gamble.* A former deputy sheriff for Santa Fe County, he established the first sex-crimes unit. He has also served as an instructor at the New Mexico Law Enforcement Academy and as an investigator for the New Mexico public defender's office.

CONNECT ONLINE

www.michaelmcgarrity.com

Read on for a look at the next installment
of the Kerney family's epic story,

BACKLANDS

Available now.

E mma Kerney woke early. Not a sound could be heard outside: no cackling of chickens in the neighbor's backyard, no braying of the ancient donkey Mr. Roybal kept in the small field adjacent to his dilapidated adobe casita, not even a whisper of wind through the bare branches of the trees that lined still-dark, quiet Griggs Avenue.

As she had every night since the outset of winter, Emma had gone to bed exhausted, half expecting to die in her sleep. And every morning, she opened her eyes to a deep fatigue that haunted her throughout the day. Her exhaustion was now so persistent, she could no longer hide it from her eight-year-old son, Matthew. Nor could she hide the sudden, gushing nosebleeds, the searing chest pains that doubled her over in agony, and the noisy, raspy breathlessness that came after all but the slightest bit of physical exertion.

There were days when she barely gathered the strength to mop a floor, cook a meal, or wash a dish. Often she had to rely on Matthew to finish her chores, and lately, out of fear she might collapse on the short walk downtown, she'd taken to sending him off to the grocer's on Main Street to do the weekly household shopping. He had done all that she asked, never failing to oblige her with other than a worried look and a tight-lipped smile old beyond his years. It broke Emma's heart to see her plucky boy give up so much time caring for her when he should be with his friends enjoying a fleeting, carefree childhood. It wasn't fair at all.

But this morning, Emma woke up feeling unusually rested. The sound of her pounding heart in her ears had subsided, her normally twitchy legs were still, and her mind was clear of worry. As she stretched her fine-boned, thin frame under the thick pile of blankets that covered her, she felt full of energy as if the defective valve in her heart had miraculously mended. Not a bone ached, her legs felt light and limber, and her feet, normally cold no matter what the season, were deliciously toasty.

For a long minute she lay still, wondering if she was daydreaming, suspicious that if she moved another inch the feeling of endless weariness would return and squash the fantasy. Finally convinced that she felt wonderfully like her old self, she pushed away the covers, swung her legs over the side of the bed, and stood. There was no light-headedness, no touch of numbing listlessness, and above all the snappish mood that had plagued her for weeks was gone.

Almost giggling with delight, she dressed quickly, hurried to the kitchen, stoked the embers in the cookstove, and added some wood before peeking out the window. Early dawn revealed a dusting of snow on the bare branches of the cottonwood tree in the front yard. Not a drop of moisture had fallen on the town of Las Cruces since late summer and the welcome sight raised Emma's spirits even higher. The start of the day had been perfect. If she kept feeling lively and normal for a change, the entire day would be wonderful.

She swooped into Matthew's bedroom and roused her sleeping son with a big hug just as Mr. Roybal's donkey announced the arrival of dawn with a long, honking bray.

"Let go," Matthew grumbled sleepy-eyed, pulling away.

"Time to rise and shine, young man," she said, turning on the bedside lamp. "How about some hotcakes, eggs, and bacon for breakfast?"

Long and lean, with square shoulders like all the Kerney men and startlingly blue eyes, Matthew squinted at his mother. "Are you feeling better?" he asked tentatively, searching her face.

Emma smiled and nodded. "Much better, and I've a great hunger for hotcakes. Now, shake a leg. You have chores to do before we eat."

"You're really better, no kidding?" Matthew asked again.

"For now," Emma said.

Matthew smiled. "Boy, I'm glad to hear that."

"So am I." She gave him a kiss on his cheek, which he quickly wiped away. Out of bed, he reached for his clothes neatly folded on the top of the small dresser that held a framed photograph of his older brother, CJ, standing stiff and proud in his sergeant's uniform. It had been taken just weeks before his death on a French battlefield during the Great War.

She couldn't look at it without stifling a sob that always rose in her throat. What a fine man he would have become if the madness of war hadn't claimed him.

She left Matthew to dress, returned to the cozy warmth of the kitchen, and set about mixing the batter, cutting thick strips of bacon, and heating the griddle. In a small Apache basket on the top of the kitchen cupboard, Emma kept all the letters CJ had sent home from the army. Tonight would be a perfect time to read them aloud again with Matthew.

Until her latest bout of illness, Emma had been writing letters for Matthew to find and read after her death. Mostly, she'd set down the happy times in her life and the people and friends she'd known, loved, and admired so he would have some knowledge of her past and his family's history. She had never hidden the fact from him that her defective heart couldn't be fixed, and she didn't shy away from the subject in the letters. However, she had kept silent about the reality of her dying soon, which until now seemed wisest. Why burden a child with such cruel knowledge? But now, with her illness more than an occasional inconvenience once easily masked and the undeniable suffering she endured, which Matthew had witnessed day after day for weeks, the subject could no longer be avoided.

She dreaded the conversation they soon must have. CJ's death still troubled Matthew, and he often became visibly gloomy at the mere mention of his brother's name. As for Emma, the simple, clear-cut knowledge that she wouldn't live to see Matthew fully grown was a wrenching sorrow that made the idea of the conversation almost unbearable. Yet she had to prepare him for the inevitable, especially since it could no longer be ignored.

She would do it soon, she vowed, but not today. Today was for celebrating.

Matthew came into the kitchen, followed by a blast of cold air; he was bundled in his coat with an armload of wood for the cookstove. As always, he'd slicked down his cowlick in an unsuccessful attempt to tame it. His cheeks and nose were rosy from the cold.

"It snowed a bit last night," Matthew said as he filled the woodbin.

"I know," Emma replied. "How wonderful. How many hotcakes can you eat?"

"Four," Matthew replied as he shed his coat and hung it on the back of his chair. "No, maybe six."

Emma raised an eyebrow as she greased the griddle. "Six?"

Matthew nodded. "Yep, you haven't made hotcakes in a long time."

Emma paused, spatula in hand. "That can't be true. You'll eat them all?"

"Yes, ma'am. Promise."

"Fair enough. Six it is. Pour yourself some milk and get the jug of syrup."

Bacon sizzled in the frying pan to be done crispy, the way Matthew liked it. She greased the griddle, poured the batter, and quickly made a stack of hotcakes she kept warm on a platter in the oven. When the bacon was done, she forked it onto plates with the hotcakes, fried two eggs over easy, eased them onto the stacks, and brought breakfast to the table.

Matthew grinned at the plate of food placed in front of him. "This looks just swell," he said.

"Thank you kindly, sir," Emma replied. The look of pleased anticipation on Matthew's face raised Emma's spirits even higher. She watched as he broke the egg yolks, poured syrup on the hotcakes, and dug in with his fork.

He ate with such happy concentration that Emma didn't venture a word to interrupt him. She turned with gusto to her own meal and only spoke when he looked up from his empty plate.

"I think I'd like to walk with you to school this morning," she said.

Matthew looked startled. "Are you sure you should?"

"Am I acting poor and sickly?" Emma teased. Minute by minute, she was feeling better and better.

Matthew studied his mother's face and shook his head. "No, ma'am, not this morning, but you've been sick for quite a spell."

"And you've been a good sport, taking on so much work and being the man of the house."

"That's okay," Matt said, visibly pleased by the compliment.

"You deserve a reward." Emma got her change purse from the cupboard drawer and gave Matthew a dollar in quarters.

Matt looked at the coins in his hand and beamed. "Wow. Thanks."

Emma snapped the purse closed and smiled. "You've more than earned it. Now, I haven't stuck my nose outside for weeks. A walk to school with you will do me good. I'll clean up the kitchen while you make your bed and feed your pony."

Matt's happy expression turned serious. "Are you sure you can do it, Ma?"

Half-convinced she wasn't fooling herself, Emma laughed and said, "Starting today, things are back to normal. Is that okay with you?"

Matt's smile returned. "That's aces with me."

"Then jingle those spurs. After school you can go downtown and spend your hard-earned money anyway you like. I'll have a nice snack fixed for you when you get home and we'll have an extra-special meal at dinnertime."

Matthew grinned, grabbed his coat, and flew out of the house to feed and water Patches.

* * *

A block away from the schoolhouse, Matthew ran ahead of Emma to catch up with two of his best chums, Jimmy Potter and Joe Pete Johnson, waiting for him at the corner. As soon as he got there, he turned and waved. Emma smiled in return, waved back gaily, and watched as the three pals raced the rest of the way to school, skidded to a stop in unison at the front of the tall double doors, and piled inside, three abreast.

It had started to snow on the short walk to school, dropping heavy flakes that raised Emma's spirits even higher. A thin white blanket now covered the dirt road and a low sky of dense clouds promised a lot more moisture to come throughout the day. Before turning for home, she watched the last few children hurry inside just as the school bell rang. It was good to be outside in the snow, good to see Matthew happy with his friends, and good to feel strength returning to her body.

On the way back, she set a steady pace, thinking she would freshen up and change into a nicer skirt and blouse before setting out to pay the monthly grocer's bill and make appointments to see her banker and lawyer. Sickness had forced her to let important matters go by the wayside and now while she felt rejuvenated it was time to put things back in order.

At home, she washed up in the small bathroom that she'd had added to the rear of the house between the hallway that separated the two bedrooms. Barely big enough to turn around in, it had a sink, a lavatory, a bathtub, and a cold water tap only, which meant bath nights required heating water on the kitchen stove and carrying it to the tub. Still, it was a great convenience compared to the old outhouse, which had been torn down and filled in to make room for the small stable that housed Matt's pony, Patches.

Over the sink was a small mirror and above it a single light fixture. Emma couldn't quite remember the last time she'd looked closely at herself, but what she saw stunned her. She'd always been slender but never so rail thin. Her pale face was bony, almost gaunt, and there were dark circles under her eyes. Quickly she applied some face cream to hide the circles and bring out a bit of color on her cheeks, touched up her lips with a light lipstick, and darkened her eyebrows with a pencil. Upon inspection, she decided she didn't look too frightening after all, just a lot older than she wished.

Outside, the subdued winter snowfall of early morning had turned blustery and a gust of wind rattled the small bathroom window above the tub. After changing into a brown skirt and a fresh ruffled blouse, she climbed back into her warm winter coat, pulled a wool cap down over her ears, put on her gloves, and stepped into a gale that was blowing wet snow sideways. After so many weeks of dust and drought, the moist air smelled marvelous. It might not have been the best weather to be venturing out in, but she felt fine and it was but a few minutes' walk to the grocer and a few more steps from there to the bank.

She hurried down the road, snow-blown wind at her back, with a half a thought to believe in miracles—she felt that good. Twenty years ago, she and her ex-husband, Patrick, had bought the house on Griggs Avenue after a doctor had warned them of the risk of another miscarriage if she remained at their remote Tularosa ranch during her pregnancy. She had given birth to CJ in that house, returned with him in her arms to the ranch, and remained there until her separation from Patrick and the divorce. Ever since, she'd lived in Las Cruces permanently, giving birth to Matthew at home there as well.

Over the intervening years, the town had grown some, especially with the recent completion of the Elephant Butte Dam on the Rio Grande eighty miles north, which created a farming and business boom all the way south to El Paso. But even with the growth, Las Cruces still gave way to open range along the wide, fertile river valley, and the small residential neighborhoods, from the modest to the most elegant, were still clustered around Main Street.

Few people were out in the bad weather and only a single truck chugged down empty Main Street. Miles away to the east across the rolling desert, the Organ Mountains were masked by a thick blanket of clouds that made the scale of the land seem less vast, more reasonable. The sky was so low, not even the prominent spires of St. Genevieve's Church or the smokestacks of the power plant were visible. As the winds eased and the snow squall diminished, everything looked tranquil and soft under a white mantle.

At the grocer's she stomped her feet to shake off the wet snow as Sam Miller came round the counter, smiling broadly in greeting, his round cheeks bright pink as always.

"Why, Emma, you're up and about," he said jovially.

"And feeling fit as a fiddle," Emma replied.

"That sure is good to hear. What all do you need this morning?"

Emma opened her purse. "I came to pay my bill and set aside a few things to pick up later for dinner."

"Happy to oblige," Sam replied as he slipped behind the counter and reached for the account book he kept on a shelf beneath the shiny nickel-plated cash register. After he read off the amount Emma owed, he studied her carefully as she counted out bills and coins from her purse. She seemed smaller, swallowed up in her heavy winter coat, and her features, while still attractive, were sunken. She looked frail and worn in spite of her good humor.

Sam counted the money, rang it up on the cash register, and then helped Emma pick out what she needed to fix Matthew an extra-special dinner.

"No need to stop back by," he said as he wrapped up a freshly dressed chicken, several baking potatoes, and the fixings for gravy and a peach pie. "I'll have my boy bring the groceries by your house around the noon hour."

Emma smiled brightly. "Thank you, Sam. That will be perfect."

"You take care not to stay out in the cold for long," Sam said with concern as he entered Emma's purchases in his account book. Through the large plate-glass window, snow was blowing hard down Main Street again.

Emma laughed as she turned toward the door. "Don't you worry about me, Sam Miller. The bank is just a few steps away."

Sam watched Emma pass by the store's front window. Most everybody in town knew she was likely to die soon from a bad heart and all, and it was a damn shame. She'd suffered hardships, especially her divorce and the loss of CJ in the war, came through it all with spunk and spirit, and made a good life for herself and young Matt. As far as Sam was concerned, Emma Kerney deserved a far better hand than the one fate had dealt.

* * *

As a single young man, Henry Bowman had come to Las Cruces with his widowed father, George, after making a sizable amount of money selling tractors door to door to farmers across the upper Midwest during the closing years of the old century. Almost immediately upon their arrival, father and son had bought majority shares in a struggling bank and quickly turned it into a successful enterprise by attracting both Mexican and Anglo merchants with attractive loan rates and personal service. With George Bowman's death five years ago, Henry took over as bank president and doubled the loan department staff to keep pace with the burgeoning real estate market. Initially, he'd moved into his father's old office without changing a thing other than placing a framed photograph of his dad on the wall above the tall wooden cabinet that held the files of the bank's most important clients. From his perch, George gazed down on his son and his clients with the look of a man who knew the value of a dollar and the importance of hard work.

Although the office furnishings were out-of-date, it didn't bother Henry at all. In fact he liked the old-fashioned ornate breakfront bookcase; the large writing desk, which held an inkstand and postal scale placed there solely for ornamentation; and the two high-backed chairs for clients, which fronted the desk. His only concessions to change were a new, comfortable solid oak revolving desk chair on casters and a mahogany standing coat rack conveniently placed next to the office door.

He rose quickly when Emma Kerney stepped into his office, helped her with her coat, and ushered her to one of the of high-backed chairs in front of his wide desk, where he joined her, scooting his chair sideways a bit to have a better look at her. In the two months since her last visit, Emma's pretty blue eyes had now become paler, her face more aged, and her cheeks hollow. A woman with a small frame and long legs that made her seem taller, she now had a slight bend to her once perfect carriage.

Emma had enchanted Henry Bowman from the day they had first met almost twenty years ago and the feeling hadn't changed one iota since. Although he'd never spoken of it to her, he felt certain that she knew.

"It's good to see you," he said with a smile.

"It's good to see you as well, Henry," Emma replied.

Over the years, Henry had become portly as a result of sitting behind a desk, and a moon-shaped bald spot had spread over the top of his head. He was a sincere, serious-minded man not given to lightheartedness or small talk.

"How is your family?" Emma asked.

"Everyone is fine," Henry replied.

"Give Martha my best," Emma said.

"Of course," Henry said, eager to move the conversation off the subject of his wife, whom Emma always made a point to mention. "I'm glad you stopped by. An interesting and profitable offer has been tendered on two of your commercial lots just west of the city limits. But before we discuss that, how are you feeling?"

Emma laughed. "First Sam Miller and now you. Seems everyone is concerned about my health. I'm fine today."

Henry shook his head sternly in rebuke. "Every soul in town who knows you knows how sick you've been with your heart condition. So again I ask, how are you?"

Emma paused. Over the years Henry had been a trusted adviser who had never pried into her personal life. When she was carrying CJ, he'd suggested it would be smarter to buy a house rather than rent while she lived in town during her pregnancy. Later, after her divorce, he'd guided her into some wise investments and profitable opportunities. He deserved an honest answer.

"You're very kind to be concerned," she said, holding up a hand to stem a look of remonstration forming on Henry's face. "Today, honestly, I'm feeling much better, but I don't know how long that will last. Not long I think, and my doctor agrees. He's told me time and again that any one of a number of things can kill me, and that it's a miracle I've survived as long as I have. So let's talk business, instead of worrying about my physical ailments. I want to make sure there's enough money to see Matthew through after I'm gone."

"It's hard to image your passing," Henry said glumly. "Not a pleasant notion to consider at all."

Emma smiled. "Now, don't get all soppy on me, Henry. There's nothing to be done, no good reason for me to complain about it, and no need be downcast. When I do go, I'd like it to be as quick as possible. The idea of being a helpless, bedridden invalid mortifies me. Now, tell me about the offer on my lots that you mentioned."

Henry composed himself, nodded, rose, and went to his desk. "In a moment. Have you put your legal matters in order?"

"I thought first I'd speak with you about finances and then visit with Wallace Hale."

"That's very wise." Henry reached for the telephone. "Let's see if Wallace can meet with us here within the hour. By then we should know exactly how much your estate will be able to provide for Matthew's care, and he can advise you on the best way to legally ensure it will serve Matthew's needs only."

Emma adjusted herself in the chair. "That's exactly what I want. Please call him."

Henry placed the call, confirmed that Wallace Claiborne Hale would join them shortly, fetched Emma's file from his locked cabinet behind the desk, settled into his chair, and read aloud the particulars of the offer on the lots. When he finished, he suggested the interested party might be willing to pay ten percent more than the asking price. If so, the net profit would be almost quadruple what Emma had paid for the land four years ago.

"The buyer wants to close quickly," he added. "Shall I approach him with a counteroffer?"

Emma nodded her agreement. "The timing couldn't be better."

"I'll see to it," Henry promised.

"With this sale and the income from my remaining properties, is there sufficient annual income to see Matthew through for at least the next ten years?"

Henry opened Emma's file, slid his chair in front of the adding machine at the corner of the desk, and began paging through documents, entering numbers. Emma Kerney owned three houses that were rented out, eighty acres of pasture near the river leased to a dairy farmer, two additional vacant commercial lots, and her home on Griggs Avenue. He ran a total of the projected annual income and deducted a reserve for taxes, upkeep, repairs, loss of rental income, and trust administration fees.

"I'm assuming you would want to sell the remaining commercial parcels and put the money into Matthew's trust," he proposed. "It could be used to make up any shortfalls in income that occur and the balance will continue to earn interest."

"Should I do that now?"

"It might be best. The interested buyer plans on building an automobile dealership and large garage on the lots. Once the sale goes through, I know several speculators who will be very interested in the remaining parcels at the same if not a slighter higher price."

"Sell them as soon as you can," Emma said.

"What about your home?" Henry asked. "Sell it also when the time comes?"

Emma's eyes widened at the unhappy thought of it and she paused momentarily. "I'd like Matthew to keep it, if possible. After all, it's his home too. He can sell it when he's grown, if he has a mind to."

"Very well." He put the papers carefully back in order and closed the file. "Taking into account expenses, there's enough to provide Matthew an annual income of fifteen hundred dollars."

"Over the next ten years?" Emma asked, relieved to hear Henry's calculations would yield that much.

"Yes, but I'm assuming we'll have rent going into the trust from the Griggs Avenue property. Matthew can't live there alone after your passing and there are no relatives to care for him other than his father."

Emma leaned forward and fixed Henry Bowman with an intent gaze. "After I'm gone, Patrick Kerney must have no rights to Matthew's inheritance or how the trust is to be used on his behalf. He can be a father to his son, if that's at all possible, but have no say-so about the money. Promise me that."

"I understand," Henry said soothingly. "But it could very well become contentious even with proper legal safeguards in place. That's what lawyers are for."

Emma bit her lip.

"What is it?" Henry asked.

Emma shook her head. She wanted to say how badly she wished for ten more years to raise Matthew, but it would only sound self-pitying. "Nothing," she said brightly.

A knock at the door and the announcement by Henry's clerk that Wallace Claiborne Hale had arrived saved Emma from further questioning. The clerk stood aside and Hale filled the open doorway, his curly hair damp with wet snow, the overcoat draped on his arm dripping snow melt on the wood floor.

"It's a blizzard out there," he announced in his booming courtroom baritone, smiling broadly at Emma, "like I've not seen before. You must allow me to drive you home after our meeting."

"Thank you," Emma said. "That would be very nice."

"Very thoughtful of you, Wallace," Henry chimed in, unhappy with himself for not having offered to do the same sooner.

Wallace Hale nodded in agreement as he sat next to Emma. "It will be my pleasure." A tall man with a thin frame and long legs, Hale had a narrow nose and thick, bushy eyebrows. He studied Emma's face. "I hope that seeing you up and about means that you are recovered from your illness."

"Not entirely," Emma replied.

Wallace smiled knowingly. "I thought not. Otherwise there would be no rush for the three of us to meet." He turned to Henry Bowman. "What is the issue I am here to address?"

"We have agreed upon a trust plan for Matthew that should carry him comfortably through ten years after Emma's death. She wants Matthew's father to be barred from access to the trust."

Wallace leaned back. "That is certainly possible, simply by appointing someone other than Patrick as the trust administrator with the power of attorney to use the funds on Matthew's behalf within a specified scope of authorized expenditures. I can have a draft prepared within a few days."

He paused and waved a cautionary finger. "However, remember that as the surviving parent, Patrick Kerney will have full legal rights to raise Matthew as he see fit. If he finds himself at odds with the conditions of the trust, he might hire a lawyer to contest it before a judge."

"Can't it be made ironclad?" Emma asked.

"Few marital and family legal issues are that clear-cut and tidy," Wallace replied. "As a result, courts and judges have traditionally more leeway when deciding upon matters pertaining to minors. I will promise you a trust document that legally meets your need to provide for Matthew according to your wishes, but I cannot guarantee the outcome of any future challenges to it brought in a court of law."

"This is not what I was hoping for."

Wallace smiled sympathetically. "Of course it isn't. But remember, your ex-husband has a good reputation as a rancher, businessman, and law-abiding citizen, which means mounting a challenge against the trust might succeed if he can convince a judge it would be in Matthew's best interest to do so."

Emma bit her lip. "Make it as difficult for Patrick as possible."

Wallace nodded. "It's too bad your ex-husband hasn't had any serious run-ins with the law. The court wouldn't look kindly upon that."

"I think maybe he did as a young man," Emma said.

Wallace raised his eyebrows. "Do you have specifics?"

Emma shook her head. "He never talked about it. That's no help, is it?"

"No," Wallace said as he checked his watch and stood. "I'm due to meet with a judge shortly. Let me get you home if you don't mind my rush."

"Not at all," Emma said as Henry hurried to get her coat.

"We'll have something for you to review by the end of the week," he said. "Think about whom you'd like as trust administrator."

Emma smiled at the men. "Both of you will do nicely, if you're agreeable. That way I'd be sure Matthew will be well looked after."

"As you wish," both men said simultaneously.

* * *

It was still snowing lightly when school got out. The heavy, wet stuff was perfect for making snowballs, so Matthew, Jimmy Potter, and Joe Pete Johnson battled their way against a gang of four older boys all the way to Main Street, until they broke off the fight and ducked inside Sam Miller's store, laughing and red-faced. Matt bought a round of hard candy with some of the money Ma had given him that morning.

The three boys lived in the same neighborhood and had been friends forever. Jimmy was the bravest, Joe Pete the toughest, and Matt the smartest and the tallest, towering a good two inches above his pals. Because of that and his somewhat serious nature, most folks pegged him as older.

On the chance they might get waylaid, they waited until the four older boys were nowhere to be seen before splitting up. As Matt was leaving the store, Mr. Miller told him that his ma had been in earlier to buy the fixings for a special dinner she had planned for tonight.

"I was glad to see her out and about," Mr. Miller added.

"Me too," Matt replied with a big grin. "What's she fixing?"

Mr. Miller shook his head. "I'm not telling. You need to get on home to find that out."

"I will."

Hearing that Ma was still feeling better gave Matt a powerful good feeling. Maybe things could get back to normal again. Still grinning, he ducked into the drugstore, hoping to find the book he'd secreted at the bottom of the used-book bin under a thick volume of famous quotes by famous people. *Flintlock and Fife: A Tale of the French and Indian Wars* was still there. He paid a dime for it and started home, eager to read it and find out what Ma had planned for dinner.

Although he was good at all his subjects in school, Matt loved reading best. Happily, the book report due in two weeks could be on any subject he wanted to write about, and *Flintlock and Fife* was just the kind of story Matt liked: brave soldiers fighting for a worthy cause, just like his brother CJ had done in the Great War.

In his dresser, carefully wrapped in a leather pouch, Matt kept CJ's medals, which the army had sent home to Ma months after his death in France. The Victory Medal had a silver star for gallantry and a Meuse-Argonne battle clasp on the ribbon. The other medal was the Croix de Guerre from the French Government, awarded for feats of arms.

CJ had been a war hero. Just about everybody in Las Cruces knew the story of how he'd run away from home, lied about his age, and become the youngest sergeant in his regiment before shipping overseas. It always filled Matt with pride and sadness whenever folks talked about his brother. He'd decided to be a soldier like CJ when he grew up, but knew better than to say anything to Ma, who would surely give him what-for about it.

At home, although keen to learn what Ma was fixing for dinner, he checked on Patches first, laid down fresh straw, broke the ice on the water trough, and fed him a bucketful of oats. After dinner he'd muck out the stall before starting in on his homework.

He stepped inside and shucked his coat. The delicious smell of a roasting chicken made his mouth water and his stomach grumble. He called out to Ma and got no answer. She wasn't in the kitchen, but a delicious-looking fresh-baked, peach pie sat on the table. A slice had been cut out and left on a plate as a snack. He wolfed it down and looked for Ma in the sitting room and her bedroom. With his heart thumping with worry, he called out to her again and knocked hard on the closed bathroom door.

"Ma, are you in there?" his voice rising.

"Yes, give me a minute."

Matt held back a sigh of relief. "Are you okay?"

"Yes. Go set the table for me."

Matt hesitated. She sounded okay, but should he ask again? Sometimes Ma said things just to keep him from fretting.

"Go on now," Emma said from behind the closed door.

"Okay."

Emma smiled at herself in the mirror as Matthew's footsteps receded. She'd prettied herself up, brushed her hair, and changed into a fresh blouse for dinner. It was going to be a wonderful evening meal with Matthew and not just because she was feeling so much better and lively. The mail had brought an astonishing surprise that would surely delight him as it had her.

She glanced again in the mirror, pleased with the results. Ever since her divorce, CJ and Matt had been the only men in her life, although it wasn't for a lack of flattering attention from the likes of Henry Bowman and a few other married men she knew about town. If she'd lived elsewhere—in a more modern city such as New York—it might have been different and she could have taken a lover. That was impossible to do in Las Cruces without inviting harsh criticism. Still, even with that disadvantage, she had what most women lacked: the freedom to live independently, answerable to no man. So she'd schooled herself to be virtuous. Given her lusty nature, it had been no easy task.

Matthew had eaten his snack and set the table for dinner. She found him sprawled on his stomach across his bed, nose in a book.

"It's about the French and Indian Wars," he explained as she sat beside him, "for a book report."

"I'll want to know all about it once you finish."

Matt nodded as he looked up at her. "You look pretty."

"Thank you. Now, will you stop worrying about me?"

"Maybe."

"Hungry?"

"Yep."

"Then let's eat. After dinner I have a surprise to show you."

"What is it?"

"You'll see."

* * *

Matthew devoured his dinner, topped off by two slices of the peach pie that he praised with each bite, and left to tend to Patches. Emma busied herself with the dishes, impatiently waiting for his return. Finished, she took the magazine, letter, and book that arrived in the mail, sat at the table and reread the letter from Gene Rhodes.

Dear Emma:

This is not a letter—it's an apology. It took this old yarn spinner more years than he'd like to admit to whip "Emma

*Makes a Hand" into a good enough story to get published.
But here it is, wrapped inside this issue of* Sunset *Magazine
with a drawing to go with it of a young gal on horseback
twirling a lasso by my friend Maynard Dixon that I swear
looks just like you.*

*My New Mexico friends—thugs, gunmen, and outlaws that
they are—tell me you've been sickly and I am grieved to hear of it.
I hope "Emma Makes a Hand" lifts your spirits. I'll surely always
remember that trail drive on the Tularosa when you showed me
and all those other boys what a heck of a fine hand you were.*

*I've also been told that you've got a son named Matt who
likes to read, so I'm sending along a copy of my book,* West Is
West, *which I inscribed to him. Tell him to read everything.*

Yours truly,
Gene Rhodes

She thumbed through the magazine to the story and read the
opening paragraph:

*Thomas Wheeler Van Eaton, known to all on the basin as Van, drew
rein in front of the Double K ranch house and gazed at the prettiest gal
he'd seen in a long, long time. Freshly beautiful she was: sparkling and
fair, hair curly, eyes bewilderingly blue, slight as a desert willow. He
had heard of Emma Kerney, her frank and friendly manner, her warmth
and sweetness, but seeing her under a cloudless sky, with a soft wind at
his back and the sun touching Rainbow Ridge, rendered him speechless.*

She thought back to the day Gene had showed up at the ranch
after a fistfight in a mining camp with a badly swollen eye and puffy

lips, asking for a place to hide out in case the law came after him. Over supper he told her he had written a short story about her that had been turned down by a magazine editor. He promised to send her a copy if it ever got published.

Not soon after, he moved back east to live with his wife and her family and over time became a highly popular writer of Western books and one of the best-loved cowboy storytellers of the Old West. Tall tales still circulated about Gene's connections to infamous New Mexico outlaws and cattle thieves of the territorial years. To many folks, that made him an intriguing character with a somewhat shady background, which only served to build his reputation as a writer who truly knew the ways of cowboys and desperadoes.

To Emma, Gene was a good man who kept his word, stood by his friends, was more honorable than most of his trail-riding companions, and was always a gentleman with the ladies. She'd read all of his books and many of his short stories, often wondering what had happened to the yarn he'd written about her. Finally, here it was in her hands for everyone in the country to read. Good memories of living on the Double K flooded her mind and brought happy tears to her eyes.

She closed the magazine and put it with the book and letter. What a day it had been! For months she'd felt her life slipping away and now it was back, vibrant and exciting. She was beginning to wonder if it was possible for a body to heal itself, for a heart to mend on its own. Nothing seemed impossible.

The back door slammed shut.

"What is that surprise you promised to tell me?" Matt asked as he stomped snow off his boots and hung up his coat.

"Come in here and I'll tell you a story," Emma replied.

Don't miss any of the
NEW YORK TIMES BESTSELLING
✷ AMERICAN WEST TRILOGY ✷
from
MICHAEL McGARRITY

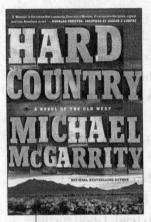

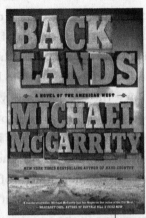

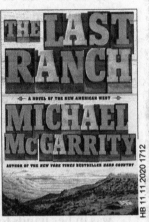

AVAILABLE IN PAPERBACK   AVAILABLE IN HARDCOVER

Follow every moment of the richly authentic grand saga of rough-hewn men and courageous women, set in the hard country of the American Southwest frontier

PRAISE FOR THE AMERICAN WEST TRILOGY

"*Hard Country* is the evocation of real people in a real land. McGarrity is an accomplished soryteller, and he writes with clarirty, perception, and authenticity."
—N. Scott Momaday, Pulizer Prize–winning author of *House Made of Dawn*

"A coming-of-age story. . . . An epic novel with a grand sweep of the West."
—*The Denver Post* on *Backlands*

"McGarrity serves up a tough but tender cowboy." —*Kirkus Reviews* on *The Last Ranch*

HB 11.11 2020 1712